New Dreams at Polkerran Point

Cass Grafton began her writing life in Regency England, enlisted Jane Austen's help to time-travel between then and the present day and is now happily ensconced in 21st-century Cornwall. Well, in her imagination and soul; her heart and physical presence reside in northern England with her ever-patient husband and Tig and Tag, their cute but exceptionally demanding moggies.

A bit of a nomad, Cass has called three countries home, as well as six different English counties, but her aspiration is to one day reunite with her beloved West Country. In the meantime, she writes feel-good contemporary romances set in Cornwall and, in doing so, manages to live there vicariously through her characters and settings.

An Ambassador for the Jane Austen Literacy Foundation, Cass is also a member of the Romantic Novelists' Association, the Jane Austen Society UK and the Society of Authors.

Also by Cass Grafton

A Quest for Mr Darcy

A Fair Prospect

Volume I - Disappointed Hopes
Volume II - Darcy's Dilemma
Volume III - Desperate Measures

The Austen Adventures (with Ada Bright)

The Particular Charm of Miss Jane Austen
The Unexpected Past of Miss Jane Austen

The Little Cornish Cove series

New Dreams at Polkerran Point

New Dreams at Polkerran Point

Cass Grafton

CANELO

First published in the United Kingdom in 2023 by

Canelo
Unit 9, 5th Floor
Cargo Works, 1-2 Hatfields
London SE1 9PG
United Kingdom

A CIP catalogue record for this book is available from the British Library.

Print ISBN 978 1 80436 599 1
Ebook ISBN 978 1 80436 600 4

Cover design by Head Design

Look for more great books at www.canelo.co

Printed and bound in Great Britain by Clays Ltd, Elcograf S.p.A.

1

MIX
Paper from
responsible sources
FSC
www.fsc.org
FSC® C018072

To Julian, who always makes my dreams come true

Chapter One

Not from the stars do I my judgement pluck

William Shakespeare, *Sonnet 14*

Horoscopes had a lot to answer for. Not that Anna Redding was superstitious – she wasn't madly into such things – but one of her housemates, Lauren, found them amusing and sometimes read them aloud on a weekend when there was time to linger at the kitchen table.

One particularly cold Saturday in November, Anna emerged from her room and hit send on the text she'd just tapped into her phone before hurrying down the stairs. She glanced at the time as she padded along the hallway: almost midday.

'There you are!'

Anna smiled as she entered the kitchen and walked over to make herself a much-needed coffee. Lauren and Georgia, her other housemate, were already at the table, and she sank into a chair inhaling the comforting smell from her mug.

'Pisces.' Lauren looked meaningfully at Anna over the top of the *Harrogate Herald*.

Anna faked a groan. 'Not another dose of Mystic Moron. Go on then. Hit me with it.'

Lauren assumed what she referred to as her newsreader voice. '*The wind of change is approaching, but is it news from a stranger or a blast from the past that will sweep you off your feet?*'

Anna rolled her eyes. 'More likely to be the icy pavements right now.' She picked up a slice of thickly buttered toast from the platter on the table and bit into it, wiping her fingers on her pyjamas. 'Is that the best she can do?'

Georgia – whose wealthy family owned the house they all shared – looked up from texting on her phone, then flicked her hair over her shoulder.

'Utter poppycock, darlings. Besides, Anna, there would be the most dreadful brouhaha from your Giles.' She also had a tendency to talk like she'd just stepped out of an episode of *Downton Abbey*.

Exchanging a smile with Lauren, Anna took another bite of toast. 'How's your head this morning?'

Lauren pulled a face. 'Felt like someone was trampolining on my eyeballs when I first woke up. Took some painkillers and went back to sleep.' She raised her mug of coffee. 'And I'm on my third of these, which helps.'

Georgia looked up from her phone again. 'Poor darling. Feeling seedy is quite the worst thing ever.'

'Mixing too many different drinks,' Anna said sagely. 'It'll get you every time.'

Lauren walked over to re-boil the kettle. 'I know. So much for spending the entire evening in a bar that sells nothing but gin.'

'I don't think we were supposed to work our way through the entire menu.' Anna laughed, despite her own somewhat tender head. They'd had such a great night out, the sort only a group of old friends can have. She stretched and got to her feet. 'I need more toast.'

Dropping some bread into the toaster, Anna glanced at Lauren where she leaned against the counter, cradling her refilled mug. Her friend had a head of neat blonde hair, stylish and short, unlike Anna, who had shoulder-length brown hair that was neither straight nor curly but annoyingly wavy and difficult to tame.

'Still tall then?' Lauren grinned up at her, and Anna smiled at the familiar refrain.

'Still short then?'

'You've no idea how much I envy you your long legs.'

Anna fished two pieces of toast out of the toaster. 'Don't. My unspeakable cousin once described me as having lofty proportions. Made me feel the size of a Georgian town house.'

Lauren's cheeks dimpled, and Anna quickly buttered the toast and followed her back over to the table. Georgia pocketed her phone and stood up.

'Lunching with Mummy. I'll bag the first shower, sweeties.'

Anna eyed Lauren across the table as Georgia closed the kitchen door.

'And then there were two.'

'All the more for us. So,' Lauren sipped her coffee, 'when's Giles getting back?'

'Sometime today.' Anna's contentment deflated a little, but she pushed aside the sensation. She'd think about it later.

'He's lucky you didn't get stolen last night.'

Anna wrinkled her nose. 'I think we experienced the pinnacle of bad chat-up lines.'

'*You* certainly did!'

They were both still chuckling about the appalling lines they'd been subjected to when the doorbell interrupted them.

'I'll get it.' Anna picked up a slice of toast and made her way along the hall. It was the postman.

'Mornin', love. Got a *signed for* in't name of A. Redding.'

'That's me.' Anna stuck the toast between her teeth and signed, frowning at the envelope. It was from her afore-mentioned much older cousin, Victoria, who, although she'd raised Anna since she was a baby, never got in touch.

Back in the kitchen, Lauren was clearing the table and loading the dishwasher. 'What've you got?'

Anna dropped a couple of bills on the table. 'No idea. My miserable cousin has sent something.'

'Hah! There you go.' Lauren pointed to the open paper. 'There's your unexpected news.'

'She's hardly a stranger.'

'She is if you never see her anymore.' Lauren waved her phone. 'Georgia sent a text – needs more tea. Do you want some?' She raised the kettle, but Anna shook her head.

'No, thanks. Besides, I'll probably need something stronger by the time I've seen whatever this is.' Anna threw Lauren an amused glance. 'Victoria must think it important if she's spent money on getting a signature.'

'I'll line up for the next shower then.' Lauren turned for the door. 'See you later.'

Anna sank back into her chair at the kitchen table and tore open the envelope, pulling out a slightly thinner one and a piece of paper containing a few lines in her cousin's handwriting: *Enclosed was forwarded on from the old address.*

Looks important. If you're in any sort of trouble, don't come running to us.

'And I love you too,' whispered Anna as she tossed the paper aside, pretending Cousin Victoria's lack of interest didn't still have the power to hurt. The envelope indicated it was from a company – Potter, Ball & Mottershead – and dated some weeks ago.

Puzzled, Anna opened it. Why would they be writing to her at an address she hadn't lived at for more than ten years?

The heading conveyed the bad news.

> Estate of Miss Margaret Joan Stratfield, deceased.

Anna's eyes filled with tears as she struggled to understand. How could Aunt Meg have finally passed away, and yet she didn't know?

Tightness gripped Anna's throat, and she swallowed hard on it, but it only intensified as a solitary tear rolled down her cheek. It didn't matter that Aunt Meg had been a prisoner to Alzheimer's, that she hadn't recognised Anna anymore. The thought of never seeing her again hurt.

Anna sniffed and dashed a hand across her eyes before fishing her mobile out of her pyjama pocket. She'd better call the hospice and find out what happened.

–

'I'm off, love. Meeting Jaydon at one.'

Anna looked up as Lauren put her head around the sitting room door. She'd barely moved from the sofa since making her call, but as soon as Lauren saw Anna's damp cheeks, she rushed over to sit beside her.

'What is it? Don't tell me Giles is being an arse again?'

Anna smiled shakily. 'No, had some sad news. My aunt Meg passed away.'

Lauren hugged her. 'Oh, Anna! I'm so sorry.' She frowned as she released her. 'Did the hospice call?'

'No, my cousin forwarded a letter from a legal firm in Cornwall, so I called the hospice to find out what happened. I was way down the call list, living so far away, but they say they still tried me. Turns out they'd written one of the numbers down wrong.'

'Was it the Alzheimer's?'

'Yes, and no. She got pneumonia and was gone within forty-eight hours. The funeral was a few weeks ago.'

Lauren glanced at the envelope on the table. 'And the letter?'

'They want me to contact them, to do with Aunt Meg's will. It must have been drawn up around the last time I stayed in Polkerran, as they had such an old address.' Anna took a sip of her drink. 'Those summers in Cornwall were the happiest days of my childhood. Quite possibly the *only* happy times.' She smiled ruefully. 'Even though we weren't related, Aunt Meg and I became very fond of each other.'

Lauren looked at her watch. 'Do you want me to stay? I can easily cancel my date.'

Anna shook her head. 'I'll be fine. Where's Georgia?'

'Gone for luncheon with Mumsie, darling.' Lauren did her best impression, and Anna laughed.

'You go. I'm going to—' She stopped as her mobile started its merry tune: Giles.

Giving her a quick hug, Lauren hurried from the room as Anna accepted the call.

'Hey, Babes.' How many times had she asked him not to call her that? 'Bit of a prob.'

'What's up?'

'One of the chaps has a spare ticket for the game at Twickenham later. Won't be heading back until tomorrow.'

To her surprise, Anna felt nothing but relief and not the slightest disappointment that watching a bunch of men get hot and sweaty running round with an oval-shaped piece of leather was more of an attraction than a night with her.

'No worries. I've got plenty I should be doing.'

'Don't sound so low, Babes. I'll be back soon.'

Anna shook her head, even though he couldn't see. 'It's not that. I just heard—' she drew in a shallow breath '—my aunt Meg died.'

Giles's voice sharpened. 'The old bird in Cornwall? Did she leave you anything?'

'Giles!'

'Sorry, Babes, but you did say she had no family.' Conciliatory now, Giles tried to backtrack. 'I mean, I'm sorry she died, but she was pretty old, and she'd been ill for years.'

'I know, but it still upset me.' Why should someone elderly dying not be a cause for sadness? 'I only wish you'd known her.'

Giles's tone softened. 'I really am sorry, Babes. Look, got to go. Call you when I'm back up north.'

'Okay. Safe journey.'

Anna checked the time before pocketing her phone. She ought to shower and get dressed. But then again, it was Saturday and she had no plans. She'd make a cushion nest in front of the fire and immerse herself in memories of Aunt Meg and those happy summers of her childhood.

Several hours later, Anna prodded her solitary supper around the plate and stared at the background of her laptop: a selfie of her and Giles at the York races last summer. Why wasn't she missing him more? He'd been away on business for a week now. Shouldn't she be desperate to see him?

Anna had always been a die-hard romantic who'd lived on a diet of love stories through her teens and dreamed endlessly of meeting that special someone, becoming a wife, mother to several children, and finally having the security of her own home. She had lived her life through the pages of her much-loved books, waiting for the thunderbolt to strike, to feel every heart-wrenching emotion of falling in love. So why wasn't she feeling like that about Giles now? Anna blinked and straightened up. Had she *ever* felt that way with him?

Her appetite non-existent, Anna placed her fork on her plate. She'd given up on her dream years ago, having failed to find anyone to stir her in such a way. The romance novels had been assigned to boxes under her bed, her bookish heart comforted by rediscovering some of the classics she'd read at school: the Brontës, Hardy, Gaskell and Austen.

Had she done the right thing – giving up? Giles was amusing company and could be quite sweet sometimes, but he'd never made her feel an ounce of what a novel's heroine described when the hero was around. Had her desire for a sense of belonging, a family of her own, led to this?

Feeling rattled, Anna glanced at the clock in the kitchen as she put her plate in the dishwasher. The house was quiet; time to lose herself in a book. Lauren hadn't returned, Georgia had gone out and although one of Anna's friends from the night before had phoned to invite her out for 'a dose of the hairy dog', she hadn't felt like it.

Anna grabbed her book – Wilkie Collins was her latest find – then looked up in surprise as Lauren came into the room.

'Didn't think I'd see you until morning.'

Dropping her oversized designer bag onto the table, Lauren pulled a face. 'Decided it wasn't worth it.'

'Oh dear.' Anna took two glasses from the cupboard. 'What happened?'

'The usual. Wanted to make things a bit more formal.'

Lauren was a serial dater, focused on furthering her high-flying career and shunning any hint of commitment.

Anna opened the fridge and pulled out an open bottle of rosé. 'Join me?'

'Absolutely. Let's raise a toast to your aunt Meg.'

They were soon comfortable in the well-proportioned sitting room – Georgia insisted on calling it the drawing room, but as Lauren pointed out every time she did, no one was so much as going to pick up a pencil in there – each nursing a large glass of wine.

'How're you doing?' Lauren sipped her wine and eyed Anna over the rim of her glass.

Anna shrugged lightly. 'Just wish I'd found a way to visit Aunt Meg since the summer, but you know how mad it's been, with all the events I've had to do.' Anna worked as a project manager for an event co-ordination company and took on assignments across the county.

'But she didn't recognise you anymore.'

'I know.' Anna reflected on her visits to the hospice in Cornwall. She'd tried to maintain them, despite the

9

vast distance. 'Aunt Meg said something strange to me. "Follow the shells." I had no idea what she meant, so I asked her.' Anna took a sip of her wine. 'She looked blankly at me. I'll never forget the confusion in her eyes, but then she said, "I don't know. Why don't I know?" It broke my heart, and she never spoke as if she knew me again after that visit, but every time I went, she would press a small shell on me as I left.'

Lauren's brows rose. 'Is that what the collection is in your room?'

Anna nodded. 'I didn't know what to do with them but couldn't face throwing them away. She must have taken them with her when she went into the hospice. After what she'd said to me, it felt like we were still connecting. Do you know what I mean?'

'Yes, of course.'

'But the time came when I went and there was no shell other than Aunt Meg. She didn't even open her eyes. I sat there for an hour, held her hand, and I wept.' Anna stopped, her eyes aching with unshed tears.

Lauren viewed her with sympathy. 'I remember you coming back from the visit. Wasn't that last Easter?'

Anna gave a watery smile. 'Yes. I managed to go a few times after that, but it was always the same. Her mind had given up on her long before her body was ready.' Feeling her voice wavering again, Anna took another sip from her glass, closing her eyes as the cool liquid flowed down her throat.

'Come on. You need distraction.' Lauren leaned forward and picked up the remote. 'What's it to be? *Strictly*? *The Masked Singer*? Or something you need your brain for?'

Anna curled up in the corner of the sofa, tugging a throw from the back to tuck around her feet. 'You choose.'

Scrolling through the options, Lauren selected the film currently showing on an obscure channel, an old romantic comedy they'd seen before, but as the credits rolled two hours later, Anna felt unsettled. It all came back to the same thing: people falling in love, getting their happy ever after.

'I think I need my bed and my book.' Anna put her empty glass on the table and got to her feet. Lauren stretched and did likewise, and Anna followed her into the kitchen and picked up her copy of *The Woman in White* from the table. Lauren started to rummage in her bag, then held up a book in triumph.

'There it is. Keen to get back to this. It's just heating up.'

'What are you reading now?'

Lauren showed her the cover: a copy of the latest bonk-buster.

'Not really your sort of thing, mate. Not so much Dickens, more *A Tale of Two Titties*!'

Anna continued to smile as Lauren headed for the stairs, then she turned back to switch off the lamps in the sitting room. Why couldn't she be more like her friend, focused on a career and not having this desire for a man to share her life?

Because it's not your dream.

'And it's as elusive as ever,' Anna muttered as she switched off the first lamp.

She walked over to stand in front of a painting of Polkerran Point hanging above the fireplace – a water-colour of the harbour at full tide in early morning, her favourite time of day, when the light was almost ethereal.

Anna looked fondly at the steps on the quay where she'd spent endless hours crabbing. She could almost smell the saltiness in the air, hear the gulls crying and the water lapping. She reached out a hand and touched the painting, consumed by the past, those summers in Polkerran, and then, with sudden clarity, assailed by the memory of Alex Tremayne, the boy who'd made her teenage heart pound.

Chapter Two

I am excessively fond of a cottage

Jane Austen, *Sense and Sensibility*

Giles arrived in Yorkshire late on Sunday, and they spoke on the phone but Anna decided against going over to spend the night. Somehow, she wasn't in the mood for him but, unable to put a finger on why, she took herself off to bed feeling as unsettled as she had the night before.

Having slept poorly, Anna was up early and in the office well before eight, where she tried to immerse herself in her work but instead kept looking at her watch. When it got to a couple of minutes to nine, she pulled the letter from Potter, Ball & Mottershead from her bag and tapped the number into her phone.

Five minutes later, she slumped back in her chair, her mind miles away. Four hundred miles away to be precise, wandering a picturesque Cornish village.

Her throat was taut, and an unexpected rush of tears filled her eyes as she grasped her mug, wrapping her hands around its warmth.

Anna's mobile started up, and she glanced at the screen. Giles.

'Hey, Babes. How did it go?'

She drew in a short breath. 'Okay. They had trouble tracking me down, were about to use a search company.'

'What did you get?'

Anna blinked. 'Other than being a beneficiary, I've no idea. They won't discuss it until they see formal ID.'

'Imagine if she left you the property! We could sell it and buy one up here!' Giles sounded euphoric. 'What a result that would be!' She could picture him punching the air with his fist.

'Giles, could you try being a bit more thoughtful?'

'What, me?' He cleared his throat. 'Sorry, Babes. Well, if it's anything worth selling, I'll get you that engagement ring.'

Anna held the phone away and glared at it before returning it to her ear. Could he be serious? Was this his idea of being thoughtful? A sensation stirred within her, a quiet outrage at his attitude.

'It's probably just a token – a keepsake for me to remember her by.'

'But the valuables must go to someone. You said she'd got no family.' Giles's tone was almost accusatory.

'I won't know anything until I visit the solicitors.' Why wasn't he listening?

'Well, think positive, and let's celebrate with a few drinks – damn, no can do this evening. Got a work thing on.' He paused. 'Got to go, Babes. Call waiting.'

Anna tossed the phone onto the desk and leaned back in her chair. She glared at the photo of Giles in its stylish frame – one he'd given to her for her last birthday – then laid it on its face. *Celebrate?* What was there to celebrate when the one person who had made Anna feel loved as a child had finally gone, and she'd missed the funeral, her last chance to say goodbye?

Lauren was in the kitchen when Anna arrived home that evening.

'Hey, how was your day?'

Anna shrugged. 'Very Monday. How about you?'

'Pretty good. Got to go to Singapore for a meeting on Thursday, so they suggested I pop to Manila from there.' Lauren worked for a global company based in Leeds and travelled all the time with her work. 'Good job I love airline food.'

Anna walked over and lifted the lid on the pot simmering on the hob. 'Smells good.'

'Cod and butter bean stew. Want some?'

Shaking her head, Anna opened the fridge and peered inside. She still had no appetite, even with the tempting smell of Lauren's stew. Ignoring the low-fat yoghurt, she grabbed a plate of leftover cheesecake and a fork from the drawer and sat at the table.

'Where's Georgia?'

'Had to stay late. She's working on the Mayor's Column. God knows why they had to give the feature a name like that!'

Anna grinned. Easily bored, Georgia drifted from job to job; currently, she was Girl Friday with a local magazine. She eyed the cheesecake. She shouldn't give in to the temptation, really. Slicing off a piece before such a foolish thought could take serious hold, Anna popped it in her mouth.

'Are you okay?' Lauren came to sit opposite, handing over a mug of tea.

Anna let the creamy dessert dissipate in her mouth. 'Not sure.' She didn't want to talk about Giles, but Lauren's kind demeanour invited her to share, so she put the fork aside and picked up the mug.

'I feel like I'm waking up. I've allowed myself to drift into a demoralising relationship. It used to be good. Giles was fun to be around. Now it barely feels like we're going through the motions.' She didn't want to think about his offhand comment about a ring.

Lauren tilted her head. 'Why don't you look into buying yourself a flat? Could you stretch to a mortgage?'

'Hah! On a birdcage, perhaps. I can't borrow enough on one wage to buy anything round here.'

'I just feel if you had a place just for you, that you felt you owned…'

Anna grimaced. 'The only thing I own right now is my overdraft.'

Lauren grinned. 'I know the feeling. Did you call the solicitors?'

'Yes, I'm going to see them, have to provide originals of my ID before they'll discuss anything. They said I could take them into a local solicitor's office, but I was planning to go down soon anyway.' Anna felt her sadness intensify. 'I suppose I don't need to now, but I want to… well, see where Aunt Meg is.'

Lauren leaned back in her chair. 'Remind me how you ended up spending your childhood summers with her?'

'She was an old friend of a neighbour from when I was growing up in Chiswick. She babysat for me sometimes when visiting from Cornwall, and then one year – I was about six – she invited me to stay with her in Polkerran Point during the school summer holidays.' Anna waved a hand. 'You remember what my cousin Victoria and her husband are like. They leapt at the offer. Of course, back then I didn't realise quite how begrudgingly they took me in when my parents died. I was too young to understand, but... well, you know.'

Lauren's look was sympathetic. 'And you don't know what she left you?'

Anna shook her head. 'They wouldn't say over the phone.'

'I'd be riddled with curiosity. What if it's an absolute fortune?'

Anna took another sip of tea. 'I doubt that very much. Aunt Meg was in the hospice for a long time. If there was any money, I'm sure it will have been used to settle the bills. I'll probably find she's left me some more shells.'

Lauren laughed, but once she'd finished her meal and started to load the dishwasher, Anna walked back into the sitting room and went to stand in front of the painting of Polkerran.

So many memories were wrapped up in that place. How would she feel going back? It was so many years since she'd been there. Even on her visits to Aunt Meg in the hospice, she'd gone no further than Bodmin, never taking the winding roads that led to the small seaside town where she'd once been so happy. A flutter of anticipation swept through her. Was it for Polkerran Point, or her hopes for Alex Tremayne still being around? Could he still be there, in the village? Amused at her train of thought, Anna brushed it aside. It had been nothing more than a teenage crush.

Turning her back on the painting, she headed back to the kitchen. It was time for wine.

–

It was early December when Anna began the long drive south, reaching Lostwithiel, the market town where Potter, Ball & Mottershead was located, without mishap.

Wendy, the efficient secretary, made her welcome and took copies of Anna's ID while chatting about nothing in particular until the door behind her opened.

'Ah, Miss Redding. We meet at last.'

Mr Mottershead, as Anna had imagined from his voice, was elderly, with a benevolent smile.

Entering his cluttered room was like stepping into a long-gone world, with no computer on his desk, though the outer office had seemed modern enough.

'Do sit, Miss Redding, please.' The gentleman waved a hand towards the leather chair beside his desk, and he eased past a pile of papers stacked precariously on its edge and sank into his own seat, picking up a document from the blotter.

'Here we are. The Last Will and Testament of Miss Margaret Joan Stratfield.' He peered at Anna over his spectacles. 'She made us her executor, you understand?'

'Yes, of course.'

'Now, where were we?' He peered at the document before clearing his throat, and then began to read aloud.

Five minutes later, a stunned Anna blinked. 'I— Excuse me, Mr Mottershead, but… are you sure? The *sole* beneficiary?'

He looked taken aback. 'My dear lady! Of course I'm sure.' He leaned forward. 'Besides, I took the instruction myself. Why would you question it?'

'It seems so much. I thought perhaps the house wasn't hers, that she was just a tenant, or that she'd left me a token, a piece of jewellery maybe. I don't know. But not this.' Anna frowned. 'How were the hospice costs covered? And the funeral?'

'We have received all and any claims on the estate. An arrangement had been put in place at the hospice to pay all invoices on a monthly basis. As for the funeral, there was ample provision in the estate, of course, should it be needed, but her friends wished to make the arrangements and one of them made an anonymous donation to cover the costs.'

'Oh.' It was a long time since Anna had been in Polkerran, but Aunt Meg had always had a lot of local friends. 'That's so lovely of them.'

'She was respected and well loved by all.' Mr Mottershead leaned back in his chair, his hands steepled on his chest. 'I remember Meg coming here to make the will. It was more than ten years ago. She had no family, as you know. She felt her age, and she wanted to be certain her home went to someone who loved it. There was no question in her mind.'

So it was real. Westerleigh Cottage was Anna's; not just somewhere of her own at last, but the only place that had ever felt like home for her. Almost choked with gratitude, Anna struggled for words.

'I'm overwhelmed. Touched, and... and so surprised.'

'She was convinced that once you were living in Polkerran Point, you would never leave.'

Anna stared at Mr Mottershead. *Live* there? She'd no desire to sell the cottage, but how could she live there when her life was four hundred miles away in North Yorkshire?

Mr Mottershead continued. 'Meg saw the damage, even ten years ago, with owners selling out to holiday lets and second homeowners. Prices have increased far beyond the reach of local people. She was adamant you wouldn't sell, expressing the hope, sat in that very chair—' he stared so meaningfully at Anna, she couldn't help but look over her shoulder as though she half expected to see Aunt Meg '—that you would make Westerleigh Cottage your home. Now, what else? Ah yes. The contents of the cottage as seen, plus several items of jewellery, here in the safe.' He waved a hand towards the back wall of his office. 'And there is, as I mentioned, also the balance of her financial accounts after any taxes – substantial, I'm afraid – to the tune of several thousand pounds.'

Quite overwhelmed, Anna tried to clear her dry throat. 'I'm a bit lost, Mr Mottershead. What happens now?'

The gentleman outlined the probate process, but when he started to talk about inheritance tax and nil rate bands, Anna found herself tuning out. The bequest was hugely significant, but give up her beloved job? Leave the house she adored sharing with Lauren and Georgia? It didn't bear thinking about. And what of Giles? Would a long-distance relationship work? Did she want it to?

Anna silenced the thought as Mr Mottershead led her out of his office and back into the present century.

'Ah, Wendy. Miss Redding and I have concluded our business for this afternoon. Would you be so kind as to make a copy of this?' He handed over the will. 'I have some calls to make, so may I request I am not disturbed?'

He shook Anna's hand, promised to keep her advised of progress with the probate, and to let her know when she could have the keys, then disappeared behind his door.

'Gone for his afternoon nap.' Wendy winked at Anna as she popped the copy into an envelope.

Stepping out into the street, Anna eyed the envelope before shoving it into her bag. It was too much to think about for now.

Her phone rang: Giles. Anna refused the call. Shivering, she looked up and down the street, then glanced at her watch. It was gone three o'clock, but there was a good hour of daylight left.

A gull winged overhead, its plaintive cry falling into the silence of a quiet, weekday afternoon in the small market town. A sensation tugged at Anna, pulling at her heartstrings, and she hurried back to the car.

It was time for a return to Polkerran Point.

–

Anna slowed the car as she reached the top of the steep road leading down into Polkerran, pulling into the small car park allocated to the hilltop cemetery. There was only one other car there on this bleak December day – a highly polished vintage Jaguar.

The sadness which had consumed her when she'd first heard of Aunt Meg's passing had returned, and she swallowed hard on the lump rising in her throat.

This won't do, Anna Redding. Pull yourself together.

Anna got out of the car just as an elderly gentleman emerged from the cemetery. His air of desolation was palpable as he walked towards the Jaguar, head bowed, and Anna's heart went out to him. So bereft!

A soft sigh fell from her lips, but she straightened her shoulders and walked determinedly through the cemetery gates, wishing she'd had the forethought to stop for some flowers at the last garage she'd passed.

It was a peaceful spot, perched on the top of the cliff with sweeping views out to sea, and Anna soon found the area of the cemetery where the most recent graves were located. There were two still unmarked by headstones, and she studied both wooden markers: one name meant nothing to her, but there lay Aunt Meg.

Heedless of the damp ground, Anna knelt down and lowered her head. It all felt horribly real, staring down at the mound of earth, and the ache in her throat intensified as tears began to fall.

'I'm so sorry, Aunt Meg.' She sniffed back the tears. 'I know you didn't know me anymore, or even realise I was there, but I feel like I let you down. I wish I could have been with you at the end.'

Anna dug in her pockets for a tissue but, finding nothing, wiped her eyes on her sleeve. Sitting back on her haunches, she drew in a shallow breath, then peered around the cemetery, starved of so much of its greenery at this time of year.

It was only as she looked back at the grave that she noticed a beautiful, hand-tied sheaf of flowers placed at its head. Anna sniffed once more.

'I'll come and see you again,' she whispered. 'And I'll bring flowers too. Thank you, Aunt Meg, for all you ever did for me. I don't have a clue what I'm going to do, but I promise to cherish Westerleigh Cottage and every single memory you helped me make there.'

Anna reached out and touched the flowers, her throat taut, but as her hand rested once more on the soil, she felt something hard beneath her fingers.

'It's a shell, Aunt Meg,' Anna murmured, putting two fingers to her lips before pressing them to the shell. 'It must have found its way to you.'

Slowly, Anna became aware of the biting wind chilling her bones. Getting to her feet, she rubbed ineffectually at a mud stain on her jeans.

Gripped by a sudden sense of being watched, Anna turned her head. A distant figure, tall and broad, stood on the edge of the treeline. Unnerved by its stillness, she shivered, but then the figure turned away and disappeared through the trees.

Chapter Three

*The most important thing in life is to stop saying
'I wish' and start saying 'I will'*

Charles Dickens, *David Copperfield*

Anna hurried back to the car, glancing over her shoulder to see if she was alone. The Jaguar had gone, and she started the engine before rummaging in her bag for a tissue, making a perfunctory effort to repair her face before setting the car in motion again.

Soon parked up in the centre of the small town, Anna was struck by the strangeness of seeing Polkerran at this time of year – the winter light on the grey sea, the bare trees and empty flower baskets, the lone Christmas tree bowed by the stiff breeze, and the strings of colourful lights suspended between the streets.

A settlement since the Middle Ages, the coastal village had formed within two arms of land embracing it from the east and west, forming a natural harbour. The run of cliffs extending from the main side of the bay extended further out to sea, topped by a small lighthouse, giving the village its name of Polkerran Point. However, due to the protected bay's crescent shape, the locals insisted on calling it 'the cove'.

Anna looked around with rising interest. The pretty cottages still hugged the hillside, with their fabulous views of the harbour and the sea, but the old-fashioned bakery had gone, replaced by a stylish coffee shop, Karma. Many of the restaurants had changed from their traditional seaside fare to more modern offerings, including a tapas bar, an expensive-looking bistro and a Thai restaurant. The traditional sweetshop was now a small deli, and one of her favourite places to hang out as a teen, the Mariners Tea Rooms, had become a holiday let, with a card displayed in the window.

The village post office remained much the same, however, as did the small pharmacy. Beyond that, there was a predominance of high-end boutiques and a couple of expensive-looking art galleries.

Anna turned her steps towards the harbour, her mind filled with memories, but before she'd gone far, a voice hailed her.

'Bleddy hell! Is that you, Anna Redding?'

Startled, Anna spun around, then smiled widely as a young woman with a pushchair caught her up.

'Oh my god, Phee Radcliffe. I don't believe it!'

Phoenix, named by her bohemian parents for her red-gold curls, was a younger local girl Anna had hung out with back in those idyllic summers. Although Anna hadn't seen her since her last summer in Polkerran, Phoenix hadn't lost her friendly smile or the soft Cornish lilt to her voice.

They both exchanged a hug before standing back to survey each other. Then, they spoke at the same time.

'Blimey, Anna. Look at you!'

'You don't look any different, Phee!'

Phoenix smirked. 'How many years has it been? You must've been a gangly teen when last I seen you.'

'It's about twelve years. You look great.' Anna glanced at the hand resting on the pushchair.

'I'm a single mother. The parents are proper proud.' Phoenix laughed. Anna remembered Mr and Mrs Radcliffe. They used to run The Curious Cavern, a quirky little shop selling all sorts of objects relating to the zodiac, including a range of the incense burners and sticks so popular in those days.

Leaning down, Anna admired the sleeping child in the pushchair. She had Phoenix's red-gold curls peeking out from under her multicoloured woollen hat and looked positively cherub-like.

'Verity Blue,' Phoenix offered. 'The blue is in honour of her eyes, which came from the father. Bit of a cheek really, to bestow them on her and then bugger off.'

'Oh, I'm sorry.'

Phoenix grinned. 'I'm not. He was worth it. Met him at the Regatta two years back. Right lush. Parked his large boat for twenty-four hours, if you take my meaning, and scarpered the next day.'

Anna leaned down to admire the sleeping child. 'She's adorable.'

'Aren't they all when they'm sleeping? She's heading for the terrible twos and right teasy lately.'

'So, I see The Curious Cavern is now a dress shop?' Anna straightened, and they turned to walk down to the harbour together.

'Yeah. Shame, really. They tried diversifying, but trade was pretty dire. People want the swanky boutiques and interiors shops these days.' Phoenix reached into her handbag for her cigarettes, offering the pack to Anna, who shook her head. 'Mum took a course and now makes handmade soaps and lotions. Some of the local shops stock them. Dad is doing gardening locally. You'll probably see his van before you leave. Hey—' she lit her cigarette and inhaled deeply '—how long be you in town? I heard about Meg Stratfield passing but didn't see you at the funeral. There's a lot of speculation about what will happen to the cottage. Plenty of agents sniffing about.'

They came to a halt beside the harbour wall, and Anna took in the view across the water towards Westerleigh Cottage, where it perched on the far side of the bay. The biting December wind blew all the more keenly here, and she wished she'd brought her scarf and gloves from the car.

'I didn't know in time. The news only reached me recently.'

'It was well attended. She'd been here a long time and had a lot of friends, bless her. Such a shame she spent the last year or so falling into her own little world in that hospice.'

There was nothing she could say to that, and Anna's gaze scanned the coastline: the jumble of cottages on the hillside, the waterfront businesses (many closed for the winter), and the vast, looming shape of the house perched on its headland directly opposite Westerleigh Cottage, beyond which it was possible to discern the small lighthouse.

Phoenix followed her gaze. 'Ah, the good old Bat House. Those were fun times we had.'

Anna's lips twitched. 'I can't believe we used to run amok in the grounds and no one seemed to care. Not sure you'd get away with it these days.' She glanced at Phoenix. 'D'you remember how scared we used to make ourselves, telling each other ghost stories about it, and then trying to peer through cracks in the boarded-up windows and screaming when we thought we saw a movement inside?'

With a grin, Phoenix began to rock the pushchair as a whimper came from the sleeping Verity Blue. 'Mum always said it was bats. It's all done up now. Local landowner bought it a while back, did it up, but then moved away and leased it out a couple of years ago to a reclusive writer. Historian. Does work for the TV, too.'

Anna was intrigued. 'Have you been inside?'

Phoenix shook her head and leaned over to pull Verity Blue's hat down over her ears. 'Keeps himself to himself. Just what the locals say, you know, the tradesmen engaged to do the work on it, and the domestic staff this writer chap uses. He's got a live-in housekeeper as well as a few dailies.'

Anna eyed the Gothic-style Bat House again. 'It's a big house, but why does one man need so many staff?'

'Probably needy. Or a bit precious. Used to people bowing to his every wish.' Phoenix looked back over at the house. 'We all had high hopes he'd throw parties and invite along some glamorous London types so we could get a geek inside, but no such luck.'

'Shame.' Anna surveyed the large property perched on the rocks at the far end of the town. It was only visible from the waterside, as a high stone wall secluded it from the public lane which ran past it down to the nearby sandy cove. 'I'd love to see inside. What's he like?'

'Don't see much of him, to be honest. Girt older chap. Always buttoned up in a shirt and tie.' Phoenix snorted. 'Even wears a waistcoat most of the time. Still, a right looker – if only he'd smile. Last time I saw him was Meg's funeral. Suppose that wasn't a time for smiling.'

Anna frowned. 'Did he know her, then?'

'Everyone in the cove knew Meg.' Phoenix rocked the pushchair again as her daughter opened one sleepy eye. 'So?'

'So what?'

'How long be you in town? Would be great to catch up, proper-like, over a drink.'

'Oh. No. I'm only here for today. I'm staying in Lostwithiel overnight, and then I have to head back up north. I live in Harrogate.'

Phoenix's forehead crinkled. 'Where's that to, then?'

'North Yorkshire.'

'Bleddy hell, that's a long way to come for such a short stay!'

It was indeed. Anna looked around and inhaled deeply of the cool but vibrant Cornish air. An emotion stirred within her, and it felt very much like excitement. 'But I hope to come back soon.'

'Sweet! Here.' Phoenix rummaged in her bag, scribbled on the lid of the cigarette packet and tore it off, holding it out to Anna. 'My mobile. Let I know dreckly if you come down for longer.'

'Thanks.' Anna pocketed it, and Phoenix dropped the stub of her cigarette to the pavement and ground it with her foot. Then, seeing Anna glance at it, rolled her eyes and picked it up, walking over to put it in a nearby metal container.

'Always one for following the rules, you were.'

Phoenix waved a hand as she turned the pushchair and retraced her steps back into the town, and Anna looked around. The light wouldn't last much longer. Turning her back on the west side of the cove, she walked across the stone bridge over the River Polwey and took the lane towards Westerleigh Cottage. There were fewer businesses here on the east side of the cove, where the steeply wooded hillside rolled down into the water in places. Her insides swirling with emotion, she trod the well-remembered streets, took in the beloved views, and tried to accept the news of her inheritance.

Anna opened the wooden gates to Westerleigh Cottage slowly. Assailed by memories, she drew in a short breath, but it hitched in her throat. Never had she arrived here without Aunt Meg there to greet her, wrap her in a warm and comforting embrace, her lovely smile lighting up her face in welcome.

Blinking away rising emotion, Anna walked around to where the house fronted on to the water and down the steps onto the lawn, turning to survey the building with affectionate eyes. Although old, it was full of charm and character; calling it a cottage was a bit of a misnomer. Westerleigh was a substantial house, built to withstand the elements in its exposed, cliff top position facing westwards across the bay and out to sea.

The view was as stunning as Anna remembered, and the lovely gardens weren't at all overgrown. Taking the steps back up to the wraparound terrace two at a time, much as she had as a child, Anna peered through the nearest window, her eyes straining against the rapidly diminishing light. She knew most of the furniture, though old-fashioned, was of good quality and in excellent condition. Aunt Meg had treasured all her things and looked after them. The last few years or so of neglect wouldn't take much more than a bit of polish to put right.

Anna smiled to herself. She was pretty old-fashioned too. She and Westerleigh Cottage would suit each other just fine.

She walked across the terrace and round to the back of the house again. Dusk was falling. It was time she returned to her hotel. She crossed the drive and almost had her hand on the gate when she heard a footstep behind her.

'Who the hell are you?'

Startled, Anna swung around. A giant of a man glared at her, a pair of fierce-looking shears gripped in his hand, his broad shoulders clad in a sweater that had clearly seen better days. Even with the fading light, she could discern his unwelcoming expression.

'Well?' His voice was deep and uncompromising.

Anna edged nearer to the gate. 'Sorry. I'm not trespassing. I promise.' She waved a hand at the house. 'I was a friend of Aunt— Of Meg Stratfield. I'm leaving.'

The man didn't move, and Anna opened the gate and shot out into the lane. Why hadn't she said it was going to be her property? Those shears probably belonged to her now anyway!

Flustered over not having more presence of mind, Anna hurried along the lane, casting a wary glance behind her. There was no sign of the grumpy giant and, relieved, Anna eschewed the small passenger ferry running between both sides of the bay, opting for a longer walk.

Her heart had calmed down after the shock of the man's sudden appearance, and she walked briskly along the main street, but as she was about to take the lane to the car park, a sign caught her eye. Walking slowly forward, Anna came to a halt beside the building: Tremayne Estates, the family business of Alex, the boy she'd fallen head over heels for during those summers.

Was it really twelve years since she'd last seen him, the boy she'd idolised? Shaking her head over her silliness back then, Anna turned away to return to her car, but as she did, she passed an elderly lady towing an old-fashioned wicker shopping trolley.

'Mrs Lovelace?'

The lady stopped and turned around. 'Yes, my lovely?' Her gaze narrowed, but then her eyes widened. 'Well, as I live and breathe. You'm Meg's little one.'

Anna half laughed. 'Well, yes and no.'

'Well, I'm blessed, you'm grown into quite the maid. What be you doin' in the cove?'

'I had to come to Cornwall to sort some things out.'

'Ah, Meg missed your visits when you was all grown up and didn't have those long summer holidays.'

Anna smiled weakly. 'We tended to meet in London once I was working. I didn't have the free time to get down here. But I missed my visits.' She looked around, raising her head to catch the stiff breeze coming in from the sea. 'I think I might be coming back now and again.'

'Well now,' Mrs Lovelace beamed, 'and wouldn't our Meg be happy to know it.' She reached out and patted Anna on her coat sleeve. 'You take care, my lovely. Meg was right fond of you.'

Anna felt a little choked up. 'Goodbye, Mrs Lovelace. I'll come and see you, when I next come back.'

'Always welcome, my lovely. You know where I am.' With that, the elderly lady walked off, and Anna continued on her way back to the car park.

She glanced at the wide-open skies as she unlocked the car. Something felt right about this: the timing, the place, the opportunity. Was this more than simply an unexpected bequest?

'Bless you, Aunt Meg,' Anna whispered as she got back into the car. 'You may just have rescued me.'

It was late when Anna got home from Cornwall on the Saturday night, and she tumbled into bed emotionally and physically exhausted, only to pass a disturbed night. Was this inheritance a blessing or not?

Rolling onto her side, Anna stared unseeingly at the curtained window, conscious it was light outside. Giles would tell her she was mad if she told him about her dream of living at the other end of the country. And it *was* madness. Her life was here. Her job, her friends.

Releasing a frustrated breath, Anna flopped onto her back. But was she really supposed to sell the cottage and buy up here? How on earth would she have the heart to do it? Aunt Meg had entrusted her beloved home to Anna's care…

She glanced at the bedside clock. Sleep wasn't going to return; she may as well get up. Anna clambered out from the tangled sheets, tugged on her old dressing gown and ambled down the stairs. Georgia had gone to Switzerland to catch the start of the ski season, but it was only eleven, way too early on a weekend for Lauren to be about.

Anna gathered the papers from the doormat and sat at the kitchen table with a mug of tea and a pack of chocolate teacakes. Turning first to the local rag, she found herself drawn to the horoscopes:

> You're a disgrace to your sign. Pisceans are
> born dreamers. Stop dismissing yours and get
> your life back on track.

She dropped the paper onto the table and leaned back in her chair. Was her dream shifting now? Should she take Aunt Meg's lifeline of a home of her own – the one thing she felt she'd never had – or stand by her relationship with Giles? Which was most likely to answer her dreams, bring her the happiness and security she longed for? She desperately wanted children, after all, and—

The doorbell pierced her train of thought, and Anna hurried down the hall.

'Sorry, love. Couldn't reach my key.' Lauren, who had only arrived back from her Asia trip a week ago, staggered over the threshold and eased past Anna, arms straining round a bulging paper carrier bag.

Anna followed Lauren along the hall. 'Stayed over at Kit's again, then?' Kit was Lauren's latest. He was in danger of outlasting the use-by date on most of the stuff in the fridge.

Lauren eyed Anna's smug expression over her shoulder. 'Seemed churlish to refuse, as he asked so nicely.' She dropped the bag onto the kitchen table and tugged off her woolly hat and gloves.

Once they were settled at the table with mugs of coffee, Anna filled Lauren in on how things had gone in Cornwall.

'Wow! So, you inherit everything, including a cottage. That's amazing, Anna.'

'I'm finding it hard to take in. But that's not all.' Anna chewed on her lip. 'Aunt Meg expressed the wish I live there. I wish I could. I loved it so much, and to have my own home… Only how can I do that? I'd have to give up my life here, my job, this—' she gestured around the warm and cosy kitchen of their much-loved house '—and… well, you know.'

Lauren raised a brow. 'Ah. I see the stumbling bloke.'

'Giles. Absolutely. I wish I could see into my own future so I make the right decision.'

Glancing at the open paper on the table, Lauren smirked. 'Is that why you were seeking celestial guidance this morning?'

'Here.' Anna turned the paper round so Lauren could read her horoscope.

'Oh dear. Mystic Moron clearly hadn't had enough caffeine when she sat down to write this week's entries.'

'I know. But it has raised a question for me. What *is* my dream? I mean, I know what it always *was*: somewhere I could genuinely call home, the happy marriage, the big family. It never felt too much to ask.'

'And now?'

'And now…' Anna bit her lip. 'It feels mean to say it, but, to misquote Shakespeare, I think I've been enamoured of an arse.' Lauren snorted, and Anna couldn't help but laugh. 'I suspect my choice is Giles or Polkerran Point.'

'Long-distance relationships can be made to work.'

Anna got to her feet, closing the paper and taking her mug over to the sink. 'They can, if both sides are equally committed.' She knew where this was headed, didn't she?

Lauren put it into words for her. 'Polkerran it is, then.'

Chapter Four

*I do not think, sir, you have a right to command
me, merely because you are older than I*

Charlotte Brontë, *Jane Eyre*

Anna wavered all morning. Part of her quivered excitedly
at the thought of moving to Cornwall – somewhere she
had shut out of her life, but where she knew her heart and
soul felt happy. The other part fought against turning her
back on everything about her life in Yorkshire.

Unable to put it off any longer, Anna called Giles,
letting him gloat about the inheritance for a moment
before mentioning her wish to live in the property. When
he dismissed it out of hand as ludicrous, stating she would
soon come to her senses, she ended the call. They were
going to meet for dinner, where no doubt Giles would
overrule her menu choices too.

Trying not to think about the evening ahead, Anna
sank onto the sofa with an old romance novel she'd dug
out and tried to lose herself in the words. It worked. Soon
completely wrapped up in the sheer passion of the story,
she didn't realise Lauren had come in until she sat down
next to her.

'Reading love stories now instead of the classics, then?'
Lauren gestured towards the book.

Anna put it on the sofa arm. 'I'm not sure it was the wisest move. It's brought back a lot of feelings from those days. Feels weird now. It's almost like I've become that insecure teenager again, suffering the pangs of unrequited love. No one could make my young heart pound like Alex Tremayne.'

Lauren's eyes widened. 'Tell me more!'

It didn't take long to explain about Alex – after all, what was there to say? It had been nothing but a crush of enormous magnitude, lasting years.

'I was six when I first went to Polkerran, and he was a lanky local boy of about eleven with a band of followers. He was heading off to 'big school' and seemed so grown up. By the time I was approaching my teens, I'd started looking for him everywhere. A glimpse of him from a distance was enough to make my entire day.' Anna shook her head. It all sounded so ridiculous now. 'I filled my diary all year, writing about him, and lived for the summer holidays.' She met Lauren's amused look with a grin. 'Blond, sun-kissed, with a smile that did strange things to my insides. Things I never really understood at my innocent age.' Then, she sobered. 'Not that he was smiling at *me*, of course.'

'Oh dear.' Lauren's cheeks dimpled. 'You did have it bad.'

'Tell me about it.' Anna picked up the book again. 'I've come to a sad realisation. My emotions were stirred more by the heroes in my old romances and by a teenage crush than they ever have been by Giles.'

'Anna.' Lauren's voice held a warning. 'You're not thinking this Alex chap will still be in Polkerran, are you? I mean, he's surely moved on?'

Anna burst out laughing, dropping the book into her lap. 'Of course not! It was a silly crush, and like I said, he never really noticed me anyway – other than as a part of the young kids in the village. They used to tease us mercilessly, had nicknames for all of us. He was barely there in the last few summers I had with Aunt Meg, and I never saw him again after I was eighteen.' She pursed her lips in thought. 'His family owned the local manor, though, so they may still have links to the place.'

Lauren raised a brow. 'And how old would this fine specimen be now?'

'Thirty-five-ish.'

Her friend snorted. 'He's probably balding and portly now from stress and too many business lunches.'

'Wait a minute.' Anna reached for her phone and opened Google Images. 'Couldn't resist looking him up.' She turned the screen to face Lauren. 'There. That's him.'

Lauren's brows rose further as she took the phone. 'Wow. Is this a current photo?'

'From some business awards event in London last month.'

'Well, then. Not gone to seed at all, has he?' Lauren sent Anna a speculative look. 'You do like your men blond, don't you?'

'Of course!' Anna winked. 'It's the only reason I love you, mate.'

With a chuckle, Lauren handed Anna the phone, and she studied the image: not overweight and thinning, but tanned, his golden hair a little more tamed but his smile as gorgeous as ever. Alex had lost the lanky frame of a youth, but he looked in good shape, and his dark business suit only made him all the more handsome. 'And he's hardly likely to be around – judging by the event, he's got some important job in London. And he certainly isn't likely to notice me if he is ever in Polkerran.'

'Don't sell yourself short. No one can resist those beautiful eyes.' Lauren struck a pose. 'All you have to do is think sophisticated. Cool, calm and collected. Make it your mantra in case fate steps in.'

'I wish it would!'

Lauren giggled then sobered. 'You do realise how you're talking, don't you?'

'Yes. I have to tell Giles it's over.'

–

As expected, when they met for dinner, Giles hadn't listened when Anna told him of her decision to move to Cornwall, speaking over her as he outlined his intention to get the cottage on the market as soon as possible and a house clearance company in to dispose of the contents. Anna had shuddered at the thought, her resolve increasing, and finally she had managed to get the message over to him that she was serious. She was leaving not only her job and Harrogate but also him.

Giles had become conciliatory as they left the restaurant, then patronising, but when his efforts proved ineffective, he'd turned to anger.

It was all Anna had needed. Once he'd started calling her selfish and mercenary, she'd found it easy to walk away from him, and although he tried to phone her over the next few days, she didn't take the calls.

There were moments when she wondered if she'd made the right decision about leaving Yorkshire, but Anna, with Lauren's support, moved forward with her plans, liaising with the solicitor in Cornwall and handing in her notice at work – though she did have a bit of a wobble when she'd done that.

She had several conversations with Mr Mottershead, who seemed delighted with her decision to make the cottage her home. Her boss, on the other hand, was less impressed. Lauren and Georgia were sad to see her go, but understood and promised to come and visit her when the summer came around.

The final weeks of the year flew by. Christmas and New Year came and went, and by the middle of January, Anna had started to pack up her old life in preparation for the move to Cornwall. By the end of February, all the necessary taxes were paid, the probate finalised, and the keys ready for Anna to collect from the solicitors in Lostwithiel.

Finally, her last night in Harrogate came around.

'How's it going?'

Lauren's head appeared round the bedroom door, and Anna smiled.

'Pretty much done. Not sure why I'm taking all my glam rags to a Cornish village.'

'Hah! Bet those fishermen know how to party!'

'I'll be sure to let you know.' Anna took the proffered mug of tea as her friend walked over to perch on the bed.

'You okay?' Lauren eyed Anna in concern. 'You look a bit out of sorts.'

Anna put her mug down to tuck a sweater into the only space left in the case. 'Oh, you know, this and that. Giving up the job I love. Leaving all my friends, moving to a whole new life in Cornwall. Adjusting to being single again.'

'Hmm.' Lauren grinned. 'You have been rather busy in recent months.'

Anna retrieved her mug and took a sip of tea as she walked over to sit beside Lauren. 'I genuinely thought my life was going to be like a book.'

'Think you were reading the wrong ones, mate.'

'Don't I know it. And here's me, newly single.' She pulled a face. 'I'm beginning to see how stupid I was. I mean, I don't regret the loss of Giles, merely the future I'd dreamed of.'

Lauren's expression sobered. 'I know, love. You were too good for him.'

'You said that once before.'

'Time you believed me.' Lauren's voice softened. 'Listen, Anna. I know how much you want the happy ever after – especially children – but I did warn you I thought you were settling for Giles as a means to an end. He's a tad too obsessed with himself and making money, and you're just—'

'Not. You were right. I think it was the only time we nearly fell out in all these years of friendship.' Anna bit her lip. 'Forgive me?'

Lauren reached out and squeezed her hand briefly. 'Of course.'

'I don't know what I was thinking. But I'm thirty, heading for spinsterhood and living La Vida Lonely. I think I'd better take up knitting and get a cat.'

Lauren rolled her eyes. 'This is the twenty-first century, not a Jane Austen novel. Besides—' she fixed Anna with a stern eye '—you're available, remember? If that Alex chap so much as shows his face and hasn't got a ring on his finger, you go for it.'

Anna burst out laughing. 'I really don't think I'm his type. He had the most gorgeous girls on his arm, even as a teen.'

'Probably gay now then.'

Anna grinned at Lauren and took another sip of her now cooling tea.

'You're a match for any of them.' Lauren got to her feet. 'Remember what I said if you see him? Repeat the mantra: cool, calm and collected. You'll be sophistication personified. Right, the girls have arrived, so I'm off to open the wine.'

Anna got up and walked over to look out of the window. Sophistication? She knew her own limitations. She contemplated the jumble of gardens and rooftops. She was sad to be leaving the house. It was the closest thing to a home she could remember having. Soon she would be seeing a totally different scene from her windows.

Anna straightened her shoulders and turned around. This was a moment to look forward, not back. And right now, it was time for one last evening of wine and giggles with her friends.

–

It was late in the day when Anna finally collected the keys to Westerleigh Cottage from Potter, Ball & Mottershead's office and headed towards Polkerran Point, soon driving along West Street towards her new home. Tired after the long drive, her anticipation over this new stage in her life felt muted by the uncertainty of taking on the unknown. She had little thought for Giles, but sadness at saying farewell to her colleagues, her friends, and especially Lauren, hung over her, tempting her mile by mile to turn and go back.

She'd persevered, though and soon stepped from the car, inhaling deeply of the bracing sea air, before turning to close the gates to Westerleigh Cottage and opening the boot. Dusk was falling and so was the temperature. She'd get the log burner lit and make a much-needed cup of tea before thinking about food.

Soon Anna surveyed the jumble of cases, boxes and bags now deposited inside the hallway. A faint musty smell hung in the air, but it would soon disperse once she'd had the windows open a few days. Feeling a little sad over being here without Aunt Meg, she closed the door and flicked the light switch. Nothing.

'Damn!'

She flicked the switch again, and again. *Where is the fuse box?*

Selecting torch mode on her phone, she made her way along the hallway to the staircase. Was it upstairs or down? She'd never given it a moment's thought during those carefree holidays.

There was something incredibly creepy about dusk. Shadows formed where there should be none; a strange stillness and heavy silence lay—

'Aargh!'

Anna dropped her phone as a dark shape shot out from under a dresser. The beam of light caught a small, skittering creature making its escape.

With a shudder, she picked up her phone and warily made her way around the house, convinced a pair of beady eyes watched her.

'Don't be ridiculous. It's a mouse. A particularly *large* mouse,' she muttered, flashing the torch here and there and popping in and out of the various rooms.

Anna found no sign of a fuse box. Perhaps only the hall light bulb was out? She flicked the kitchen light switch hopefully, but nothing happened other than the sound of scurrying feet again.

Then, she spotted the rear door leading on to the paved terrace, which overlooked the garden and the sea beyond. It unlocked with ease, and she placed her phone on the table before stepping out into the half-light and drew in another breath of the crisp sea air.

Memories assailed her as a gull swung low overhead, its mournful cry drifting away on the wind. She shivered again, hugging her arms to herself as she walked to the edge of the terrace, bordered by its ivy-clad wall, and looked across the cove. There were lights shining out from the Bat House – she must try to remember to use its proper name, Harbourwatch. The reclusive writer was at home.

She turned slowly on her heel to look at the small town of Polkerran – nestled in its embrace of tree-clad cliffs – and her spirits lifted. Perhaps it was more exciting than nerve-racking to be back.

Anna returned to the house and grabbed her phone, shining the torch around. The fuse box must be upstairs, but as she reached the bottom step, she heard a noise outside. She hesitated, then walked over and opened the door a fraction to peer out. The same broad-shouldered giant of a man as before had emerged from the garden shed. Before she could give in to the temptation to close the door, he looked over and saw her.

'You again!'

He crossed the driveway to stand in front of her. He was as tall as she remembered, though she could barely discern his features in the now near darkness. Strangely, she didn't feel threatened.

Anna cleared her throat. 'Yes. I live here.'

The man seemed to still, his gaze raking her face. Then, he took a step closer. 'Why are you in the dark?' He reached over and flicked the light switch, then swore, and Anna blinked. Whoever he was, he seemed to be in a very bad mood. 'Here, give me that.'

He took the phone from Anna before she realised his intent and shone the torch along the hall. Then, he strode past her, opening the door to the cellar and disappearing from view. A minute and a muffled curse later, the lights flickered into action. Blinking in the sudden glare, Anna eyed the man warily as he returned to the hall. He had handsome features, marred by the irritated look on his face. His dark hair was short-cropped, greying at the temples, and he had piercing blue eyes, which narrowed as he studied her closely.

'You were in the graveyard a few months ago, before I found you snooping around here.'

Anna bristled.

'I was not snooping! And this is my house now.'

His gaze narrowed further. 'You can't stay here tonight.'

For a stranger, he had very clear ideas about what she should or shouldn't be doing.

'And you are?'

'Getting impatient. Are you seriously thinking of living here in these conditions?' He waved a hand round at the dusty, neglected interior.

'Yes, I am.'

The man's attention turned to the haphazard pile of cases and boxes. 'You'd better come home with me. Supper will be ready soon. I'm sure we can make it stretch to three. Grab what you need.' He made for the door.

'Don't be ridiculous.' Anna knew she sounded patronising, but really, this man! 'How stupid would I be to go with a complete stranger?'

'Technically, this isn't our first meeting. But it's your choice. Enjoy your evening.'

He had gone before she had a chance to respond, and she closed the door with a snap.

'Good riddance,' she exclaimed, then eyed the jumble of luggage and possessions with regret. She was tired and hungry, and whoever was preparing supper was probably far less grumpy, had a few social graces and – more importantly – hot food!

Chapter Five

It is home, and I can't put its charm into words

Elizabeth Gaskell, *North and South*

Anna woke early after a fitful night's sleep. The strangeness of the house, the memories jostling for attention, and the eeriness of the dusty emptiness of what had once been a welcome home all coalesced in her sleepy mind.

Once up, she drew back the curtains, then wiped her finger over the sill. Dusty. She pushed open the window, looking down on the once familiar garden, surprisingly in good shape. Had the grumpy giant been doing some work, looking out for a sick neighbour? He hadn't come across as the generous, charitable type.

Cormorants dipped and swayed on the dancing waves, and a seagull swooped low across the garden as Anna followed its flight over the expanse of sea where it fed into the cove.

'Beautiful,' she whispered. 'And this is now my home.'

She hurried into the bathroom, shivering and wincing through a cold shower, wishing she'd thought to find the immersion heater the night before. She'd certainly need hot water for the cleaning she had to do.

Anna made a perfunctory effort at tidying her bed and headed downstairs, keeping a wary eye out for the large mouse. There were no provisions in the kitchen other than the few supplies Anna had brought with her, and as she consumed a bowl of cereal and a cup of tea, she made a list of the groceries she needed. Before long, she was on her way to the shops on the far side of the cove.

Her shopping soon completed, the sturdy wicker basket she'd found in the pantry weighing heavily on her arm, Anna took the little passenger ferry back across the water.

Within five minutes, she reached the narrow lane to the cottage, a little out of breath and pink in the face. She half expected to see the man from the previous night as she passed the properties along the lane. He must surely have been a neighbour – if only she'd had the presence of mind to ask him what he was doing in Aunt Meg's shed! She eyed each property as she passed, trying to recall who used to live there all those years ago and wondering who still did. Many had key boxes by the door, suggesting they were now holiday lets.

With relief at not seeing the bad-tempered neighbour again, Anna reached the gates and closed them behind her, only to see another man coming around from the side of the house – a younger, bearded, fair-haired specimen, his long hair in a ponytail and sporting paint-spattered dungarees.

As soon as he saw Anna, he waved and came over. Not much taller than her, he looked friendly and nothing like the grumpy giant, so she smiled.

'Morning.' He held out his hand. 'You must be the new owner. Welcome to Polkerran. I'm Daniel Tremayne.'

Anna shook his hand. Could Daniel be a relation of Alex's? It was impossible to say she saw any family likeness with all that facial hair.

'Thank you. I'm Anna Redding.' Then, she frowned. 'I only arrived late last night…'

Daniel grinned. 'And half the village will know by now. Thought I'd pop over to say hello and, as I'm a local handyman, ask if anything needs doing. You know, house having been empty for so long.'

'That's very kind.'

'I've had a look at the exterior. Shall I come in? It won't take long to check things out.'

'Oh. Yes, of course.' Anna reached for the basket, but he beat her to it.

'Allow me.'

'Thank you.'

She led the way, and Daniel followed her into the kitchen and put the basket on the counter. He began to walk around, eyeing the woodwork and giving the skirting a prod.

'I'm hoping it only needs a little TLC.'

He pulled a notepad from his back pocket. 'Probably best if I go room by room and make a note of things and then you can say yay or nay?'

'Yes, of course.' Anna bit her lip. 'I think there might be holes in the skirting as there's a very big mouse running around.'

Daniel raised a brow. 'Mouse? Is that you being optimistic?'

'Probably. I slept better thinking it was more Stuart Little than Peter Pettigrew.'

Laughing, he headed for the hall. 'Right. I'll get on, so I can leave you in peace.'

Anna put away her groceries, then went to find the immersion heater, flicking the switch and reassured by the instant gurgling from the tank. She heard Daniel's footsteps on the stairs now and again, and then he was back outside, so she busied herself filling the kettle and setting it on the Aga.

'Think I'm done.' Daniel's cheery face peered round the boot room door, and Anna walked over to meet him.

'What's the verdict?'

He screwed up his eyes as he studied his list. 'Depends on your budget. It's mainly cosmetic, although—' he glanced around the kitchen '—this and the bathrooms could do with a serious update.' He looked back at his list. 'The outside woodwork needs a fresh coat of paint, of course, but indoors everything seems well-maintained. Bit of wear and tear, and the front door needs a bit of work, but should come up well.' He turned the list over. 'Couldn't see any holes in the skirting. I'll need to get down in the cellar, see what's what, but that can wait until I've got my tools with me.'

Thinking of the pattering of tiny feet on the floor-boards, Anna chewed her lip. 'And that will be?'

'Six months? That okay?'

What?

'No!'

'Only joking!' Daniel smirked. 'You should've seen your face. I can start on Monday if you like?'

'Oh, yes, that's great. Wait, don't you have any other work?'

'Not as an odd-job man. I'm taking a bit of a sabbatical from the day job, so keeping myself busy with this sort of stuff is ideal. Don't worry—' he seemed to sense her concern '—I'm not usurping the locals. Doug's company is so busy it really would be months before they could do anything other than an emergency call-out. He's been using me as a contractor. He knows I can handle the basics.' He scribbled on his pad. 'That quote okay for you?'

'That's fine.' Anna hoped it was. Her knowledge of how much it should cost was negligible. 'So where will you start?'

'On the outside woodwork, while this mild weather holds. Oh, and the cellar of course.' He winked, and Anna couldn't help but laugh. At least Daniel was friendly, unlike the man she'd seen coming out of the shed.

She followed him down the hall.

'Do you know a neighbour from round here, tall, not overly friendly? I saw him twice, maybe. Seems to be using tools from the shed?'

Daniel shoved his pad and pencil into his pocket. 'I've only been here for about six months, and I don't know everyone this side of the cove but people help themselves to things round here. With the house being empty so long, I'm not surprised. They bring them back again,' he added quickly, then grinned. 'I doubt you'll see him in the shed again now there's someone living here.'

Did she detect a familiarity about his smile under that facial hair? Anna opened the door, then said hesitantly, 'Are you related to the Tremaynes who used to live in Polkerran? I know there was a family of that name when I came down for the summers.'

'That's my aunt and uncle. They're still here.' Daniel stepped out onto the driveway. 'I don't think Aunt Bella would ever give up the distinction of owning the local ancestral pile. In fact, I've been hanging out there. Wasn't sure how long I'd stay, but I think I'm in for the duration so I'll probably look for my own place soon.' He gave a cheery goodbye, and Anna closed the door on him and leaned back against it.

So, Alex's parents still lived in Tremayne Manor. He'd come to visit, surely…

Stop it, Anna. Determined to squash her speculations, she set off for the kitchen. It wouldn't be good to have all this dust lingering with painting to be done. She'd have a quick cuppa and then make a start on the cleaning.

–

Anna was exhausted by the evening. She'd started on the bedroom and bathroom in the eaves, wondering if perhaps she should make it her own. For now, she'd instinctively taken her old room, but the other looked so lovely with its beams, the bed covered in freshly laundered bedding, and the brass bedstead and furniture polished. She'd swept the floor, given the rugs a good beating in the garden, washed the curtains and given the adjacent bathroom a thorough clean. It was old-fashioned in its fittings but perfectly serviceable. An hour later, she'd moved her things up there, and fell into bed happier than she'd felt in a long time.

Despite her tiredness, however, something woke Anna in the middle of the night. She opened one eye, then another. Had she heard a sound? She switched on the bedside light, squinted at the clock in its brightness, then froze. It wasn't a sound; it was a movement on the bed, next to one of her legs.

Convinced it was the large mouse, she eased her leg away. As suspected, a dark shape lay hunched up on the covers. Anna began to slide closer to the edge of the bed, but as she did so, the creature raised its head, then turned to look at her, and she gasped.

The 'large mouse' turned out to be a rather scruffy black kitten, and it skittered off the bed and disappeared under the dresser.

Unable to coax it out, Anna hurried downstairs to fetch a saucer of water, but as she turned away from the fridge, she noticed a light across the cove. She walked over to the window to peer into the darkness. The reclusive writer kept late hours.

–

Anna found no sign of the kitten the next morning, but the water had gone, so she left it in peace wherever it hid and got ready for the day ahead.

It took another three long, tiring days to clean the entire cottage, but Anna had some help from old Mrs Lovelace's daughter. She'd bumped into them both on a walk in the village, and when she'd said what she was doing, Jean Lovelace, who ran the ice cream shop, which wouldn't open again until Easter, offered her services to help.

By the end of it, Anna was proud of the gleam of the wood of the well-loved furniture, the fresh smell of the linen on the beds and how well the floors had come up.

She had come across the kitten as it darted away from her now and again. A missing cover where the tumble dryer air vent should be seemed to account for its presence, but Anna was keen to befriend the creature and had put out more water and some cat food she'd picked up at the local shop, hoping to encourage it to venture downstairs.

She and Jean had gone on to wash the entire contents of the linen press on the landing, emptied every kitchen cupboard to clean them, and Anna busily made a list of things that needed replacing.

The kitchen was a joy of rediscovery. She'd spent so many happy hours in there with Aunt Meg. It was a large room, with flagstone floors, hand-fitted wooden units, a Belfast sink, a large pine dresser, a comfortable sofa, a wood burner, and a large scrubbed pine table set in the bay window to make the most of the views.

The only rooms she'd still to sort out were the study at the back of the house, and Aunt Meg's bedroom. The study, which overlooked the driveway and gates, was a good size but contained several boxes which appeared to be crammed with paperwork and books.

The room was also home to things Anna remembered from her childhood visits, and her fingers rested gently on the musical figurine on the desk which she'd listened to with so much delight, then smoothed over the old polished wooden box on the sideboard which Aunt Meg had treasured. The lid didn't seem to open anymore, and she walked over instead to study the prints on the wall of Polkerran in all seasons. As she turned away, a line of shells on the windowsill caught her eye.

'Follow the shells...' Anna murmured as she picked up one and studied it.

Aunt Meg had loved to walk on Cornwall's beaches, choosing specimens to add to her collection. But what had she been trying to tell Anna? And why? If only she'd been able to remember.

Eyeing the daunting jumble of boxes, Anna closed the door on the sight. It could wait for now.

Walking into Aunt Meg's bedroom had aroused all sorts of emotions, the faint smell of lavender sufficient to bring tears to Anna's eyes as she took in the familiar things, including the old-fashioned dressing table set she had loved to use.

The bed was neatly made. In fact, the whole room was tidy, and Anna inspected the wardrobe, still filled with Aunt Meg's clothes, and the drawers of the dresser, which were likewise full. Throwing open the windows to let the chilly air into the room, Anna smiled wistfully at yet another row of shells on the sill. She rested a gentle hand on the old velvet toy rabbit propped up at the end of the sill, looking a little worse for wear. For as long as she could remember, it had sat on Aunt Meg's bed among all the needlepoint-covered cushions. Anna had loved to cuddle it when she was younger.

Walking over and sinking onto the counterpane, her eyes were instantly drawn to the faded photograph in a frame on the bedside table: a young Meg with her baby sister, who had not survived infancy.

Keen to shake off a lowness of spirits, Anna rose from the bed, closed the window and turned for the door. She paused as she opened it, a hand resting on the selection of handbags suspended on a hook, filled with affection for Aunt Meg. Then, she drew in a long breath. She would tackle this room at a later date too.

Daniel was right, though. Despite a thorough clean, the appliances all needed replacing. It would take a chunk of the money Aunt Meg had left Anna. Time to find a job – but where?

Chapter Six

I am Heathcliff

Emily Brontë, *Wuthering Heights*

Over the next few days, Anna's new life fell into a pattern. Daniel would arrive promptly at eight every morning (a hangover from his days at a desk job, he said) and would set to work, stopping for coffee, some of Anna's home-made biscuits and a chat around eleven, and often joined by whomsoever decided to pay a call.

This was a fond memory for Anna from her summers in Polkerran. On the days she wasn't out and about in the village, crabbing on the harbour wall, trailing around in the hopes of seeing Alex, or hanging out with Phoenix and her friends, she'd stayed in the kitchen, helping Aunt Meg with baking or preparing that night's supper dish, only to be constantly interrupted by friends and neighbours calling in for their daily dose of coffee, cake and gossip.

She'd met several of her neighbours now, but Daniel had been right. She'd not seen the man from the first night again, and although she kept a wary eye out for him when going up and down the lane, he hadn't yet emerged from any of the nearby cottages.

There had been progress with the kitten, too, who looked a little less bedraggled than when Anna had first seen him and, having filled his belly, now sat on the window seat having a thorough wash. Being a foundling, she'd named him Heathcliff, hoping he'd prove to have a more appealing nature than Emily Brontë's original.

'Any chance of a coffee?'

Anna spun round as Daniel's hopeful face peered around the door.

'Of course. Come in. The kettle's just boiled.'

He walked over to the sink to wash his hands. 'What smells so good?'

'Scones.' Anna waved a hand towards the wire rack where they were resting. 'You can have one when they've cooled.'

'You're an angel, Anna Redding. Can I have a permanent job here?'

She smiled as she poured hot water into the coffee pot. 'I don't think I could afford you.'

Barely had they taken a seat at the table when the door from the boot room opened.

'Had her Devon clothes on as usual.' Mrs Lovelace beamed at Anna. 'Morning, my lovely. Been tellin' Jeannie here 'bout Lady T.'

Anna got up to fetch more mugs and poured coffee as they settled at the table, one ear on the conversation. 'Lady T' was Mrs Tremayne, Alex's mother, who seemed to have earned the title through her dedication to acting the role, even if she wasn't actually entitled to it.

'Don't mind me, young Daniel,' Mrs Lovelace continued as Anna placed a mug in front of her. 'I know she'm your aunt and all that, but her Lord of the Manor airs don't go down well with the locals any more now than they did years back.'

With a laugh, Daniel picked up his mug. 'Aunt Bella's living in the wrong century, I'm afraid. Uncle says she wants the locals to be beholden to the manor like they used to.' He yawned, hand over his mouth, then realising three pairs of eyes were watching him, grinned. 'Sorry. Late night down the Three Fishes with the boys.'

Mrs Lovelace shook her head. 'You'm a nice young man,' she admonished. 'Why don't you look for a nice young woman to stay home with?'

'Maybe he prefers men,' added Jean with a wink at Daniel.

'I appreciate your concern, Mrs L. Thanks, Anna.' He took the plates from her and passed them around as she fetched the scones, jam and clotted cream. 'But I don't seem to meet the sort of person I'm interested in.'

A further commotion came as the boot room door opened again, this time to admit Phoenix and Anna's neighbour, Nicki.

'Alright?' Phoenix viewed the pile of scones as she fell into a seat. 'You'll be putting the local cafe out of business if you carries on like this, Anna.'

'Oh dear.' Anna bit her lip. 'That would be awful.'

'Where's your young'un this morning?' Mrs Lovelace passed plates to Phoenix and Nicki.

'Mum's looking after her for a few hours. I need to get over to St Austell. Thought I'd drop by afore catching the bus.'

'So, what's happening this morning?' Nicki sipped her coffee and looked around.

'Just askin' young Daniel here why he's not dating.'

Nicki smirked at him. 'Again?' Nicki was married to a local fisherman and had two little boys in the village school. 'Perhaps you'd do better if you let me loose on this.' She tugged on his ponytail, but Daniel laughed.

'I'm fine. Honestly. I've got plenty going on. Besides, my cousin is coming home at Easter, and he always draws the ladies into town.'

Anna's attention was caught. Did he mean Alex?

'Now, young Daniel. Don't you go gettin' in with his crowd. You'm be safer on one of those online dating things, wouldn't he, Jeannie?'

Jean leaned in and lowered her voice. 'One of my friends tried it. *He* prefers men, as it happens. He's dating a chap from up country now, but it seems to be going okay.'

'What about that other thing for young'uns, Jeannie? We read about it in the paper the other day. Tinder or somethin'.' She pronounced it like 'kinder', and Phoenix snorted as she spread jam onto her scone.

'How're you settling in, Anna?'

Anna smiled at Nicki. She'd been such a help to her in these early days, pointing her in the right direction for things. She worked part time at the Point Hotel's beauty and hair salon, fitting her shifts around her husband's work.

'It's going well, thanks. I'm loving waking up to that view.' They looked out of the large bay window, through which the stunning seascape at the mouth of the cove could be seen. 'And everyone's so warm and friendly.' Except for the grumpy giant. 'Only downside is I feel like I'm rattling around here on my own.'

'Good job you and Heathcliff discovered each other, then.' Daniel nodded towards the kitten, fast asleep on the window seat.

'He's getting used to me, so I think he'll be good company, but I miss living with my housemates. There was always someone to talk to, something going on.' Anna smiled wistfully. 'The evenings can be very long.'

'Not a fan of the telly, then?' Jean asked kindly.

'I had an aerial installed when the internet was sorted out. Keep meaning to buy one.' Anna smiled at Jean's friendly face. 'Relying on my laptop too much.'

'Have a word with Ray down the end.' Mrs Lovelace gestured towards the lane. 'He'll get one for you and set it up dreckly.'

'Yes, I will. Heathcliff isn't much of a conversationalist yet.'

Nicki chuckled. 'Perhaps you should get a job.'

'That had crossed my mind, but most of the village isn't open until Easter, is it?'

'That'll be here before we know it.' Phoenix spooned a healthy dollop of cream on top of the jam. 'They've had chocolate eggs in the Spar since January.'

Mrs Lovelace and Jean exchanged a glance, then both turned to look at Anna. 'There's a job going at Harbour-watch if you're interested.'

'The Bat House?' Phoenix's eyes widened. 'Rather you than me, Anna.'

Nicki turned to the Lovelaces. 'For the writer? How did you find out he was looking, Mrs L?'

'From Cleggie. D'you remember Mrs Clegg, Anna my lovely? Keeps house for the girt man now, used to help Meg from time to time with the occasional big clean.'

'Yes, of course.' Anna took a sip from her mug. 'What sort of hours is it, do you know?'

Jean Lovelace shook her head. 'Not sure, but he needs a typist to help out with a book he's writing.'

Her interest piqued, Anna glanced out of the window and across the cove, and Phoenix nudged her. 'Great chance to see inside.'

'Is he a novelist? Is he famous?'

Nicki shrugged. 'Name's Seymour. Keeps to himself mostly, but I think he writes non-fiction. Bit of a history buff. Does work for some shows on the telly, and so on.'

Mrs Lovelace nodded. 'He's one of them sociable historians.'

Phoenix snorted. 'Nothing much sociable about him. Probably why he doesn't care about fashion.'

Anna frowned, uncertain. 'Is he elderly, then? He seems to have a lot of people looking after him.'

'I suppose he is quite old.' Phoenix pulled a face.

Daniel got to his feet, shaking his head in amusement. 'Oh, the eyes of youth! Well, I'd best get on. It's set to rain next week, so I need to finish off outside.' He drained his cup and walked over to the ancient dishwasher with it, and Anna couldn't quash her curiosity. Leaving the other locals to continue their chat, she joined him in the kitchen.

'So, will your cousin be staying with your aunt and uncle as well?'

Daniel turned to face her. 'Yes. It's his home too. Do you know Alex?'

Not exactly.

'Er, yes and no. I mean, I know who he is from when I used to visit many years ago, but we weren't exactly acquainted.'

'I'll introduce you, then.' And with that, he left the room to continue his painting, and Anna sank back into her seat beside Phoenix, to find them talking about someone in the village who'd had a fall.

'He's one of them repercussionists.' Mrs Lovelace shook her head. 'Proper teasy he's missing the competition next weekend.'

Anna glanced at Nicki in confusion.

'Plays in the local brass band,' she whispered.

'Ah, okay.' Anna concealed her smile and offered the coffee pot once more, but everyone declined and made moving noises, and under cover of the commotion, Nicki followed Anna as they carried things over to the sink.

'It's classic Mrs L. She could give Mrs Malaprop a run for her money.'

Anna laughed. 'I remember now. I came into the kitchen once, when I was about eight, and heard her telling Aunt Meg the Tremaynes were shooting peasants. I was petrified until my aunt explained to me later.'

Chuckling, Nicki waved and followed Phoenix, Mrs Lovelace and Jean out of the house, and Anna walked over to the window. She'd wondered whether her path would cross with Alex Tremayne's. Now she knew it would.

–

Mrs Lovelace was back the following morning with news. The job was part time – afternoons only – and involved nothing more than transcribing. Mrs Clegg had arranged with her employer for Anna to call that afternoon (with a typically vague 'around two-ish') to see if she was suitable for the job, and Anna hurried upstairs after a quick lunch to get ready.

She rummaged through her wardrobe before selecting a plain shift dress in navy blue and a pair of formal heeled shoes. She shrugged into her coat, then hesitated. She wouldn't normally have gone to an interview in anything other than one of her business suits, but it felt over the top for Polkerran. Then, she grabbed her bag and opened the door. It would have to do. Besides, this was hardly a high-flying role. It was a typing job, one she could do standing on her head.

Twenty minutes later, Anna arrived at the door to Harbourwatch and tugged firmly on the old-fashioned bell pull set into the high wall surrounding the house, screening all but its rooftops and chimneys from view.

There was no response at first, so she tried again.

'Alright, alright. I'm coming!'

The door swung open to reveal Mrs Clegg. 'Oh, it's you, dearie. Come on in.'

'Sorry, Mrs Clegg. I didn't think you'd heard me.'

'Oh, now don't you mind me, young'un. Daisy – she's the daily 'elp – hasn't turned up. And then Old Patrick – he's the odd-job man – decided to 'ead off to get more logs and isn't back, and then I've 'ad a right morning of it with him upstairs.' She paused and eyed Anna with interest. 'My, you'm grown into a right maid. Who'd have thought it?'

Anna smiled weakly, and Mrs Clegg gestured at the stone staircase rising from the large and lofty hallway. 'He's alright. Just has some bad days.' She lowered her voice. 'Lovely man, really. Divorced, you know. Nursing a broken 'eart, we reckons. Never seems to date anyone.'

Anna bit her lip. If him upstairs was an elderly, needy, broken-hearted man, he didn't sound like he'd be much fun to work for. Still, if she didn't earn a bit of money, she wouldn't be able to stay in Polkerran Point.

She looked around full of curiosity as she followed Mrs Clegg across the flagstone entrance hall and up the stairs. After all, Phoenix would want details. Everything seemed well-maintained, no doubt thanks to Mrs Clegg and her daily help.

'Ready, dearie?'

They'd come to a halt outside the first door along the landing, and Mrs Clegg rapped firmly on the polished wood and pushed the door aside, gesturing for Anna to enter.

'Miss Redding, Master Oliver.'

Master Oliver? Anna threw the housekeeper a startled look. Surely she didn't have to call him that? Mrs Clegg merely smiled warmly at her and closed the door.

Turning back to face the room, Anna waited. There was no acknowledgement from the man at the large desk under the bay window, which framed a wonderful vista of the sea. As Phoenix had implied, he dressed formally in a shirt and waistcoat, a suit jacket hanging off the back of a chair. The only sounds were the muted cries of the gulls and the tapping of a keyboard.

Anna looked around the generously sized room, now serving the purpose of a home office. Two of the walls were made up of bookcases reaching as high as the cornicing and were stacked with books, and she longed to go and study the spines.

Aside from the desk under the bay window, there was a second, smaller desk and chair by a side window, two armchairs either side of a fireplace containing a roaring log burner, and, to her surprise, a dog and a cat curled up together on the rug. Both raised their heads, but deeming her unworthy of further interest, returned to their dreams.

'Nice to meet you too,' Anna muttered under her breath.

'What did you say?'

Anna's gaze flew back to the man who'd now risen from his chair to face her and instinctively she took a step backwards.

'It's you!'

Chapter Seven

Is not general incivility the very essence of love?

Jane Austen, *Pride and Prejudice*

The grumpy giant raised a derisive brow.

'Of this I was never in doubt.'

'I thought you were a gardener. Or a neighbour. Not a...'

The mocking brow rose higher.

'I— I was simply—' Anna gestured towards the animals '—admiring your pets.'

The man grunted. 'The feline isn't mine.'

Oliver Seymour was as Anna remembered: aside from the grumpiness, good-looking, tall and broad-shouldered, with dark hair and piercing eyes. He wore wire-rimmed glasses today on his Roman nose, and a sardonic expression.

'So, you want to work for me.'

Did she? Anna was tempted to say, 'No thanks, I've changed my mind,' but then she remembered her need for a job.

'You'll do.'

Anna's gaze snapped to his. 'But... but you haven't asked me anything. Or tested my typing speed or...' Her voice trailed away under his look.

'I'm not looking for a conversationalist. You'll do fine. I can't imagine you came here for the job if you can't do it. Mrs Clegg knows better than to suggest it.' He raised his chin. 'She said she knew you. Does she?'

'Yes, of course. She was a friend of my aunt's. Well, not really my aunt, I just called her that.' Anna paused. 'Why does Mrs Clegg call you Master Oliver?'

He didn't answer for a moment. After all, he'd said he wasn't looking for a conversationalist.

'She was in service all her life. I've asked her not to, but old habits die hard.'

Anna smiled. 'I like it. It's sweet.'

A grunt was the only response to this, and Oliver Seymour turned back and retook his seat.

'The desk is over there. Go and power up the Mac and I'll give you the first chapter.' He didn't look at her again, merely resumed his tapping on the keyboard. 'Oh, and there's no need to dress up. There's no one here to see whether you look like a typist or not.'

Bristling, Anna resisted the temptation to tell him he didn't look much like a successful social historian either, but then she realised she didn't know what one was supposed to look like. Did they all wear business suits and ties? Surely he approved of formal dress? Then, she brushed it aside. Facts were facts. If this is where she would work, and only he and the housekeeper would see her, she may as well turn up in her pyjamas.

She put her coat and bag on one of the armchairs and took a seat at the smaller desk, adjusting the chair to the right height before turning her attention to the Mac. Thankfully, she was used to using one.

He reeled off the password, and Anna tapped it in quickly before grabbing a pencil and writing it down.

'Here.' He had risen from his desk and pulled a stack of papers from a tray. 'The first draft was typed up by the last girl. I've made several notes and changes to the first few chapters. You'll find it stored under *Haunting History* – file's called Edit 4.'

Anna scribbled down the details, took the papers without a word and began to peruse them, conscious he still lingered. She bent her head, relieved when he walked back to his desk, then raised her eyes to peer at his back. Several notes and changes were an understatement. Every page was covered in pencil, with arrows and annotations and goodness only knew what else.

'Why did she leave?' Anna bit her lip. She hadn't really meant to ask.

Oliver didn't turn around. 'Because I told her to.'

Sensing conversation, if it could be called that, had ended, Anna turned her attention to the papers and before long was completely engrossed. Though unaware of his writing until now, she found herself gripped by the topic – the run-up to the Battle of Sedgemoor – and although she made a perfunctory attempt at starting the edits, she soon turned page after page, unable to stop herself.

'I was wrong, then.'

Anna started and looked up. Oliver Seymour towered above her once more.

'Sorry?'

'I see no evidence you can actually type.'

Warmth rushed into her cheeks. 'Yes, I can. I mean, I will. Now. Sorry. I got wrapped up in reading ahead.'

'I'm flattered,' he said drily. 'I'm going out. There's a door key in the desk drawer you can have. Leave me a note of your hours and let yourself out when you're done for today.'

Anna breathed out slowly as he picked up his jacket and left the room. Her mind buzzed with questions she'd liked to have asked him, such as why he'd been in Aunt Meg's shed and how he knew his way around the house well enough to know exactly where the fuse box was.

Perhaps he'd mellow with time and she could ask him then? Turning her attention back to her work, Anna had all the amendments to the first few chapters done by late afternoon. There was no further sign of Oliver Seymour, but Mrs Clegg appeared around four with a cup of tea and a plate of biscuits. Anna consumed them gratefully, and once she'd done all she could, printed out the fresh pages and stacked them neatly.

Logging out, she donned her coat, picked up her bag, and carried the pile of printing over to the large desk under the window. There wasn't a space anywhere for her to put it without laying the papers on top of something else. Anna leaned forward and placed it instead on the keyboard, but then her eye was caught by the foolscap notepad open to the right-hand side. It bore a long list – further research, she assumed, having now gained the gist of his work – but then she drew in a sharp breath. Clearly written on the bottom left of the page and underlined were the words *Follow what shells? Where? Why?*

Anna backed away. It must be a coincidence, that's all.

The light outside had altered. If she wanted to fit a walk in, she'd best hurry, and with relief, she let herself out of the room and made for the front door and freedom.

–

Anna eyed her *Poldark* calendar in the kitchen (one of her leaving gifts from work). March hurried its steps, much as the clouds scuttled across the skies, buffeted by the spring winds. Easter loomed on the horizon.

Looking up from studying her bank statement as the boot room door opened, Anna smiled warmly as Phoenix came in with Verity Blue.

'Alright?'

Folding the statement, Anna put it in a drawer. She'd think about her finances later.

'You're early today.' She crouched down and held a hand out to Verity Blue, who hurried over and took it. 'Hello, beautiful.'

'Anny! Cake!'

Anna smiled. 'Hmm, I think I know my place.' She ruffled the child's curls and straightened up. 'Come on then, let's see what's in Verity Blue's special tin, shall we?'

Sitting at a small table more suited to her height, Verity Blue tucked into the two miniature cupcakes Anna had produced for her, and Phoenix carried the usual crockery over to the pine table as Anna brewed the pot of coffee.

'Wasson, mate? Feeling at home now?'

'Absolutely. I love it.' Anna placed the pot on the table and turned around as the door opened and Mrs Lovelace came in.

'Where's your Jean this morning?'

'Gone up country with a friend.' Mrs Lovelace took her usual seat, selecting a biscuit from the plate. 'Wanted a few days away before the emmets get here for the season.'

Anna frowned. 'Emmets?'

'Tourists.' Phoenix grinned. 'Like you used to be.'

With a laugh, Anna offered the sugar bowl. 'Whereabouts have they gone, Mrs Lovelace?'

'Brissle, to see some show. Margie, that's the friend, she's been a-wanting to see *Cats*.' Mrs Lovelace sniffed as she picked up a spoon. 'Dunno why. She's allergic to 'em.'

'Daniel not here this morning?' Phoenix glanced out of the window. 'Didn't see his van.'

'He's finished the outside.' Anna checked Verity Blue's feeding cup. 'Can she have some more?' Phoenix nodded, and Anna walked over to the sink. 'He's coming back next week to do the front door.'

Nicki put her head around the door. 'I thought I saw people arriving.'

Anna hurried to put the kettle on again as Nicki headed for the table and Phoenix attended to a rather messy Verity Blue, wiping her face and then bringing her to sit on her lap.

'How's it going, working for the big man?' Nicki grinned. 'Cleggie reckons he's nursing a broken heart. His wife left him, you know.'

'They divorced real quick,' piped up Phoenix.

Anna was puzzled. 'How do you all know so much about him? I thought he kept himself to himself.'

Nicki grinned. 'He does. Half the village googled him when he arrived in Polkerran. You're going to be our best source outside of that. So?'

'It's going fine.' Anna looked around at their expectant faces. 'Well, he's engrossed in his work most of the time. I'm not even sure he knows what I look like.'

'Yes, but what about *him*? What's he like?'

Nicki was certainly persistent, and Anna pondered the question. Did she have any idea what Oliver Seymour was really like?

'Well, he's certainly not as elderly and decrepit as I was led to believe.' She threw an amused glance at Phoenix.

'You said he was old and implied he dressed like an ageing professor.'

'I think I said he was *quite* old,' Phoenix pulled a face. 'Anyway, he is. He's got to be in his forties, hasn't he?' She snorted. 'And he wears waistcoats!'

Nicki waggled her eyebrows. 'That's considered quite sexy since the England footie coach started doing it.'

Anna's attention drifted towards Harbourwatch, but then she frowned.

'I need to keep an eye on the garden. It's going to be a huge challenge to keep it in order. I was surprised to see it in such good shape with Aunt Meg having been in the home for so long.'

'I think Oliver Seymour used to do some of it.' Nicki waved a hand in the direction of the village. 'I've seen him helping out at a few of the gardens on this side of the cove, elderly residents mainly.'

Anna's interest was piqued. Hadn't she been wondering about that? 'Why?'

Nicki shrugged. 'No idea.'

Phoenix looked up. 'He befriended Meg when he came to the cove. Probably doing her a favour. Normally, Dad could help, but he's rammed at the moment, what with spring and everything.'

'How about Tommy the Boat?'

'He doesn't sound like a gardener, Mrs Lovelace.'

'Retired, young'un.' The lady rummaged in her pocket, pulling out a tissue. 'Still does half-hour trips for the emmets in season, but he'll turn his hand to anything going. He'll see you'm right.'

'I'll get him to call round, Anna.' Nicki fished out her mobile as it rang and went over to the other side of the room to answer it.

'Did Ray down the end get your telly sorted?' Phoenix bit into a biscuit.

Anna smiled. 'Yes, but the evenings are still pretty lonely.'

'Why don't you open up as a B&B?' Phoenix leaned forward. 'How many bedrooms have you?'

'Four I'm not using: three with sea views, plus the bunk room at the back.' Anna looked at the eager faces round the table. 'Won't that upset those already trading?'

Phoenix shook her head. 'In peak season, there be more people wanting rooms than there are rooms available. The hotel's too expensive for many, and those that only want one or two nights can't do the self-catering cottages. There's only one B&B on the west side now, since Polly and Ken retired and moved up country, and nothing this side of the cove.'

The idea appealed to Anna, and she mulled over what changes she'd need to make and what they might cost.

'You'm certainly a fair baker.' Mrs Lovelace smiled kindly at Anna as she tucked the tissue up her sleeve. 'How's your cooking, young'un?'

'Not bad. I can definitely rustle up a good full English.'

'That be all you need, my lovely.'

Nicki walked back over, pocketing her mobile. 'Got to go, ladies. There's a client up at the hotel in a panic over a dye gone wrong.'

Anna started to clear the table once Nicki had gone, with Mrs Lovelace soon after her.

'D'you remember that summer when I tried to dye my hair blonde and it went green?' Phoenix picked up Verity Blue's cup and joined Anna at the sink to rinse it.

Anna grinned at the memory. 'I'd have been horrified, but you loved it, kept it for the whole season.'

Phoenix chuckled, sweeping Verity Blue into her arms and waving a cheery goodbye. Anna closed the door on them, conscious of a frisson of excitement. Why not turn Westerleigh Cottage into a B&B?

Glancing at the clock, she grabbed her keys and bag and headed out. There was no time to think about it now. It was a mild day and a pleasant walk over to Harbourwatch, and she was enjoying taking in the changes to the village as everyone geared up for the season's start.

As she crossed the bridge, Anna reflected on her new life. When the locals gathered round her kitchen table, she was in her element, watching them enjoy whatever she'd been baking and entertaining her with amusing anecdotes about village life. But she'd begun to enjoy working at Harbourwatch, too, especially as Oliver's ever-looming deadline for his manuscript meant more hours. In fact, she'd started going over much earlier, half expecting Oliver to tell her to go away again. So far, he hadn't.

Anna considered the enigma of Oliver Seymour as she walked through the little town. Despite her initial reservations, they had fallen into a smooth working pattern. At first, she had relished the times when he was out at a meeting or gone to London or Bristol for the day. Lately, however, she found herself happier when he was there. It wasn't that they chatted – he hadn't been joking about not wanting a conversationalist – but with Anna's genuine interest in his work and her blatant enjoyment of it, Oliver seemed content to answer her questions about the book now and again. She merely had to gauge his mood by the day.

Nearing Harbourwatch, Anna glanced at the skies – today, the pale, wispy blue of spring. After work, she would go for a walk along the cliffs before picking up any groceries she needed. She smiled as she reached work, happier than she had been in many years, the future she had given up with Giles now a distant memory.

Exchanging greetings with Old Patrick, the odd-job man at Harbourwatch, Anna let herself into the house, popped her head round the kitchen door to say hello to Mrs Clegg and then headed up the stairs, running her hand along the well-polished banister. Daisy, the daily help, was on the landing arranging some flowers on a side table, and Anna admired them as she passed. It did seem an excessive amount of assistance for one man, even if the house was quite large, especially as Mrs Clegg lived in and was available 24/7 if needed.

Shrugging her bag further onto her shoulder, Anna reached for the door handle. Her curiosity was at its height. If Oliver was in one of his more receptive moods, she might even ask him about it.

Chapter Eight

I would always rather be happy than dignified

Charlotte Brontë, *Jane Eyre*

Oliver was at his desk, speaking testily into his mobile. 'I know the price is inflated. Just get the necessary drawn up. I want to acquire it before they do, you understand?' Oliver paused. 'Not my problem.' He ended the call as abruptly as he did most things and turned to his laptop.

With a last look at the beautiful morning outside, Anna paused by his desk.

'Morning.'

He grunted a response, as was his habit, and Anna sat at her desk, picked up the latest pile of amended notes and set to work.

Oliver had his head down, scribbling into his notebook, and apart from swearing under his breath every time the desk phone rang, said nothing for the first hour. When it rang for the fourth time, however, he dropped the pen on the desk and his head into his hands, and Anna got to her feet.

'Perhaps if you answered it the first time, they wouldn't keep trying to reach you. Don't you have an answerphone you can set it to?'

Slowly he raised his head and turned to look at her. 'If they leave a message, they will assume I have received it.' Oliver gestured towards the desk phone. 'I prefer it this way. Besides, if they don't have my mobile number, they'll be someone I don't want to talk to.'

The phone stopped ringing again.

'Yes, but surely...'

He raised a hand. 'Fine, fine. You answer it next time. I'm not here.'

Anna turned her attention back to her typing, but she'd barely edited the next paragraph when the phone started up again.

A growling noise emanated from Oliver, and she hurried over to his desk and picked up the receiver.

'Good morning, Anna speaking.'

'Put him on the bloody line, whoever you are.'

'May I ask who's calling, sir?' Anna assumed her best professional manner.

'No, you damn well can't. Now put him on.'

'I'm afraid, sir, if I don't know who is calling, I'm unable to put you through.'

Anna looked out of the window at the expanse of sea and sky as she tried to shut out the swearing on the other end of the line.

'Goldsworth, okay? It's Gerard Goldsworth, from Pattison's Rural Estates. Now put him on. I know he's there, and I want to know what the bloody hell he thinks he's up to.'

Anna picked up Oliver's pencil and scrawled the name on his pad, and he shook his head.

'Sorry to keep you, sir. It seems Mr Seymour is unavailable.'

When the indignant man had finished his tirade and ended the call, Anna replaced the receiver, eyeing the connection point on the wall.

'Would you like me to remove this?' She studied Oliver's untidy desk. 'What about your mobile? Should we put that somewhere else too, so you don't get interrupted when you're writing?'

Expecting nothing more than another grunt, Anna started when Oliver tossed his notepad onto the desk and turned his head to look at her. Was he mad at her for the suggestion? He'd made it all too clear she was here to work on his manuscript and nothing more.

'I'm not writing.'

Expansive as ever. However, Anna was relieved his grumpiness this morning didn't seem to extend to her. After all, she didn't know what had made him fire the previous typist.

Oliver tapped the notepad with his finger. 'Making notes.' He got to his feet and Anna took a step back. 'Move the phone out.'

'And your mobile?'

He picked up his jacket from the back of the chair. 'I only switch it on if I think someone important might get in touch.'

'But how *do* people contact you? I mean, you must have someone wanting to liaise with you over the book? Work and things?'

Oliver draped his jacket over his arm and turned for the door. 'Not my problem. They'll find a way if need be.'

'But Oliver, you said you wanted to go through the next chapter. Where are you going?'

He paused, his back still to her. 'I'm taking part in a flash mob.'

What? Anna opened her mouth, but no words came.

Glancing back over his shoulder, Oliver shook his head at her. 'Do you believe everything you're told, however unlikely?'

Anna smiled begrudgingly. 'You were joking.'

He turned away again. 'I've got an appointment in town.'

'But when will you be back?'

'When I'm ready.'

With that, he left the room, and Anna released a frustrated breath. He was a nightmare!

Despite his brusque manner overall, though, Anna continued to enjoy her afternoons working with Oliver. On the one hand, the typing didn't really require her to use her brain too much, which meant she could be completely absorbed by the content. For all his abruptness, Oliver had a way with written words that astounded her.

His book could have been dry as dust, but somehow, he managed to present fact almost as though it were fiction, and Anna soon found herself looking for his previous works and lapping them up. She had no intention of telling him, of course. She'd either get no response, the habitual raising of one brow, or a snub.

When she walked into the office the following day, Oliver was on his mobile again, and Anna dropped her bag by her desk and walked over to stroke Thumper, Mrs Clegg's elderly cat. Dougal, the resident dog, was nowhere to be seen.

'I want the contract signed by the end of this week or I'm pulling out.'

Anna rolled her eyes at Thumper, who ignored her and tucked her head back down, and she walked back to her desk, unbuttoning her coat.

'So, get it sorted.'

Oliver ended his call and dropped his phone onto the desk. He ran a hand through his hair, not recommended for someone with such a short cut. He looked like a disgruntled hedgehog.

Hiding her smile, Anna dropped into her seat and picked up where she'd left off the day before. Oliver tapped away on his keyboard again, and she was soon lost in her work, and before she knew it, Mrs Clegg had come in with a tray of much-needed coffee and the post.

'Now you make sure you drink that while it's 'ot, Master Oliver,' she chided him as she poured him a drink. She walked over and placed a saucer of water next to Thumper, who raised her head briefly, ignored it and went back to sleep.

'Shall I give the post to Anna?'

Anna walked over to help herself to coffee from the tray, holding out her hand for the post as she passed, but Oliver swung around in his chair and eyed Anna with surprise, as though he hadn't realised she'd arrived.

'No, I'll take it.'

Mrs Clegg handed it to him, winked at Anna and left the room. Returning to her desk, the warm mug in her hands, Anna read through what she'd typed. She sipped at her drink, conscious of Oliver opening his letters. It would be nice if, now and again, he shed his cloak of inscrutability. Anna choked back a laugh. It made him sound like a moody Harry Potter!

'Did you say something?'

Anna turned around in her seat. 'No, nothing.'

A grunt was the only response. Oliver's attention was on the letter he held, and he got to his feet, reaching for his mobile, and left the room.

The rest of the afternoon fled by in a similar pattern, with Anna making great strides in her typing and Oliver seemingly exasperated by someone who wasn't sorting a contract as quickly as he'd like. Was he signing up for another book deal?

Anna glanced at her watch soon after five, then started as Oliver loomed at her side.

'You'd better go. You've been staring at the screen for too many hours as it is.'

Surprised, Anna looked up at him. 'But it's what I'm here for.'

'You're not here to ruin your eyesight. Go and get some fresh air. I need to go out.'

'Can I do anything to help?'

Anna gestured towards the pile of post on his desk, only some of which he'd opened. Oliver said nothing for a moment, and she fidgeted under his scrutiny.

'I doubt it.'

No 'thank you for the offer' then? Anna blew out a frustrated breath as he turned away.

By the time she'd logged out, donned her coat and said goodbye to Thumper, who'd now been joined by Dougal, Oliver was still staring at his cluttered desk.

She should simply say goodbye and leave. So why hesitate? There was a hint of dejection about his shoulders, something not quite right with his demeanour, and Anna stepped towards him.

'Er, Oliver?'

She'd expected zero response, but he swung around to face her. 'Are you sure there's nothing I can do?' His expression wasn't encouraging, but Anna drew in a quick breath, then let her words out in a rush. 'I have plenty of time on my hands. If you need help with anything else… I'm good at admin, and it would free you up to focus on your work more. I don't know how you find anything.' She gestured at the chaos on the desk, then raised her eyes to his. 'I don't mean to interfere.'

'You don't?' Oliver raised the habitual sardonic brow, and Anna wished she'd left when she'd had the chance. The man was impossible!

'Sorry. Just thought I'd offer. I'll leave you to it.'

She hurried from the room and sped down the stairs, grateful to soon be outside and inhaling the cool March air. Clouds had built up over the afternoon, and it looked like rain, so she turned her steps towards the town and was soon on the ferry bobbing across the cove. Not really the weather for a walk; she'd curl up with her latest read and Heathcliff, and try to forget the assessing look Oliver had thrown her as she left the room and why it had made her feel flustered.

–

Oliver was at a meeting in Bristol the following day, and Anna continued with her work, methodically transferring his edits to the file, typing up a new chapter – Oliver preferred to write longhand – then sitting back to enjoy reading the text. She chattered intermittently to Dougal and Thumper and welcomed the interruption of Mrs Clegg with some afternoon tea and biscuits around three. It was peaceful now the phone had been moved out and Oliver's mobile wasn't going off all the time.

Anna mulled over what Oliver had said, that he only switched it on if he expected a message or call from someone important; it had been on a lot this last week. Was it to do with this contract? He'd mentioned his agent. Perhaps it was her, trying to contact him. Poor woman.

Her phone rang.

'Hey, Nicki, hi!'

'So sorry to call you at work, Anna, but I need to ask a quick favour. Any chance – and please say if you can't – you could have the boys one weekend in May?'

'Yes! Yes, of course!' Anna smiled widely. Nicki's boys were lovely. A tad mischievous, but good company. 'Where are you going?'

'One of my oldest mates is getting married. Wasn't sure we could go, but Hamish reckons he can risk a couple of days off, and I can rearrange my shifts, but there are only two rooms left in the hotel we want to stay in, so I need to get it booked.'

Anna was about to respond when the door opened and Oliver walked in.

'Oh! I didn't think you'd be back so soon.'

'Change of plan.' Oliver threw his coat on a chair and sat down, pulling the post towards him, and Anna walked over to the window, lowering her voice.

'Sorry, Oliver just came back. Go for it, Nic. Let me have the dates when I next see you.'

'What if you're full with guests?'

Anna shook her head even though Nicki couldn't see it. 'I've not made much progress yet – I doubt I'll be up and running until summer.'

Pocketing her phone, Anna glanced over at Oliver. He was engrossed in his post, and she settled back at her desk, excited already for May. Having Liam and Jason to stay would be fun.

By the time the Easter weekend arrived, Polkerran Point bustled with activity. With the schools already on holiday across the country, the visitors had begun to arrive, and all the small businesses were putting finishing touches to their hanging baskets and window displays.

Anna awoke on Good Friday to cloudy skies. A hint of spring lingered in the air, and she walked out onto the terrace with her mug of tea, warmly wrapped in her dressing gown, and padded over to stand near the wall. The view of Harbourwatch from here was quite stunning. Although the exterior from this distance merely looked much as she had known it – dark and forbidding – the improvements to the interior had much influenced her impression of it. Not to mention her job there had become important to her, and either Oliver's abruptness with her had eased further, or she had developed an immunity to it.

A sudden gust of wind swept across the terrace, and Anna wrapped the gown closer across her front and turned away. Her mobile rang as she entered the house, and she snatched it up. Phoenix.

'Hey, what's up?'

'Anna, my lover.' Phoenix's tone wheedled, and Anna smiled knowingly. 'They've asked me to do a shift in Karma this afternoon as they're so busy. Mum's away and Dad's on a job up country. I don't suppose you could—'

'Of course I can. What time and for how long?'

'Just before two, for about three hours? You're a gem. See you dreckly!'

Anna grabbed the last piece of buttered toast from the plate, along with her half-finished mug of tea, and took the stairs two at a time to the bedroom. Verity Blue was adorable, mischievous, a little out of control, but she was a salve to Anna's need for children in her life, and she appreciated any opportunity to look after her.

–

The afternoon was fun but messy. Conscious she had finger paint on her shirt and several locks of hair stuck together with the glue Verity Blue had so generously shared with her, Anna welcomed the clearing skies to wrestle the child into her pushchair and go out for a reviving walk. They were due to meet Phoenix outside Karma, and that would leave Anna free to go home and shower and feel sticky-finger free.

A half hour later, Verity Blue sat contentedly on her lap, munching her way through a small ice cream, spreading much of it on Anna's jeans. With a contented sigh, she looked out over the cove, her heart full.

From this vantage point on the harbour wall, she could see both Westerleigh Cottage and Harbourwatch, each perched on their respective cliffs, with the lighthouse out on the far point. She must walk out there one day.

Anna adjusted Verity Blue's position on her lap, dropping a kiss on top of her burnished curls, her mind returning to work.

She looked forward to getting back to it on Tuesday. The book was coming along well, and Oliver seemed confident of getting it in by the deadline. Would he have any need for her after that? There must surely be edits to come back? But what then? Disappointed at the thought of her job coming to an end by the summer, she looked around at the bustling town, filled with Easter visitors.

There were plenty of opportunities in the shops and cafes for seasonal workers, but that wasn't going to fill the void of not working for Oliver.

Anna blinked. *A void? Really?*

Brushing the thought aside, she reached for her tissues as Verity Blue turned a beaming face to her, her mouth liberally spread with ice cream. Perhaps the B&B was the best option to look into going forward. Time she made some proper enquiries.

'You're beautiful,' Anna whispered into the child's ear as she tucked the damp tissue back into her pocket, and Verity Blue chuckled and leaned back against Anna.

'Birdies! Birdies!' She pointed at a couple of cormorants near the shore, and Anna clapped her hands.

'Well done, sweetheart. Birdies indeed.'

A sudden breeze came in across the cove, and Anna swept her hair out of her eyes, conscious of the sticky mass of glue again, but then something caught her eye and she almost gasped: Alex Tremayne was barely steps away from them.

Chapter Nine

Fate is a cunning hussy, and builds up her plans
as imperceptibly as a bird builds her nest

Elizabeth Gaskell, *Wives and Daughters*

Anna's insides swooped unexpectedly as she took in the figure sauntering along the harbourside. Alex's attention, on the other hand, was with his mobile, oblivious as ever to the startled pair of eyes watching him approach.

Heart pounding, Anna turned back to face the sea. Paint on her shirt, ice cream on her jeans, glue in her hair? After all these *years*? She held her breath as Alex passed behind them, relishing the sound of his voice and his laugh again, then let it go in a rush as he moved away.

Sophistication, Lauren had prophesied. *Cool, calm and collected*. Anna rolled her eyes. Fate was seriously having a laugh.

Half an hour later, she waved goodbye to Phoenix and Verity Blue and hurried through the town, wary eyes darting everywhere for any sign of Alex.

All those years of teenage yearning, of dreaming of his noticing her, and the first time their paths almost cross in over ten years, she looked like this? It had to be the first time she was thankful for being invisible to him!

Desperate to get home, Anna paused on the corner by the post office. She really needed to pick up some milk, and the small store on the other side of the cove would be closed by now.

She walked into the Spar, paid for her purchase and stowed it in her bag. Time to get home and indulge in that shower – no, make it a bath. She would have a really good soak.

Pausing in the doorway, Anna peered out of the shop. There was no one between her and the bridge, and—

'Oh! Sorry.'

With a small gasp, she took a step backwards as two men came striding in through the door and nearly knocked her sideways. Fate, up to its old game again.

Anna stared wide-eyed at Alex. 'It's okay.' She tucked the sticky piece of hair behind her ear and hauled her bag further forward in an attempt to hide the paint marks on her shirt. She had one foot out of the door when Alex spoke again.

'Hey, have we met?'

Clutching the bag even tighter, Anna glanced over her shoulder. He was frowning, but still impossibly good-looking. 'No. Yes. Sort of.'

She fled out of the door, her heart pounding as she hurried towards the bridge, keen to get out of sight, but she couldn't resist a quick look back down the street. Alex Tremayne remained outside the shop, his attention still on her.

'Hey, Anna!'

A voice hailed her as she sped past the chemist, and she turned around.

Jean Lovelace smiled. 'You look like you're running away from something.'

Or somebody? Alex's assessing glance had been unnerving. Anna summoned a smile. 'No, no. In a hurry to get home, that's all.'

'I'm heading back as well. Let's take the ferry.' Anna fell into step with Jean, thankful to have someone to talk to, and soon they were on board the ferry and bobbing their way across the water.

'I used to envy the idea of term starting up and the local kids taking this to school and back every day.' Anna raised her head to the breeze, thankful for its coolness on her flushed cheeks.

Jean grunted. 'You wouldn't in winter. Gales blowing, rain lashing and little shelter from it. A bedraggled caravan of school kids trudging up yonder hill to sit by inadequate radiators, steam rising from their clothes!'

Anna smiled, then turned in her seat to look over towards the harbour. There was no sign of Alex anywhere now. Her skin tingled. How could one small encounter turn her back into that quivering teenager?

A soothing bubble bath later, Anna dried her now glue-free hair and headed down to the kitchen to prepare supper. She felt more herself now, and rather amused at her reaction to Alex, but as she looked around the room, memories came flooding in.

Hadn't she been in this very kitchen, night after night during those long summers, first as a mere ten-year-old, then later as a teenager, longing to be glamorous and full of scintillating conversation, as dear Aunt Meg listened, consoled, brought home-made lemonade and soothing words? Well, glamour and scintillating conversation had been decidedly lacking. Anna laughed to herself. Ridiculous.

It was only as she inspected the vegetable rack for garlic that she realised she'd run out.

'Damn.' She looked at her watch. Thankfully, the Spar would still be open.

Shrugging into her jacket, she grabbed her purse and keys and half ran down the lane to the ferry, hopping from foot to foot as she waited for it to come in. Once back in the shop, she grabbed the garlic and paid for it, all the time looking around in case Alex lurked behind the shelves.

With a shake of her head, she stepped back out into the street. She was a right idiot. Her stomach gave a mild rumble, reminding her of the planned supper, and she turned back towards the ferry only to walk straight into Alex. He grabbed her arms to set her back on her feet as she stumbled, and Anna froze.

He said nothing for a moment, his eyes roaming over her face. Then he smiled, and her heart fluttered.

'Are you sure we've met? Think I'd remember you.'

'It was years ago.' There. That was the longest conversation they'd ever had! Aware of his amused expression, Anna pulled herself together. 'I used to spend all my summers here.'

Alex eyed her keenly. 'Good lord! We didn't date, did we?'

Chance would've been a fine thing. Anna shook her head. 'I was a child – a summer visitor. I used to hang out with Phee Radcliffe and her friends.'

He scrutinised her features. Then, the corners of his mouth twitched. '*Bambi*? You're that lanky kid who used to come down every summer?'

Anna felt a blush stain her cheeks.

'Hey, Bambi? It is you, isn't it?'

'Yes, it's me. Anna. How—' she cleared her throat '—how are you, Alex?'

He raised an amused brow. 'You remember my name.'

He really had *no* idea! 'You're very formal.' He bowed. 'Are we properly introduced now?'

Anna's heart danced. She felt like her entire face was smiling, from her chin to her hairline.

'So, what do you think of the old cove?' Alex waved a hand in the general direction of the town.

'It's as lovely as I remember.'

He glanced at his watch, and Anna bit her lip. Was she boring him already?

'Fancy a drink?'

Anna blinked. 'A— Er, a drink?'

'Yes, you know. That wet stuff they serve in glasses. Think they've heard of it, even here in deepest Cornwall.'

Seriously? Alex Tremayne was asking her for a drink! If her eighteen-year-old self had been here, she'd have squealed in delight. As it happened, Anna glanced at her own watch and made a point of shrugging. 'Sure. I have a bit of time.'

Alex gestured down the road and they turned their steps along Fore Street towards the Ship Inn. 'Lucky me.'

Anna followed Alex into the pub, hardly able to credit it, her supper long forgotten.

'What do you want?'

'Oh. Wine, please. Dry rosé.'

Alex placed their order, then turned around and leaned against the bar. Apart from a couple of visitors tucking into some sandwiches and beer near the fireplace and a group of young people playing pool, they were the only ones in.

'So, what brings you to Polkerran so early in the season? Crabbing on the harbour?'

'My aunt Meg left me her house.'

Alex raised a brow, but somehow Anna felt he already knew.

'Kind of the old bird. That's the big cottage on the cliff?' He gestured vaguely towards the other side of the cove.

'Yes. I think she felt I was almost family.' Anna wished she didn't sound so apologetic.

'Still. Generous all the same. Must be worth a fortune with the location and views.'

'I suppose it is.'

Anna took a sip of her wine, completely uninterested in her new home. She was standing in the pub having a drink with Alex Tremayne, for heaven's sake!

'So, what do you do here in this great metropolis?'

'I work for Oliver Seymour.'

Alex snorted. 'The History Man? You deserve a medal.'

'I enjoy it.' Anna spoke defensively.

Alex took a slug of his beer. 'And before you came here?'

'I was a project manager.' Anna wished she could give a more exciting answer, like 'I worked in television' or 'I was a chef'. 'What is it you do?'

'Private client work mainly. Up in the City, though it takes me all over the world.'

He'd get on well with Lauren.

'I've been thinking...' Why was she tempted to tell Alex? He'd hardly be interested. 'I thought I might explore setting up a B&B.'

Alex coughed on a last mouthful of beer. 'Excuse me.' Then he waved a hand at the table. 'Another wine?'

Anna eyed her still half-full glass. 'Oh, I don't know.'

'What don't you know, Bambi?' He leaned forward, and Anna was ensnared by those gorgeous eyes. Words simply wouldn't come.

'I'll take that as a "yes". Go and find a seat and I'll join you.'

Anna looked around, then walked over to a table with a wooden settle and two stools in the far corner and sat down. Her heart pounded twice as fast as normal, and her palms sweated. Was this really any way for a grown woman to behave? She squashed a ridiculous urge to check her ID to prove she was thirty, not thirteen.

She raised her eyes to Alex, who leaned nonchalantly against the bar while their drinks were prepared. Her brain had turned to mush. How could she think of anything remotely interesting to say to him?

'Cheers.' Alex placed two glasses on the table, but before he could take a seat, the door to the pub swung open and a young woman came in.

'Alex! Darling!' She rushed over and threw herself into his arms, and he laughingly held her away from him.

'Claudia, sweetheart. As low-key as ever.'

'Why didn't you say you were coming back this weekend? Daddy will be most put out if you don't join the shoot on Sunday.'

Anna wished she could've sunk into the flagged floor. This must be Alex's girlfriend. She was everything Anna was not. Not only did she have hair that shimmered and moved the way hair did in those impossible TV adverts, but she was dressed in the latest fashion. Lauren would go green if she saw those boots!

'No can do, Claud. Got to leave after brunch. Date in town Sunday evening, and I'm off to Henley on Monday to see mates.' He turned towards where Anna sat, looking from one to the other and wishing she was somewhere else. 'Do you know Anna? She's the new owner of Westerleigh Cottage across the cove.'

Claudia's surprise was evident. 'Really?' Then she turned to Alex. 'Forgive me, darling. Is this one of your private clients?' She turned back to Anna. 'He's such a dark horse. Sorry if I didn't understand. I'm Claudia Bond-Smythe. We live at Pengillis.'

Anna shook the extended hand. 'No problem, and no, I'm not a client.'

'Anna inherited from Meg Stratfield who used to live there. Isn't that great?'

'But I thought—'

'So, shall we see you at the dinner party next weekend? I'm sure Mother has invited you and the family. I'll be back for it.'

Claudia looked from Anna to Alex. 'I only got down from Bristol this instant, so I haven't been home yet. I saw your car outside.' She smiled at Anna. 'Will you excuse us a moment?'

She grabbed Alex's sleeve, and he threw Anna an apologetic look as Claudia dragged him over towards the door, hissing something at him. Turning away, in case he saw her looking, Anna picked up her unfinished glass and took a sip. Her empty stomach rumbled again, and she wrapped an arm around it.

'Shhh,' she cautioned. 'This really isn't the time.'

'Take no notice of Claudia. We've known each other since we were little kids. Acts like my big sister half the time.'

Anna almost rolled her eyes as Alex rejoined her. Men were so obtuse sometimes. 'She's very glamorous.'

'Is she?' Alex shrugged. 'Can't say I've noticed.'

He picked up his glass, threw the stool a cursory glance and came round to sit next to Anna on the bench, causing her pulse to up its speed from a canter to a gallop. She racked her brains for some conversation but ended up falling back on the mundane.

'Tell me a bit about your work in London.'

Alex raised a brow. 'Boring as hell, darling.' Then, he leaned close to her and whispered in her ear. 'I acquire things for people. Things they really want, and they pay me a hefty commission.' He placed a finger under her chin and turned her head to face him. They were very close, and she could see the gold flecks in his brown eyes. 'Sometimes, I acquire them for myself.' He ran the finger down her cheek, then laughed and picked up his glass.

Anna snatched up her half-empty glass and drained it. Good grief, he was potent stuff up close!

'So… tell me about these B&B plans. I might be able to help.'

'Really?' Anna put her glass down carefully.

With his background in business, Alex came up with things that hadn't even crossed her mind, and by the time their second drink had been consumed, he'd suggested Anna come along to the dinner party at his parents' home the following weekend so they could talk more about her plans.

Stunned by her good fortune, Anna walked back to the cottage, all thought of supper long gone. Who needed food when Alex Tremayne had asked for her number?

Chapter Ten

It's merely change of weather. We must expect change

Charles Dickens, *Dombey and Son*

In typical English holiday weekend style, the heavens opened on Saturday morning and it poured all day long.

'No going outside for you today, Heathcliff.' Anna stroked the young cat's now groomed fur as they both sat on the window seat in the kitchen observing the sheets of rain falling from laden skies. He didn't seem remotely bothered, curling up in a ball on the cushion, but Anna was. How could she accidentally bump into Alex again if confined to the house? Would he even come down into town in this weather, or stay up at the manor house with his family?

She sat at the table with a notepad and pen and opened the laptop. She would do some research for the bed and breakfast project. That way, if, no, *when* she saw Alex again, she'd have more questions and that would help her feel less vulnerable.

Anna pursed her lips. Did she feel vulnerable around him? Then she smiled sheepishly at the purring mound beside her.

'My heart does, Heathcliff. That's what feels at risk, even after such a short time.'

The cat raised his head briefly, but as Anna's attention had returned to the screen in front of her, Heathcliff tucked it back down, no doubt returning to his mouse-hunting dreams.

An hour later, Anna straightened and stretched her arms. Her shoulders were aching, and her eyes felt scratchy from looking at the screen. She glanced at the notepad and flipped it closed. She'd found out all she could online. It looked like a phone call to the local council office would be in order on Tuesday, along with enquiries on how to gain a Food Hygiene Certificate.

She looked at her watch, got to her feet and wandered listlessly around the cottage, ending up outside Aunt Meg's study. Perhaps now would be a good time to start sorting through all the boxes?

Ten minutes later, a mug of hot chocolate in hand and a Spotify playlist sounding out from her phone, Anna perched on a chair and surveyed the scene. There were several boxes stacked against the wall from when she and Jean had done the cleaning and a large bookshelf filled with books, many of which she'd enjoyed during her visits.

She turned around in the desk chair. Light poured in from the large window fronting on to the driveway at the back of the house, despite the grim weather, but then she noticed the trail of shells on the windowsill.

'You really loved collecting your shells, Aunt Meg,' she whispered as she got to her feet. What had she meant by 'follow the shells'? Where might they lead, and why?

'This is nothing but a line of shells,' Anna muttered as she looked at the sill. There also wasn't anything out of the ordinary about the solid cottage walls at either end.

One of Anna's favourite tunes came on, and she put her mug down and danced a few steps over to the nearest box, flipping the lid open and peering inside. It appeared to be full of old books, which turned out to be diaries, some ranging back to when Aunt Meg would have been a young woman.

Ignoring the more recent ones, Anna dug deep and pulled out a diary dated 1962. She bit her lip and looked around. Diaries were usually private, the personal thoughts of the owner, and not meant for other's eyes.

'I hope you don't mind, Aunt Meg,' she said softly. 'I'd love to read about your life back then.'

–

Pushing open the door to Karma, Anna threw back her rain-soaked hood and looked around. There were a few tourists huddled over the tables near the stylish log burner, which emitted a welcoming glow, and a young couple in one of the booths, but it wasn't Phoenix behind the counter today, just a cheery young man.

Anna ordered a hot chocolate, selected a cookie and relaxed into one of the squashy sofas by the window. A definite improvement on being alone in Westerleigh Cottage; some background noise, the murmur of conversation, the hissing of the coffee machine, and the occasional tinkle of the bell as the door opened.

She pulled the diary out of her bag and became engrossed in Aunt Meg's world when she was a woman in her twenties, not much younger than Anna was now.

Her chocolate grew cold, but she barely noticed as she devoured the entries. They weren't made every day, but on the occasions Aunt Meg had chosen to write, she usually covered several pages. Anna didn't recognise any names, and it wasn't clear where Meg was teaching – in a village school somewhere in Cornwall – but every now and then, some words were thickly crossed out, and several pages had been removed.

To her dismay, it was clear Aunt Meg still felt the loss of her little sister, even then. The latest entry read: *Today would have been Sarah's birthday. How the grief lingers.* Saddened, Anna closed the diary, but then a sharp rap on the window made her start, and looking up, her heart did a double thump. Alex grinned at her, and she waved tentatively, quickly putting the diary down as the door opened and he came in.

Anna willed the easy colour not to flood her cheeks; she didn't succeed.

'So, this is where you hide away.' Alex hung his dripping Barbour on the back of a nearby chair, running a hand through his hair and leaving it adorably tousled.

Anna smiled. 'Only when the skies are weeping. What brings you into town in this?'

Alex rolled his eyes and flopped onto the sofa beside Anna, whose heart rate picked up again. His leg stretched precariously close to hers. 'One gets rather stir-crazy at home. Mother can be quite suffocating.'

'Perhaps if you came home more often, she'd be less attentive. She probably misses you and the chance to look after you.'

Alex raised a brow. He was so close, and he smelt delicious. 'Perhaps I shall come home more often in future, if

99

I can find someone else who'd be prepared to look after me.'

He held Anna's gaze, and she swallowed hard. Was he flirting with her?

Anna grabbed her mug of cold chocolate and took a gulp, only to choke on it and endure the ignominy of Alex having to pat her on the back.

'Looks like the depressing weather has drawn the equally depressing History Man out.' Alex inclined his head towards the window, and Anna cleared her throat and turned to look.

Sure enough, Oliver opened the passenger door of his car, holding an umbrella as he helped Mrs Clegg out. She was carrying a wicker basket, and he passed the umbrella to her and walked back round to the driver's side, seemingly heedless of the weather.

Anna looked back at Alex. 'He's not depressing. What makes you say that?'

Alex pulled a face. 'Living in the past? Antisocial? Do-gooder?' He shrugged. 'Everything I'm not, thank god!' He got to his feet. 'Want a top-up?' He indicated the empty mug, and although Anna didn't really want another drink, she nodded. If he was willing to keep her company, she'd be a fool to say no.

Anna took in Alex's lean frame as he lounged against the counter, waiting for their order. The boyish charm that had made her heart pound as a young teen had matured into overwhelming good looks. There was no other word for it: he was gorgeous.

Anna looked away as Alex turned his head suddenly and caught her staring. How embarrassing! She may as well be that gauche teenager again. She watched the few people braving the elements as they scurried along the pavement. Oliver's car had gone, and she wondered fleetingly what he did with himself over this long weekend.

'Are you too warm?'

Alex placed two mugs on the table and resumed his seat by her side.

'Oh, no, not at all. I think perhaps I drank my hot chocolate too fast.'

Alex said nothing to this, but then he spotted Aunt Meg's diary, leaning forward to pick it up.

'Unusual reading matter.'

'It's one of Aunt Meg's from years ago. It's fascinating to read about her life back then.'

Alex grinned as he put it back on the table. 'The Swinging Sixties? Sex, drugs and rock and roll?'

Anna shook her head. 'If it was, that's not what she's writing about. She seems to enjoy documenting everyday life, everyday occurrences. Quite a few recipes I shall have to try out, books she has read, and so on. At least, so far as I've read. There are so many up at the cottage, it will take me all year to get through them.'

Alex lowered his cup. 'So, when do they start?'

'Not sure. I dug as deep as I could for this one.' Anna pointed at the one on the table.

'But they're all old?'

'I don't think so.' Anna paused. 'I'm sure I remember her occasionally writing in a diary when I used to visit her.' Then, she smiled at him. 'You seem very interested in them. Do you enjoy reading life stories?'

'Lord, no. Thought it might be worth publishing. Another possible income stream. Anything vintage sells these days.'

'Oh no, I couldn't. Besides, it really is only about everyday life. No scandal or intrigue.'

'Shame.' Alex glanced at his watch. 'Damn. Have to leave, I'm afraid. Said I'd pick up some wine and they close at four on a Saturday.'

They both looked up as the bell tinkled.

'Hello, Mrs Clegg,' Anna called, giving a small wave as the lady entered with her basket. 'What are you doing out in this awful weather?'

'Alright, dearie?' The old lady smiled and walked over, giving the umbrella a shake, but the smile faded when she saw Alex. 'Just picking up a few bits for dinner. Master Oliver's been working all day and didn't stop for lunch. I want to do something a bit special for 'im.'

'Don't you get time off at the weekends?'

'What would I do with time off?' Mrs Clegg's smile widened. 'Best to keep busy. Besides, writers don't get weekends. Master Oliver needs feeding today as much as any other.'

Alex got to his feet. 'I'll be off.' He picked up his coat from the nearby chair, but as he passed Mrs Clegg, she raised her chin.

'Back then, are you?'

'Like the legendary bad penny.'

Sensing some sort of tension, Anna looked between the two of them, but Mrs Clegg turned away.

'I've some shopping to do. I'll see you on Tuesday, dearie.'

'Bye, Mrs Clegg. Enjoy the rest of the weekend.'

The elderly lady ambled over to the counter to place her order, and Alex rolled his eyes, then grinned.

'Catch you later.'

Anna watched him stride down the street, then sank back into the sofa. All these years, then twice in as many days. What had fate got in store for her next?

It was only as she made her damp way home that she realised Alex still hadn't given her any details about the dinner party.

–

Easter Sunday brought better weather, with no rain and some broken cloud, hurried on its way by a stiff and somewhat chilly breeze.

Anna didn't linger when she went outside to get some logs from the store, and Heathcliff, having had his fur ruffled by the wind, soon took up his usual position on the window seat. She turned to another of Aunt Meg's diaries: 1972. Soon engrossed, she barely noticed when lunchtime came and went until Heathcliff's indignant mews alerted her to the hour. She put the diary aside with reluctance.

So, Aunt Meg had longed for love as much as Anna did, and although she had a home of her own – it was clear she now lived at Westerleigh Cottage – it was obvious her life felt empty at times.

'I wonder how she managed to buy such a property on a teacher's salary?' Anna mused, but Heathcliff merely mewed again, totally disinterested in the answer.

Anna fed the kitten, her mind wrapped in thoughts of Aunt Meg as a woman in her thirties, living alone here in Westerleigh Cottage. No wonder she set so much store by Anna's visits when she had retired. If only Aunt Meg had been her formal guardian, instead of Anna's cold and unfeeling cousin and her feeble husband. How different might all their lives have been?

Eating a quick lunch, Anna eyed the diary warily. Was it sensible to read on, or would it disturb her more?

When her mobile rang, Anna pounced on it. Lauren, up in Harrogate.

'Hey, how's it going?'

A rush of homesickness caught Anna's breath. 'Oh, it's fine. All I could ever hope for, but it's a bit lonely.'

'What about your frequent visits from the locals? Don't they happen at weekends?'

'Rarely, and it's Easter. Everyone seems to have plans except me. I'm not feeling sorry for myself, honestly. It's been such foul weather. I think I'm going a bit stir-crazy.' Anna sank onto the sofa and curled her long legs up. 'How are you? Has the newbie settled in?'

Lauren laughed. 'Let's say there's a different dynamic now we have a man in the house.'

'He did seem rather keen on sharing with women, didn't he?'

'I wouldn't mind, but he keeps borrowing my mascara.'

'And what about Georgia?'

'She's off visiting friends in Scotland – hardly seems to be here lately.'

'What about her job on the mag?'

'She gave it up. Seems the Mayor was pressing for a bit more personal attention to his column, if you get my drift.'

'Ewww.' Anna grimaced. 'That's awful. Did she report him?'

'No. I told her she should, but she's been a bit distracted. Her mother's putting pressure on her to settle down. Apparently, there's some bumptious cousin called Algernon or Aloysius or something similarly pompous they want her to marry, and Georgia's not having any of it. "Utter bollocks" was her last comment on it before she hightailed it off to the Highlands.'

'Poor Georgia. Perhaps she'll meet some gorgeous laird and elope, like they did in the old days. And what about you? Still seeing Kit, or have you sent him to join all your other cast-offs?'

There was a pause. 'Not yet.'

'Wow. He *is* lasting well. Are you hooked at last?' Anna's eyes widened at Lauren's uncharacteristic hesitation. 'Lauren?'

'Kit gets me. Like no one else ever did. We're both focused on the same things, you know?' A huff of breath. 'Never mind me. What about the blond hunk? Seen any sign yet?'

'I might have.' Anna grinned.

'Tell me now. I insist!'

Settling back into the sofa, Anna related her encounters with Alex in the past forty-eight hours. Barely had she ended her call when the doorbell pealed, and she hurried to answer it. The locals all used the boot room entrance, so who could it be?

'Oh!'

Alex stood on the doorstep.

Chapter Eleven

*He then departed, to make himself still more inter-
esting, in the midst of a heavy rain*

Jane Austen, *Sense and Sensibility*

Wishing she'd stopped to check her hair in the hall mirror, Anna opened the door wider. 'Come in. If you want to, that is.'

'I do want to.' Alex removed his coat, and Anna tried not to ogle the jeans hugging his hips and the close-fitting shirt emphasising his lean frame. She hung the coat on the stand and led the way down the hallway into the kitchen, turning around to find Alex immediately behind her.

'Oh!'

'You just said that.' The corner of his mouth twitched. 'Am I such a surprise?'

'Yes. I mean, no, not now, because I know you're here. But you were.' Did that make any sense? 'I thought you said you had to be back in London today.'

Alex followed her into the kitchen, and she threw another log onto the wood burner before turning to face him.

'I do. Heading off now, but was passing so thought I'd call in.'

Anna shifted uneasily under his steady look. Thank heavens she'd washed her hair that morning, though she wished she'd put on clothing a little more becoming than stretchy leggings and a well-worn shirt. She suddenly noticed the chipped varnish on her toes and stuffed her feet into her slippers. Alex, however, had turned to look around the room rather than at her.

'Would you like a cup of tea or coffee?' Anna gestured towards the Aga. 'The water's not far off boiling.'

'Shame to waste it then.' He walked over to the table in front of the window. 'Stunning views, even in this weather.'

'I know.' Anna came to stand beside him, hardly able to believe he was here at Westerleigh Cottage. Her teenage self would have been quivering. 'I can't believe I live here, even after several months.'

'I can't believe it either, Bambi.' Alex turned to face her. He was so close, and he still smelt delicious. Did he have any idea how much she wanted to run her hands through his thick, blond hair?

The sudden opening of the boot room door made her start, and tearing her gaze from Alex's, she took a step back and peered around him.

'Hey, Anna. We wondered if you—' Nicki fetched up short when she realised Anna had company. 'Oh, hi, Alex. How's life in the big city?'

'Invigorating. How's life in the small town?'

Nicki raised her chin. 'Quiet. Suits us perfectly.'

He smiled faintly, then sauntered over to sit on the sofa, and Anna hurried over to Nicki.

'What's *he* doing here?' she hissed as Anna joined her by the door. 'I didn't see him come up the lane!'

'I'm not entirely sure.' Anna bit her lip. 'I think he was just passing.'

Nicki smirked. 'Really? It's hard to "just pass" when you live on a no-through lane.'

Anna's discomfort must have been visible, because Nicki patted her on the arm. 'Take no notice of me. I popped round to see if you wanted to join us. We're holed up inside playing games with the boys. We'd planned a picnic, but the ground's so wet from yesterday, we're going to have it inside instead.'

'Oh, I – er...' She glanced over her shoulder. Alex's attention was with one of her magazines. 'Can I come round in a bit?'

'Of course. Come when you're ready.'

Anna closed the door on Nicki's retreating back and looked over at Alex.

'So. Tea or coffee?'

He looked up with a smile, then tossed the magazine aside and got to his feet. 'Tea, please.'

His smile had been able to do strange things to her years ago, but it had never been directed at her back then. The full impact was impressive, and Anna turned away. Time to focus on things like tea and water and how to put them together... though how to make a drinkable pot with her insides careering around like a drunk on a bouncy castle she didn't know.

'So, er, how do you know Nicki and Hamish?'

They had taken seats at the kitchen table with their mugs of tea and a plate of cupcakes, freshly baked by Anna that morning.

'Most people in Polkerran know each other.'

'Yes, so I'm beginning to find out.'

'I think she used to come to the manor to do mother's hair back when she first moved here – before she took up with the fisherman, that is.'

Anna sipped her tea. Alex's tone was a little derogatory, but she put it down to the fact he'd grown up in a manor house on a large estate. She supposed it would give you a superior view of things.

He eyed the kitchen now, and Anna smiled. 'It's a lovely room, isn't it? Did you ever come here before?' She knew he'd not visited during her own stays with Aunt Meg, but he'd been in the village all his life until he left for London as a young man.

'Only as far as the hall.' He looked around appreciatively. 'Needs some updating, but it's the view that will sell it.' He waved at the windows. 'Can't be beaten here in Polkerran.'

Anna frowned. 'It's not for sale.'

'No, I know. I spoke figuratively.' He gestured towards the window again. 'Not even Harbourwatch commands such a view, for all its size.' He glanced at Anna. 'How's it going, working for the History Man?'

'Great. Do you know him well?'

'In passing. Mother's been trying to court his company ever since he arrived – without much success, I might add.'

'The house has been beautifully renovated. Do you know who owns it?'

'Rick Devonshire, grew up in the cove. Bought it, did it up, never lived in it.' Alex drained his cup and glanced at his watch. 'I'd better go.'

He shrugged into his coat as Anna opened the door, but as he made to go past her, he stopped. He was so close, they were almost touching as he studied her intently before glancing at her lips. Anna caught her breath, then released it in a rush when he smiled.

'Thanks for giving me some shelter on this miserable day. And enjoy the—' he faked a yawn '—board games next door.'

'It'll be fun. They're good company. I'm glad Nicki came round.'

'And I'm glad—' Alex lowered his voice and leaned towards her '—that you came back to Polkerran.' Before she could realise his intention, he kissed her firmly on her lips, and then he'd gone, disappearing into the rain, and Anna closed the door and sank back against it, heart pounding in her chest.

She'd been so wrapped up in him, she'd forgotten to ask so many things: all those questions about the B&B; and she still had no details over timing, dress code, and so on for the dinner party; and by far the most important of all, why oh why had he kissed her?

—

'Your turn!'

Reluctantly, Anna took the console from Nicki's youngest, Jason. 'But I'm so bad at this!'

'There has to be someone who comes last,' said Liam sagely, the eldest at six, as Anna stepped in front of the screen.

'Make this the last round, boys,' Nicki called from the kitchen. 'Time we had our picnic.'

Jason whooped and high-fived his brother.

Their father got to his feet with a guffaw. 'It's okay, Nic. It's Anna's turn. She'll be ready in about three seconds.'

Anna rolled her eyes at Hamish and promptly delivered exactly what he'd predicted.

'Right, boys, time to help with the blanket.'

Everyone set to with their tasks, and Anna went to help Nicki carry the plates through, placing them on the blanket they'd laid in the small sitting room, while Hamish fixed them all a drink.

Looking around as the boys munched happily, the open fire giving out a lovely glow over the scene, Anna took a sip from her glass. Despite Alex's words, there had been no mention of board games – not that she'd have minded. She was definitely better at Trivial Pursuit than Dragon Quest!

They passed an entertaining hour enjoying the meal, and Anna leaned against the sofa, contributing to the interactions now and again but mainly a contented observer of Nicki's family life.

Anna's offer of help with clearing up was refused, so she sipped on her refreshed glass as the boys were persuaded to do their bit in collecting up the paper plates and serviettes. She smiled to herself as Liam, casting a peep towards Hamish – who was busy adding a log to the burner – shovelled the remaining sausage roll into his mouth.

Anna got to her feet and joined Nicki in the kitchen, dodging the boys as they shot back into the sitting room, begging their dad for a new round on the PlayStation.

'At least let me help with the washing-up.'

Nicki grinned and tossed her a tea towel as Hamish resumed the game-playing with the boys.

'Have you known Alex long?'

Anna picked up a tumbler, smiling wryly. 'I'm not sure.'

Nicki raised a brow as she rinsed a glass under the tap. 'Intriguing.'

'Not really. You know I used to come here for the summer when I was a child? Alex and his gang of teens were always around. I hung out with the younger local girls. It's how I met Phee.' Anna placed the glass in the cupboard and picked up another. 'So I've known of him for years, but he barely knew of my existence.'

Nicki threw her a puzzled look. 'So how come he called on you? I assumed he knew you through your aunt Meg.'

'We bumped into each other a couple of times this weekend, got talking. I had the impression he was bored stuck in the house by the weather yesterday and simply wanted to get out. Do you know him well, Nicki?'

To Anna's surprise, Nicki pulled a face. 'Not really. Nor do I wish to.'

'Why?'

'Oh, don't mind me.' She glanced towards the sitting room and lowered her voice. 'When I first came to Polkerran, and he came home for a visit, we'd sometimes be at the same social event. I used to see him when I went up to the manor to do his mother's hair, too.'

'I get the impression you don't approve of him.'

'He's alright.' Nicki dried her hands and turned to face Anna. 'Just be careful with your heart, Anna. He's got such charisma. It's hard not to fall under his spell.'

'Did *you* fall under his spell?'

Nicki didn't answer for a moment; then, she glanced towards the sitting room again, where the noise indicated quite a battle going on. 'For a while. I think every female of a certain age in Polkerran Point has been bitten by the Alex bug at one time or another.' She turned around and leaned against the sink. 'Hamish doesn't know, and I'd rather he didn't.'

'Of course.'

'Alex is a player, bit of a ladies' man. That's all I'm saying. Watch yourself, and—'

'Nic!' A shout came from the other room, and Nicki smiled. 'Take no notice of me. I'm an old married woman. Alex can be a lot of fun.' She squeezed Anna's arm gently as she passed. 'I'm coming. Is it my turn again?'

–

The skies had cleared when Anna woke on the Monday, and she saw to Heathcliff's needs before treating herself to a full English. It didn't hurt to practise, after all.

She ate it at the table, her eyes staring fixedly at Harbourwatch, but her thoughts on Alex. *Why* had he kissed her? She felt agitated but unable to put a finger on the reason. Then, she shook her head as she placed her knife and fork neatly on the plate and got to her feet. Time she found something to do instead of dwelling on such a trivial thing. She had a strong urge to go to work, even though it was still a holiday. Oliver would think her mad.

An hour later, Anna pulled into the car park adjacent to the cemetery and picked up a posy of spring flowers from the garden at Westerleigh. It was a chilly day, with a brisk breeze, and she wrapped a thick scarf around her neck in an attempt to keep her hair from blowing all over the place. Head down against the wind, she hurried over to the low stone wall and fetched up in front of the recently erected headstone.

'They've done your stone, Aunt Meg!' Anna whispered as she leaned forward to read it. She would have to ask Mrs Lovelace if she knew who had arranged for it. It was brief, giving her name, dates of birth and death, and then the words 'Selfless Love'.

The graveyard was well-tended, and Aunt Meg's own spot already sported some colour from the miniature spring bulbs, which must have been planted in the winter. Comforted, Anna filled the stone vase with water from the tap and chatted away as she arranged the flowers, knowing it was foolish but feeling the need to talk.

When she'd finished, she stepped back, tucking her hands into her pockets. Then she shuddered as she became aware of the cold wind again, and with a final pat of Aunt Meg's headstone, she hurried back to the car.

What should she do now? The rest of the day stretched before her, empty now Alex had left town. She paused at the exit to the car park, then turned the car to the left and drove down to Fowey, stopping by the community centre, which currently hosted a large antiques fair. She browsed the stalls, bending down to read the price ticket on a small table before becoming aware of someone beside her.

'Oh, hello.'

Oliver didn't answer, merely gestured towards the table. 'It's reproduction.'

'Is it?' Anna smiled, feeling a little awkward. 'I wasn't bothered about its age. I liked the look of it.' He had an uncanny knack for making her feel like a bit of an idiot.

She spotted a wooden box tucked under his arm and, catching the line of her gaze, he brought it out to show her. 'Is that...?' She looked up at him, but with the light behind him it was hard to read his expression. 'Isn't that a tea caddy?'

Oliver raised a brow. 'No, it's a large snuff box.'

'Oh!' Anna eyed it warily. 'But—'

He smirked. 'Yes, it's a tea caddy. Sarcophagus in style, see?' He held it out to her, and she took it from him.

The wood was polished and smooth, a real piece of living history, and Anna smiled. 'Aunt Meg has one of these. Not that she kept tea in it or anything, but she was very attached to it.'

'She showed it to me once. In the study?'

'Yes.' Anna smiled, thinking about the times she'd seen Aunt Meg polishing it. 'I like it. I love old things.'

Oliver made a faint sound, then cleared his throat. 'That's... fortunate.'

'Why?' Anna handed the caddy back to him.

'With the work you're doing for me.'

'Oh, yes, of course.' Anna cast a longing glance at the small table. She couldn't justify buying things she didn't need. She turned away, only for her attention to be caught by an attractive young woman glaring at Oliver across the stalls.

'Er, Oliver?' He raised a brow. 'Do you know that woman over there?'

His gaze followed Anna's. 'Yes.'

The woman turned on her heel and left, and Oliver shifted the tea caddy from one arm to the other.

'She doesn't look very happy to see you. Did you do anything to upset her?'

'Isn't that a rather personal question? She could be a scorned lover.'

Anna blushed. 'I'm sorry.'

'Don't be. She isn't. I'd best get along.'

'But—' Anna watched the back of the departing woman, and she became aware of Oliver shifting beside her.

Then, he sighed exaggeratedly. 'If you really must know, she was your predecessor.'

'Oh.' Anna bit her lip. 'Still, I am sorry. I shouldn't have pried.'

Oliver shrugged. 'She didn't take too well to being sacked.' He raised a hand as Anna went to speak. 'She had a tendency to snoop through my papers. I found it inappropriate.' He gestured around the hall. 'If you need any advice, let me know.'

'Thank you.' Anna smiled at him. 'Are you looking for anything in particular?'

'A few pieces for set decoration.'

Anna's eyes lit up. 'How exciting!'

'Is it?'

'A new historic production? Why not?' Anna gestured at the caddy. 'Is that for it?'

Oliver shook his head. 'This is mine.' He glanced around the packed fair. 'I'm off in search of a foot-warmer. See you later.'

Anna smiled faintly as he strolled away, then cast one last look at the table before moving on, heading for the exit until a lady hailed her from behind one of the tables. She didn't think she knew the stallholder who'd beckoned her, but walked over anyway.

'It *is* you! You used to visit old Meg Stratfield at the hospice!'

Anna smiled. 'I remember you now. You were on duty the day I got a puncture. Helped me sort it out.'

'I'm retired now.' The lady gestured at the various items of bric-a-brac on her table. 'Just indulging one of my interests.'

'I wish I could have visited Aunt Meg more often, but it was such a long way.'

The lady smiled kindly. 'She didn't know. She didn't know anyone for some time afore she passed.'

'But she did have plenty of visitors, didn't she? There was often a newspaper in the room or fresh flowers.'

The lady nodded. 'Oh aye. Friends came from the village, some quite regular. And there was another man who came a few times.' The lady frowned. 'Mind you, she had days when she got quite agitated round him.' She eyed Anna with sympathy. 'Part of the symptoms, I'm afraid. She could get quite worked up with all of us at times.'

They exchanged a few more words before Anna excused herself. She felt bad enough about not being there for Aunt Meg in her final months without the reminder.

Time for some fresh air.

Chapter Twelve

For what do we live, but to make sport for our neighbours, and laugh at them in our turn?

Jane Austen, *Pride and Prejudice*

Once back home, Anna took a long walk on part of the coastal path but, fed up with her own company, she then headed down to the local pub for her supper, content to read her book and pause to people-watch. Gavin and Sebastian, who owned The Lugger, had only recently tied the knot, and they were regaling the locals with tales from their honeymoon in Thailand, including Anna in their friendly banter.

Tuesday dawned fair and mild, typical after a long holiday weekend, and Anna had barely finished hanging out some washing when Daniel came around the corner of the house.

'Just the person I need to see.'

He smirked. 'And those are the perfect words to cheer you up when you're in the pits. Got any cake, Anna?'

'Why so glum?' Was it because his cousin had gone away again? Alex seemed to have that effect. She'd certainly felt out of sorts yesterday.

Daniel sank into his usual seat and grabbed a biscuit from the plate. 'Thought I'd got myself a date but she blew me off.'

'Oh, that's a shame.' Anna busied herself with the coffee pot. 'A visitor?'

There was no answer, and Anna glanced over at Daniel but his attention was with his phone.

She soon had the table laid up with the usual: a pot of coffee, mugs, sugar, milk and a plate of chocolate brownies she'd made the previous day.

Daniel shoved his phone back in his pocket and smiled. 'Excellent.' He reached for a slice and took the mug of coffee from Anna. 'You're a treasure, Anna Redding.'

'I have my motives.' Anna sank into the seat opposite, keen to grab a moment before anyone else appeared. 'Daniel, you know I'm thinking of opening a B&B?'

He nodded as he munched.

'I phoned the council this morning to find out what I need to do. I've got to register with them at least twenty-eight days before I start taking guests, and then they send round an Environmental Health Officer to do an inspection, but before that happens, I need some work done on the house. That includes setting up a separate food prep area so I can keep Heathcliff out. I thought perhaps the utility? I want to upgrade the appliances, too.'

'Of course. What about the sinks in the bedrooms?'

'They're in good condition for their age, but I think if I'm offering guests a room, I do need some power showers in both bathrooms. It's a shame I don't have any en suite rooms.'

'You won't have any problems. Not with this view.' He gestured towards the window. 'But yes, I can sort that for you.'

'Thanks, Daniel. You're the treasure, not me.'

His smile faded. 'Wish Claudia thought so.'

Claudia? *Claudia* was the girl he tried to get a date with?

'Claudia Bond-Smythe?'

Daniel looked surprised. 'You know her?'

'Not really. I was introduced to her briefly.' Her drink in the pub with Alex seemed ages ago.

Daniel put his mug down. 'Known her for years. Asked her out this weekend. It didn't go well.'

'I'm so sorry.' Anna eyed Daniel's paint-splattered overalls, the long ponytail and the copious facial hair. He was a lovely man, with warm brown eyes and an engaging smile, but with Claudia's glossy finish, it would be like trying to pair a solid workhorse with a dressage pony. Perhaps if Nicki gave him a makeover...

'Wasson, my lovelies?'

Anna and Daniel looked over as the door opened to reveal Mrs Lovelace, followed shortly by Nicki, who carried a large black bin bag, which she stowed by the door before joining the others at the table.

'Anything you need to tell us, Nic?' Daniel dipped his head in the direction of the discarded sack.

'Collecting for the stall sale.' She smiled at Anna as she handed her a plate. 'Raising funds for the Christmas lights.'

Anna was puzzled. 'Isn't it a bit early?'

'Goes on all year.' Mrs Lovelace jabbed a finger towards the bin bag. 'They goes door to door to see if anyone has anythin' they don't want or need no more.'

'They really go to town when the lights are launched.' Daniel took a sip from his mug. 'Probably the high-light of the village festive calendar, other than Biffy Bates squeezing into his Santa suit and turning up at the Three

Fishes with a full sack.' He waggled his eyebrows mean-ingfully, and Anna and Nicki were in stitches.

'I might have some things for you.' Anna wiped her eyes, thinking of all of Aunt Meg's clothes still hanging in her wardrobe. She hated the thought of removing them, but she'd already decided a charity shop was the best option. At least that way, someone would benefit from them. The wardrobe certainly didn't. 'I'll put a bagful of bits and pieces together.'

Busying herself with the coffee pot, Anna glanced at the clock. She had a couple of hours yet before she needed to get ready for work, which was a good thing as everyone was clearly up for a good chat.

'All going well at the big house, Anna?' Nicki took a bite of a brownie. 'These are lush!'

'Thanks.' Anna sank back into her chair. 'Yes, I'm enjoying the job. Oliver's an amazing historian, and his writing is so absorbing. It's a real treat, to be honest. Not really like work at all.'

'Still keeps himself to himself, do 'e?' Mrs Lovelace's face was alive with interest.

'I'm not sure I've worked him out. I mean, he's taciturn, almost to the point of rudeness sometimes, but I think half the time it's because he's so wrapped up in what he's doing he doesn't realise how he comes across.' Anna smiled as her gaze drifted out the window towards Harbourwatch. 'He's always very nice towards Mrs Clegg though.'

'Cleggie never has a bad word about him.'

There was a pause as Mrs Lovelace went to the bathroom and everyone had their mugs topped up, but although Anna was pretty certain Oliver wouldn't appreciate being their topic of conversation, she couldn't shake the feeling she was missing something.

'He must enjoy gardening if he helped look after Aunt Meg's garden, but why would he then employ someone to look after his own?'

Nicki shrugged. 'Pots and hanging baskets aren't really gardening, are they? Maybe he appreciated the physical workout this garden brought. He's in pretty good shape, after all.' She smirked at Anna, who rolled her eyes. 'That, or he's a bit of an eccentric.'

'That's what I thought at first. I mean, he's got all the house staff, but this chap doing the pots and so on seems really odd. It's a big house, but the paved terraces aren't like having to maintain Tremayne Manor with all its manicured grounds.'

Mrs Lovelace sniffed. 'They definitely have a team of gardeners for all those acres. Ruined it in recent years, too. Used to be laid out by that Calamity Brown.'

Anna exchanged a small smile with Nicki. 'I didn't know "Calamity Brown" had designed the grounds at Tremayne. How fascinating.'

'Much good it did him. Her Ladyship's had it all reworked now. Young Phoenix's dad was one of the gardeners on the job a few years back. All the villagers was jumping.'

Anna topped up the plate of biscuits, her mind still on the enigma that was Oliver Seymour.

'He's considerate. At least, towards Mrs Clegg, and Daisy, and Old Patrick.'

Nicki turned in her seat. 'You didn't hear about what happened to Cleggie, then?'

Anna looked up. 'No. Why? Is she okay?'

Mrs Lovelace tapped her nose. 'It's not widely known. Mr Seymour asked Cleggie to keep it to herself. Only told me, she did. And then I told Nicki.'

'Told you what?'

Nicki picked up her cup. 'Mrs Clegg was a tenant in a row of cottages on Deeping Lane, all owned by the Tremayne estate. The whole run has, one by one, been sold to out-of-towners, all willing to pay a premium. Locals didn't get a look-in at those prices, so now they're all second homes or holiday lets. Once Cleggie's lease was up for renewal...'

'It wasn't renewed.' Anna chewed on her bottom lip. 'What did she do?'

Daniel leaned forward. 'Yes, go on. I hadn't heard this. I wasn't living here back then.'

Nicki sighed. 'It was all very sad. She was very distressed. She's retired. Only got a small pension. The rent had been a peppercorn one, as she and her husband had lived there for decades. He worked for the Tremayne estate all his life. The council were looking for a small flat or bedsit for her in Bodmin. She was so upset about leaving the cove and perhaps not finding room for her pets. But then someone stepped in.'

'Oliver?'

Mrs Lovelace folded her arms. 'Gave her a home and a job. Took in her animals. She lives rent-free and gets a wage, too.'

'What about the others?'

'Old Patrick were right devastated when his wife died last year.' Mrs Lovelace shook her head. 'Wed these fifty years or more, they were. Went into a terrible decline. Then, he gets a call, sayin' Mr Seymour needed someone to do odd jobs and maintenance. Part time, about twice a week, but Cleggie says it's done him so much good. Given him a reason for livin', made him feel wanted, so he tends to pop in every day to see if there's anythin' he can do.'

'And Daisy?'

Nicki smiled. 'She's not trained for anything. When the Mariners Tea Rooms shut down, she wasn't sophisticated enough to get a job in the coffee shop or any of the boutiques. Cleggie told Mr Seymour, and he offered her the job of helping her out at busy times.'

'He doesn't entertain though, or have visitors.'

'Daisy still goes in every day. She loves it. Feels wanted too.' Nicki looked around. 'He's probably got no idea we all know.'

'He doesn't seem to go out much, other than to business meetings,' mused Anna. 'I've not known him do anything remotely sociable.'

'Mrs L has a theory about that, don't you?' Nicki turned in her seat to face the elderly lady.

'Aye.' Mrs Lovelace nodded. 'You'm mark my words, young'uns. One-woman man is our Mr Seymour. Never been seen out with a young lady here in the cove, has he?' She eyed her audience keenly. 'He still be hung up on his ex-wife. That's what I reckons. One woman only for him.'

Daniel leaned back in his chair. 'He was out last night, as it happens.'

Everyone exchanged a look, and Nicki grinned. 'Don't tell us he finally did have a date?'

Daniel picked up the last slice of brownie, but when he realised three pairs of eyes were fastened on him, he paused. 'What? Oh! No. I was coming out of the Three Fishes, quite early on, and passed him. Looked like he'd been walking that dog of his. He was helping old Charlie back to his cottage.'

Anna threw him an indulgent look. 'Walking the dog is hardly "out", Daniel.'

'Charlie's proper teasy of late. You'm mark my words.' Mrs Lovelace looked around sagely.

Anna got to her feet. 'So who's this Charlie?'

Nicki and Daniel spoke in unison: 'Charlie the Crab!'

Anna smiled to herself as she carried the empty plate over to the sink and turned on the tap. She'd discovered quite early on that people were defined by where they lived or what they did. Aside from Ray down the End, the electrician, there was Brian up the Top, a plumber, Tommy the Boat, the retired fisherman who did trips for the visitors in the season, and Colin the Cod, who ran the village chip shop.

Charlie the Crab was a new one, however. 'Don't tell me,' she turned around as the sink filled with water. 'Another fisherman.'

Daniel stretched his arms above his head. 'Nah. He's a bit too fond of the sauce. Most often seen walking sideways as a result.'

Anna turned back to the sink, conscious of a wave of contentment sweeping through her. Polkerran Point, with its stunning views, happy memories and its funny people, warmed her heart.

Aren't you forgetting something? whispered a voice in her head. Oh yes, and Alex. The boy she'd fallen hard for all those years ago.

The one who'd kissed her.

Chapter Thirteen

There is always a 'but' in this imperfect world

Anne Brontë, *The Tenant of Wildfell Hall*

Anna arrived at Harbourwatch not long after her visitors had left, her encounters with Alex over the weekend playing like a film in her head. She laughed softly as she let herself into the house. It was a good job Oliver was out at a meeting in Plymouth this morning and wouldn't see the inane grin on her face.

Popping her head round the kitchen door, Anna was surprised not to see Mrs Clegg. There was no sign of anything being prepared for Oliver's lunch either, or even of the coffee pot being warmed.

A noise came from the utility room, and she pushed open the door only to find Oliver in there.

'Oh! What on earth are you doing?'

There was silence for a moment before Oliver straightened, a packet of dog food in his hand.

'You really can't tell what I'm doing?' Dougal tucked into his bowl, and Anna released a huff of breath.

'Of course I can. I meant, being here. What about your meeting?'

Oliver dropped the packet onto the countertop and strode past her back into the kitchen, and Anna patted Dougal on the head before following.

'I'm not in it.' He picked up the pot from the stove, then lowered it again.

'But where's Mrs Clegg?'

'In bed, feeling unwell. She had a fall last night. Nothing broken, but she's a bit dazed and confused. The doctor's coming as soon as surgery's over.'

'But what about your meeting?' No response. 'Oliver?'

'I postponed it.'

'But—'

Oliver held up a hand. 'That's three sentences beginning with "but", which is three too many.'

Tempted to say 'but' again, Anna drew in a short breath. 'Fine. Here.' She held out her hand for the pot. 'I'll make the coffee.'

He handed it over and left the room. 'Thank you,' she muttered under her breath. 'Much appreciated.'

Oliver's head appeared around the door. 'Did you say something?'

'Just talking to myself.'

She set the pot to warm, flicked the switch on the kettle and hurried down the hallway to the door at the end, which led, so Mrs Clegg had said on her first day, to the annexe where she lived. There was no answer when she tapped at the door, so she went in.

There were three doors leading off the inner hallway. The first one was a small kitchen, the second a sitting room crammed with some worn-looking furniture, all sorts of knick-knacks, and in a cage by the window, two budgies.

Anna tapped on the last door and opened it slowly to peer into the room. 'Mrs Clegg?' she whispered. 'Are you awake?'

'Come in, dearie.' The voice sounded weak, but Mrs Clegg, when Anna walked over to the bed where she lay on top of the counterpane, smiled faintly, and Anna took her hand.

'Is there anything I can get for you? Oliver says the doctor is coming soon.'

Mrs Clegg's eyes closed for a minute. 'So good to me, is Master Oliver. He's 'ad no breakfast. Been looking after me since last night when I took ill.'

'I'm sure he can look after himself. But what about you?'

Mrs Clegg didn't seem to have heard Anna. 'Who's going to feed 'im? What about his lunch?' She grabbed Anna's hand. 'If I don't make 'im stop, he'll work on and on and on.'

'Don't you worry about that. You must focus on getting better. I'll pop along now and see what I can rustle up for lunch. I'll be back to check on you soon.'

Anna hurried back to the kitchen, racking her brains for a simple meal to prepare that wouldn't eat too much into her precious typing time.

She took the coffee tray up to the office and the next hour flew by, as Anna made her way methodically through the latest edits, stopping now and again to refresh the mug on Oliver's desk and let Dougal out for a run around the walled garden.

Then, she popped along to Mrs Clegg with a cup of tea, but the lady was fast asleep. Anna looked at her watch just as the doorbell rang. She quickly ushered the doctor into Mrs Clegg's room and waited in her sitting room for his verdict. There were so many things spread around the room: old photos in china frames, a collection of small brass animals, a silver trinket box and a pile of *People's*

Friend magazines. A bag of knitting rested by one of the armchairs and a book lay on the side table, topped by a pair of glasses.

The doctor was swift in his assessment, getting straight on the phone.

'She needs to go into the hospital, hopefully for no more than twenty-four hours.'

'Is it serious?'

'It could become so if we don't act. Looks like a nasty UTI. We need to assess her kidneys.'

Anna fetched Oliver, and he helped Mrs Clegg to her feet when the ambulance came and into a chair to wheel her outside. Anna carried out the bag she had packed under the lady's instruction.

With Oliver gone to the hospital with Mrs Clegg, Anna tried to focus on her work, but soon after he returned, she slipped from the room to get lunch ready. Engrossed as she was in preparing a salad to accompany the three-egg omelette simmering in the pan, she wasn't aware of Oliver's presence until he spoke.

'I'm going to have to increase your pay.'

Anna glanced over her shoulder. 'Please tell me you like eggs?'

'Yes.' He frowned as he inspected the pan on the stove and threw her a puzzled glance. 'What about you? Are you not eating?'

'Oh! No. I mean, I thought I'd take Dougal for a proper walk. I'll grab a sandwich from Karma.'

'We'll share this, then we'll walk Dougal together. I need to sound something off you.' He glanced out of the window. 'I'll treat you to an ice cream.'

Their lunch had been consumed in silence, and when the dishwasher had been stacked, Anna fetched Dougal and attached his lead and followed Oliver out of the door.

She felt a little awkward. Other than bumping into him at the antiques fair, she'd never had anything to do with him outside of the cocoon of the office, and while she was pretty comfortable with their working pattern, she knew very little about him.

Oliver didn't seem to feel the need for small talk, though. He walked with a confident stride, and although Anna had long legs, she had to make an effort to keep up. It was only as they fetched up outside the ice cream shop that he turned around, handing Dougal's lead to her.

'Any preference?'

'Chocolate, please.'

He smirked. 'Predictable.'

'What do you mean?'

He looked back over his shoulder as he entered the shop. 'I had you down as a traditionalist.'

Anna turned her back on the ice cream shop and looked out over the harbour. What did *that* mean? Did she bore him?

'I'm not good at pretending I'm someone I'm not, Dougal.' She bent down to pat him on his head, and he peered adoringly back at her.

'You wouldn't be working for me if you were.'

She spun around. Oliver had come back to the door. 'Cone or tub?'

'Cone, please.'

He took on a pained expression. 'Sprinkles or—' he looked back over his shoulder '—smarties or caramel chunks?'

'Oh, er, nothing, thanks. Just the ice cream.'

'Traditionalist.' He headed back into the shop, and Anna smiled.

He returned within minutes with three unadorned cones: a chocolate one, which he handed to Anna, and two vanilla, the smaller of which he offered to Dougal, who wolfed it down in one. 'Special dog ice cream. Shall we walk?' He gestured across the road and they walked towards the harbour wall.

It was such a mild day after the unpleasant weekend, with a hint of the summer to come, and Anna felt awash with memories of her childhood as they sat on a bench to look out over the water.

'I used to sit on those steps for hours.' She gestured over to where some holidaymakers were gathered.

'Crabbing?'

'Yes. Did you ever...?' She hesitated. Oliver was always so immaculately turned out in his shirt and tie and his waistcoat, she couldn't picture him as a little boy, getting stuck into the bait bucket.

'There are so many possible endings to that sentence.'

Anna couldn't help but laugh. 'Sorry. I was wondering if you ever did that sort of thing: went on holiday to the seaside, sat on the harbour wall for hours, crabbing or fishing.' She glanced at him, and he raised a quizzical brow.

'Is there any reason why I wouldn't have?'

'No, of course not. I was...' Anna turned away to look across the harbour again. He was impossible. 'I know some people aren't so lucky.'

'I wasn't.'

Anna turned back. 'Oh. I'm sorry.'

'Don't be. I'm not.' She bore his scrutiny for a moment. 'I grew up abroad.' Oliver fished in his pocket and pulled out a neatly pressed white handkerchief. 'Here.'

'Oh, thanks.' Anna eyed it warily. It was immaculate. Was she really supposed to wipe her fingers on it? Reluctantly, she did so before handing it back.

'You missed some.'

Her eyes widened as he reached over and dabbed the handkerchief near her bottom lip. 'See?' He held it up to show a small patch of brown.

Mortified to think she'd had ice cream around her mouth, like a child, Anna felt warmth fill her cheeks. 'Thank you,' she whispered.

Oliver appeared unfazed, tucking the handkerchief back into his pocket and stretching his long legs out in front of him. A family gathered on the little beach below them, which only became exposed as the tide receded, and they watched them in a comfortable silence for a moment.

Anna smiled as the little girl of the family, paddling in the shallows in her bright pink wellies, held up a large shell, crowing with delight.

'So cute.'

Oliver grunted. 'I don't do children.'

'Oliver!' Anna spluttered. 'Children aren't something to be *done*!'

'Come on.' Getting to his feet, Oliver unwrapped Dougal's lead. 'Let's take this hound for a run.' He waved a hand towards a side street, which led to an open patch of ground where dogs could be exercised, and Anna fell into step beside him again.

'You haven't asked what it is I wanted to talk to you about.'

It wasn't a question, and if she'd said it, he would have seen no need to answer, but Anna wasn't Oliver. 'I assumed you'd mention it when you were ready.'

'You assumed correctly.'

They emerged from the lane and passed through a gate into the grassy area before he let Dougal off the lead. Watching the dog tear across the field in search of who knew what, Anna smiled.

'He's lovely. Where did you get him?'

'I didn't. He was outside the gates when I got home one night. When I went out the next morning, he was still there, so I asked Mrs Clegg to feed him. Fatal mistake. He's been a fixture ever since.'

'Did you never try to find his owner?'

'No.'

'Why did you call him Dougal?'

Oliver turned his head, and she fidgeted under his piercing look. 'It's a dog's name.'

'Yes. Of course.' Anna was confused. 'But then, what about Thumper?'

'I didn't name her.'

'But it's a rabbit's name!'

Oliver's brow rose. 'Really? Is that official? There's a list of rabbit-only names?'

Anna's lips twitched. 'Yes, probably. Online somewhere.'

'People need to get out more.'

With a laugh, Anna surveyed the open field. 'It's from *Bambi*. I loved that film, even though it made me cry.'

Oliver blew out a breath. 'Disney crap.'

'Oliver!' Anna looked at him in disbelief. 'Every child grows up on a dose of Disney.'

'Not me. Never saw a single one.'

'Never?' Anna sobered. What sort of childhood had this man had?

Oliver eyed her in silence for a moment. Then, a glimmer of mirth shone in his eyes. 'Got you again.'

Torn between exasperation and amusement, Anna shook her head. 'Why do you *do* that?'

'Easy target? Bit hard to resist, I'm afraid.'

'So you *did* know Thumper was a rabbit...?'

His gaze roamed over the expanse of long grass. Dougal was having a good run around. 'You shouldn't believe everything you're told.'

So she had begun to learn where Oliver was concerned! Anna glanced at her watch. Time moved on, and she pulled her thoughts together. 'So, are you ready now?'

'For what?'

Anna rolled her eyes. 'What did you want to talk about?'

'Work.'

Obviously. 'What about it?'

'I'm leaving Harbourwatch in September.'

'Oh!' Disappointment flooded Anna. 'I— That's a shame. Are you buying something here in Polkerran?'

'No.'

'So why are you leaving?'

'Why not? I only took the lease on the house for three years. It's convenient timing. The owner is coming back. The book's as good as written. There'll be some structural edits, and once it's done, I'm due to go on a two-week lecture tour. Then, I'll start packing up.'

'Won't all the schools and colleges be over for the summer?'

'Precisely. I go to conferences, seminars and summer schools aimed at mature students, scholars and researchers. They like to use empty university campuses.'

Feeling a little stupid, Anna said nothing.

'I need you to help me with it.'

'I can't come with you! I have Heathcliff to look after, and I'm trying to set up a business.'

Oliver turned to look at her. His face was inscrutable. 'I'm not asking you to accompany me.'

Anna felt even more stupid. 'Sorry, of course not. So what—'

'Are you prepared to take on more work? I need someone to organise the itinerary, sort out travel, accommodation, and so on. There will be talks to type up and slides to prepare.'

He spoke in an offhand manner, as though he didn't care either way whether she took him up on it, but Anna leapt at the chance.

'I'd love to. I used to be a PA, so I'm more than capable.'

'I know that.' Oliver put two fingers in his mouth and whistled, and Dougal came running and patiently submitted to having his lead attached.

They walked back to the house in silence, but it felt far more comfortable to Anna than when they had left. She didn't like to think about Oliver leaving Polkerran at the end of the summer, though – poor Mrs Clegg, Daisy and Old Patrick!

Chapter Fourteen

It is not everyone, who has your passion for dead leaves

Jane Austen, *Sense and Sensibility*

Mrs Clegg made a swift recovery in hospital and was soon discharged into the care of her niece, who came over from Falmouth to collect her.

Anna started to go over to Harbourwatch earlier still, so there was time to deal with the book edits, start on the itinerary and prepare some lunch. Busy liaising with various people on Oliver's behalf, and trying to be a calming influence when his patience wore thin, she enjoyed herself.

As Thursday lunchtime approached, Anna hurried down the stairs, stacked the coffee things in the dishwasher and opened the fridge. Thankfully, she'd made a quiche the day before with Oliver in mind. She'd rustle up a small salad and once the quiche was warming in the oven, she'd heat up the home-made soup she'd also brought over in a flask. With a couple of rolls, that should suffice.

They had eaten the soup in silence, but as Anna cleared the bowls away and brought over the quiche, she felt the need to break it.

'What brought you to Polkerran?'

'My car.'

'Very funny. You know what I mean.'

Oliver got up and fetched the bowl of salad, placing it in the centre of the table, and Anna cut a slice of quiche and passed the plate to him as he retook his seat.

'Enlighten me.'

'Why pick this particular coastal village? Cornwall is full of wonderful boltholes for someone wanting to shut themselves away to write, and there are plenty more remote than this one. If you didn't want to socialise or put up with the locals' gossip, why not rent a barn conversion up on Bodmin Moor?'

'I'm not averse to civilisation.'

With a smirk, Anna piled salad on her plate. 'Just people. And conversation.'

Oliver took the bowl from her. 'This is a conversation, isn't it?'

Yes, but hard won! Typically, silence fell as they ate their lunch, and when they had cleared the table and filled the dishwasher, he held the kitchen door open for her and then followed her along the hall.

As they mounted the stairs, however, he said, 'A connection brought me here.'

Anna cast him a curious glance as they reached the landing. 'And this house is ideal, isn't it? So cut off from the world on one side by the high wall and the sea on the other. Perfect for a writer.'

Oliver said nothing as they returned to their respective desks.

'Do you know the owner of this house, then?'

'No.' Oliver started to type on his laptop and with a shake of her head, Anna turned to her own. Conversation duly ended.

Friday commenced in similar fashion, with a manic morning in the office, enhanced by Oliver's need to leave after lunch to fetch Mrs Clegg home from her recuperation in Falmouth.

'You like history.'

Anna eyed Oliver across the kitchen table when they paused for lunch. He'd insisted she join him again, though he'd drawn the line at her doing any more catering and had sent Daisy off to get sandwiches for them.

As usual with Oliver, it wasn't a question, but Anna chose to answer it all the same.

'It was my favourite subject at school, and I never lost my interest for it.' She paused as Oliver topped up her glass with some of Mrs Clegg's home-made lemonade. 'I wish I'd studied it at uni, but I went down the English Lit route instead.'

For a moment they munched quietly on their sandwiches. She wanted to ask Oliver about his own love of the subject: what had set him off in the first place? What had surprised him most in all his research around his writing? Did he plan to write any more books?

'I can sense the myriad of questions on the tip of your tongue.'

Taking a sip of her lemonade, Anna pulled a face. 'I've always had a readable expression. I'm not very good at concealment, I'm afraid.'

Oliver got to his feet. 'Concealment is not something I want in anyone around me.' A strange look crossed his face, but it was gone in an instant. 'Tea?'

He picked up the kettle, and Anna shook her head. What had that look been for? Had he been bitten by deceit before?

'So can I ask a question?'

He leaned against the worktop. 'No.'

Fine!

'I'll make myself a hot chocolate.'

A grunt was the only response to this as Oliver filled the kettle and switched it on, and Anna busied herself.

'It will make you sleepy.'

She looked up. He nodded towards the hot chocolate in her hand, and Anna smirked. 'No, it won't. I drink it all the time. It's my secret indulgence. Doesn't everyone have one?'

He didn't answer, and she busied herself clearing the table as Oliver made his tea, and once they both had a full mug, she followed him out of the kitchen.

'Come with me.'

To her surprise, he didn't go straight back upstairs to the office but along the main hallway to a part of the house she'd never seen before, fetching up by a pair of panelled doors.

Mystified, Anna followed Oliver into the room, then gasped.

'It's like an antiques shop!' Oliver looked a little sheepish, and Anna's heart went out to him. 'This is your secret indulgence.'

He didn't answer her, gesturing around the room, and taking it as an invitation, she wandered around, admiring the cabinets of silver – things she often saw on her favourite antiques shows such as snuff boxes, pin cushions, card cases and several things she couldn't identify.

'What's that?'

Oliver came to stand beside her, then tugged the glass door open and reached for the item, handing it to Anna, who laid it on her palm.

'It's a nutmeg grater.'

'It's beautiful,' she whispered, and to her surprise, Oliver laughed.

'Why are you whispering?'

'Because of its beauty and age.'

'You know it's old? How old?'

Anna all but rolled her eyes at him. 'Of course I know it's old. You wouldn't have it here if it wasn't. As for *how* old...' She hazarded a guess. 'Early 1800s?'

Oliver raised a brow and took it from her. 'Not bad. It's George III. What about this?'

He handed her an unusually shaped implement, long and narrow, not a spoon exactly, and she weighed it on her hand, then looked for a hallmark.

'It's a marrow scoop. What can you see?'

Anna screwed up her eyes. It was tiny, but she could make out an anchor.

'Birmingham!' She announced with satisfaction.

Oliver took it from her and replaced it in the cabinet. 'Do you know about antiques?'

'Not really.' Anna strolled further on, aware he followed her, her hand trailing across side tables, fine chairs and a bookcase filled with what were clearly early editions of novels. 'I love watching the TV programmes. You know: *Bargain Hunt, Flog It!, Antiques Road Trip.*'

'I enjoy them too – but more behind the scenes.'

Anna spun around. 'You do work for them? I've never seen you on screen.'

'I'm not an expert, I'm a historian. I get consulted from time to time on various stories but never on camera. Not for them, anyway.'

Anna smirked at him. 'I'm surprised you love these inanimate objects so much if you don't like concealment.

Don't you find things of historical interest often have secret pasts?'

Oliver walked past her and picked up a heavy object from a table. 'Like this?'

'Oh!' Anna let out a small gasp. He held up a very old pair of handcuffs, fashioned from rustic iron. 'Very *50 Shades*. I bet they could tell a story.'

'Precisely.' He put them back in place. 'Well, this is it.' He waved a hand around the room. 'I couldn't bear to put it all in storage.'

No wonder he needed such a big house.

'I expect there will be antiques up at Tremayne Manor.'

Oliver raised a brow as they turned for the doors. 'You've not been inside?'

Anna came to a halt as he opened the door and moved aside for her to go through. 'Never had the chance until now.'

He followed her along the hallway towards the stairs. 'And now?'

'I'm going to a dinner there tomorrow night. It'll be my first glimpse.'

Oliver said no more as they returned to the office, but once inside, Anna eyed him with curiosity. 'Why did you show your antiques to me?'

He looked surprised as he sank into his chair. 'You have an appreciation for history.'

Smiling to herself, Anna took her own chair. He was an enigma, her boss, but every now and again, he had a certain appeal.

'Oliver?'

There was no reply, and Anna turned to face her computer. Business as usual, then.

'What?'

She spun around in her chair to find he'd turned too. 'I was curious...'

'You always are.'

'I know. Bad habit. Sorry. But why is the Birmingham assay mark an anchor? I mean, it's about as far from the sea as you can get.'

'That may be so now. In the past it was a vast port.'

Staring at him, Anna tried to think back to her history and geography lessons at school but couldn't recall anything of the sort. 'How... I mean, what happened to...'

'The sea?' Oliver shook his head and turned away again. 'So gullible. It's thought it's because Matthew Boulton – who fought for Birmingham and Sheffield to have their own marks – stayed at the Crown & Anchor tavern in London while lobbying for Royal Assent to the Assay Bill.'

'So that's why Sheffield has a crown?'

'Precisely.'

'It's a good job the Slug & Lettuce didn't exist back then.'

Oliver made no response to this, and Anna smiled again as she turned back to her keyboard. Yes, she was right.

For all his abruptness, she quite liked Oliver Seymour.

–

Oliver set off at two thirty to pick up Mrs Clegg and hadn't returned by the time Anna left for the day. She'd finally got confirmation from Alex of the time for the dinner party, but when it had come to anything else, he'd been vague, saying it was like any supper, nothing too fussy. What did *that* mean?

When it came time to get ready on Saturday, Anna went up to her room and eyed her reflection. She knew she wasn't bad-looking. She had large eyes, smooth and clear skin and a good figure, though probably a bit too curvy for the current fashion. But somehow, she'd always felt very 'girl next door', so how on earth was she supposed to turn into the elegant, sophisticated sort of model she knew Alex admired in the space of two hours?

Anna released a huff of laughter. Was she really thinking for one minute a man like him would ever consider *dating* her? But he had invited her, hadn't he? And he had kissed her…

The memory of the sudden pressure of those lips against hers turned Anna's insides to mush, and then she gasped. He'd probably meant to kiss her cheek. What if she'd moved her head when he wasn't expecting it? This galling thought was interrupted by a voice from downstairs, calling, 'Hey, anyone home?'

Nicki! Anna hurried down the stairs to find her peering round the kitchen door.

'What are you doing here? I thought it was quiz night down The Ship.'

Nicki was an avid team member and proudly claimed never to have missed a quiz night.

'Doesn't kick off until nine. I'm here to help.' She waved the bag she carried and followed Anna down the hall into the kitchen.

'With what?'

'With you.' Nicki eyed her up and down keenly. 'Yep. You sure need it.'

Anna pouted. 'Is it really that bad?'

'You're perfectly lovely as you are.' Nicki grinned. 'But is the divine Mr Tremayne going to be there?'

Anna couldn't halt the blush from stealing into her cheeks, and Nicki grinned. 'No time to waste then. Go shower and wash that hair, but don't dry it. I'm in charge of your styling tonight.'

'But he said it was an informal dinner party with a few friends.'

Nicki pulled a face. 'Not sure he's got that many friends, but it will be rammed with people, and even though the food is likely to be informal, the people, not so much. The women especially will be dressed as if it's Lady's Day at Ascot.' She chuckled. 'Though perhaps minus the fascinators.'

'I thought you didn't approve of Alex.'

Nicki's face softened. 'Pay me no mind, Anna. He probably needs the love of a good woman to sort him out. He's a bit of a ladies' man, but that's all.' She smiled. 'Now, let's get to work.'

'I really don't think—'

'Good. Best that you don't. Off you trot.' Nicki was clearly in 'mother' mode as she ushered Anna towards the door and began unpacking her bag.

-

An hour and a half later, Nicki admired her handiwork. She hadn't allowed Anna to look in the mirror once.

'Not bad, even if I do say so myself.'

Anna looked up from staring at her nails. They felt strangely unlike her own, which they should, because they weren't. Nicki had taken one look at Anna's short, neat nails and tutted.

'Not a chance you'll hook him with these babies. He's all about glamour, love, not efficiency.'

'What if they come off?'

'They won't. That's an industrial-strength glue I've used.'

Anna's mouth formed a round O. 'But how do I take them off when I want to?'

'I'll tell you about it another time. Come on, we haven't got long, and you need to get dressed. What are you wearing?'

'Can't I look at myself yet?'

'No. You can look two minutes before going out the door.'

'But then it will be too late to change anything!'

'Precisely.' Nicki beamed at her and Anna raised a hand to the waves dancing against her cheeks.

'I thought you were using your straighteners to give me that smooth, glossy mane I've always coveted.'

Nicki shook her head as they left the room. 'All the women will look like clones. Long hair, straightened to within an inch of its life. You need to stand out.'

Anna's step faltered as they reached the stairs. 'Do I have to?'

'Yes.' Nicki urged her onwards. 'Now show me what you've chosen to knock Alex dead.'

A quick inspection of the black trousers and cream striped shirt and a roll of Nicki's eyes was enough to warn Anna that something else would be pulled out of the bag of tricks.

Chapter Fifteen

She meant to be impertinently curious

Jane Austen, *Emma*

A young girl relieved Anna of her coat when she arrived at Tremayne Manor and, when she enquired after the location of a bathroom, tottered down the hallway, feeling like she'd never worn high heels in her life. The sound of voices and laughter spilled from a vast room to her right, and Anna shuddered. Never had she felt so socially inept!

She closed the door of the spacious toilet and caught sight of her reflection in the ornate mirror above the sink, almost not recognising the young woman before her. To be fair, Nicki had done a tasteful job of glamorising Anna. Her mouse-brown hair framed her features in soft waves, bearing a sheen she'd never been able to achieve. It was a flattering style and gave no hint of having taken so long to achieve. Thankfully, Nicki had foregone pressing false eyelashes on her because her own were so thick, but the acrylic nails still clung to Anna's own in a completely unnatural way.

Opening her bag with all the elegance of Edward Scissorhands, Anna extracted a tissue, blotting her skin out of habit, but unnecessarily. Nicki had done a very professional job with the make-up, too.

Anna turned to face the full-length mirror on the opposite wall. Sharing a similar shapely frame to her friend, she had allowed herself to be dressed in one of Nicki's former 'pulling' dresses, as she had called it: plain black, which Anna approved of, but hugging every curve of her body, which she did not, and exposing quite a length of leg because she was so much taller than Nicki.

'You know what the style mags say,' Nicki had admonished, as Anna tugged at the hemline. 'Show your cleavage or show your legs, but never both at the same time.'

Anna felt horribly self-conscious, turning this way and that as she eyed herself in the mirror. How was anyone supposed to eat anything dressed in such a way? Where was all the food to go?

She opened the door and stepped out into the hall as two women passed her. They both shone with glamour and sophistication, but clearly hadn't read the article about neck versus hemline. How was *this* a casual supper? Anna walked back along the hallway. She hesitated outside the room from which all the noise was emanating, debating on whether to turn tail and simply go back home, when a voice spoke behind her.

'Allow me.'

What on earth is Oliver doing here?

He pushed the door aside, and Anna whispered 'thank you' and walked into the room.

Conscious he had come to stand beside her, she threw him a quick glance, only to discern his very obvious double take.

'I didn't realise it was you.'

Anna frowned. 'You see my back all the time when I'm working for you. How could you not know it was me?'

A faint smile touched the corners of his mouth. 'Perhaps it's because you're normally sitting down.'

Warmth flooded Anna's cheeks. 'Oh.' Was he paying her a compliment? Oliver remained by her side but said nothing more, and Anna blurted out: 'I didn't know you were coming.'

There was no response for a moment, and she glanced up at him.

'Oliver?'

He shrugged. 'Last-minute decision.'

'I didn't know you knew the Tremaynes.'

Oliver regarded her in silence for a moment, then said, 'Should you know everything?'

'But—'

'I've done business with them in the past.'

Anna longed to ask what sort, her curiosity at its height, but a young lad had appeared before them with a tray of champagne, and she reached for one, forgetting about the false nails giving her a reach she didn't normally have and knocking the neighbouring one backwards.

'Oh no! I'm so sorry!'

As the fizzy liquid dripped from the tray, Oliver offered a clean and neatly pressed handkerchief to the nonplussed waiter who had been liberally showered in champagne and took a glass for them both before steering Anna over to the side of the impressive drawing room.

'Interesting colour.'

Anna put a hand to her face, but Oliver laughed, something he did so rarely, she blinked.

'I meant the nails.'

'Oh.' Anna drew in a sharp breath. 'My friend thought it was… sophisticated.' She studied the dark red of her false nails.

'You have no need to try and be sophisticated.'

'What do you mean?' Anna bristled, then took a long swig of her drink. At least she wasn't so tightly under regulation that she didn't know how to enjoy herself. Who carried neatly pressed white handkerchiefs these days, anyway?

'I can see you're a little preoccupied. I'd better pay my dues to the hostess.'

Before Anna could speak, Oliver had gone. She hadn't even had the chance to ask him about Mrs Clegg. Looking around uneasily, Anna tugged at the hemline of her dress. Supper had better be easily digestible.

'You're looking very glam, Anna.'

With relief, she turned around at the familiar voice.

'Oh, Daniel. I'm so pleased to see you.' She gestured around the room. 'I don't know anyone here.'

'You're not missing much.' He glanced around at the guests, air kissing and shrieking loudly over each other's conversation.

Daniel had left his long hair loose tonight. It was good to see him in a formal shirt and trousers though, and his beard looked like it had been given a trim.

'You've scrubbed up well.' Anna smiled as he turned to face her.

'You don't look too bad yourself.' He grinned, his brown eyes warm. 'I'm keeping my head down. If my aunt spots me, she'll probably tell me to don a waiter's garb and serve the masses.'

'She wouldn't!'

His lips twitched. 'Probably not. She does make me feel like an interloper, though. Time I moved out.'

'You're not leaving Polkerran?' Anna would miss him, and not only because he was handy to know.

Daniel didn't answer, and she followed the direction of his attention. Claudia had entered the room. She looked stunning; her sleek black flowing locks a match for Daniel's in length, but straight and shiny, and she was poured into a yellow sheath of a dress, the neckline trimmed with black feathers.

Daniel continued to stare at Claudia, so Anna hastily placed her empty glass on a nearby table and nudged him in the arm. 'So, you wouldn't leave Polkerran, would you?'

'No.' Daniel remained fixated on Claudia. 'No. I'm not giving up.' He turned to Anna. 'I'm going to rent a cottage for bit. Got the chance to—'

'There you are!'

Anna's heart rate stepped up a notch as she turned to Alex with a smile. 'Hi.'

He looked gorgeous, his black shirt setting off his colouring, his smile as adorable as ever.

'I'll catch you both later.' Daniel raised his glass to his cousin and Anna was pleased to see him heading in Claudia's direction.

'Thought you'd decided not to come.' Alex leaned forward and kissed her on the cheek, and Anna schooled her expression into one of nonchalance. In her heels, they were pretty much the same height, their eyes on a level.

'I was a little late arriving and ended up chatting to someone.'

People pressed all around them, and Alex took a step closer.

'Shame on whoever it was for keeping you from me. I've just escaped from the History Man.' He faked a yawn, and Anna bit her lip.

'I didn't know Oliver was coming.'

'Didn't expect him to, to be honest. Mother sent out the invites, though. She'll be made up to have finally snared him.'

'I wonder what drew him out. He doesn't socialise in general.' Anna looked around, but there was no sign of Oliver.

Alex placed an arm about her shoulders, and all thought of anyone else fled from Anna's mind.

'Let's not talk about him. I want your attention fully on me.' He steered her across the room, and Anna willed the ready colour not to flood her cheeks.

'Here.' He lifted two glasses of champagne from a passing waiter's tray and handed one to her, and Anna took it carefully, mindful of her nails. 'Here's to Meg Stratfield for bringing you back to the cove and into my life.'

Anna wasn't sure what to say to this, but she was happy to raise a toast to Aunt Meg and took a cautious sip of her drink. She wasn't overly fond of champagne, but it appeared to be the only thing on offer.

'Now, tell me. What have you been doing with yourself in my absence?'

'Not a lot.' Anna wished she had something scintil-lating to say. 'I've got an appointment at the local council on Monday about the bed and breakfast, and Daniel is busy updating the bathrooms, and so on.'

'Sounds like a good start. Let me know if I can—'

'Alex, darling! Your mother says it's time we ate.' Claudia joined them and looped an arm through his before turning to Anna with her Tipp-Ex-white smile. 'It's like herding cats, trying to get everyone to sit.' She glanced at Alex from under her lashes, and Anna wondered how he could resist her. She was gorgeous. 'Darling.' Her voice had become pleading. 'If Araminta

Byfleet doesn't eat, she's going to keel. I swear she's downed half the champagne on her own.'

Alex rolled his eyes but excused himself from Anna and allowed Claudia to drag him out into the hallway. A few seconds later, a loud gong sounded and the throng of people, barely breaking conversation, turned as one towards the imposing double doors leading into the dining room.

Feeling a little lost again, and still not recognising anyone she knew, Anna held back a little and took another sip from her glass, only to meet Oliver's gaze over the rim. Defiantly, she drained the glass and placed it on a nearby table, but before she could tag along behind the stragglers, he crossed the room to join her.

'I'll escort you in.'

He gestured towards the doors, but Anna held back. When would he ever think to ask rather than direct? A simple 'may I' or 'shall I' wouldn't go amiss.

'I don't need escorting, thank you.'

'I don't recall saying you did.' He eyed her intently. 'Are you always this prickly?'

Anna's eyes widened. 'Me? Prickly?'

'As the proverbial pear.' He placed a hand under her elbow and gently steered her across the room.

'I'm never prickly!' Anna bit her lip as they crossed the threshold. 'At least, not usually.'

'Must be my company, then.' Oliver shrugged. 'You'll have to try and rein it in, I'm afraid. Look.'

They had come to a halt by a massive table already laden with a variety of serving dishes. According to the neatly printed place cards, they were to sit next to each other.

Taken by surprise at the relief sweeping through her, Anna searched the people milling around, seeking their places and taking seats. Where was Alex? It wasn't until she took her seat, Oliver to her right and a rather loud-voiced elderly gentleman to her left, that she saw him come into the room and take a place beside his mother, who presided at the head of the table, her husband at the opposite end. Claudia was on Alex's other side. Across from him was a young man, eyeing Alex with blatant admiration.

Alex had seen her, and he smiled, just as his mother raised a hand to the two wine waiters near the door.

'It's a little formal for such informal food,' she said, almost to herself.

'Maximum effect, minimum expense. Sums the Tremaynes up.'

Anna glanced at Oliver, but he watched Alex. Surely he would approve? He was always so formal in his attire.

'I thought you'd be seated next to the hostess.'

'The advantage of accepting the invitation at the last minute. Too late to rejig the place settings.'

'So why did you—'

'Best not to ask.'

Anna sat back in her seat. Infuriating man! She looked over at the gentleman on the other side of Mrs Tremayne. She appeared perfectly happy with her dinner companion, who showered her with attention. Anna smiled faintly. She couldn't imagine Oliver would be so rewarding.

'Watch your step with Tremayne.'

Her gaze flew back to Oliver, but his attention was back on Alex.

'Why?'

Typically, he didn't answer her.

'Wine, madam?'

153

Turning to the waiter, Anna smiled. 'Yes, please. Red.'

When both she and Oliver had a glass, he raised his to her. 'Here's to an evening of surprises.'

Anna touched his glass with her own. 'So, does that mean you're going to launch into conversation? Be chatty, even?' Damn! The champagne must have control of her tongue.

Oliver, however, inclined his head. 'Gauntlet thrown down. Duly taken up.'

To her utter surprise, Oliver was true to his word and, what was more, an amusing dinner companion as they tucked into their soup. It also surprised her to find they had some shared feelings about growing up. He admitted to not being close to his mother, who didn't seem overly enamoured of having a child.

'Sounds like my cousin,' Anna conceded as the waiter topped up their glasses again.

'Cousin?'

'Victoria. She's quite a bit older than me. I was raised by her and her husband. My parents died when I was a baby so I remember nothing of them other than...' She hesitated. She never talked about this to anyone. Why was she telling Oliver?

'Other than?' Oliver offered her the bread basket, but she shook her head.

'For some reason, I have a feeling of being loved. That even though I have no exact memories of being with them, I have a fondness for them. I suppose that's a bit fanciful, really.'

'Cherish it. I wish I could say the same. My mother had little time for me. I was always in the way, preventing her from doing things she'd rather be spending her time on. I think everything about me annoyed her. I was nothing like her, you see. She was dainty, petite and – if you can use the word outside the nineteenth century – delicate. I was too robust, too keen on running and jumping and climbing, like all healthy kids.' He glanced down at his person. 'She once described me as "too large to be allowed".'

Anna laughed. 'Oh dear. She definitely would've got on well with my cousin.'

Conscious the elderly gentleman to her left was offering a platter of finely sliced roast lamb so that she could take some, Anna smiled at him as she helped herself. She passed it on to Oliver then, and accepted the accompanying selection of vegetables, glancing over to where Alex sat. His attention remained on Claudia, oblivious to the adoring demeanour of the young man across the table.

That's two of us, wanting to hang on his every word. Anna would have loved to be seated on his other side, though she probably wouldn't have been able to eat a thing. Oliver, despite his aversion to conversation in general, was someone she felt surprisingly comfortable around.

'Families are overrated.'

Anna swallowed a mouthful of wine, her startled gaze flying to meet Oliver's.

'I'm sorry you feel like that. I can't imagine having a mother who—' Anna stopped and bit her lip. 'Ignore me. I don't remember mine, so I can't talk.'

Oliver's expression remained unmoved. 'Having family does not presuppose a happy upbringing.'

'Cousin Victoria is certainly proof of that.'

There was a short silence as various other dishes were passed around, catering for different diets, but then Anna frowned.

'Why did you get married?' Lord, she was being nosy! Oliver would tell her to shut up in a minute, or simply get up and leave.

'I thought I was in love.'

'Oh.' Anna wasn't sure what to say to that. Things had become a bit personal – her fault – and she sought a more general topic.

'Mrs Clegg will be missing looking after you this evening after being away.' She glanced at Oliver as she passed a platter of Dauphinoise potatoes to him, half expecting no answer. After all, it wasn't a question.

'Someone picked her up. There's a Women's Institute evening in the village hall. Suspect she wants to fill everyone in on her hospital stay.' Oliver shook his head. 'Locals gossiping – Polkerran's favourite pastime.'

Anna studied him thoughtfully as he ladled potatoes onto his plate, leaning back a little in her seat so the waiter could pour sauce over her lamb. 'Who brought you here?'

Oliver turned to look at her, lowering the platter slowly, and she swore there was something wary about his expression. 'This dinner party? Or Polkerran Point?'

'Polkerran. You said the other day it was a connection?'

With a shrug, Oliver handed the platter on to his neighbour, declining the sauce. 'Don't we all have people we know, but don't really know? Networks can be useful sometimes.'

'And how did you become friends with Aunt Meg?'

For a moment, Anna thought he would ignore her. Then, he turned in his seat to fix her with his blue gaze.

'A shared loved of nurturing things that matter.' He shrugged. 'Gardening. There isn't much of a one at Harbourwatch. It's all terraces, trees and pots. I like getting my hands dirty. Meg needed help to maintain the

156

extensive gardens at the cottage, so I stepped up. It was a win–win.'

He turned to face his plate, his expression inscrutable, but Anna was reminded of the man she'd seen maintaining the hanging baskets at Harbourwatch.

'I'm surprised you have so many staff around, if you dislike intrusion on your privacy and have no time for the locals' love of a good gossip.' She was fishing, but she doubted he'd confirm what the others had told her. Anna mused fondly on the gatherings around her kitchen table. 'I found it a huge comfort when I first arrived – the locals, their company, that is – not so much the gossip.'

'Perhaps that's because you aren't the subject of it.'

'If you were less secretive, they'd have less to speculate on.'

Oliver ignored this, picking up his glass and draining it.

Anna supposed it must be the wine making her so chatty with him. 'I learnt so much about the village and the occupants during those early months. I love how people are defined by their job or where they live, or—'

'By the stupid things they do or say?'

'That's a bit harsh.'

Oliver looked a little contrite. 'It may be.' Then, he smiled. 'So, you've heard all about Charlie the Crab and Tommy the Boat?'

'And Ray down the End, Mary up the Top. It's an endless array.'

'What about Billy Two Feet?'

'No, but—' Anna eyed him warily. 'What's so odd about having two feet?'

'He doesn't, he's only got one leg.'

'Oh no!' Anna's hand shot to her mouth. 'How awful. What happened?'

Oliver shook his head. 'Gullible as ever. No, even he has two legs, and two feet. That's not where the name comes from. Apparently, ask him anything and his answer is "two feet".'

With a smile, Anna leaned back in her seat so the waiter could top up her wine. 'So... how big was that fish?'

'Precisely. How far down was the drop? How much rope do you need? There's a rumour that when he dies, he's asked to be buried two feet under.'

Anna grinned, then sobered quickly as she recalled Oliver intended to leave at the end of the summer. Why did that bother her? She took a sip of her wine.

'Why don't you stay longer in Polkerran?'

Oliver took a drink of his own wine. 'There's nothing to keep me here now.'

'Now?'

'Besides, I told you, the owner's coming back from abroad.' He turned to answer a question from the lady sitting on his other side, and Anna applied herself to her food, uncertain where her sense of disquiet came from.

Once again, she thought of Mrs Clegg. She seemed to have her entire life in her rooms at Harbourwatch. What would happen to her and the others when Oliver turned his back on Polkerran?

The niggling worry was swiftly forgotten, however, when Anna realised that one of her dark red nails had come off. So much for the industrial-strength glue!

Looking around her seat in dismay, she couldn't see it. Warily, she lifted her side plate. Nothing.

'I think it shot into the vegan dish as it passed.'

Startled, Anna turned her head only to find Oliver leaning towards her. They stared at each other for a second.

Then, a hand flew to her throat as Anna spun around to watch the progress of the asparagus and bean casserole around the table. The lady opposite helped herself to a good dollop.

'How can I get it back before someone sees it?' Her voice was a strangled whisper, but Oliver heard her.

'I wouldn't worry. That's Araminta. She's too half-cut to notice it's not an overly crunchy kidney bean.'

Chapter Sixteen

Love is a possible strength in an actual weakness

Thomas Hardy, *Far from the Madding Crowd*

'I'll walk you home.' Oliver came to stand at Anna's side as the guests began to leave.

Anna bit her lip and glanced over to where Alex was in conversation with Claudia. She had a feeling they were arguing.

'There's no need. It's not far.' She didn't want anyone to know she'd got her slippers in her bag, ready to swap her heels for them. Typically, Oliver ignored her.

'Get your coat.'

With a final glance at Alex, who looked up and smiled his gorgeous smile, she left the room, her heart fluttering.

By the time she'd extracted her coat the row of old-fashioned pegs in the hall, she found Oliver waiting by the main entrance. Two women tried – and failed – to engage him in conversation, and he left them in mid-sentence to approach Anna. He was an attractive man if you liked the silent type, with his height and breadth of shoulders and that aquiline profile.

'Anna!'

She spun around. Alex had joined them.

'You're not leaving? The night is young yet.'

The chime of the hall clock indicating it was one o'clock in the morning contradicted him, and Anna laughed.

'I think I'd better go.' Anna gestured back towards the drawing room, where the sounds of revelry were growing louder. Oliver had come to stand beside her, and she smiled at Alex. 'You need to enjoy your friends' company. Oliver is going to see me back.'

'Allow me. I've hardly seen you this evening.'

'You can't leave your guests.' Anna looked between the two men. Oliver's face was unreadable.

'Technically, they're Mother's guests. I can do as I please.'

'It seems my services are no longer required. See you Monday.'

Anna watched Oliver turn on his heel and leave the house with a pang of regret. He had these odd moments of kindness, but she felt sometimes they cost him.

'Thank god.' Alex grabbed Anna's hand, sending a tingling along her skin. 'I thought the History Man would never take the hint.'

'So why did you invite him?'

'I didn't. Like I said, Mother did. Not like him to accept, to be honest. Quite a coup – except he's hardly worth the company.'

He'd been an entertaining enough dinner companion though. Anna drew in a short breath, unsure why she wanted to defend Oliver, but all thought of him was swept aside as Alex drew her closer.

'It was good seeing you at supper.'

Anna couldn't help but smile. 'I was at the other end of the table.'

'If you'd been next to me, I wouldn't have been able to look at you.'

'Oh!' She didn't really have any words, conscious as she was of his closeness.

'Shall we?'

'Shall we what?'

A smile tugged at the edge of his mouth. 'Make a move? Get you home?'

'Oh! Yes, of course.'

He helped her into her coat and took her bag from her, and she eyed it regretfully. It would be a long walk home in heels, but nothing on this earth would have her get the slippers out in front of him.

Anna tried not to be aware of Alex next to her as they walked down the hill into the town. He lit a cigarette as they crossed the bridge, offering one to her, and she shook her head. They kept up a desultory conversation, which suited Anna fine, as she struggled to keep a coherent thought in her head. Was it the drink she'd consumed, or the potency of being so close to Alex? Her heart thumped so hard she thought he must surely be able to hear it, and it urged her into conversation, asking him about his work in London, and once he'd started, he seemed happy to continue.

They soon reached her front door, and she pulled her keys out, but when she turned to say thank you and goodnight, he was right behind her.

'Oh! Do you— I mean, would you like to come in? For a coffee or something?'

'Something might be nice.'

Heat flooded Anna's cheeks and, flustered, she flicked on the hall light, tossed her coat onto the settle and hurried down to the kitchen. Busying herself with the kettle, she wasn't aware he'd come to stand behind her again until she turned around.

'Now. Where were we?'

Anna swallowed quickly. He was so close, she could see the blends of brown and gold in his eyes, smell his cologne mixing in with the cigarette smoke. Then, she held her breath as he raised a hand and touched the curl by her cheek.

'There's something in your hair.'

'What is it?'

Not the missing nail!

'My hand.'

Alex's hand cupped the back of her head, drawing her closer. Then he kissed her, slowly, languorously, and Anna melted into him, the few coherent thoughts she'd kept hold of floating away as a long-ago dream became reality.

Anna's hands slipped, tentatively at first, to his shoulders, then to his neck and finally into that golden hair she'd so longed to touch.

When they broke for breath, he continued to hold her incredibly close. She could feel the firmness of his shoulders under her hands now, hoped he couldn't hear the frantic beating of her heart. She really shouldn't be this easy.

Unsure if relieved or disappointed when he released his hold on her, Anna turned her attention to the now boiled kettle, her mind racing, and her skin warm and tingling.

'So.' Alex rested a hand on her right shoulder.

'So?' Anna strove to focus on pouring hot water into two mugs.

The other hand landed on her left shoulder, but she tried to ignore it. Swallowing hard, she added milk to her mug. 'Do you want milk? Sugar?'

'No. I'll tell you what I want.'

He took the milk from her unresisting hand and turned her to face him. 'We never had a chance to talk about the bed and breakfast.'

'Oh!' *Seriously?* Anna tried to hide her confusion, but he put the milk down and took both her hands in his.

'I have a suggestion.'

Trying to school her features into one of interest, Anna waited.

'I propose we explore the bed options first. We can pick up on the breakfast in the morning.'

He pulled her into his arms, and she went willingly. Sometime later, she led him up the stairs. There was no way he could see her room, awash with the clothes she'd tried on before Nicki came to her rescue. Aunt Meg's room was out of bounds too. Would it feel wrong to take him into her childhood one?

Alex started to kiss her neck as she led him along the landing, and before she could lose herself in him again, she pushed open the door to the spare room, thankful it was clean and ready for... well, *this* wasn't what she'd anticipated.

Turning her around, Alex's mouth descended on hers again, and as she felt his hands reaching for the zipper of her dress, Anna pushed aside all other thought.

Worrying about being easy was so last year.

–

Anna eyed herself resignedly in the bathroom mirror the next morning before stepping into the shower. The curls from the previous night had dropped, a smudge of mascara rested under one eye, and she looked tired – an image so different from the glossy, perfect girls who had graced the table at the dinner party.

By the time she'd seen Alex on his way, however – he had to be back in London by the afternoon – Anna had begun to accept he must like her. She'd prepared a light breakfast of smoked salmon and scrambled eggs on a slice of toasted home-made bread, all good practice for the B&B, though the presentation would have to improve for her guests. It hadn't helped that Alex kept coming over and kissing her on the neck when she tried to put everything on plates.

He'd promised to call her that evening and would be back the following weekend so they could 'continue their conversation', as he put it. Anna chuckled as she stripped the bed in the spare room. There really hadn't been much talking. Gathering up the sheets, Anna was unable to suppress her excitement at the thought of Alex returning the following weekend. How was it in one night he'd made her feel more than Giles had in all their time together?

Once the washing machine was on, she set Spotify playing and tried to suppress the churning of her insides every time she thought of Alex. She needed to be active, keep busy. Looking around as she hummed along to a favourite tune, her eye landed on the paperwork for the Food Hygiene Certificate which she'd completed the previous day.

The best use of her time would be to press on with her preparations for guests, and with that in mind, she headed down the hallway towards the dining room, but before she'd gone a few paces, her phone rang. She tugged it from her pocket, her heart leaping around like a mad thing in hopes it would be Alex, even though he must surely still be travelling. It was Lauren.

'Hey, how's tricks?'

'Good. How about you?'

They had a catch-up chat, but Lauren wasn't likely to hold off for long. She'd known the dinner party had been the night before.

'So? Did he spoon-feed you while gazing into your lovely eyes, speechless with admiration?'

Anna laughed. 'Hardly. We were almost at opposite ends of a very big table.' She couldn't resist telling Lauren about how Alex had walked her home, though.

'Wow, he's a fast mover!' Lauren paused, but Anna said nothing. 'Anna? Don't tell me—'

'He stayed the night.' The words came out in a rush.

'What has happened to you?' Lauren's tone was amused. 'That sea air must be pretty potent. Where's the cautious Anna we all know and love?'

'She's thrown restraint to the wind at last.'

'I can tell from your voice you're happy. I'm so pleased for you, Anna. When will you see him again? Didn't you say he works in London?'

'Yes. In finance. Does stuff for private clients, acquisitions, and so on.'

Lauren let out a whistle. 'Good money, then.'

Anna shrugged, even though Lauren couldn't see. 'I suppose so.'

'I know, I know. That wouldn't bother you.' She hesitated. 'Be careful, love.'

'Why is everyone telling me to be careful?'

'Are they?'

'Well, not everyone. But you, Nicki – she's my neighbour – and Oliver.'

'Oliver?' Lauren's voice was sharp. 'Why on earth would your boss say that? Is he avuncular?'

With a snort, Anna walked over to the window. Harbourwatch looked much as always. 'Hardly. But he's... I don't know.' She launched into how lovely he'd been the previous evening, keeping an eye on her, amusing her over the meal, and then offering to walk her home.

'Interesting.'

'Is it? Anyway, he didn't need to, because Alex did. But that's enough about me. What's happening with you and Kit? Is he still around, or have you sent him packing?'

Lauren made a small noise. 'I'm not sure what's happening – to me, anyway. I really like him. Same ambitions, driven by the same passions.'

'Sounds promising. Shall I go and buy a hat?'

A derisive sound was the only response to this. 'Well, I'm off to the States on Thursday for almost three weeks, so we'll see if I still feel the same when I get back.'

Once the call had ended, Anna returned to the kitchen. The dry weather tempted her outside. The dining room could wait. She made a quick lunch and headed out for a long walk on the cliff path to her favourite secluded outcrop of rocks. She stood for some time, staring out to sea, recalling how she'd sat there as a teen, dreaming of falling in love, of Alex suddenly realising she was the girl for him. Then, she smiled. Her horoscope had said it was time to stop dreaming, and now she could.

While her supper simmered on the stove, she poured herself a glass of wine, trying to be patient waiting for Alex's promised call. There was nothing on TV to hold her attention, and having finished reading the 1978 diary, she headed into the study to choose a new one.

Digging deep into the box, she pulled one out from lower down the pile: 1990, the year Anna had been born and before Aunt Meg had met her. She straightened up, but as she did so, she dislodged the diaries at the top of the pile and two of them fell to the floor, some pieces of paper falling from them.

Dropping 1990 onto the dresser, Anna bent down to pick everything up. One of the items was a photo, clearly taken around the time of the one on Aunt Meg's bedside table, and turning it over, she read the faded ink: *Last photo of Sarah, October '53.*

Anna studied the baby's face with sadness. She was propped up in the corner of a chair, the velvet rabbit Aunt Meg had kept all these years nestled beside her. 'Poor little mite,' she whispered before dropping a kiss on the photo and opening one of the fallen diaries and replacing it and putting it back in the box.

The second piece of paper was a recipe, undated, and Anna flipped open the second diary to return it, then stopped, her eye caught by some words scrawled in the margin: *He's been here again. I want him to leave me alone.*

She closed the book slowly. The diary was from two years ago, and rattled, Anna placed it back in the box, grabbing the one from 1990 and hurrying back into the kitchen. She didn't like to think of Aunt Meg having to deal with anyone she didn't like. Curling up in a corner of the sofa, she called Heathcliff over and when he'd stretched out next to her, she did her best to lose herself in the minutiae of life in Polkerran in 1990.

About an hour later, and true to his word, Alex called her, leaving Anna in no doubt whatsoever that he intended a repeat of their encounter on the following weekend. When the call ended, Anna hugged her arms around her middle and tried to wipe the smile off her face. She glanced around at the kitchen where she'd spent so much time with her aunt Meg over the years, and then raised her eyes to the heavens.

'You know how I pined for Alex, Aunt Meg. He was so worth the wait. Thank you for bringing us together.'

—

Anna was running late on Monday. Having had to work Sunday at the hotel salon, Nicki had only just been round to remove the false nails, and as she wanted all the details on the dinner party as she worked, it had taken far longer than Anna had anticipated.

Hurrying down the lane, Anna took the ferry across to save time, waving at Jean Lovelace behind the counter in the ice cream parlour as she passed. Glancing at the grey skies, Anna couldn't help but think she'd find business rather quiet today.

'Morning, Mrs Clegg.' Anna popped her head around the kitchen door, inhaling the smell of coffee. 'How are you feeling?'

'Much better, dearie.'

'Shall I take the tray up?'

'He's already 'ad one.' Mrs Clegg looked a little troubled and shook her head as she wiped her hands on a tea towel. 'I don't know, my lovely. Sommat's upset 'im, make no mistake.'

'Oh dear.' Anna bit her lip. 'I hope it's not the manuscript. I'd best go up.'

'I'll bring a fresh tray dreckly.' Mrs Clegg turned to the kettle and Anna walked up the stairs, attempting to suppress her happiness and adopt her usual efficient work manner. She didn't think Oliver would have much time for lovesick mooning.

'Morning.' She closed the door, unsurprised when the only response was a grunt.

Settling into her seat, she blew a kiss at Dougal and Thumper, and the latter stretched before curling up in a tight ball.

'Exactly what I feel like doing,' Anna muttered under her breath as she logged in. It was good things were so busy here, or she'd be taking a nap on her keyboard before too long.

'Here. I've redrafted the last chapter. Then there's the bibliography, acknowledgements and appendices to come.' Oliver dropped a sheaf of paper onto her desk.

Anna picked it up and looked up at him. His face was unreadable; gone was the almost charming dinner companion from the weekend. For a long time, or so it felt, he regarded her in silence, but then his mobile rang, and he muttered an expletive before turning to snatch it up.

'Seymour.' There was a pause, then, 'About time.'

Anna drew in a short breath. Mrs Clegg was right. Oliver wasn't in the best of moods this morning. Perhaps he felt as tired as she did? Shutting out the conversation behind her, Anna focused on the new chapter, trying to decipher Oliver's handwriting. With the book nearing completion, she had some anxiety about whether he would continue to need her once he'd set off on his tour. September and beyond she refused to think about.

'I have to go out.'

Anna looked up as Oliver shrugged into his jacket. 'I thought you said you needed a full day in the office?'

'I changed my mind.' He frowned. 'What happened to your nails?'

Anna inspected her now shorter, slightly discoloured nails. 'Nicki had trouble getting the false ones off. Ironic, really, with one of them leaving of its own free will on Saturday.'

'Why remove them? She could have replaced the missing one.'

'They weren't really "me".' Anna let out a huff. 'And I doubt they would have been compatible with a keyboard.'

Oliver said nothing, his face as inscrutable as ever.

Just as I'd extolled his improved manner to Lauren...

Anna gestured at the pages of edits on her desk. 'I can't read your writing on some of this.' She knew she could probably have worked it out, but for some strange reason, she didn't want him to leave.

'Do what you can.' He picked up his car keys and headed for the door, but Anna followed him.

'Oliver? Has something gone wrong?'

He stopped, his hand on the door handle, but didn't turn around. Then, he blew out a breath. 'It would seem so.'

With that, he was gone, and Anna returned to her desk. If she was quick with the work, she would be free this afternoon. It was a shame Alex wouldn't be around.

The door opened, and she turned around expectantly. 'Did you forget... Oh, hi Mrs Clegg.'

The housekeeper came in with the tray of coffee, the anxious look still on her face. 'Now he's gone out. Had no breakfast, and who's going to feed 'im at lunchtime? He doesn't look after himself, poor man.'

Anna refrained from pointing out that the poor man didn't appear to be wasting away. Nor did he elicit her sympathy.

Chapter Seventeen

I mentally shake hands with you for your answer,
despite its inaccuracy

Charlotte Brontë, *Jane Eyre*

Left alone again, Anna completed the edits, made a few calls in relation to the lecture tour and updated the itinerary. By two o'clock, she felt extremely hungry and, unable to do any more until Oliver reappeared, she left the updated edits on his desk and hurried from the house, emerging into a blustery, grey afternoon.

Anna glanced up at Tremayne Manor as she headed along the road, the turret of its tower visible above the treetops of the park surrounding it. What was Alex doing today? Hugging her arms to herself, she scooted through the main street, intent on taking the passenger ferry back across the water, keen to get into some jeans and boots and get out on the cliff path for a walk.

As she turned down towards the harbour, however, she realised Oliver's car was in the small short-stay car park, and as she reached the corner, where the wind blew her hair across her face for a moment, he emerged from a cottage on the harbour-front, turning to call a cheery farewell to whoever was inside.

Anna paused, her hopes of fresh air and the stretching of her legs sinking rapidly. Was he going back to work? Before she could move, however, he was back in his car and turning it in the direction of the main road. Throwing a curious glance at the cottage, which sported an estate agent's board with a SOLD sticker blazoned across it, Anna resumed her walk. Oliver already seemed in better spirits. Perhaps, like her, he needed to get out for a while.

—

When she wasn't working with Oliver, Anna focused on getting the cottage ready to receive guests. Everything seemed pretty straightforward, once she'd looked into it.

Daniel busied himself fitting smoke alarms, turning the sizeable utility room into a second kitchen and updating the bathrooms. She'd applied for the appointment for the Environmental Health Officer's inspection, but despite chasing, no one seemed in any hurry to call her back with a date.

Anna's next task had been to set up a website, and she tried to teach herself the purpose of the various components on the dashboard. Alex had promised to help when he came down at the weekend, and what with speculation over how that would go, the B&B preparations and longer hours with Oliver, it was Friday before she knew it.

The next couple of weeks sped by in similar fashion. Oliver was deeply immersed in a final read-through of his book, and Anna kept herself busy with the tour preparation and did her best to anticipate his needs, all the time counting the days to the next weekend and Alex's return.

Although Anna loved being with Alex, they didn't do much or go anywhere other than the occasional walk along the cliff path to her favourite secluded beach. On the nights she didn't cook for them, they got a takeaway. He hadn't taken her to Tremayne Manor either, and she hadn't liked to ask him why. Perhaps someone had choked on that missing nail and she was banned from the house?

When she'd asked him why they didn't go out, he'd kissed her thoroughly, dismissing her concerns in an instant, then said he valued being alone with her without the intrusion of others and needed the downtime because his job was so stressful.

Feeling guilty, Anna had never mentioned it again. If he didn't feel like going out to dinner, that was fine. She happily planned and cooked the meals every weekend, loving that it gave him the chance to unwind. He always popped over to see his parents for a few hours on a Sunday before heading back to town, but he'd yet to ask Anna to go with him or invite her up to town one weekend so that he didn't have to travel.

To Anna's amusement, Alex – who professed his only reading tastes to be financial reports – had taken to flicking through Aunt Meg's diaries.

Before long, the early May holiday weekend was upon them. Wrapped in Alex's arms on the Sunday morning, Anna listened to his even breathing. Dawn had broken and soft light filtered through the curtains. She ought to get up soon. Alex hadn't been too happy about her having Nicki's boys on the next bank holiday weekend, but she'd managed to persuade him it would be good practice at having someone else in the house for when she could start taking guests.

Anna eased onto her side. The delay in getting her business going was frustrating, what with the woman she had to deal with constantly not returning her calls and failing to make the appointment for the essential inspection.

With this being a long weekend, it felt like a missed opportunity, but perhaps she'd be able to pick up some trade as the summer approached. After all, short breaks were all the rage these days, especially for bikers and walkers, and the house was ideally situated by the coastal path, with plenty of storage available for guests' equipment.

'Alex,' she whispered, unsure if he'd hear her.

Silence, then, 'What?'

'I have to get up.'

He grabbed her arm. 'Not yet.'

She smiled and rolled over to face him. 'Yes. Now. It's gone eleven. Heathcliff will be climbing the walls.'

Alex scowled, but even doing so he looked cute, and Anna's heart did a small leap. How had this happened, this gorgeous man in her life, in her bed? She leaned across and placed a kiss on his pouting lips, and then melted into his embrace as he returned the kiss.

Sometime later, she rolled away from him, then saw the clock on the bedside table and gave a small yelp. 'I really *do* need to get up! Poor Heathcliff.'

'It comes to something when the cat is higher up the importance scale than me.' Alex lay flat on his back, staring at the ceiling, but then he looked over at her as she swung her legs out of bed and smiled. 'Good job I know my place.'

Anna reached for her dressing gown and headed for the door. Alex's place seemed to be solely in her bed. They hadn't been out all weekend again, even for a drink.

Placing the kettle on the Aga, Anna opened the door for Heathcliff, who shot into the kitchen from the boot room, mewing loudly. He didn't take kindly to being banned from Anna's bed when Alex was around, but Alex hated cats. He wasn't too fond of dogs either, unless they were out on a shoot and bringing back dead pheasants.

Taking a mug of coffee upstairs and leaving it on the bedside table for Alex, who appeared to have fallen asleep again, Anna headed for the bathroom and an invigorating shower. She had breakfast to prepare right now, and something for dinner. It was so nice Alex wasn't heading back to London halfway through Sunday, as was the norm, and she wasn't going to waste the day speculating on where things might be going.

Anna was sat at the table by the window, trying to work out how to change the background on her new website, when Alex came into the room. He walked over and put his arms around her, nuzzling her neck and causing all sorts of havoc with her heart.

'Alex!' Anna swatted him away, laughing. 'I'm trying to get this sorted. Can you help me?'

'Come on, out of the way.'

She got to her feet and he dropped into the chair. 'What is it you want done?'

'I want the background to be a pale blue, so the banner sits nicely on it. That sort of watery blue the sky goes sometimes.' She gestured at a lovely sketch of the cottage perched on its rocky headland. 'But I can't get the shade right.'

'I'm expensive, you know.' Alex looked up at her with a smirk. 'Sure you can afford me?'

With a contented smile, Anna turned for the kitchen. 'I know. Coffee, lots of it.'

'And breakfast?' His tone was hopeful.

'All ready, just keeping warm for when you got up.'

He blew her a kiss and turned back to face the laptop, and with a contented sigh, Anna hurried over to the newly installed coffee machine. Life was good.

It was even better that afternoon, when Alex suggested they pop up to Bodmin as he wanted to do a drive-by on a farm, which had recently come onto the market with a rival company to Tremayne Estates. Anna enjoyed the drive, wrapped in a cocoon of happiness, and when they parked up in the town centre and Alex found the agents open and a rather inexperienced-looking young man alone in the office, he told Anna to go for a walk while he tried to charm some details out of him.

Anna happily window-shopped for ten minutes or so, then turned around to retrace her steps. Alex stood outside the agent's office now, beside a young woman who seemed to be entreating him. Anna slowed her steps. Unless she was mistaken, it was the same girl who'd glared at Oliver at the antiques fair.

Alex detected her approach, and he waved a hand before speaking to the girl again, who threw a hasty look in Anna's direction, then hurried away.

'Who was that? A friend?'

Alex took Anna's arm as they strolled back to the car park. 'Not exactly. An acquaintance.'

Anna frowned. 'You sound annoyed.'

'Not at all.' He dropped a kiss on Anna's cheek. 'Remembered she works at the local council. Asked her to see if she could chase up the appointment for your inspection.'

Touched, Anna dropped a reciprocal kiss on Alex's cheek. 'Thank you.'

Alex grinned. 'Now—' he paused as they reached the car and opened his door '—shall we head back, or do you fancy a walk around the grounds at Lanhydrock first?'

Enjoying being out and doing normal 'couple' things, Anna smiled widely. 'Lanhydrock, please!'

—

To Anna's delight, the appointment with the Environmental Health Officer finally came through, and the inspection took place. Anna's website was live, with contact details and some gorgeous photos of Westerleigh Cottage, and she'd prepared an advert for a Cornish magazine as well as joining a local B&B association. Before long, she started to get booking enquiries, and Dickie the Chippy, the local carpenter, came to put up the lovely wooden sign she'd commissioned.

With all the volume of work Oliver now gave her, Anna had started going over to Harbourwatch as early as ten o'clock most days, so she'd barely had time to host her impromptu coffee mornings, but today, the Thursday before the late May bank holiday weekend, she had a welcome respite. Oliver had been asked to do an on-camera slot as part of a local history programme, and he'd told her to take a well-earned day off.

She popped over to St Austell, sourcing room trays for the tea and coffee, toiletries and other sundries to make her potential guests' stay as comfortable as possible, and then spent an hour emptying the wardrobe and dresser in Aunt Meg's room, reverently folding everything neatly and putting it into a bag for the local charity shop. The bags hanging on the back of the bedroom door she would give to Nicki for the sale, and the shoes could go into the recycling skip in the main car park.

Feeling they added to the homeliness of the room, she left the other treasured items in place, other than the photo by the bedside, which Anna took up to her own room.

Back down in the kitchen, Anna glanced at the clock. Daniel had finished installing the new kitchen solely for the guests' food, and was now busy fitting a new washing machine. Her first guests were due to arrive the next day, and she turned her attention to unpacking her purchases. She'd barely made a start when the door opened and Mrs Lovelace came in.

'Alright, my lovelies? Wasson, young Daniel?'

'Morning, Mrs L.' Daniel peered round the boot room door. 'I'm putting a new washer in.'

'Well now, isn't that nice?' The old lady sat at the table, and Anna moved the packaging onto the sofa.

'Cup of tea, Mrs Lovelace?'

'That would be just the thing, young'un.'

Daniel grinned at Anna as he joined them at the table. 'Only the freezer for the utility now, and I'm done.'

'I'm so grateful, Daniel.' He'd refused to accept any payment for installing the new appliances, which Anna appreciated more than he could ever know. She'd made a serious dent in the money Aunt Meg had left her having the second kitchen put in and paying for the sign to be made, never mind the advertising and the new towels.

A decent dishwasher and washing machine were essential, however, if she was to manage her business efficiently.

There was a disturbance as Christie the Post called, and when she'd gone on her way, munching happily on one of Anna's biscuits, she opened the newly delivered box.

'*Westerleigh Cottage. Come stay a while, you won't want to leave.* Great tagline, Anna.' Daniel held one of the business cards out to Mrs Lovelace to inspect. 'Nice drawing, too.'

'Phoenix did it. Isn't it lovely?' The sketch of Wester-leigh Cottage emphasised the charming rose growing over the pergola on the terrace. 'I'm using it on the website as well, only in colour. I can't believe I have my first guests arriving tomorrow.' She laughed. 'And Nicki's boys staying, too!'

'Ah, young'un, Meg would be so pleased to see the house comin' to life. She was getttin' quite worked up, you know, about what would happen to it.'

Anna frowned. 'Why, Mrs L?'

Mrs Lovelace sipped her tea. 'Got quite agitated afore she started to take ill. All sorts of things would upset her.'

'I remember her confusion starting, bless her.' Anna sighed. 'We used to write to each other often. The lovely, old-fashioned way, pen and paper. I've still got all her letters. I suppose I should've recognised the early signs. She would repeat herself, telling me stories she'd told me in the previous letter, and asking me the same questions over and over.'

Mrs Lovelace's head bobbed up and down. 'Worried about gettin' executed. That was the problem.'

Daniel threw Anna an amused glance. 'Say what, Mrs L?'

'Her will, young'un. She seemed a lot better when she'd got it done.'

Partly distracted by the post, Anna only half heard Mrs Lovelace, but then she realised what she'd said and looked up from the letter she held. 'But the will was written years ago.'

Mrs Lovelace shrugged. 'Was it, dearie? Seems like it was only a couple but then, I'm getting on, aren't I? Asked me to witness her signature, she did. At this very table.' She beamed at Anna and Daniel and finished her tea. 'Best be goin'. Got to get me to the chemist for some ointment.'

'Are you okay, Anna?' Daniel had taken his mug to the sink, where Anna stared deep in thought at the taps.

'What? Oh, yes. Sorry. Miles away.' She summoned a smile. 'I'll take all these things upstairs.'

She gathered her purchases and the box of cards and carried them up to the first-floor landing, dropping them onto the bed of the first room she came into, then went to the window, watching the sea crashing onto the rocks below Harbourwatch. Did Mrs Lovelace misremember the date she'd witnessed Aunt Meg's signature?

Suddenly anxious, Anna hurried up to the top floor and tugged open the drawer to the dresser and pulled out her copy of the will. Then, she sank back onto her bed, her mind in confusion and her heart pounding. Either Mrs Lovelace was right, or she was seriously losing her mind, and if the former, she had a major problem.

If the old lady really had witnessed Aunt Meg's signature on a will, it wasn't the one leaving the cottage to Anna.

Chapter Eighteen

There is always a pleasure in unravelling a
mystery, in catching at the gossamer clue which
will guide to certainty

Elizabeth Gaskell, *Mary Barton*

After sending a quick WhatsApp to Alex, Anna called Mr
Mottershead, her insides churning with uncertainty. He'd
been no help, really. Having been Aunt Meg's solicitor
in all the many years she had lived in Cornwall, he had
no reason to suppose there was another, later will. After
all, he'd hardly have processed the earlier one if he had.
He also had no pearls of wisdom to impart on how Anna
could find out what was in it, if it really did exist, other
than looking through Aunt Meg's papers.

When Anna asked if there was a central database somewhere in cyberspace, where every will ever drawn up was
logged, he said not. He then passed her to his secretary,
Wendy, who mentioned the Probate Registry and the
National Will Register, but as both only recorded wills
that had passed through probate, she felt it unlikely they
could help.

Wendy did, however, offer to contact the secretary of
the local Law Society, who would be able to email their
members to see if Aunt Meg had been a client at any

time. She listed the information she would need Anna to provide (dates, addresses, etc.) and taking the lifeline with gratitude, Anna agreed to call her back as soon as she had it.

Ending the call, Anna walked down the stairs as though in slow motion. Alex, when she checked, hadn't responded.

She tucked her phone away as she entered the kitchen. Daniel eyed her with some concern. 'You're awfully pale.'

Anna summoned a smile. 'I'm fine. A bit tired, I think.' Her mind raced, but Daniel threw her a serious look before turning back to finish his task.

She looked at her watch. It was nearly lunchtime, but she had lost all appetite. What time had Oliver said his recording ended? Was it an all-day thing? She couldn't think straight.

'Daniel, you okay if I pop out? Just take the door off the latch when you go.'

'No problem. You *sure* you're okay?'

'Yes, fine. I'm fine.' Anna smiled faintly and headed into the hall, grabbing her bag and keys, and ten minutes later she reached Mrs Lovelace's cottage.

There was no reply. She must still be out shopping. Anna looked around but couldn't see her in the street, and a quick check at the chemist confirmed she'd been in, but they didn't know where she'd headed.

Anna walked over to lean on the railing bordering the harbour. What could she do? How could she find out if her fears were justified? Her normally organised thoughts were in tatters.

Pulling out her phone, she chewed on her bottom lip, then shot another message over to Alex. Would he find it an intrusion? She had never tried to contact him during working hours before.

Her phone rang almost instantly, but her hopes were quickly dashed. Someone making enquiries about the B&B rooms, and she took a booking for a date in June, feeling none of the excitement she'd anticipated.

On her return to the house, Anna dug out the information Wendy had asked for and called her. Then she prowled restlessly from room to room, her heart clenched in her chest, a slight nausea sweeping through her from time to time. What if she lost the house? Where would she go? She'd given up her whole life in Harrogate for this. How could her dream be under such threat? And what about the money? She'd spent a lot of it! What if *that* wasn't hers either?

When her phone rang again, she snatched it up: Alex. Anna connected the call with relief.

'Alex, something awful has happened.'

'Got to be quick, darling. Going into a meeting in five.'

'It sounds like there might be a more recent will. More recent than the one leaving Westerleigh Cottage to me.' No response. 'Alex? Are you there?'

'Yes. Sorry, don't quite understand?'

'Mrs Lovelace. She's the old lady I told you about who calls on me, Aunt Meg's old friend. She said this morning she witnessed Aunt Meg's signature on a will, but this was about two years ago. My will was over ten years old.'

'Christ.'

Anna was touched he understood the shock. 'I know. I don't know what to do. I contacted Aunt Meg's solicitor, but he knows nothing about another will.'

'Can't you ignore it?'

'No, I can't!'

'Look, got to go. I'll phone over the weekend, and we can talk about it.'

'I thought you were coming down tomorrow?' Anna's disappointment was extreme. She couldn't face being alone after this awful discovery. What about the supper she'd put so much effort into preparing?

'Last-minute engagement cropped up. You've got those kids staying, haven't you? That'll be company for you. Got to dash. I'll call you.' Alex blew a kiss down the phone and was gone, and Anna's arm dropped to her side as her screen went blank.

Damn. Damn, damn, damn.

—

Despite her disappointment over Alex not coming down, and her anxiety over the possible later will, Anna looked forward to the distraction of having Jason and Liam to stay and, at least now, she wouldn't have to worry about keeping Alex happy at the same time.

Friday, however, didn't go as well as she'd hoped. Firstly, when Mrs Lovelace called with Jean, she was adamant about witnessing Aunt Meg's signature and that it was on a will, and her daughter confirmed it, saying she was present at the time, definitely no more than two years ago. When Anna asked if they remembered who the other witness was, neither Jean nor Mrs Lovelace had any idea. It was too soon to hear back from Wendy, and when she got to Harbourwatch, Oliver piled the work on.

Anna tried hard to keep her mind on it, though worries about the new will were always in the back of her mind, and then Nicki started texting her over this or that in a completely un-Nicki-like flap, so unused was she to going away without the children.

In the end, she phoned Anna with a long list of last-minute things worrying her. Conscious Oliver had stopped tapping on his keyboard, Anna edged towards the door, speaking as quietly as she could.

'Don't worry, Nicki. I'll be back around five.' She glanced at her watch, then bit her lip. She'd be lucky. 'No, truly. I've only got one booking for the weekend. It'll be fine. Go and enjoy the wedding.'

Anna ended the call and hurried back to her desk, casting Oliver's back a wary glance. He had yet to resume his tapping. She'd best get on if she was to be home for the promised hour.

'These need a few changes.'

Looking up at Oliver as he handed her some pages, Anna chewed on her lip. 'Do you need me to do these first, or work on the itinerary? I can't stay late tonight.'

'Do what you can. The rest can wait.' His gaze held hers for a moment. 'What's troubling you?'

Anna longed to talk about her worries. It ate away at her, her stomach churning every time she so much as caught a glimpse of Westerleigh from the window. She itched to get on Google and search for any pointers on finding missing wills, but she shook her head.

'Nothing. I'm fine.'

'Liar.'

Anna eyed Oliver warily. It would feel good to talk about it, but was her boss really the person to pour everything out to? What if she got upset? Besides, Alex knew. He'd help her sort things out.

Oliver pulled his chair over and sat in it. 'You can trust me.'

Anna knew it, and Alex wouldn't be here for a week. She really did need to unburden herself to someone.

It took her a while to explain, because she blurted it out in all the wrong order, but Oliver let her talk herself out. His expression was unreadable as Anna related all she knew and the response from the solicitor so far. Then, he asked a few pertinent questions and agreed her best option, until businesses opened again on Tuesday, was to continue her ongoing search through Meg's papers to see if anything among them shed some light on the mystery.

Anna leaned back in her seat. 'I'll probably just find more shells. There's a small box full of them on the desk, and I emptied it this morning in case she'd buried something in there. I'll start working through the papers over the weekend if I get a minute.' Anna eyed Oliver warily. 'Are *you* okay?' He had gone rather pale, and she wasn't surprised when he didn't answer and got to his feet.

Picking up the papers he'd handed her earlier, she turned back to her desk, and Oliver did the same, taking his chair with him.

Sipping her cooling tea, Anna set to, accompanied by the tapping of Oliver's keyboard. It felt better to have talked about it. Now she didn't feel she needed to hide her worries.

Thankfully, the amendments weren't too difficult, and she updated the files quickly before turning her attention to Oliver's complex travel arrangements. She still awaited a couple of confirmations and, not wanting to disturb him, went onto the landing to chase them by phone.

By the time she came back into the room, Oliver was no longer at his desk but staring out of the window. It was a beautiful May day and Anna longed to be outside. She glanced at her watch again. She really needed to go in the next ten minutes.

Hurrying back to her desk, Anna added the new details to the travel plans and set the printer in motion. Oliver wasn't fond of being given everything electronically, as she'd found out early on. He found charging his phone low priority, so relying on it wasn't an option.

'I have to go out.'

Anna looked up. 'I'm nearly done. I'll see you on Tuesday.'

Oliver said nothing, but he didn't leave, and Anna stirred uneasily under his scrutiny. Then, he turned on his heel and left the room, and she leaned back in her chair and let out a small laugh.

Despite his avoidance of social pleasantries, she found herself enjoying her hours with him more and more. Perhaps he had rubbed off on her?

–

Anna arrived back at Westerleigh at twenty past five, out of breath from running up the lane from the ferry, to find Jason and Liam bouncing up and down on their heels waiting for her outside their cottage. There would be little chance for research this weekend.

'Anna! Did you make those little cakes?'

Jason clapped his hands together. 'Oh yes! They're epic!'

'Mum says we have to be at our best.' Liam wrinkled his brow. 'But we're not sure what that is.'

Anna smirked as she reached them and opened her gate.

'Just be yourselves, boys!'

'Where do you find a horse with no legs, Anna?'

'I've no idea.' She put the key in the lock.

'Where you left it, silly!'

Liam and Jason crowed with laughter, and barely had she opened the door, the boys charging past her down the hall to the kitchen, when Nicki and Hamish arrived with a small bag of their things.

'I think everything's there.' Nicki peered into the bag. 'Here's the key to the cottage in case they desperately need anything.'

'I wouldn't tell them you've got it.' Hamish winked at Anna.

Taking the bag, Anna smiled. 'Please don't worry about them. Everything will be fine.'

They followed Anna into the house, and the boys said a noisy goodbye before Anna shooed the parents on their way.

'Call me if you want to check how they are, but we'll be fine. Honestly!'

She waved them off, but the boys had run back into the kitchen, intent upon devouring more of the small cakes Anna had made.

'I think that's enough for now.' Removing the plate to their joint protests, she shook her head. 'How will you have room for your supper if you fill yourself with cake?'

'Mum asks us that every day.' Jason giggled, but Liam shook his head.

'Not *every* day, Jase.'

Jason rolled his eyes and grinned at Anna. 'Can we go to our room?'

Half an hour later, the boys' things stowed in the cupboard in the cosy bunk room at the back of the house and their toothbrushes placed in one of the bathrooms, Anna watched from the window as they raced around the garden, their shouts drifting in through the windows thrown open to the gorgeous sunshine.

Would she have this one day? A family of her own, playing in the garden of Westerleigh? Or would she become another Aunt Meg, alone and living for the days when other people's children came to visit? Then, her insides lurched uncomfortably as she remembered Mrs Lovelace's words. Would Westerleigh even be hers in the future?

Her mind drifted towards Alex, and much as she knew she ought to quash the dream, she couldn't help but imagine them living together... if not here, somewhere else in Polkerran, raising their family. Was she being a fool?

The sound of a car outside roused her from her speculations, and Anna glanced at her watch. Her first guests were here. She smoothed her hair and straightened her shoulders as she walked down the hall.

Time to put a happy face on and pretend all was right in her world.

–

The weather held on the Saturday morning, a rarity for a bank holiday weekend, and Anna's guests tucked into their breakfast, full of compliments for the stunning view from their room and eager to get out and walk some of the South West Coast Path. Anna offered to make them a packed lunch, which they accepted with pleasure, and she waved them off before turning her attention to the boys, who'd been giggling late into the night together and therefore slept longer in the morning.

Once fed, washed and dressed, Liam and Jason headed outside to explore the farther reaches of the garden, and

Anna hurried upstairs to attend to her guests' room and clean the bathroom.

It was nearing midday by the time she had finished upstairs and dealt with the constant interruptions from the boys, and she replenished the hospitality tray with freshly baked cookies as the doorbell went.

'Oh. It's you!'

She half expected Oliver to make some sarcastic remark, but he didn't.

He raised the basket he carried. 'Some treats for your young guests.'

Anna's eyes widened. 'How kind. I didn't even tell you they were staying.'

'You told Mrs Clegg.'

Hugging her arms around her waist, Anna smiled. 'Well, I thank you both.'

Was that almost a smile touching his mouth? Then she realised he still held the basket.

'I'm sorry! Come in.' She closed the door and led him along the hall to the welcoming kitchen, and Oliver walked over to place it on the table.

Should she offer him a drink? It was sweet of him to have brought the treats over, after all.

'It's noon, would you...?' Her confidence faltered as he eyed her keenly. 'I— er... wondered if you'd care for a glass of wine or something? I don't have beer, I'm afraid.'

Oliver raised a brow. 'I came in the car.'

'Oh yes, obviously. Tea, then? Or coffee?'

'I only drink coffee—'

'In the morning. Yes, I know. I just thought...' Her voice trailed off, but then the door to the boot room opened, and both boys came rushing in, only to fetch up short when they saw the visitor.

To Anna's surprise, Jason and Liam exchanged a look, then said formally in unison: 'Hello, Mr Seymour.'

Chapter Nineteen

*My hour for tea is half-past five, and my buttered
toast waits for nobody*

Wilkie Collins, *The Woman in White*

Oliver leaned down and held out a hand first to Jason,
then to Liam. 'As we're not in school, you may call me
Oliver if you wish.'

Anna's heart melted as both boys shook his hand seriously, clearly proud of acting so grown up.

'School? Is that how you know each other?'

'Mr Seymour.' Jason stopped as Liam nudged him hard
in the ribs.

'*Oliver.*'

Jason rolled his eyes. 'Oliver came to class last year. It
was 'mazing!'

'Fights!' Liam made a swishing motion with his arm.
'And lots of blood! Awesome.'

To Anna's astonishment, Oliver laughed.

'It sounds like I was warmongering, but I simply told
them about the Battle of Shrewsbury.'

Anna smiled at the boys. 'And lots of blood?'

They both beamed widely, and she turned to Oliver.
'Do tell.'

'It was 1403, one of the bloodiest battles in English history. Always popular at school age.'

'It was *epic*, wasn't it, Liam?'

Liam nodded, his russet hair flopping onto his forehead. 'He had weapons to show us too! Will you come back one day, sir— Oliver?'

'If I'm invited.'

The boys turned their attention to Anna. 'We're starving. What's for lunch?'

'Tomato soup and some sandwiches.'

'And what's for supper?' Liam looked eagerly around.

'Spaghetti Bolognese, and if you eat it all up, ice cream and chocolate sauce.'

With a whoop, both boys began to high-five, and when they'd done it several times to each other, they high-fived Anna and then Oliver, who looked startled, but after a momentary hesitation raised his hand at a suitable height for them to reach.

'Are you staying, sir? I mean Oliver.' Liam came to a halt, a little pink in the face from his exertions. 'Anna is a 'mazing cook.'

Oliver said nothing, and Anna went to his aid. Tomato soup and sandwiches would hardly appeal to him. 'I think Oliver needs to get home, boys.'

'No, I don't.'

'Oh.' Anna threw him an exasperated look. Why did he always do this? 'Well then, do you want to stay? Join us. There's plenty.'

Jason and Liam leapt up and down. 'Stay, stay, stay!'

Oliver looked from the boys to Anna. 'If you're sure. I'd hate to see these boys go hungry because I ate all the sandwiches.'

The boys crowed in delight. 'Can we watch TV? *Down on the Farm* is on CBeebies soon.'

Liam shook his finger at his brother. 'Mum said we weren't to watch TV, Jase, 'member?'

'Oh.' Jason looked a little crestfallen, and Anna exchanged a look with Oliver.

'Why don't you tell Oliver all about your trip to France next month? He's bound to know some really gruesome history about the country.'

Grinning with anticipation, the boys turned to Oliver, who raised a brow at Anna.

'Sorry, but I need to get on with lunch.'

He surveyed her intently for a moment, and she thought he would make some excuse and leave, but then he turned back to the boys. 'And I shall attempt to earn my keep. Right, follow me.'

He headed for the door to the patio, and Jason and Liam fell into step behind him, marching as though going off to war. Anna smiled at their bobbing heads as they passed by the window and down the steps after their gallant guide.

Then, she looked at the clock and hurried over to the fridge. Lunch wasn't going to ready itself.

Anna's preparations were interrupted by her phone: more potential guests, drawn to Cornwall by the lovely weather, which she accepted, even though they planned to arrive during that same afternoon.

Then, she walked out onto the terrace. The second room was ready, but these guests were vegans. Although she already had soya milk and vegetarian sausages to hand, they'd requested almond milk and she'd need some fresh avocados. She chewed on her lip. A quick trip to the farm shop at Pengillis should sort it out. Should she ask Oliver if he would go?

Laughing under her breath as Liam launched himself at Oliver and almost knocked him from his feet, she eyed her boss in amusement. He seemed to be taking the boys in his stride considering he'd said children weren't his thing.

Oliver looked up as Anna came down the steps onto the lawn.

'Ah, the cavalry. Your time's up, boys.' Both Jason and Liam stopped their pretend sword fight to look at Anna.

'Sorry to interrupt the battle.' She turned to Oliver. 'Lunch is ready, but I have new guests arriving in a couple of hours and I need to get over to a shop, so once we've eaten, I have to—'

Oliver held up a hand. 'You'd like me to go so you can get on.'

Surprised at how much she didn't want him to leave, Anna shook her head. 'No, don't go. I mean, there's no need. It's just...' She glanced over at the boys, who'd resumed their mock fight and were paying the boring adults no attention.

'I'll take them fishing.'

Anna blinked. 'Are you sure? I only need an hour, but I can take them with—'

Oliver came up the steps, stopping on one that left his blue-eyed stare on a level with hers. 'I said I'll take them. I need to pop over to Port Wenneth this afternoon. We can sit on the harbour there and while away a couple of hours.'

'I'd need to ask Nicki if it's okay.'

'Then go do it.'

Anna hurried back to the kitchen, grabbed her phone and sent Nicki a text, wondering if she'd see it, but within seconds, a response came: *Fine by us!*

Lunch was soon over, and the boys were ready for their adventure. Anna wasn't sure how Oliver felt about suddenly being in charge of two young children; his expression, when he wasn't talking to the boys, resumed its habitual inscrutability. Watching him wrestle with the booster seats and put the boys in the back of the car when they were so full of excitement was entertainment in itself, but Anna made herself turn away and focus on what she needed to do. The time would fly by.

And it did. Her guests arrived a little early, but she was ready for them and they were delighted with the light-filled, pretty bedroom she'd prepared for them, as well as the dairy-free cookies she'd managed to find. There was no trace of her own childhood in there anymore, but the room was charming nonetheless, and she'd made them a tray of tea and set it out in the guests' sitting room and handed them a selection of maps and leaflets about local attractions before hurrying back to the kitchen to start preparing the Bolognese sauce for supper.

A quick glance at the clock as she peeled and sliced onions showed it to be close to five o'clock. Surely Oliver should be back by now? Before anxiety could take hold, she heard the sound of childish chortles and the boys came running around from the back of the house, across the terrace and in through the door.

'We had a 'mazing time, Anna.'

'Oliver is cool.'

Wiping her hands on a towel, Anna opened the fridge. 'Juice, boys?'

They hurried to take a seat at the table and she carried it over to them. 'Just one biscuit or it will spoil your meal.'

'I think *Anna* is cool.' Liam eyed the biscuit with pleasure.

'So, what did you catch?'

'Nothing,' Jason said, beaming.

Anna hid her smile. 'You seem rather proud for having caught no fish.'

'We tried crabbing, but Oliver said the water wasn't warm enough.'

She caught a movement from the corner of her eye. Oliver had walked into the garden, looking across the water towards Harbourwatch. He had such a presence. His tall frame, the way he carried himself, was attractive... Anna blinked, turning to Jason, who tugged on her arm.

'Anna! Guess what? We saw a cone fish.'

Curbing her amusement, Anna said seriously, 'Interesting. I've never heard of a cone fish.'

Liam eyed her sagely. 'Floating in the harbour. Oliver said it happens when the tide is right.'

'And we saw a glove fish too!' Jason grinned. 'Oliver said it's where they get fish fingers from.'

'Can we have fish fingers for tea?'

Anna smiled at Liam. 'Not tonight, but perhaps tomorrow.'

She looked up as Oliver came in through the door. 'Cone and glove fish?'

He shrugged.

'Port Wenneth isn't Polkerran. There were a few things floating in the water and the boys were curious about them.' He spoke quietly, and Anna started to smile.

'No shopping trolley fish, then?'

'They're freshwater. Tend to frequent rivers.'

Oliver turned out to be good company and, since their outing, much more relaxed around Liam and Jason. He kept the boys amused over supper with more of his gory tales from history, and all three of them cleaned their plates with gusto, with Liam declaring Anna the best cook ever, after his mother of course.

Anna chivvied them both to get washed and ready for bed, and they came back down to say goodnight to Oliver, who held out a hand again, but both boys clearly felt they had moved beyond such formalities. They launched themselves at him with a hug and begged him to come up and tell them a bedtime story. Meeting his surprised look over their heads, Anna bit down on a smile. He could be quite endearing.

Anna busied herself clearing the table and putting the dishwasher on. Oliver would doubtless leave as soon as he came back downstairs. She would get on her laptop and do some research about will tracing, so she could start contacting people after the holiday weekend, and if she had time tonight, she'd also go into the study and start assessing the paperwork.

When she heard Oliver coming back down the stairs, she dried her hands and walked over to the door into the hall.

'Are they asleep?'

Oliver started. He'd been staring at the bowl of shells on the console table that Anna had brought with her, the ones Aunt Meg had kept handing to her when in the hospice.

'Er, not quite.'

Anna smiled. 'Don't tell me. You got them so excited with your tales of battle, they now can't sleep.'

He looked a little sheepish, and her smile widened. She could see a new side to him today, and she liked it.

'Please thank Mrs Clegg for the basket. I hope she's not overdoing it. I'll see you on Tuesday?'

The sardonic brow was back. 'Am I being dismissed?'

'No! Not at all. I thought you'd be wanting to get off. Go home.'

Oliver walked towards her. 'Does the offer of a glass of wine stand?'

It was Anna's turn to raise a brow. 'What about the car?'

He stopped in front of her. 'I dropped it back home earlier. The boys wanted to see some armour I'd told them about. We walked over. So?'

'So?'

'Wine?'

'Yes, of course.' Flustered, Anna hurried back into the kitchen and headed for the fridge, welcoming the blast of cool air on her warm cheeks. Research would have to wait. She'd get up early tomorrow instead. 'White, red or rosé?'

'Red, please.'

He took both glasses from her when she'd poured, and they settled in opposite corners of the comfortable sofa in front of the log burner. Heathcliff eyed them warily from the hearth, then lowered his head and resumed his dozing.

'So.'

Anna glanced at Oliver. 'So?'

'Who taught you to cook? Was it your cousin?'

'Sadly not.' Anna reached for her glass. 'She had little interest in it, or in helping me learn anything, actually.

Aunt Meg taught me everything I know about cooking. I often wonder if my mum loved it as much as I do.'

She eyed Oliver over her glass as she took a sip. If he asked questions, did that mean she could as well? 'What about you?'

'I can cook if I have to.'

Anna smiled faintly. 'No, I meant, what about your parents? Did they teach you things?'

Oliver took a drink from his glass. 'Not really. We moved around a lot with my father's job. He lives in Dubai now. We don't see a lot of each other.' He placed the glass on the table. 'My mother died about four years ago.'

'I'm sorry. Not that long before you came here to Polkerran, then.'

'How do you know how long I've been here?' His eyes narrowed. 'Ah. The gossips.'

'You did mention your three-year lease was coming to an end. And even if it was 'the gossips', they don't mean any—' Anna's phone rang, and she snatched it up. Alex. 'Excuse me a minute.' She hurried down the hall to the study, closing the door.

'I miss you.' Anna ran a hand through the box of shells on the desk.

Alex snorted. 'You're supposed to!'

'You'll definitely come down next weekend?'

He hesitated. 'I'm not sure. I'll let you know when I know what my plans are.'

Anna's heart sank. Was he fed up with her already? 'Have I done something wrong?'

'Of course not. I have a lot of claims on my attention, that's all. You don't know what it's like.'

'I do at the moment.'

'How so?'

'Guests at last. Two rooms occupied, and I've got Nicki's boys here, as you know, in the bunk room.' She hesitated. 'And Oliver's here.'

'Poor you. Do you take in every waif and stray?' He grunted. 'I don't think you're going to be cut out for this B&B business, Anna.'

'Why ever not? Alex?'

There was silence at the other end, and then she heard a male voice and assumed from the muffled sound of Alex's reply that he'd put his hand over the phone. 'Look, got to dash. I'll call you in the week. And don't get too cosy with the History Man.'

Anna wished she hadn't told him about Oliver. 'Don't be silly. Why on earth would I do that?'

'He's interested in the house, you know, not you.'

'What do you mean?'

'Couldn't stay away from it, by all accounts, when your aunt Meg lived there. Quite obvious he has some sort of design on it. He's obsessed with buying up property in Polkerran. Beaten Tremayne Estates to two lately.'

It wasn't possible. Oliver wouldn't do that... would he? But then he seemed to know Westerleigh Cottage incredibly well. Hadn't he gone straight to the fuse box that night she moved in? Hadn't he walked out onto the terrace earlier as if he knew exactly where to go?

And Oliver knew about the shells...

Chapter Twenty

Do not give way to useless alarm... though it is right to be prepared for the worst, there is no occasion to look on it as certain

Jane Austen, *Pride and Prejudice*

Troubled, Anna ended the call and walked slowly back into the kitchen. Oliver stood at the sink, washing the dishes that wouldn't fit in the dishwasher, and Anna eyed him warily. Then she pulled herself together. This was ridiculous. She'd been working closely with the man for months now, and she was surely a good enough judge of character on her own.

There was something incredibly touching about Oliver today, the domestic scene, the fact he'd actually shed the jacket he'd been wearing and rolled up his sleeves. The tie remained in place, but he was... different. At home, almost.

'I'm seeing another side of you.' Oh lord. She'd said it out loud.

Oliver draped a damp cloth over the rail on the Aga and turned to face her.

'There hasn't been much chance for dish drying at the office.'

'Yes, I know, but...' Anna blew out a breath. 'You know what I mean.'

'Invariably.' Oliver looked at his watch. 'Let's have a truce. I'll curb my instinct to state the obvious if you do too. Think we can last another hour? Then I'd best go.'

For some reason, she felt relief he would stay a bit longer. Probably she missed Alex's company. 'I'll get more wine.'

Anna curled back up into her favourite corner of the sofa. Time to ask the question.

'Why are you interested in shells?'

Oliver took the sturdy armchair opposite, more suited to his large frame, his long legs stretched out in front of the burner. A strange look filtered over his face, and he didn't answer for a moment, staring at his feet. Then he raised his head, his piercing blue gaze on Anna. 'Am I?'

Anna cradled her glass in her lap. 'You were looking at some of them. Aunt Meg loved shells.' She tried to dispel the feeling she touched on matters she shouldn't. 'I wondered if you liked them too.'

'Not particularly.'

'Did Aunt Meg ever talk to you about them?'

Oliver said nothing for a moment. Then he took a drink from his glass. 'Not a lot you can say about shells.'

Anna bit her lip. She didn't like to say she'd seen the words written on his notepad on her first day working for him without sounding as though she'd snooped. Oliver didn't like snoops.

'Shall I?' He gestured towards the fire.

'Yes, please.' Deciding it best to let it go, Anna watched Oliver stack another log in the wood burner. 'I'm going to miss using it when the proper warm weather comes.'

'I've always loved a real fire.' Oliver retook his seat and reclaimed his wine glass.

Anna pulled a face. 'My only experience of it came from being here, and it was rare Aunt Meg used it in the summer. Sometimes, though, if it had rained for a few days and become quite chilly, she'd get it going, and I'd sit and stare into the flames for ages, my mind away on adventures.'

With a blink, Anna took a slug of her wine. Where had that come from? Oliver would be bored rigid.

'So, what was home like? No roaring open fires, I take it?'

'Oh, no!' Anna put her glass on the coffee table. 'I grew up in a modern house. Cousin Victoria and her husband had one of those new builds so prevalent in the early nineties, with the fake timber. "Mock Tudor" was the awful phrase?' Oliver nodded. 'Appalling. Of course, back then, I didn't really think about it, but my childhood was...' Anna mulled for a moment. 'Let's say, they didn't hide the fact I was a drain on their more than adequate resources.' Her smile was a little sad as she picked up her glass again. 'What they never understood was that I didn't want private lessons or new clothes all the time. All I wanted was their love.'

'And you were an only child?'

'Yes. I was so thankful when Aunt Meg threw me the lifeline of spending my summer holidays here in Polkerran.' She looked fondly round the room, then recalled Alex's words. 'How did you know where the fuse box was?'

'Sorry?'

Her curiosity came to the fore as a guarded expression crossed his face. 'When I moved in and the lights weren't working. You knew exactly where to go.'

'I did some basic DIY for Meg, helped her maintain things – not overly well.' He smiled faintly. 'Hence my familiarity with her shed, too.'

It made perfect sense, and Anna picked up the previous conversation. 'Didn't you have anything good in your childhood?'

Oliver took a slug of wine before answering. 'No.'

'Why not?' Gosh, this wine was taking effect. Anna eyed her almost empty glass warily, but Oliver leaned over and picked up the bottle, topping up both their glasses before he responded.

'My father was constantly away on business and, as I said before, I never quite bonded with my mother.'

'That's so sad.'

'Is it?'

Thinking of how much she wished for children of her own, Anna felt uneasy. Was there a chance her own child might not love her in return? She was in no doubt she would be overwhelmed with love for any child she had.

'So, you were an only child too?' She wasn't sure how many more questions she could get away with before Oliver's habitual shutters came down.

'Yes. I did see quite a bit of my cousins. Two. Much younger. I think they thought I was rather odd.'

Anna bit the inside of her cheek so as not to laugh. 'In what way?'

She half expected him to not answer or to evade the question. After all, the conversation had become rather personal. To her surprise, however, Oliver took a drink from his glass, then leaned back in his seat, his attention on the flames in the log burner.

'I had a fascination, even as a young child, with the past. History, or more specifically, the history of *things*. I wanted to know how people lived, worked, played. I was pretty obsessed with the day-to-day "tools" of life.'

'From any particular era?'

Oliver shook his head. 'Not really. My younger cousins thought I was strange because I'd rather spend time talking to my grandparents, exploring their garden shed, hauling around an old decrepit pair of skis, than sitting down with the latest video game.'

'You had video games back then?'

'I'm not—' He stopped, eyeing her in an assessing manner. 'You're teasing me.'

Anna smirked. 'Perhaps I'm not the only gullible one.'

With a smile, he returned his gaze to the fire.

'So, tell me about the skis.' Anna wasn't really interested in old skis, but he had a lovely voice, deep, masculine and clipped. No superfluous 'umming' and 'ahhing', no repetitive words. She enjoyed listening to him.

'When I was about fourteen, I went on a school trip to Switzerland. We stayed in Zermatt. Have you been there?'

Anna shook her head.

'It's this amazing, car-free town in the Alps, nestled below the Matterhorn. You've heard of the Matterhorn?'

'The Toblerone mountain?' Anna smirked. 'Oh yes.'

Oliver rolled his eyes. 'Heathen. Well, the whole history of the first successful ascent fascinated me. You know, the race to the top, the daring, the challenge, and then the tragedy of the descent. But when I visited the rather makeshift museum – there's a new one now, very well done and impressive – I was struck by how basic the climbing equipment was. And their clothing – nothing protective per se, just tweeds and a jaunty hat! Unbelievable, yet they did it.'

'And this started you off? On the social history path?'

'Yes.'

A companionable silence settled on them, broken only by the crackling of logs.

Then, Anna returned to a thought that was troubling her, especially in the light of today. 'And you say you don't like children?'

'I've never tried them.'

Anna laughed, then sobered. 'Seriously, Oliver. Don't you want to have a family one day?'

'No.' He stirred in his seat. 'Can we change the subject?'

'Yes, of course. Sorry.' Anna felt awful, conscious she had pushed Oliver too far. Yet he was an anomaly. Did he have no idea how much the boys had enjoyed his company?

Leaning forward, Oliver placed his glass on the table. 'I wouldn't want to put a child through what I had growing up – or rather, didn't.'

Anna's heart broke for him, but she didn't press him. 'I can't wait to have children.'

Oliver raised a brow. 'Plural? How many do you plan on having?'

'Well, two as a minimum.'

'Traditionalist.'

'But I'd love to have four if possible.'

He grunted. 'Good luck with that.'

Leaning forward, she emptied the bottle into both their glasses. 'You're such a cynic. Why aren't you prepared to give it a go?'

'I did. I got married. Wasn't surprised when it didn't work out.'

'Oh no. What happened?'

'I wasn't thinking beyond the bedroom at the time.'

Anna felt heat creep into her face, and she took a slug of her wine, trying to push away a sudden image of Oliver in bed with a faceless woman.

She cleared her throat. 'I think you're right. We should change the subject.'

Oliver leaned back in his seat. 'Tell me about Alex.'

Almost choking on her wine, Anna hurried to place her glass on the table between them. 'There's nothing to tell.'

'Really? Do you often fall into an affair with someone you've barely met?'

'I've known Alex for years.' He'd touched on a nerve. She'd felt all along she'd been too easy.

'Known?' Oliver's look was intent, and she stirred in her seat.

'Well, known *of* him. We weren't exactly friends, but I feel I know him well because I've seen him grow up.'

'Impressive. I thought he had a bit to go on that front.'

Anna frowned. 'You don't like him? Why? He doesn't like you either.'

'I know.'

She waited, but he added nothing more. '*Why* doesn't he like you?'

Oliver's expression was blank. 'I have no idea, and absolutely zero interest in finding out.'

Silence fell for a while, with Oliver's attention drifting back to the flames and Anna's fixed on her normally taciturn boss.

'So?' A few minutes later, Oliver looked over at Anna.

'So?' She eyed him warily.

'How is looking into Meg's papers going?'

Leaning back in her seat, Anna smiled ruefully. 'It isn't. I've had so little time this weekend, with the boys here, to look through the boxes.'

'I can pick a couple up tomorrow if it would help, go through them for you?' Oliver leaned forward, placing his glass on the coffee table. 'Are the boxes the only place Meg kept anything like that?'

'There were papers in the desk drawers. I thought they might contain the most recent or most relevant things, but there was nothing. I did wonder if she took anything with her to the hospice, but I've emptied the small suitcase they returned and it only contained clothes, a couple of books and last year's diary.'

Oliver sat forward in his seat. 'I can't imagine there was anything lucid in there.'

Anna shook her head. 'Very few entries, and those were almost impossible to read and made no sense. There was a page torn out, though. From the early part of the year. I'm assuming she messed up whatever she tried to write. Poor Aunt Meg.'

'And no other personal belongings?'

'No, just her—' She leapt to her feet. 'Her handbag! Mr Mottershead handed it to me with the keys to the house.' She hurried out into the hallway, tugging open the door to the cupboard under the stairs. She had hung the bag on the hook on the back of the door and then forgotten about it!

Hurrying back into the kitchen, Anna realised Oliver had got to his feet and walked over to the window, and she joined him, placing the bag on the table.

'It's silly, but it feels wrong to go rummaging in Aunt Meg's handbag without her permission.'

Oliver glanced at her. 'Only way to find out what's in there.'

Anna opened the catch and peered inside, then said weakly, 'Oh dear. Not more shells!' She slowly upended the bag and the contents skittered out onto the table, and Oliver's hand shot out to stop a glass vial from rolling onto the floor.

Aside from the shells, there was a purse containing a bank card and some change, a pencil, a prettily embroidered handkerchief and the glass bottle in Oliver's hand. No papers of any sort.

'Oh well, worth a try.' Anna placed everything back inside apart from the shells, then held her hand out for the glass bottle, which she eyed with interest.

'Is this a perfume bottle?'

'Yes, cut glass with a silver lid. Edwardian.'

Anna inspected the delicate cap. 'I can't make out the hallmark.'

'Chester.'

'Oh.' She looked up at Oliver. 'How do you—'

'I've seen the bottle before.'

Anna popped it back into the bag and closed it, but Oliver had turned away.

'I need to get home.'

He headed for the hallway and Anna followed him to the door, standing on the doorstep as he walked to the gate. He turned around as he opened it.

'Try not to worry. There really isn't much you can do until you hear back from Mottershead's secretary.'

'I'll try my best.'

And then he was gone, swallowed up by the darkness, and Anna went back into the house, puzzled by how empty it suddenly felt. Oliver wasn't an easy conversationalist, unless he felt like putting himself out, but she hadn't wanted him to go.

—

The good weather held overnight, and once all the guests had eaten a hearty breakfast, Anna urged the boys into action.

'Upstairs to do your teeth, and then we'll sort out a picnic and go to the beach.'

She felt so much better this morning about everything. It had been too late to get on the laptop last night, but she'd managed to make a small start on her research this morning, in between cooking breakfast for her guests and the boys waking up.

Before they set out, Oliver turned up with the car to collect a couple of the boxes from the study, selecting two that seemed to contain more recent papers and were therefore more likely to deliver.

Once the guests had set off for their respective days out, and Liam and Jason were happily tucking into their bowls of cereal, Anna hurried up the stairs to tidy the guest rooms, remake the beds, restock the hospitality trays and give the bathrooms a quick clean.

Then, it was off to a small beach on the other side of the cove, not far from the lighthouse, where the boys busied themselves for a couple of hours, making a huge sandcastle as Anna sat digging her toes into the warm sand. She wondered what Oliver had planned today, other than going through the boxes. There'd been something on his mind before he left, she was sure. What could it be?

Then, she dismissed the thought. No doubt it was work.

'Right, I think you've earned an ice cream after all that hard work, boys. Let's tidy up and head into town.'

Wiping the crumbs from their faces, smiling at the juice moustaches they now bore, Anna followed the boys as they raced up the steps from the beach, the cool bag over her shoulder and the towels in her arms. She would miss their company when they went home.

–

Anna opened her curtains on the Monday morning to a sky thick with cloud. The glimpse of summer had been too good to last.

Both sets of guests checked out after their breakfast, and Anna waved them off with a satisfied smile. They had been very complimentary, and one couple had already booked to return in the autumn for a whole week. She finally had her business up and running!

When she returned to the kitchen, the boys were getting restless for their parents' return. Keen to get started looking through Aunt Meg's papers, Anna encouraged them to sit at the table with paper and crayons and suggested they draw a picture to describe what they'd been doing over the weekend.

She sat at the other end, her laptop open and chatting to them as she scrolled through website after website, jotting down things to follow up later. The boys had barely finished their masterpieces when Nicki walked in from the boot room, followed by Hamish, and both boys rushed over to hug them, talking non-stop.

They'd all gone before Anna realised the drawings were still on the table, and she picked them up, intending to pop next door to drop them off, but as she stepped outside, she stopped. Sweeping her hair from her eyes as a sudden breeze whipped it across her face, she took in the childish drawings depicting a black cat, an array of cakes and biscuits, some swords, several strangely shaped fish and, on Jason's, the giant sandcastle they'd built.

Anna hugged the drawings to her as she walked round to the gate. Liam had included two stick-like people, clearly a man and a woman, arm in arm. Despite the man's height and the brown-haired woman, surely this was meant to be Nicki and Hamish? She tried not to notice the heart he'd drawn above their heads, unevenly coloured in with a red crayon.

Once back home, Anna tried to keep her concerns over the second will at bay, but it was so much harder with only herself for company. She found a stack of paperwork in the old cupboard in the study, and she worked methodically through each piece, then put it aside when it didn't deliver what she needed. Stopping for a break, she stripped the beds upstairs and put a load of washing on, then cleaned the bathrooms and carried the trays down to the kitchen.

Anna knew she ought to think about shredding the paperwork she'd checked, but she returned it to the cupboard for now and turned her attention to the boxes stacked against the wall. Carrying the nearest one into the kitchen, she dropped it on the table and made herself a hot chocolate. She felt vulnerable and under threat. She had embraced Westerleigh as her home so completely, imagined living here for the rest of her life. How could her dream be at risk?

Her gaze drifted towards Harbourwatch. It had helped to tell Oliver about it, but she could hardly run to him every time she needed distraction. She could picture his expression if she turned up on his doorstep uninvited.

Anna drained her mug and turned her back on the view. Before she could get started on the next pile of papers, however, her mobile pinged, and she tugged it from her pocket.

Perhaps it would be Oliver, or Alex?

Chapter Twenty-One

It is the nature of truth to struggle to the light

Wilkie Collins, *Man and Wife*

Anna tapped in a quick reply, and two minutes later, she sat cross-legged on the sofa as Lauren's cheerful face appeared on her laptop screen.

'What's up, mate?'

'Oh Lauren!' Anna drew in a long breath. 'I'm so worried. I think I'm going to lose the house.' Saying the words out loud made it seem all the more real, and Anna felt her skin grow cold.

Lauren looked stunned, but then she sat forward. 'Hey, are you okay? You're awfully pale.'

Anna smiled sadly. 'Yes. I'm fine. I'm frustrated by how little I can do about it at the moment.'

'I don't understand.' Lauren frowned. 'How can you lose it when it's yours?'

As succinctly as she could, Anna filled Lauren in on what Mrs Lovelace had said and her failure to find out anything more so far. 'If this later will exists, then the cottage might not be legally mine.' She needed someone to reassure her, tell her everything would be okay. 'I wish Oliver was here to talk to. He has this ability to make everything seem okay.'

Lauren leaned even closer to the screen. 'Hold on, hold on. So there may be a later will, but from what you've told me over recent months, Mrs Lovelace is a bit of a gossip. It doesn't mean it's fact. Is there any chance she's making this up?'

'But that's just it. She does gossip, but she wasn't talking about someone saying they were a witness on a will. She said *she* was. Besides, her daughter's pretty down to earth, and she agreed with it being about two years ago.'

'Okay, but don't assume the worst, Anna. Even if there is a later will, it doesn't mean the bequest to you of the cottage has changed. It may be that, with the earlier will having been drawn up so long ago, your aunt Meg decided to leave some other things to various friends, and so on.'

'Then why didn't she have a codicil drawn up?'

Lauren shrugged. 'I don't know. Would it suffice? If she'd already bequeathed everything in its entirety to you?'

Anna shook her head. 'I've no idea. I don't know how any of it works. Mr Mottershead was completely flummoxed, but his secretary is trying to help.'

'Are there any clues among your aunt's papers? I know you said there were boxes of stuff. What are you up to, anyway?'

Anna pulled a face. 'I was about to start wading through one of them when you messaged.' Then, she smiled. 'Oliver took a couple away too.'

Lauren raised a brow, then smirked. 'Did he now? And Alex?'

'Couldn't get here this weekend.'

'But you told him?'

'Yes, in the week, about what Mrs Lovelace said, and I was going to see if he had any ideas when he got here, but he said something had come up.'

A frown creased Lauren's brow. 'I worry about you, Anna. Doesn't this ring bells over how things became with—'

'Alex isn't Giles.' Anna knew she sounded defensive, and to her relief, Lauren smiled.

'Of course he isn't. I just wish I was there with you.'

'Me too.' Anna looked around the charming kitchen. 'I miss having company. Having guests in the house is nice, but I only really see them in passing. Part of me can't wait to get back to work with Oliver in the morning.'

'Erm, Anna?'

'What?'

'You do realise you talk about Oliver far more than you talk about Alex?'

'No I don't!'

Lauren merely raised a brow again. 'Okay, I'll leave you to your searching. Call me in the week when you know more.'

They ended the call, and Anna turned to the box and opened it. It smelt musty. Some of these papers must be years old. She glanced at her watch. She'd spend an hour or so looking through them, and hopefully Wendy would call in a few days with some news.

It was exactly as Oliver said: until that happened, she couldn't really do much else.

–

Tuesday morning dawned, and Anna made her way downstairs checking her to-do list in her head. Both guest rooms were ready again, and at the moment she only had one room booked and not until later in the week. She smiled as she made coffee and wandered over to look out of the window, as she did every morning. She felt better for being proactive, and although the first box she'd checked hadn't provided any clues to the missing will, she was determined to fill every spare moment working her way through the rest. It would be good to see how Oliver had progressed with his boxes.

She also intended to follow up on some of the things she'd discovered through her research: aside from searching the papers of the deceased for the will, correspondence with a legal firm or business cards, recommendations ranged from contacting the local Law Society (already in Wendy's capable hands), the Society of Will Writers, and the Solicitors Regulation Authority.

Anna's gaze landed on Harbourwatch. Hopefully, she'd find a few moments during the day to whizz off a few emails.

She smiled as she turned away from her beloved view. Oliver had been a bit of a revelation over the weekend. She'd had no idea he would be a natural with children. Nor did he, it seemed.

An hour later, with the dishwasher doing its job, Anna poured fresh beans into the coffee machine and fetched the milk, unsurprised when the door opened and Daniel came in.

'Morning, Anna.'

'Hi!' Anna topped up the water in the machine. 'Give me a sec. I'll get you a coffee.'

'Brill.' Daniel sauntered over to get a mug from the cupboard. 'How's business?'

'Not bad.' Anna smiled at him as he leaned against the counter. 'Had a busy first weekend. Two rooms in use and, of course, Nicki's boys here.'

'In at the deep end.' Daniel's eyes creased. 'And I hear you had a helping hand.'

Anna opened her mouth, then closed it. 'I— Did you mean Oliver?'

Daniel smirked. 'Don't worry, I won't tell Alex.'

'Daniel!' Anna turned to put some small cakes out onto plates. 'It's not like that. He must have been at a loose end, and he was a useful pair of hands.'

'Was he now? I'm definitely not telling Alex that!'

'*Daniel!*'

Daniel started to laugh at Anna's appalled expression. 'Okay, okay.' He held up a hand. 'I get it. The big man helped out – with the boys.'

'So, what are you doing here?' Anna glanced pointedly at the clock. 'Got no odd jobs on at the moment?'

'Nothing much.' Daniel paused as Anna washed her hands and poured them a coffee. 'I've got a new project though. A bit hush-hush at the moment, but it's taking up most of my time. Got an appointment at the bank, so thought I'd drop by before I go to it.'

They walked over to sit at the scrubbed pine table. 'Sounds intriguing.'

'Not really. Trying to stem the gossip as long as I can, you know how it is.'

'Oh yes, I do indeed.' Anna looked over her shoulder as the door opened, then said quietly, 'And here's some more.'

She was unsurprised, really, to see Mrs Lovelace come in. If Daniel knew Oliver had been round over the weekend, then so must most of the village.

By the time Anna had supplied Mrs Lovelace with a cup of tea and placed more plates of goodies on the table, Nicki had arrived. She was eager to hear how the first B&B guests had felt about their stay, but then the conversation turned to Liam and Jason.

'The boys are full of their weekend, Anna. Hamish is already talking about us going away again so they can come back.'

Daniel grinned. 'A victim of your own success, Anna.'

'To be fair, they're full of talk about Oliver too.'

Anna suppressed a sigh. She thought she'd dealt quite nimbly with the questions Mrs Lovelace had about Oliver and how he came to be there. Now, she could see the old lady's eyes light up as she questioned Nicki about what Oliver had been doing with the boys.

'He's besotted, the girt man is.' Mrs Lovelace cast a sly look at Anna, but Daniel laughed.

'That's a bit hasty, Mrs L!'

She folded her arms across her chest and eyed Daniel beadily. 'You'm mark my words, young'un. Doesn't go out much, never been seen datin' since he came here.' Mrs Lovelace looked around at her audience. 'Still hung up on his first love, Cleggie says. A one-woman man.' She frowned. 'Now what's that word? I can never remember it. Begins with "m"…'

'Monogamous?' Nicki winked at Anna.

'That's the one! Until now.' Mrs Lovelace nodded knowingly. 'So what's drawin' him out? I reckon his eye's on a different maid these days.'

Anna was about to protest at the absurdity of the elderly lady's words, but she didn't think Oliver would appreciate being discussed. Feeling disturbed by the turn of the conversation, she walked over to glance out of the window at Harbourwatch instead.

Daniel's phone went, and he walked outside onto the terrace to take the call. Not wanting to be swept into any further conversation about Oliver, Anna left Nicki to chat with Mrs Lovelace and headed into the boot room to move a bundle of towels to the tumble dryer, but then she became aware of a voice outside. Daniel must have walked along the terrace and around the corner.

She tried not to listen as she turned the dial on the machine, but his voice carried clearly through the open window.

'No, that's fantastic. I'll get the contract back to you by the end of the day. Thank you, Mr Seymour.' Anna straightened up slowly as Daniel paused. 'Oliver. Yes, of course.'

What contract? Anna tried to push her curiosity aside. It was none of her business. She switched the machine on, thankful for the noise it made, but it seemed Daniel had ended his call because when she walked back into the kitchen, he came in through the door to the terrace.

'Got to love and leave you, ladies.' He picked up a biscuit and waved a hand as he left the room, and Anna sighed resignedly as Nicki offered Mrs Lovelace a refill.

It didn't look like they were leaving any time soon.

–

The week flew by, with one-night guests and the hours Anna put in at Harbourwatch. Every spare moment beyond, she passed either working methodically through more boxes of papers, sending emails to various organisations, or on Google, desperately seeking an answer over what to do in her circumstances.

She did hear from Wendy after a few days, but disappointingly, all she was able to confirm was that none of the local legal firms had Aunt Meg listed as a previous client.

Before Anna knew it, it was Friday, and Alex was due in Polkerran. She dismissed a sudden inexplicable wish to be alone as she walked to work. He'd be a welcome distraction from her incessant thoughts.

What with her worries over the cottage and the wisdom of having set up a business there, she was also relatively distracted at work, and a growing awareness of Oliver didn't help. Something had changed since the day he'd spent at the cottage and the evening by the fire, talking and laughing. She just didn't know what.

When lunchtime came around, Mrs Clegg popped her head round the door to see if Oliver wanted to eat at his desk, as he usually did, but to Anna's surprise, he said he'd come down to the kitchen.

Anna was already digging around in her bag for the sandwich she'd made at home.

'You'd better join me.'

She looked up at him in surprise. 'That sounds ominous.'

He shook his head as Anna got to her feet and followed him from the room. 'Thought it might be easier to talk at the table.'

'Did you find anything?' Anna's heart felt like it had crawled into her throat.

'Nothing to help you, no.'

'Oh.' Her heart slid back into position as they walked down the stairs.

Mrs Clegg fussed around them, putting out Oliver's meal and a plate for Anna's sandwich and making tea. Then, she left them alone, and they ate in a companion-able silence for a few minutes, but Anna's curiosity was at its height.

'So you've found nothing of interest in the boxes yet?'

A strange look crossed Oliver's face, gone in an instant. 'Nothing of a legal nature. I'll drop them off over the weekend.' He paused. 'I take it Tremayne's visiting?'

'Yes.'

'I won't disturb you. I'll leave them under the porch by the front door.' He picked up his knife and fork. 'What about you? Any joy?'

Anna shook her head. 'I've been through a couple, but most of the paperwork was dated years ago. I know I need to eliminate every box, in case she popped anything to do with the second will into the nearest one to hand, but I don't hold out much hope.'

Oliver poured them both a glass of water. 'And nothing else has come up in your online searches?'

'I've whizzed off emails to any organisation that comes up, in case they can point me in a new direction, but no joy so far.' Anna bit her lip as he passed the glass to her.

'You look guilty.'

She let out a huff of laughter. 'Not really. I keep getting distracted.'

'By?'

'Strange laws, like it being illegal to handle a salmon in suspicious circumstances.'

Oliver grinned. 'When I lived in the States, I heard of a couple. Apparently it's illegal for rats to leave a ship in Tampa Bay, and against the law to put tomatoes in clam chowder in Massachusetts.'

Anna smirked. 'Good old Google. It comes up with all sorts of links when you put in anything to do with wills.'

'Such as why did Shakespeare leave his wife the second-best bed.'

'I know! Who got the first?' Anna shook her head, amused.

Oliver drained his glass. 'I think my favourite is the German poet, Heinrich Heine. He left his entire estate to his wife provided she marry again, "because then there will be at least one man to regret my death".'

'You and your aversion to marriage!'

Oliver turned his attention back to his meal. 'Shows I'm not alone, though.'

Anna eyed him thoughtfully as she popped the last bit of sandwich into her mouth and chewed. Then, she picked up her glass. 'Why did you want to talk?'

'I find it a useful way to express words out loud.'

'Very funny.' Anna sipped her water. 'I thought you had something to tell me.'

'So did I. It can wait.'

'Oliver! Now I'm riddled with curiosity. If it isn't to do with the missing will, is it about work?' Perhaps he had changed his mind, and wasn't going to leave after all? Hope surged through Anna, and she looked at him expectantly.

Oliver leaned back in his chair, pushing his empty plate away, but said nothing.

'Should I start guessing?'

'I'd rather you didn't.'

Anna waited, watching him carefully, trying to gauge if he'd stand up and say it was time to get on with their work or expand on why he'd suggested they eat together.

'Don't look at me like that.'

Result. She assumed an innocent expression. 'Like what?'

A smile tugged at his mouth, and he held up his hands. 'Okay. I wondered if you'd do some research for me.'

'Oh.' Torn between confusion over why he couldn't have asked her up in the office and happiness that he had more work for her, Anna took another sip of her water. 'Yes, of course. To do with the book?'

He shook his head and got to his feet. 'A new project. On... on the lost villages of England. Tea or coffee?'

Pleased they were staying longer and that he was inclined to talk further, Anna smiled. 'Hot chocolate, please.'

Oliver rolled his eyes at her, but turned to make the drinks, and Anna opened the notes app on her phone, ready to jot down Oliver's thoughts. This job kept getting better and better!

–

By the end of the day, Anna opened the gate to Westerleigh relieved to be home. Oliver had clearly felt the need to make up for time lost over lunch, and she had ploughed through as much as she could while also starting on the research he'd asked for, namely into a small village, known as Hallsands, in Devon, once home to over a hundred people, which was all but wiped out one night by a severe storm. Added to the heavy week she'd had away from the office (the constant stripping, washing, drying, ironing of the bedding before remaking the beds, the cleaning and the breakfast cooking was time-consuming), Anna was thankful she had no bookings this coming weekend. Alex would be delighted. It was a shame he had no interest in history. She could have talked to him about the new project with Oliver.

Preoccupied with her thoughts, Anna glanced over at Harbourwatch as she laid the table for supper. Oliver seemed to be on her mind a great deal lately.

Ridiculous. Anna turned away. Luckily, she'd already prepared their dinner the day before and it only required heating up while she made a salad. She had a feeling it would be an early night.

Chapter Twenty-Two

...smiled in his sleep, as though these marks of pity and compassion had awakened some pleasant dream of a love and affection he had never known

Charles Dickens, *Oliver Twist*

Anna had persuaded Alex to come for a walk along the cliffs to her favourite cove on Saturday afternoon, and then they enjoyed a meal at the large granite table on the patio. Anna had found her attention drawn repeatedly to Harbourwatch, and she wondered what Oliver did with his weekends. Mrs Clegg had implied he kept working, and for some reason, it made her feel sad.

Alex was uninterested in Anna's dilemma over the cottage, dismissing the talk of another will with a shrug. When she told him she intended to go through all her aunt's papers to see if she could find it, he had merely laughed and wished her luck. She would need it.

By Sunday, the fine weather had passed and thick clouds hung over the cove with a threat of rain in the air, so they ate breakfast at the kitchen table, but the clatter of the letterbox drew Alex into the hall in search of the financial pages of the Sunday newspaper.

'What's the History Man doing?'

Anna looked over as Alex came back into the room holding the paper.

'What do you mean?'

Alex gestured back along the hallway. 'Just seen him in the driveway.'

Anna had to quell a sudden urge to go and talk to Oliver. 'Oh. He said he'd drop the boxes back – he took some to look through.'

She got up and began to clear the breakfast things.

'Sounds highly suspect to me. Why's he poking his nose into your business?' Alex dropped into his chair at the table, but Anna didn't respond. It would be nice if Alex had some interest in her concerns. She bit her lip; how horribly disloyal of her.

'Can you clear this end first?' Alex gestured at his used table setting and waved the newspaper, and Anna was hit by a flashback to life with Giles when she'd stayed over at his for the night.

She bit back on the temptation to tell him to do it himself, and by the time she'd finished cleaning up and been out into the garden, ostensibly to pick some fresh flowers for the vases but really to check if there was any sign of Oliver – there wasn't, merely the two boxes, as promised, on the front doorstep – Alex had gone up to shower and dress.

The pretty B&B sign swung gently in the breeze as Anna headed back into the house carrying the first box, the flowers lying on the top. 'Please let me be able to stay,' she whispered under her breath.

By the time she went back into the house with the second box, Alex lounged on the settle in the hallway, still holding the newspaper.

'Time I was off.'

'Oh!' Anna looked at her watch. 'It's not even midday. I thought you were going back this evening?' She'd planned to cook them a traditional roast for lunch, something she never bothered with for herself. Cooking for one was never much fun.

'Want to avoid all the weekenders heading back later in the day.'

'Okay.' Was part of her relieved? What was going on with her? Anna summoned a smile. 'See you next Friday, then.'

'I'll call you. Might be late getting down here.' He tossed the paper aside and got to his feet, taking the box and putting it on the console table. Then, he caught her close, kissing her thoroughly, and Anna melted into his arms. No, of course she wasn't relieved. This was right. This felt heavenly. She held onto Alex's shoulders as he drew the kiss to a close, then dropped a final one on the tip of her nose.

'And don't take in any guests. I've a fancy for trying out some of those other bedrooms.' He winked at her, and she shook her head at him.

'I'm trying to get a business going here, Alex. Weekends are more likely to bring people.'

He opened the door, then looked back over his shoulder. 'I'm serious, Anna. I'm not prepared to share you.'

He blew her a kiss, and she turned away as the door closed and picked up the discarded flowers. She had no intention of taking bookings for the next weekend. Oliver's book had to be with his agent by Saturday latest so they could read it over the weekend, and if this past week was anything to go by, the following one would be long and busy. He'd already said he might need her to work late on Friday, and she'd willingly agreed.

Looking around the kitchen as she filled a vase with water, Anna sighed. Alone again, naturally. Then, she hurried over to the boot room door.

'I'm so sorry, baby.'

Heathcliff shot into the room, mewing indignantly, and she scooped him up and let him snuggle up against her, purring loudly.

'I have the day free now, Heathcliff. Let's make a start on another of those boxes, shall we?'

–

The notices had gone up in the village for the fundraising sale for the Christmas lights, and Anna filled a bag for life with a few bits and pieces from around the house before fetching the handbags she had removed from Aunt Meg's room. She started to check they were empty, and as she picked up the last one, Nicki's head appeared round the boot room door.

'Last call for any bric-a-brac or accessories.'

'Perfect timing.' Anna held up the bag. 'I hope they go to good homes. They're a bit old-fashioned, but well cared for. I've kept a couple, ones I remember Aunt Meg using.'

'Vintage is all the rage these days.' Gathering up the bags, Nicki dropped them into her bin bag and picked up the bag for life, and Anna waved her off before resuming her search through the next box in the study, making her way through several piles of letters, many of which were ones she had sent to Aunt Meg over the years. There were other letters of business, letters exchanged with friends outside of Cornwall and some old bills, but everything so far was dated further back than two years ago.

Despite being so busy at work and exhausted when she got home, Anna continued the search every night, breaking off now and again to browse one of the diaries for light relief. She thought she'd had a breakthrough one evening. As she turned the final few pages of a three-year-old diary, Aunt Meg mentioned a solicitor's appointment.

Anna made a quick call to Wendy the next day, but when she called her back, it was only to confirm there was nothing on the file that suggested Meg Stratfield had been in contact with them around that time, nor was there any record of an appointment.

She skim-read the most recent diary she could find, other than the one found in Aunt Meg's handbag. There were hints of what was to come in her writing – a certain paranoia growing. The locals were right about someone trying to persuade her to sell the cottage, but she didn't say who it was. There were comments like *He was here again, He won't stay away, even though I've told him I'll never sell.*

Her heart breaking for Aunt Meg and her anxiety, Anna felt upset and unsettled. Had she made the new will under pressure? With her health in decline and her mind starting to weaken, had she succumbed to this man in the end and made the property over to him on her death? Would that stand up in court if it could be proven she had not been fully of sound mind at the time? Yet more questions, and not a single answer in sight.

–

Friday soon came around, and knowing she needed to work late, Anna had gone home around six o'clock to prepare a meal for Alex and leave it for him to heat up.

'Smells good.'

She looked up in surprise from laying the table for one. 'You're early!'

Alex walked over and put his arms around her. 'Meeting cancelled this afternoon. Decided to make the most of it.'

He bent his head to kiss her, but Anna broke away from him after a few seconds. 'I can't stop long, Alex. I've made coq au vin and it's in the oven now, along with some rosemary and garlic potatoes. There's bread in the bin.'

She hurried over to get a glass for him, but when she turned around, he hadn't moved.

'Where are you going?'

'Back to work.' Anna walked over and placed the wine glass on the table, then touched his arm when he didn't look at her. 'Alex? I did forewarn you when we spoke in the week, said I had to work Friday evening.'

'What, *all* of it?'

'Possibly. The book has to go off to Oliver's agent tomorrow, and—'

'Fine.' He strode over to the door into the hall. 'I'll see you when I see you.'

'But where are you going? I made you dinner.' She gestured helplessly towards the oven, but Alex had gone.

'Alex?' Anna hurried after him, and he stopped by the front door.

'What?'

'I'm sorry, okay? Oliver needs me.'

Alex whirled about. 'Really? And I don't?'

Anna drew in a short breath, studied his handsome features and, for the first time, found them lacking. His mouth could be quite cruel sometimes, his eyes without warmth. For all Oliver's brusqueness, his eyes were never cold. For all his mocking brow and liking his own way, he did at least consider others.

'Fine.' Alex turned away and walked out of the door, and Anna ran after him.

'Alex, please.' He stopped again, only he didn't turn around, and she walked round to face him, squaring her shoulders. 'You know it's not like that. My job is important to me, especially with the delays I've had setting up the B&B.' Anna spoke firmly, confident she was in the right. 'Surely you understand that? I mean, your work often takes precedence, doesn't it?' She waited, her insides doing somersaults the envy of any self-respecting acrobat, but her mind was clear.

He held her gaze rigidly for a moment, then released a huff of breath. 'Fair comment.' He smiled reluctantly, then pulled her to him, stroking her hair as she laid her head on his chest. 'I don't like sharing you, be it guests or Saint Seymour, the History Man.'

Anna raised her head. 'Don't—'

'Okay, okay.' Alex raised a hand as he released her. 'I won't call him that.'

'It's a one-off. He has to get the manuscript off this weekend, and he needs my help.'

Alex raised a cynical brow. 'All weekend?'

'Don't be silly. It's only this evening, and perhaps a few hours tomorrow. I'm sorry I'm not there to share dinner with you, but we'll have tomorrow night instead. We could even go out.'

'We'll see.' Alex kissed her briefly. 'Drop me a WhatsApp when you're free tomorrow.'

Anna frowned. 'You're not staying?'

Alex opened the car door and put his bag on the back seat. 'May as well go and see the parents as I'm at a loose end.'

Anna watched him go, then glanced at her watch. It was nearly seven. She went back into the house, switched off the oven, grabbed her bag and keys and, leaving the outside light on, hurried down the lane. Luckily, the ferry had come in.

She focused on Harbourwatch as the little boat chugged its way across the cove, keen to get back and stay as late as need be. For Alex, she barely spared another thought.

Mrs Clegg shook her head as Anna passed her on the stairs carrying down an untouched tray of food.

'It's not right. Master Oliver hasn't eaten a thing all day.'

'He'll survive.' Anna hurried up the stairs. She could happily have eaten the meal Oliver had shunned. She was famished!

Oliver seemed remarkably calm when she entered the room, his attention fixed on the printout on his desk. Anna took in the breadth of his shoulders, and then the back of his neck and the gap between his hair and the whiteness of his collar.

Then, she swallowed quickly. Why on earth had she had the sudden urge to reach out and touch him?

This wouldn't do at all!

'Oliver?' Her voice came out in a squeak, and she cleared her throat. 'You didn't eat anything. Do you want some coffee?'

Half expecting the customary lack of response or a grunt at being disturbed, Anna was surprised when he looked up and swung around in his seat.

'You're back.' He said nothing more, a faint smile on his lips, and an inexplicable feeling swept through Anna as she took a step backwards. With his blue eyes fixed on her in such a way, it felt as though they were suddenly very close to each other, and heat invaded her cheeks.

'I'll pop down and fetch some.' She turned for the door and fled down the stairs, unsure what had just happened, then shook her head. Ridiculous.

Mrs Clegg was nowhere to be seen but had left a pot of coffee on the stove and a tray laid out with the necessary, and Anna was back outside the door to the office within minutes.

'Come on, Anna. It's only Oliver,' she admonished herself as she nudged the door open with the tray.

Only he was no longer at his desk.

'Well, that was a waste of time, wasn't it?' She addressed Dougal, who had raised his head when she came back into the room.

'No.'

'Oh!' Anna turned around, the tray still in her hands, only to find Oliver standing by the bookcase, an open book in his hands.

He walked over, tucked the book under his arm and relieved her of the tray, placing it on the table.

'Do you want some?' He picked up the pot.

'Yes please.'

A kick of caffeine would certainly help, though she thought longingly of the wine chilling in the fridge at home. Anna checked her mobile as Oliver poured. No conciliatory text from Alex. Did he really not understand?

To her surprise, it didn't worry her the way it would have done a few weeks ago. She wasn't blind to the fact that he only seemed to have one interest in her.

'Sex,' she muttered under her breath.

'Sorry?' Oliver raised a brow as he handed her a mug, and she felt the heat from earlier steal into her cheeks again.

'Checks. I said "checks".' Anna waved a hand at the next chapter on her desk. 'I mean, I need to do some checks before I give this one back to you.'

Oliver said nothing, merely turned back to his desk and resumed his reading. Throwing Dougal a culpable look, she retook her own seat.

Two hours later, the clock on the landing chimed ten, and Anna looked up owlishly. Eyes scratchy with tiredness, her back ached from hunching over the keyboard. She gripped her stomach as it let out a rumble of protest.

'Go home.'

Anna turned in her seat. Oliver still had his back to her, tapping into his laptop.

'Are we done?'

'You are.'

'But I stayed so I could help!' Anna got to her feet and walked over to stand beside him, only this time he didn't look up, simply continued to type.

'You did.'

'So, is it ready? Will you get it off okay tomorrow morning? Do you want me to—'

Pushing back in his chair, Oliver swung around to look up at her. 'No. Possibly. And no.'

Yet again, no 'thank you'. Anna drew in an impatient breath. She wanted to go home so badly, so why didn't she just leave? Tiredness and frustration with herself battled within her. Frustration won.

'Why are you like this?'

Oliver raised a brow. 'Like what?'

'So... so abrupt sometimes.'

'Why use more words than are necessary? Did you fail to understand me?'

'No, but— You're impossible!'

Oliver said nothing, turning back to his desk. Anna suppressed the urge to stamp on his foot, followed swiftly by the wish he would change his mind, ask her to stay longer with him.

Anna snatched up her coat and bag and hurried from the room, throwing a quiet goodnight at him. She doubted he heard her, but she had to get out of there.

What had happened to her? Why did she have these strange thoughts about someone who clearly had no interest in her – or any relationship? Wasn't she happy – over the moon – to be dating Alex after all this time?

Despite her tiredness, Anna all but raced through the town. The ferry had stopped for the night, and she hurried over the bridge and along the lane towards Westerleigh, her mind a whirl of confusing thoughts.

–

Unable to face eating so late at night, Anna curled up on the sofa with Heathcliff and a glass of wine, trying to unwind, and most of all, trying not to think. Soon immersed in Dickens' *Our Mutual Friend*, she almost succeeded.

Once ready for bed, she walked over to her window and pulled the curtain aside. There was a light on in the office at Harbourwatch, and she bit her lip. Oliver worked too hard.

Anna struggled to get to sleep that night, and several times she got up to stare across the water. The light still shone from the windows. Oliver hadn't even closed the shutters.

Up early, she fed Heathcliff and hurried back around the cove to Harbourwatch. It was gone seven, but she knew there would be some last-minute changes to make and she could get a head start before Oliver appeared.

Dougal and Thumper were upon her immediately, and she calmed them as best she could, conscious the house was silent apart from their enthusiastic greeting, but the lamps in the hallway were still on. Surely Oliver wasn't still writing?

Hurrying up the stairs, Anna stopped outside the door to the office, her hand hovering above the handle. Why did her heart pound like this? She leaned her head against the wood. There was no sound within of tapping keys.

She peered into the room, and then her heart lurched unexpectedly. Oliver was slumped over his desk, the light from the desk lamp spilling over his dark hair and broad shoulders. Anna hurried over to him, the animals now in her wake. Was he ill? Had someone attacked him? There was no sign of blood...

Get a grip, you idiot. This isn't an episode of Midsomer Murders*!* Anna bit back on rising amusement, then leaned forward to switch off the lamp. The sunlight streamed in through the bay window, and she blinked.

Oliver's shoulders were moving with each breath.

Should she wake him? How could she without touching him, and why was she so wary of doing so? Anna walked over to the window. What was this reluctance? All she had to do was give him a shake. Perhaps she should leave the room and then come back in making lots of noise...

'Anna...'

'Oh, you're awake!' Filled with relief she swung around.

Only he wasn't.

Chapter Twenty-Three

Oh! That gentleness! How far more potent is it than force!

Charlotte Brontë, *Jane Eyre*

Oliver hadn't moved since she'd entered the room, though his eyelids were fluttering... Hadn't she read that was a sign of dreaming?

Anna walked slowly towards him, studying the visible side of his face. Dark lashes, an angular cheekbone, and a dusting of five o'clock shadow on his chin did little to detract from his attractiveness. His aquiline nose was in stark relief against the white of the paperwork beneath his head. A pencil still rested in his hand. He looked different; his features so much more relaxed than when he was awake.

A frisson stole through Anna. It felt incredibly intimate to watch Oliver sleeping, as though she were some sort of voyeur. Warmth filled her cheeks, and her insides began a tentative dance as she took in the hand holding the pencil. He had long, slender fingers, reflective of his tall frame. She couldn't remove her eyes from him, her gaze now returning to his features, taking in the firm mouth, almost touched with a smile as he slept, the high cheekbones, his arched brow and—

A mew from Thumper roused her. Embarrassed by staring for so long, Anna cast a glance towards the animals. They gazed back. She had to wake Oliver up.

'Er, Oliver?' Anna spoke hesitatingly, her voice no more than a whisper, and Dougal eyed her beadily. She could swear the dog rolled its eyes.

Give him a shake – a gentle one.

Anna stretched out her hand, held it above Oliver's shoulder, then placed it gently. It continued to rise and fall slightly beneath her touch, and she was conscious of the warmth and firmness of his body through his shirt.

Suddenly, his eyes flew open and Anna snatched her hand away, stepping back hastily.

'Oh good.' Her throat was dry. 'You're awake.'

Oliver sat up suddenly. 'Ow.' He rubbed his neck, then turned to look at her, and Anna's insides capered anew under his scrutiny. He swallowed visibly; had he coloured up? She tried not to stare, but he had removed his tie and waistcoat, and she wasn't used to seeing him so informally dressed. 'What time is it?'

Anna dragged her eyes away from the base of his throat and looked at her watch. 'Seven fifteen.'

Getting to his feet, Oliver stretched his arms above his head, then stilled. 'Why are you here?'

'I wanted to press on with any changes. Thought I'd get a head start.'

He didn't respond to this, turning for the door, but as he went through, he said over his shoulder, 'I'll grab a quick shower and then we can go through the final changes.' Then, he stopped and poked his head back around the door and said hopefully, 'Coffee?'

Anna rolled her eyes at him. 'Obviously.'

Pushing aside the awkwardness of the last few moments, she hurried out of the room.

The sooner this book was done, the better.

–

Oliver's late-night vigil had paid off. Once Anna had transferred his final edits to the electronic file and made sure the bibliography was complete, the manuscript was ready to send off, and by midday winging its way through cyberspace to Oliver's agent, who had wanted to look it over before sending it on to the publisher on Monday.

'Let's get some lunch.'

Anna looked up in surprise from tidying her desk.

'That's very kind of you, but I have to go.' She felt strangely sad about it.

Oliver didn't respond, his face an inscrutable mask. Then, he turned back to his desk. 'Another time, then.'

'I'd have loved to, honestly. But I have to—'

'I'll see you Monday. No need to come in until the afternoon.'

Feeling dismissed, Anna said goodbye and reluctantly left the room. She hurried through the house, called a farewell to Mrs Clegg, busy dusting the drawing room, and shot out of the side door and onto the lane.

Why this sudden urge to run away? Was it the temptation of accepting Oliver's invitation to lunch? Then she let out a huff of laughter. This was Oliver. It had hardly been an invite, more of an instruction. Anna tugged her phone from her pocket and tapped a quick message to Alex to let him know she was free.

She was worn out. A soak in a bath would be the perfect thing, with a hot drink and some of her favourite music. Half hoping Alex wouldn't respond, she set off for the ferry and was soon back on her own side of the cove.

Stopping at the small coffee shop-cum-bakery opposite where the ferry docked, Anna placed her order and dug around in her pocket for her purse.

'Hey, Anna!'

Anna turned around. 'Oh, hi, Nicki.'

'Thought I saw you through the window. Are you headed back home?'

'Yes, I'm done for the day.' Anna handed over some money to Shari, who owned the quaint little cafe. 'What about you?'

'Just dropped the boys off with Tommy the Boat. He's running a class every week for the village kids. Taking the kayaks out in the cove. They don't venture far, but it keeps them out of mischief for an hour or so.'

Picking up her cup of hot chocolate, Anna tucked the bulging paper bag under one arm and followed Nicki back out into the street.

'Were you doing what I think you were doing?' Nicki sounded amused, and Anna cast her a wary glance.

'I'm not sure. What do you think I was doing?'

Nicki smirked as they made their way up the lane. 'Buying baked goods when you can make them yourself better than anyone.'

She'd been caught out. 'I feel so guilty, with everyone coming to me for morning coffee and cakes. I feel less so if I pop in now and again to buy a few things from Shari.'

Nicki was still chuckling about it when they parted at her garden gate, and Anna pushed her own gate aside, relieved to be home again.

She fed Heathcliff and walked out onto the patio, nursing her takeaway chocolate. What was Oliver doing now? She could hardly believe he'd put his feet up. Hopefully, Mrs Clegg would be allowed to fuss around him, make sure he made up for not eating in recent days.

A sudden image of him asleep at his desk flew into her mind. Had Oliver really been dreaming about her? The strange frisson once again took hold of her, and frustrated, Anna turned away. This wouldn't do!

She put the cup on the patio table and checked her phone. Still no response from Alex. Signals were so patchy in Cornwall. If he'd gone somewhere outside Polkerran, he might not be able to respond. Conscious he'd be displeased, when she'd said she'd only be a few hours at Harbourwatch, she put a call through to him, half expecting it to go to voicemail.

'Yes?'

'Alex, hi. Did you get my message?' Anna turned back to look across the water.

'Yeah. Sorry. I'm at the yacht club.' He said nothing more, and Anna chewed on her lip.

'So… do you want to meet up? I'm free now. The book's gone off.'

'I'll be here another hour or two. I'll come to you for dinner, shall I?'

Part relieved, part annoyed, Anna wasn't sure which emotion was prevalent. 'Are you ashamed of me?' She tried to backtrack. 'I mean, do you not want me to join you? Or for us to go out somewhere for a change? I hear the new bistro in town is pretty good.'

'Nah, I prefer staying in. Besides, the bistro isn't up to London standards.'

'Have you been there already?'

A pause. 'Yes. I went there last night, as it happens, when you blew me off.'

'I didn't! I had to work.'

'You *chose* to work, Anna.'

Over you, and you don't like it, do you?

Anna's stomach churned, but she would not be cowed by his attitude. 'Yes, I did. It mattered.' *And you don't.* 'By all means come round for supper. About eight?'

'Fine. I'll see you later.' The line went dead, and Anna dropped her phone onto the table.

What was she doing? She'd been swept away by Alex finally noticing her, romancing her. Did she not love him?

Perhaps, but with sudden clarity, she realised she didn't always like him.

–

Monday couldn't come soon enough for Anna, and although her usual callers arrived for their coffee and cake, she remained distracted, puzzled even, over why she couldn't stop thoughts of Oliver popping into her mind at random moments, and when they did, her fickle heart bounced all over the place.

Despite Oliver's instruction to not come in until the afternoon, Anna barely waited five minutes after seeing the last of her visitors out the door before hurrying to tidy herself and setting off for Harbourwatch. Now the book was with the publisher, her entire focus was on the new research and Oliver's upcoming trip, but as she made her way up the stairs to the office, Anna paused. What troubled her about the latter?

'Morning.'

Anna looked up. Mrs Clegg was on the stairs, a warm smile on her face.

'Hello, Mrs Clegg. How's things this morning?'

'Not too bad. He seems in quite a good mood.'

Anna smiled as they passed. Probably relief at getting the book off his desk, though to be fair, he'd said there would be structural edits to come yet.

The week flew by yet again, with Anna growing increasingly agitated as to why she found herself flustered around Oliver and fretting over only having one more box to search. None of the companies she'd contacted had come up with anything helpful, either.

To top it all, she'd had several one-night bookings during the week, mainly walkers, and turning the rooms around, along with her hours for Oliver, had left her sprawled on the sofa most evenings, stroking Heathcliff and incapable of doing more than losing herself in her book.

Anna arrived home on the Friday night longing for a glass of wine. The weekend, now it was here, would be no let-up as the B&B was fully booked. Alex wouldn't be pleased, but somehow Anna couldn't bring herself to care.

As it happened, Alex was fairly accepting of the guests in the house this time, and even took Anna into Polkerran for a coffee on Saturday afternoon. Things were changing, though, and she could feel herself becoming immune to his good looks and charming smile. Knowing him better had made her understand herself more clearly. Perhaps both Lauren and Oliver understood Anna better than she did herself: prone to being easily taken in by blond charmers and gullible to boot.

Realisation was a balm, however. A crush was simply that. It wasn't love. It had put Alex on a pedestal, one that could never survive the cracks permeating it.

When he'd said he had to leave straight after break-fast on Sunday to have lunch with his parents, Anna had almost welcomed the news. It would give her the best part of a day to finish going through the last box.

The fact her mind was soon distracted by having to see Oliver off on his travels the next day escaped her entirely.

–

On Monday morning, Anna studied the detailed itinerary she'd prepared. It was strange. When she'd first started to work for Oliver, she'd relished the days when he was out and, even more so, the times when'd he gone away for a few nights to attend meetings in London or do some research. Then, she'd played her music as she worked, stopping now and again to chat to Thumper and Dougal.

But today, Anna felt disgruntled as she placed the itinerary into a clear folder and then picked up Oliver's tickets. He would be gone for two weeks, and that was the longest trip since she'd worked for him. He'd also made no mention of her continuing to do so once the structural edits were done. Besides, he would leave in September.

'Where's Master Oliver?' Mrs Clegg peered round the door, and Anna placed the folder on her desk and got to her feet. She didn't want to think about Oliver leaving Polkerran or why it made her sad. 'Taxi's here to take 'im to Par.'

'Went off to shower and change about half an hour ago.' Anna glanced at her watch. 'I'll go and check on him.'

She followed the housekeeper out onto the landing.

'When do you leave, Mrs Clegg?'

'My niece should be here around noon.' She smiled at Anna and patted her arm. 'I'm that thankful to you, Anna. Looking after the birds for me.'

Mrs Clegg planned to stay with her niece in Falmouth again during Oliver's absence, taking Dougal and Thumper with her.

'It's no trouble. I'll be over fairly regularly as I've some research to follow up.'

Mrs Clegg hurried back down the stairs, and Anna walked along the corridor to where Oliver's room was. She pressed her ear to the door. Nothing. Had he gone downstairs?

She tapped. 'Oliver? Are you ready?'

There was no answer, and she bit her lip, reaching tentatively for the handle. Should she go in? What if he was still getting dressed?

Pushing the thought away, Anna straightened her shoulders, tapped more firmly and waited. 'Oliver?'

'Yes?'

With a start, Anna swung about. He was behind her, fully dressed, thankfully, and shrugging into his jacket.

'I didn't know you'd come out.'

He raised a brow. 'Is there something I'm supposed to have told you?'

'No! I didn't mean "come out". I meant—' She stopped, eyeing him sternly. 'You knew what I meant.'

'Indeed. Now stop with the chatting. You'll make me late.'

He turned on his heel and Anna, closing her mouth with a snap, hurried behind him back into the office.

'Do you have—'

She handed him the smaller folder. 'Itinerary, accommodation, contact details, evening engagements, etc.'

'And my—'

'Here.' She thrust the ticket wallet at him. 'All labelled and in date order for each trip.'

'And it's—'

'First class. This trip is carriage K, seat 13.'

'Is it the—'

'Quiet coach and yes, it's an individual seat.'

'Handouts?'

She passed a slightly larger folder over. 'All ready for copies to be made as and when. Your slides and meeting notes are in there, too, along with the memory stick.'

He said nothing for a moment, then took the folder from her. 'I'll see you in a fortnight then.'

Oliver turned to put everything into his briefcase.

'It'll be quiet without you.'

He straightened and turned to look at her. 'I'm not known for being noisy.'

Anna rolled her eyes. 'You know what I mean.'

He observed her closely. 'You look sad. Is it the cottage? Did you find anything?'

She shook her head. Funnily enough, that wasn't what made her feel low. 'No, I've been through the last box and there's nothing.'

He didn't speak for a moment, then turned for the door, and she took an involuntary step after him.

'Have a good trip.'

'I'll do my best.'

'Wait!'

Oliver stopped, and Anna snatched up the packet of food she'd prepared. 'I almost forgot. Train food can be pretty inedible sometimes.'

'Even in first class?'

'It's still railway food.' She held the wrapped package out to him. Then, he reached out and took it and was gone.

Turning around, Anna surveyed the room, feeling even more flat. She shook her head. Oliver's desk was in as much disarray as ever. How could someone so neat in appearance make so much mess? She walked over to see if there was anything she could do to tidy it up, but having once done that and been at the receiving end of his displeasure over not being able to find anything, she wasn't likely to do it again.

Suddenly, the door flew open, and she spun around as Oliver walked back into the room.

'Did you forget something?'

'Yes.'

He stopped in front of her, his blue eyes raking her features, and Anna could sense the telltale pink filling her cheeks. 'Can I—' Her insides were lurching around like a malfunctioning washing machine. 'Can I do anything to help?'

A faint smile tugged at Oliver's mouth. 'I think it's too late for that.' To her surprise, he reached out a hand and rested it against her cheek. She wanted to lean into its firmness and warmth. 'Thank you, Anna.'

'Oh,' Anna mouthed. 'For what?'

'Everything,' he said softly, then he withdrew his hand, turned on his heel and left the room again.

Anna was transfixed, her heart pounding, wanting to go after him.

'If this is the start of a crush, you can think again,' she muttered to herself. 'Getting a crush on the boss is a really bad idea. Besides, you're with Alex.'

Her feet didn't appear to be listening, and she flew along the landing to the vast window at the end, which fronted on to the driveway. Within a few minutes, Oliver appeared, stashing his travel bag, holdall and briefcase in the boot and getting into the seat beside the driver without a backward glance. Anna watched as the car eased out of the gateway, and then she drew in a deep, steadying breath.

She needed to get herself sorted out in Oliver's absence.

Chapter Twenty-Four

The distance is nothing when one has a motive

Jane Austen, *Pride and Prejudice*

It was early afternoon on the Friday when Anna ended a call with Alex, dropping her phone onto the bed. It was no surprise he wasn't coming down again this weekend. Too much work, he said. She didn't believe him for a second.

Perhaps he was fed up of the journey to Cornwall after a hard week's work? Maybe she should again try suggesting she go up to town? Then she almost laughed out loud. Even with her propensity for dreaming, she knew where she and Alex were headed.

Getting to her feet, Anna walked over to the window to look at the view – one she never tired of – but instead of gazing at the open seas beyond the mouth of the cove, she was drawn instead to study Harbourwatch, and a smile touched her lips. Oliver was a strange mixture of parts: taciturn, always wanting his own way, but he was also a kind, considerate man. She missed him. Anna turned away from the view, suppressing a desire to call him. He'd hardly appreciate it.

She scanned through his itinerary in her mind. With the first half of his tour over, he was due to spend the weekend with friends in Glasgow. She could hardly intrude on his free time. Besides, Oliver being Oliver, he'd have his mobile switched off.

Anna picked up her phone before heading downstairs. Was she feeling lonely again, now her weekends stretched before her, empty apart from anonymous guests? Or did she miss Oliver when she popped over to the office for a few hours? The memory of his face when he'd returned to the office rushed into her head. He never bothered with thank yous; his touch against her skin had been so gentle.

Involuntarily, Anna's hand rose to her cheek as an inexplicable flutter flickered through her again, a warm sensation, followed quickly by sadness at knowing he would be away for another week.

'Enough.' She admonished out loud. 'Find yourself something to do, for goodness' sake!'

She hurried down the stairs, thankful the doorbell chimed as she reached the hall. Some of her weekend guests had arrived.

Wandering into the study sometime later, Anna surveyed the boxes she had now been through, stacked once more against the far wall. Was it really, as Alex had said all along, a wild goose chase?

She looked around the room, more than a little despondent. She needed caffeine. Once the kettle had boiled, Anna wandered back into the study. Perhaps if she went back through the diaries preceding this last one, the name of this faceless man would be mentioned? A disturbing thought, and she shuddered. No. No diaries today. She spent the next few hours getting lost in organising the boxes she'd already searched through, before suddenly noticing the time.

'Time for some supper,' she called over to Heathcliff as she returned to the kitchen, who raised his head, then stretched on his window cushion before jumping down.

She fed the kitten, eyed the fridge's contents, then shut the door. She felt out of sorts and in no mood for cooking. Pulling on her jacket, she headed out and down into the town, joining the queue at Colin the Cod's. Clutching the warm package to her chest, Anna inhaled the comfort of fattening food as she walked back home, her eyes on Harbourwatch across the cove.

She hated seeing it with no lights on, especially the office and what she knew to be Oliver's room. A sadness she couldn't account for filled her for a moment, and she sniffed as she opened the gate to Westerleigh Cottage.

'Hey, Anna, wait!'

Spinning around, she saw Nicki hurrying out of her gate, waving a white envelope.

'Glad I saw you passing. I was going to come round with this.' She held the envelope out to Anna, who took it instinctively.

'Turned up in a zip pocket in one of those handbags of Meg's. Hasn't been opened, but it's so old now, doubt it's important. Thought you ought to have it all the same.' She stopped, then touched Anna gently on the arm. 'Are you okay?'

Slowly, Anna raised her eyes to Nicki. Her throat tightened, her insides clenched. 'Yes, I'm fine.' She summoned a smile. 'Thanks for this. I'll see what it is.'

Nicki waved a hand as she turned back home, and in a daze, Anna pushed aside her gate, hurried to open the door and closed it firmly, falling back against it. The aroma of chips no longer tempted her. All she could think of was the sealed envelope in her other hand. It bore Aunt Meg's name and address, typewritten. There was a franking mark for a legal firm in London, and the date was some two years ago.

Unsure whether she even wanted to open the envelope, Anna hurried down the hall to the kitchen, dropped the parcel of food on the worktop and, before further doubt could take hold, tore it open. Her mouth moved silently as she perused the words, her heart sinking.

Why had Miss Stratfield not returned, duly signed and witnessed, the will she had asked them to prepare? Would she please contact them as a matter of urgency?

Anna sank back in her seat. What should she do? If only Oliver was here… She had hoped the letter might give her some answers, but all it raised was more questions. She glanced at her watch, then tugged her phone from her pocket and dialled the legal firm's number: the answerphone was pleasantly voiced, but unhelpful. She'd have to wait until Monday morning.

Wriggling out of her coat, Anna read the letter through again. Brief as it was, she did have proof now. Proof a second will was drawn up. And there was someone to contact about it at last, though why a London firm was involved was a complete mystery.

An hour later, changed into her favourite loungewear and nursing a large glass of wine – probably her third, but she'd lost count – Anna sat cross-legged on the sofa in the kitchen, Heathcliff curled up at her side. She felt decidedly squiffy, despite having finally eaten her supper.

Anna grabbed her glass and drained it, then closed her eyes as the liquid slid down her taut throat. It was the proof she'd dreaded finding but had known she had to seek. And if Westerleigh turned out not to be hers, who *could* it belong to?

Then, she opened her eyes and sat up. It had to be here! The newer will had to be in the house. This company had clearly drawn it up. Mrs Lovelace had said she witnessed it nearly two years ago. What had stopped Aunt Meg from sending it back? Perhaps she had become too disorientated or forgetful by then? Anna would never know. But it had to be here somewhere! If only she knew where else to search. If only Alex hadn't let her down again – he could have helped her look... .

Anna yawned widely, then glanced at her watch: close to midnight. She ought to go to bed; her head was a pile of mush. She picked up her phone. Should she message him? Would he even answer?

Chewing on her bottom lip, Anna got unsteadily to her feet. She needed water. Ten minutes later, perched on the edge of her bed in her pyjamas, she drank thirstily from her glass, then patted the bed for Heathcliff to join her. He kneaded the pillow next to Anna's for a moment before curling up in his customary position at the foot of the bed, and she kicked off her slippers and got in.

For a moment, she lay there, convinced the wine and her tiredness would bring sleep quickly, but within a few minutes she sat up again and reached for her phone.

Tapping a quick line, she hit 'send' before she could change her mind, then fell back against the pillows, drifting into a wine-fuelled sleep.

–

Sunday wasn't the best morning for Anna. She'd had a disturbed night, full of inexplicable dreams, and Heathcliff, fed up with her tossing and turning, had given up around four o'clock and moved to the windowsill.

When she finally woke properly, unrefreshed and with a pounding head, she had a vague feeling she'd done something she shouldn't but couldn't for the life of her think what it was.

Had she phoned Alex in her tipsy state and demanded he come and help her? How awful if she had! She burrowed through the tousled sheets to find her phone. Damn. Flat battery.

Once breakfast for her guests ended, and Anna saw them on their way, she took her pounding head into the study and sank into the chair by the desk. The letter from the London solicitors lay there, taunting her, the words etched on her mind.

She looked around the room slowly, unable to move quickly in her delicate state. The will had to be there, somewhere – except she'd been through *everything*! She picked up the letter and put it into the latest diary she'd been reading and placed it in the desk drawer. She couldn't call these solicitors until Monday anyway. Better use of her time would be to strip the two rooms that had been in use.

Forcing down a weak cup of tea, the only thing she could face, she walked over to where her phone lay charging and picked it up. She'd better check whether she'd tried to call Alex. The fact he hadn't responded didn't bother her; she didn't want to see or speak to anyone, and—

The doorbell intruded, but she decided to ignore it. Whoever it was could go away. Only they didn't. This time, they rapped the door several times in quick succession, and with a growl of frustration, Anna padded down the hall, her phone still in her hand.

A glance at herself in the mirror confirmed this wasn't the best time for callers, and she opened the door with reluctance, peering round its edge.

Oliver stood on the doorstep.

Anna's eyes widened, the door falling open as her hand dropped to her side. She'd been so surprised, so relieved to see him, she'd nearly thrown herself at him.

'But – but you're in Glasgow.'

Oliver merely raised a brow.

'I don't understand.' Anna put a hand to her still pounding head. 'What are you doing here?'

'You sent me a text.'

A surge of dismay swept through Anna. *No!* She'd sent a drunken text to *Oliver*? Of all people!

'I'm so sorry,' she whispered. Her throat felt tight, and she swallowed hard on it. 'But you only switch your phone on if you're hoping to—'

He held up his phone to show Anna the screen, and she read her text from the previous night. She clenched her own phone tightly, her skin paling.

> Awful mews. Need kelp, Anna xx

'Felt pretty certain Heathcliff wasn't pining for some seaweed.'

Anna's embarrassment was profound, but it wasn't the typos in the message, it was the two little kisses at the end. What had she been thinking?

'I'm so sorry. You're in the middle of your lecture tour.'

'Thank you for letting me know.' There was something different about Oliver; he seemed less confident than usual. 'Er... is Tremayne here?'

'Alex? Oh, no. He… well, never mind.'

'I didn't like to call in the middle of the night, but I sent you a message.'

Anna held up her own phone. 'It died in the night.' *Might have been less embarrassing if I had.*

'Any chance I can come in? It's been a long drive.'

'Of course. Sorry.' Anna stepped aside so he could walk in, then followed him down to the kitchen. 'How come you drove?'

'I decided to hire a car for the weekend.'

'Oh. I'll make some coffee.'

She busied herself with preparing the drinks, her pounding head worse than ever. What had she done? All the preparation, all the commitments…

'What time did you leave?'

Oliver stretched his long arms above his head, then took off his jacket. 'About nine hours ago.'

Feeling worse than ever, Anna poured the coffee and walked over to hand him a mug. 'I'm so, so sorry.'

'Don't be.'

His fingers brushed hers as he took the mug, and Anna's skin tingled.

'But what about the rest of the tour?'

Oliver walked over to look out of the window, and Anna followed him. 'Oliver?'

'I have to go back tomorrow, but I managed to move a couple of things. Today, as you know, was a rest day.'

'It's too far!'

'All I need is a good night's sleep. And plenty of this.' He raised the mug. 'Now tell me the awful mews.'

–

The tablets Oliver had produced worked quickly, and Anna started to feel more herself, especially after he almost force-fed her some dry toast and more tea. He'd been particularly interested in her account of someone trying to pressure Aunt Meg to sell up, once he'd read the solicitor's letter, and, leaving him to peruse some of the more recent diaries, Anna excused herself to get a shower.

She took care in drying her hair, added a small amount of make-up and tugged on her best jeans. Now she felt less exposed, more able to be positive.

When she returned to the kitchen, however, the diaries lay discarded on the table and Oliver had the fridge door open.

'What are you doing?'

He didn't answer, so she walked over to stand beside him. 'Oliver?'

He picked up a cucumber and a pack of cherry tomatoes. 'You're getting out of here for the rest of the day.'

'But I can't! I've got to keep—'

Oliver closed the fridge door, put his spoils on the worktop and turned to place a gentle finger against her mouth. Anna stared up at him.

'You have no guests today. You told me – the last ones left after breakfast. You've run out of boxes to search. There can't be anything so pressing you can't take some time out.'

He removed his finger, but Anna could still feel its firm pressure, and she ran an unsteady tongue over her lip.

'But I had every intention of—'

'What?' Oliver lifted the lid on the bread bin and pulled out a small loaf. He looked over his shoulder, then walked back to stand in front of Anna. 'You had every intention of spending the day mulling over every possible outcome from the letter, culminating in your assumption you have to leave your home.' He eyed her keenly. 'Yes?'

Anna's mouth opened, but no words came out, so she closed it with a snap.

'And I'm staying here tonight.'

'What?' Anna's eyes widened. 'No, you're not!'

'I thought you said you had no guests?'

'I don't.'

'So now you do.' He studied her startled expression for a moment, then smiled faintly. 'Harbourwatch is cold and empty. Mrs Clegg is away. You need company to stop you spending another evening racking your brains over questions you can't answer. And I'll help you if there's more places to search.'

'There's no need for you to stay. I'm pretty much out of options here.' Anna drew in a frustrated breath. She felt flustered by the idea of Oliver staying in the house, and she had a feeling she'd begun to understand why. There was no way she would let him have his way! 'So, where are we going? And why are you raiding my fridge for food?'

Oliver inspected the remnants of the quiche Anna had made the previous day. He held the plate out to her. 'Have you got anything to wrap that in?'

'Yes, but that's my supper for this evening.'

'No need.' Oliver waved an arbitrary hand. 'I'll treat you to supper.'

'But I don't want—'

Swinging around, Oliver placed his finger against her lips again.

'Don't. You'll only regret it when I make you sit and watch me demolish a huge plateful later.'

He turned away and started opening and closing drawers, then pulled out a roll of plastic film.

'Why do you insist on having your own way all the time? You're impossible.'

'So I've been told before.' He sighed exaggeratedly, and Anna bristled on his behalf.

'By whom?'

'By you. Now, where do you keep a basket?'

Half an hour later, as Oliver sped the car along the A390, Anna reluctantly admitted to enjoying herself. He looked different again today. She'd noticed instantly, of course, that he didn't wear a tie, and he sported the habitual white shirt but a more casual one, open at the neck, with navy chinos. But that couldn't be it, could it? Was that... did he have a five o'clock shadow again? It was rather becoming on him.

Anna cleared her throat and tried to contemplate the green landscape around them. 'I'm glad I got to have so many holidays in Cornwall as a child. Did you come to Cornwall when you were young?'

'I told you, I didn't grow up in England.'

Anna glanced at Oliver, but his attention remained firmly on the road. 'So where...?'

'All over.'

Nothing more was said as he guided the car through slower traffic near St Austell, but soon they were on open roads again. Anna knew she should curb her curiosity, but it was a fault she'd never really mastered, and Oliver was such a closed book, she couldn't resist trying to pry open a few more pages. It didn't help she found him so damned attractive lately either.

'I can hear your brain whirring.' Oliver threw her a quick glance. 'You may as well say what you're thinking.'

Probably best not to. He might crash the car if she told him.

'Okay. If that's an invitation?'

'If I don't want to answer you, I won't.'

Fair enough. Anna eased into the comfort of the leather seat. 'It would be nice to know a bit more about each other. Because we work together,' she added hastily. It wouldn't do for him to think she was crushing on him. *Bloody hell.* Who was she fooling? She *was* crushing on him! Warmth flooded her cheeks again.

'My curiosity is at its height as to what is making you go that colour.'

'You really don't want to know.' Anna put her hands to her face. 'I've never conquered it. Been colouring up like a beetroot since childhood.'

'Then I won't press you for the cause on this occasion.'

'Thank you. So, tell me some of the places you've lived.'

Oliver didn't answer for a moment, and Anna cast him a glance. Then he shrugged.

'A couple of years in Europe. Six in various States in the US. Two in Singapore, but none of them long enough to feel fully at home or learn the languages. I can get by in a few of them, but American always eluded me.'

Anna laughed. 'Have you been back to any of them since you were in charge of your own destiny?'

'I'm not sure I am.'

'Am what?'

'In charge of my own destiny. Fate has an odd way of intervening when I least expect it.'

Anna's curiosity was high again, but she wasn't sure she wanted to ask about fate. It had a funny way of upsetting her own life.

They were driving down a narrow lane now, with glimpses of the sea through the overhanging trees.

'So, have you? Gone back at all?'

'Sometimes.'

Anna blew out a frustrated breath. 'Oliver!'

'What?' He glanced at her, but she could tell he was amused. 'You ask the questions. I answer them. It's not my fault if you don't ask ones that give you the answer you want.'

'You're impossible!'

'And you're repetitive. How many times have you called me that?'

More than you'll ever know.

'I heard that.' Anna blinked, but then Oliver added, 'Here we are.'

Chapter Twenty-Five

All sorts of thoughts cross one's mind – it depends upon whether one gives them harbour and encouragement

Elizabeth Gaskell, *Wives and Daughters*

Anna looked around as they pulled into a small car park. 'Trebutwith Bay. I used to love coming here as a child.'

'A good place to find yourself, I think.'

Not sure what he meant, Anna said nothing, and soon, they were side by side on a tartan rug on the sands, the picnic basket between them. Anna sat cross-legged and looked around. The beach was fairly secluded, and apart from a family down by the water and two couples flat on their backs to their left, it was peaceful.

Oliver stretched his long legs out on the rug. They extended way beyond its length, but he didn't seem to care, kicking off his shoes, and Anna tried not to fixate on his bare feet. For some reason, she'd imagined he wasn't a man to shed his socks lightly, but his feet, though not tanned exactly, were not pale either. They were also very long...

Trying not to pursue this line of thought, Anna placed her sunglasses on her nose and pulled her hat lower over her head to hide her face. These thoughts were idiotic and would not do. Oliver was a grown-up, and all this proved was that she was not!

Unable to help herself, Anna glanced at Oliver again. His thoughts seemed elsewhere as his blue gaze roamed the horizon, and she turned her head towards the shore where the waves rolled gently onto the sand. Why did he seem even more attractive to her today? She'd acknowledged he was a good-looking man before now, but she felt very aware of him, of how close he was to her.

Anna edged a little nearer to the edge of the rug. She felt tense and happy all at once, excited but also agitated. Yet she felt strangely comforted by Oliver's presence. Her despair of the previous evening felt out of proportion. Anna grimaced. The alcohol surely hadn't helped.

She positioned the hat more carefully and leaned back on her elbows, stretching her own legs out on the rug. Then, conscious of the silence hovering between them, she sought for something to say.

'Why do you think Aunt Meg went to a London solicitor?'

Oliver didn't move for a moment, but then he turned his head and his eyes scanned her face. He still didn't speak, and conscious of his intense look, Anna pressed on.

'It's odd, isn't it? I mean, Mr Mottershead said he'd been her solicitor for decades, ever since she came to Cornwall all those years ago. Was she trying to hide a bequest, do you think? But from whom? Oliver?'

A strange expression filtered across his face as he turned back to look out to sea, and Anna couldn't help her gaze from travelling across his broad shoulders. If only she could reach out, smooth her hands over them…

'Dwelling on it won't provide any answers. See what you can find out tomorrow first.' Oliver glanced back at her. 'Set your mind free for a few hours. You'll feel all the better for it.'

'Easy for you to say,' muttered Anna as he turned away again.

'You have no idea.'

Anna studied Oliver's back, but he said no more, and she turned her attention to laying out the impromptu picnic.

They talked idly as they ate, touching on how his tour had been going, but as Anna started to tidy things away into the basket, Oliver got to his feet.

'Come on,' he gestured along the beach. 'Let's walk it off. I'm going to fall asleep if I don't move.'

Scrambling to her feet, Anna ran a hand through her windswept hair, flicked the lid closed on the basket and grabbing her flip-flops, set off after him across the sand. It wasn't a hot day, but warm enough, and the sand was soft between her toes, a childhood comfort, and she smiled as she tried to catch up with Oliver's long stride.

'I will miss this.' Oliver had slowed his pace, Anna walking by his side now as he gestured towards the open sea beyond the rocky cove.

Anna's mood lowered in an instant.

'Can't you stay longer? Find another property to rent – or buy one?'

He didn't answer at first, and they had reached the rocks bordering one end of the cove before he turned to face her. 'No.'

'Why not?' If he wanted to be abrupt, so could she.

He bent down to study a rock pool. 'Because I can't.'

Fine. All the brightness of the afternoon faded, and Anna's mood sank. Polkerran Point without Oliver didn't seem right, somehow. When had that happened? It was this damned crush. Perhaps the sooner he went the better? She'd had her fill of crushes lately.

Oliver's not your normal style, though, is he?

Anna blinked, then silenced the inner voice. She didn't want to think about it.

When they returned to the rug, they lay side by side, hats over their faces, dozing in the weak sunshine. Anna listened to Oliver's even breathing. Would he fall asleep after his early start and long drive? She wouldn't blame him. She could easily fall asleep herself. The gentle lapping of the waves, the plaintive cry of a seagull and the sand trickling through her fingers were lulling her into a world years away from now.

Back then, she'd dreamed of falling in love, assumed she would be swept away by someone who, of course, would be completely potty about her too. And here she was, still searching for… something, someone. Anna's eyes opened. She'd been fooling herself again, hadn't she? Was there really any such thing as love – deep, abiding, all-consuming love? Did Oliver know what it felt like?

'Did you love your wife?' The words tumbled out unbidden, and Anna sat up quickly, her hat falling to one side and a hand to her mouth.

There was silence, and she slowly released a breath, her lids closing in relief. He was asleep.

'Why do you ask?'

Her eyes flew open. 'I— Er— I don't know. Forget I did. It was impertinent.'

Anna felt dreadful and made to get up, but without raising his hat, Oliver restrained her with his hand on her arm.

'Curiosity's not a crime.'

Sitting back, Anna swallowed quickly, conscious of the loss of warmth on her skin as he released her. 'I'm sorry.'

'Don't be.'

'I think I've been questioning what love is lately.'

Oliver grunted from beneath his hat. 'Tell me about it.'

Anna bit her lip.

'Oliver?' He raised his hat and squinted at her. 'Would you... do you mind telling me what happened? Why it didn't work out?'

The hat dropped back into place. Then he said, 'We fell out of love, if we were ever in it.'

'Oh.'

'Why?'

Anna tried to sound nonchalant. 'There's so much speculation.'

'Idle village gossip.'

'I suppose so. But if you don't refute it, it continues.'

'Why does it matter? I don't care what people think.'

Anna released a huff. 'Don't I know it! But I don't like people maligning your reputation.' She thought of Alex and his scornful opinion of Oliver.

Oliver, however, started to laugh under his hat and it wobbled, and Anna smiled. He did it so rarely. 'You sound like you live in a nineteenth-century novel.'

'So I've been told before.'

Oliver sat up suddenly, tossed the hat aside and fixed her with his compelling stare. 'We were very young. Rushed into it after a few months. The marriage lasted less than a year. It was a relationship, if you can call it that, founded on lust. Sometimes it takes a while to see that. We got a divorce. Hateful word. I never intended it, but turned out it was a better decision for both of us than saying "I do" in the first place.'

'That's different to the rumours. They say you've only ever loved one woman. You never date, or so the locals say. They think you're still hung up on your ex-wife.'

'Do they? How very... sentimental.' Oliver sighed. 'Helena was a beautiful woman.' He took one of Anna's hands in his, and she held her breath. 'Still is, for all I know, but it was an external beauty. Just took me a while to realise it.'

Anna willed her heart to stay calm. 'Maybe next time, it will be the opposite.'

He didn't release her hand, but Oliver turned away to view the horizon again. 'I don't intend to go down that road.'

'But why not?'

'Because it only leads to unhappiness.'

Anna tugged at his hand, and he turned to look at her again. 'No. It led to unhappiness once.'

'And that's more than enough.'

She shook her head at him. 'I'm glad I don't approach life like you do.'

Oliver shrugged. 'I've enough in my life to compensate.'

'I shouldn't have asked.'

Oliver's expression was surprisingly open. 'Like I said, curiosity is not a crime.' He smiled faintly, a thumb moving against the back of her hand, and Anna drew in a short breath as he lowered his voice. 'And I don't date because I've yet to find someone I'd rather spend time with over my work.'

A strange look crossed his face, and the blue of his eyes, still fixed on hers, deepened as Anna became conscious of the warmth of his firm grip on her hand. Filled with a jumble of feelings, she felt inexplicably drawn to him. Was he leaning towards her?

The squeal of a gull above their heads broke the spell, and they both pulled back abruptly, and Oliver released her hand before picking up his hat.

'Come on.' He got to his feet, then bent to pick up the picnic basket. 'Time we headed back.'

—

Sitting beside him in the car as he drove back up the lane from the cove, Anna tried to peep discreetly at Oliver's profile, but as soon as she did, he looked at her. Fidgeting in her seat under his piercing glance, she looked hurriedly out of the window instead.

Seconds later, she slowly turned her head back again, forcing herself to face forward, but she found it impossible not to glance over at his hands on the steering wheel: strong, capable hands. What would they feel like touching... *No!*

Anna's hand flew to her cheek, and she turned to stare out of the window again. This had to stop!

'Are you okay?'

'Yes. Yes, fine, thanks.' Her voice came out in a squeak.

Nothing more was said as they reached the junction with the main road, then turned along it back towards St Austell.

Anna couldn't look at Oliver. Her skin tingled, and her insides tumbled all over the place. Then he broke the silence.

'Am I right in assuming marriage is important to you?'

Thankful for the distraction for her wayward thoughts, Anna grasped at it. 'Oh yes! I grew up wanting it all: to fall in love, to get married, turn a house into a home, and raise a family there.'

Oliver grunted. 'You'll be saying you want a pack of dogs and a donkey next.'

'And chickens.'

'Chickens?'

Anna nodded firmly. 'Yes. The dream won't be complete without the chickens. And a cat.'

Oliver flicked a glance at her. 'You seem to be doing things in reverse.'

Anna smiled. 'I love Heathcliff, but he wasn't planned.'

They continued in silence for a while but then Oliver spoke again. 'I was right. You are a traditionalist.'

'Is that wrong?' Anna risked a glance at his profile, but this time he kept his eyes on the road.

'No.'

'Perhaps you should adopt a pet.'

There was a pause. 'I have Dougal.'

Anna let out a huff of breath. 'But he isn't yours, really. I mean, he's been taken in by you.'

'Adoption doesn't always make things your own either.'

Oliver's voice was bitter, and Anna frowned. How had this nonsensical conversation led him down a road he was unhappy about?

'Er, Oliver…'

'No.'

'No?'

'I wasn't adopted.' He threw her a brief look. 'My mother gave birth to me. She raised me in the proper sense: a roof over my head, clothes on my back, food on the table. I had a good education, private lessons in riding, music and languages I never mastered.'

'But not love.' Anna felt saddened, recalling their previous conversation about how they were both raised.

They'd reached a junction, but Oliver didn't continue on towards Polkerran Point, taking the road to the left. 'No one should bring a child into the world if they can't love it.'

They stopped at a roadside pub, and Anna reluctantly told Oliver he'd been right, she was too hungry to simply watch him devour a plate of food. They tucked into their fish platters, the conversation touching on many things but not marriage, families, nor the missing will and its implications. Despite her underlying anxiety that she might give away some hint as to how she felt, Anna found she could quite put it aside to enjoy the meal.

As they returned to the car, however, Anna stopped to look up at Oliver in the falling dusk.

'Why did you stop here?'

Oliver unlocked the car. 'I thought you'd be more comfortable not in Polkerran.'

'Why?'

Oliver merely raised a brow, but she fixed him with a meaningful look, and he held his hands up.

'Okay. I assumed you'd rather not become victim to the locals and their gossip.'

'Why would they talk about me?'

Oliver said nothing as he opened the car door for her.

'Oh.' She shook her head and slid into her seat. 'But we work together. Everyone knows that.'

He closed the door on her and walked round to get into his own seat. 'And how often have we had a meal out?'

Anna chewed her lip. 'What do you think they might have said?'

Oliver assumed a thoughtful expression as he started the engine. 'Man rarely seen in public eats food while his companion looks shiftily around. What's she trying to hide?'

Laughter rose to Anna's lips. 'Very funny. Why would I have anything to hide?'

Oliver set the car in motion. 'You're seeing Tremayne. He might not approve.'

It was almost dark by the time Oliver pulled the car into the driveway at Westerleigh. Anna glanced at him as she opened her door and the interior light came on. He looked exhausted, as well he might.

Perhaps a strong coffee would keep him awake until he got to Harbourwatch. Feelings of guilt for his having come so far threatened to return. Pushing open the door to the house, she looked back over her shoulder. Oliver was barely two steps behind her and carrying a holdall.

'What are you doing?'

'I'd have thought it was obvious.'

'It's not.'

'Checking in.'

'But I said there was no need.' Anna moved aside as he crossed the threshold.

'And I said I would.' Oliver dropped his bag on the settle and turned to face her.

'But what if anyone finds out you stayed the night?'

Oliver raised a brow. 'Are you worried about your reputation?'

'No. Yes. I mean, yours.'

Amusement flashed in his eyes. 'And we're back in the nineteenth century. I'm a paying guest. No one questions you having other male guests, do they?'

'I suppose not.'

'So?'

'So?'

'What's the room rate?'

'You can't pay to stay here!'

'I thought we'd established I'm overbearing and insist on having my own way?'

'Fine! I'll show you where to go.' It was a good thing she'd prepared Aunt Meg's room at last.

Chapter Twenty-Six

Wearily she went to bed, wearily she rose in four or five hours' time. But with the morning came hope and a brighter view of things

Elizabeth Gaskell, *Wives and Daughters*

Anna closed the door of Aunt Meg's room with a snap and hurried back down the stairs and into the kitchen. Perhaps Oliver was so tired, he'd fall straight asleep.

'Nice room. I think I'll sleep well.'

Or perhaps not.

Anna spun around as he came into the kitchen.

'But what about the morning? What if my usual callers turn up, hoping for coffee and cake?' Anna chewed her lip. 'You'll have to get up early and go.'

Oliver gave a short laugh and walked back down the hall to drop his keys on the console table. 'That's no way to treat your guests.'

'You're not a guest!' Anna hurried after him, and he swung around so unexpectedly, she almost ran into his chest.

Raising her chin with a finger, Oliver held her gaze for a moment. 'I think you'll find I am.'

Anna was keenly aware of their closeness. 'Right.' Fine. She cleared her throat and turned back towards the kitchen. 'Would you like some wine?'

'Not if I'm drinking on my own.'

'I think I'll manage a glass. Don't worry, I'm in no danger of repeating last night.'

'Pity. I've never received a drunken text before. It was quite enlightening.'

Anna turned away. What the hell did that mean? Did he know she had weird thoughts about him?

Five minutes later, Anna placed two glasses of red on the coffee table.

Oliver picked up his wine and walked over to the window, though it was too dark to see much from it. 'What will you do if you don't find the will?'

'I don't know.'

'You could stay here.'

Anna looked aghast. 'Oh no! I couldn't do that. Not if this isn't my home. I feel like a usurper already.'

Oliver turned around. 'You're not going to leave?'

'I don't want to, but how can I stay here when I may not legally own it?'

Oliver walked over and picked up one of Aunt Meg's diaries from the coffee table before sitting beside Anna on the sofa. 'You realise these solicitors may not be able to tell you anything if you're not a beneficiary under this newer will? How do you plan to find out what it contains if that's the case?'

'I *have* to find it.' Anna spoke with more confidence than she felt. Conscious of Oliver's closeness, she studied him from under her lashes as he flicked through the diary. There was something very appealing about him as he pulled out his glasses and put them on.

'But if you can't?' He didn't raise his head from the page, and Anna let out a huff of breath.

'I don't *know!*' She tried to think clearly. 'You know I said Aunt Meg had told her friends someone was pressurising her to sell, but she wouldn't say who? I did wonder...'

Oliver lowered the diary. 'Go on.'

Anna held his gaze. 'I— Well, I wondered, with her illness starting, whether she gave in, left it to this... person in the later will. It's the timing. About two years since the will Mrs Lovelace witnessed, and not much later Aunt Meg was properly diagnosed with her illness.' Her voice trailed away under Oliver's fixed look. There was something she couldn't interpret on his face.

'She mentions it in the later diaries, and—'

The diary toppled from Oliver's hand, and they both went for it at the same time, banging heads.

'Ow!' Anna rubbed her forehead as Oliver sat back up, the book in his hand. 'Sorry.'

'So am I. Hope that doesn't lead to another headache. These diaries—' He looked at the spine of the one he held. 'This one is from the nineties. When are they dated from?'

'They go way back, as far as the sixties. But I've been through the most recent ones, page by page, and there are no clues as to a name. Of course, when I call these London solicitors tomorrow, they may be able to solve the whole thing.' Anna drew in a sharp breath. 'I'm scared, Oliver.'

He put down his glass and, to her surprise, took her hand and squeezed it briefly before releasing it. 'You will be fine. Text me when you've spoken to them but remember they probably won't discuss anything over the phone.'

'Will you have gone by nine, then?' Anna was unaware how wistful she sounded as a faint smile touched Oliver's lips. She had hoped he'd still be here, even though she knew he had to get back to Scotland to resume his tour.

'I thought you wanted me long gone before the locals turned up?'

Anna bit her lip. 'Sorry. That was rude of me.'

Oliver shook his head. 'It's irrelevant. I have to be on the road early. I've moved my morning meeting, but I have to be there for a two o'clock lecture.'

Anna felt terrible for all the disruption. 'I'll do you an early breakfast.'

'No, you won't.'

'But—'

'I leave at four a.m., Anna, and that's too early to eat, never mind cooking.'

'But—'

Oliver leaned over and placed a finger against her lips. 'I thought we'd moved on from the "buts".'

Anna blinked as he dropped his hand, and she reached for her wine, her lips still tingling from the pressure of his finger.

The sooner Oliver returned to Scotland the better.

–

Not long after four the following morning, Anna eyed herself owlishly in the hall mirror. Oliver must have thought she was mad, not only getting up at silly o'clock but then watching him reverse out of the gates like a mother hen overseeing her chicks.

She turned away from her troubled expression and walked back into the kitchen, where she surveyed the fallout from her even earlier morning baking session. Oliver may not have wanted breakfast, but she couldn't bear to think of him being hungry on his long journey north.

Was that true? Releasing a frustrated breath, Anna set to cleaning up, but as soon as she was done, she made herself a fresh coffee and walked out onto the terrace. It was still dark, with a cool breeze that had arisen overnight, and she shivered. Unable to help herself, she glanced at her watch. Oliver had only been gone half an hour. He wouldn't have even reached the Tamar, so why did it feel like he was a million miles away?

Anna stared over at Harbourwatch, silent and grave, perched on its high cliffs opposite. She'd known she would miss Oliver when he went off on his trip, but she hadn't anticipated the depth of her disappointment over his prolonged absence. Seeing him, albeit briefly, hadn't helped either. Now she felt the gap left by his departure even more. How was she going to feel when he left for good at the end of the summer?

Anna drained her mug. She couldn't think about that now. Time to shower and dress, because as soon as nine o'clock came, she had a phone call to make.

—

Barely had Anna ended her call with the London solicitors when her phone started up: Oliver!

'Hi. Where are you?'

'Services on the M5. How did it—'

'Oh, Oliver, you were right. They wouldn't tell me anything!'

Silence, then: 'We knew it was a possibility.'

'Yes, but I hoped… I don't know. That there would be *something* they could say.'

'So?'

'I'm going to call Mr Mottershead again. He might be willing to act as intermediary.' Anna let out a huff of breath. 'I wish I understood why Aunt Meg had done this!' There was no response at the other end of the phone. 'Oliver? Are you there?'

'Yes. Look, call him. See if he can help. If not, he might have a suggestion over what to do next now you're a step further on.' He paused. 'I think you should let it go.'

Anna blinked. 'How can I?'

He grunted. 'Because if you never find the signed will, there's nothing you, or anyone, can do about it. Just think about it.'

Anna nodded, even though Oliver couldn't see her. 'Yes, of course. Sorry. I'm feeling panicky again.' *Now you're not here.*

'Well, stop it. I have to get going.'

'I know. Sorry.' Guilt over his having come such a distance because of her stupid text flooded her mind, and Anna closed her eyes in mortification.

'Anna, why do you keep apologising?'

Feeling flustered, Anna raised her weary lids. 'I feel bad for causing you all this… this disruption.'

A sound came down the phone. 'I'm getting used to it.'

Anna was still frowning when the call ended. What on earth did he mean? She hadn't been disruptive at the office, as far as she knew.

A plaintive cry from Heathcliff drew her attention, and she scooped him up in her arms and settled on the sofa with him before connecting a call to the office of Potter, Ball & Mottershead.

Mr Mottershead called back late in the day. He'd spoken to the London solicitors and regretted the only thing he could tell her was that Anna wasn't a beneficiary under the more recent will. However, as the solicitors did not have a signed and witnessed copy, there was nothing they could do either. He had tried to reassure Anna – these things happened. People asked for legal documents to be prepared sometimes and that was as far as it went.

Partly reassured someone wasn't going to suddenly appear on the doorstep and throw her out on the street – poor Heathcliff – Anna remained unnerved by knowing Aunt Meg had changed her mind about leaving the house to her.

She felt like an interloper, the sock that had slipped into the knicker drawer uninvited.

It had been a busy week of guests, however, and more had arrived by Friday evening. Alex had put off coming down to Cornwall again, and Anna had done what she'd known she must and told him to forget it altogether. She was unsurprised when he'd agreed with alacrity, saying it had been a blast and no hard feelings. She'd disconnected the call and shoved the phone deep into her pocket. There were more important things on her mind than her suscept-ibility for fair-haired, charming men.

Anna curled up on the sofa with Heathcliff and her latest reread, but then a message came through and she snatched up her phone. Pushing aside the disappointment of it not being from Oliver, Anna tapped a quick response to Lauren and soon she was back on the sofa with a glass of wine and her laptop, her friend beaming at her from the screen.

'Hey, how's it going?'

'Good. You? Still on your longest date ever?' Anna grinned. 'What's it now? Seven months?'

Lauren smirked. 'About that.' Then, she sobered. 'Neither of us is ready to settle down in a grown-up sense, but we seem to be pretty serious. No idea where it's going, and he's in Brazil on business at the mo!'

'So you can indulge yourself with *Love Island*?'

'Absolutely! Back-to-back episodes I missed. Heaven!'

Anna laughed too. 'Sounds more fun than my evenings lately.' She quickly filled Lauren in. 'Most of the stuff I went through is fodder for the nearest shredder. It's like Aunt Meg hoarded every letter, statement, bill she ever received. They go back decades.' Anna took a sip from her glass. 'Now we know for certain I'm not a beneficiary of the new will, but as no one has a signed copy, Oliver thinks I should let it go.'

Lauren raised a brow, smirking. 'Does he now? I thought you said he wanted to help you?'

'Well, he's away, isn't he? But he says there's probably nothing more I can do.'

'Oh he does, does he? And when was this?'

Anna rolled her eyes at Lauren. 'When he calls me. Why wouldn't he?'

'Why indeed.' Lauren peered beadily at her. 'You're not becoming a smitten kitten, are you?'

Well aware of her crush, Anna hesitated, and Lauren whooped.

'Stop it, Lauren! It's just… I find him…'

'Irresistible?' Lauren chuckled.

'No!' *Yes*. Anna drew in a short breath. She secretly enjoyed being able to talk about Oliver. 'There's something so reassuring about him, solid and trustworthy. I know he's there for me if I need him.' Anna tried to ignore the sensations rising in her breast at the thought of him. 'Alex, on the other hand, was as available as a Portakabin loo at an Ed Sheeran gig and about as helpful when one had a pressing need.'

Lauren grinned. 'And talking of Alex—' she lowered her voice and leaned towards the screen '—I see no sign. Another Friday he's blown you off?'

'We agreed to call it quits.' Anna took another sip of her wine. 'It wasn't going anywhere. Never understood why he showed any interest in me, but whatever it was, it seems to have worn off. You were right, as you so often are. Alex was just another Giles.'

'It's human nature to lean towards a type that attracts you, love, not a sin!' Lauren took a sip from her own glass. 'It's good to hear you don't sound too bothered.'

Anna shook her head. 'It's funny, really. That crush sustained me for years and years. He's still gorgeous to look at, of course, but I've come to realise I don't like him very much.'

'No broken heart?'

Anna thought for a moment. 'Nope. Nothing. I think I can honestly say I've got deeper feelings for—'

'Oliver?' Lauren crowed at Anna's expression.

'*No!*' Anna leaned over and picked up her book from the coffee table. 'I was going to say John Thornton.' She waved her copy of Elizabeth Gaskell's *North and South* at the screen, trying to ignore the swoop of her insides as her thoughts plunged rapidly in Oliver's direction again. 'We were curled up on the sofa together when you called.'

'Strange bedfellows!' Lauren leaned back in her seat. 'I wonder if you protest too much about Oliver.'

Unable to find a response to this, Anna was thankful when her phone pinged, and she lunged for it.

'Text from Oliver.'

Lauren smirked again. 'He's so into you.'

Anna clutched her midriff as her insides swirled. 'Don't be daft. He's my boss. He's a lot older, and—' She stopped when Lauren snorted. 'What?'

'He's only in his forties, love.'

Anna ignored her. 'I think he sees me as someone who needs his support. He's a thoughtful man, that's all.' She glanced at the text, aware of disappointment. 'Oliver's been invited to a dinner at the last minute.' She raised her eyes to her friend's. 'He can't call tonight.'

'You are so in denial.'

Anna changed the subject, ignoring Lauren's smirk, and they chatted for a few more minutes, and when the call ended, she walked over to put her glass in the dishwasher. The house was full of guests, with all the rooms but Aunt Meg's in use, and she needed to be on the ball in the morning.

A glance at the clock was sufficient to send Anna upstairs. Oliver would be setting off on his train journey south by midday on Sunday. For once, the weekend didn't stretch unendingly ahead; it felt like it had purpose, and she was excited. Anna stopped suddenly on the stairs to her attic bedroom.

Was she more preoccupied with thoughts of returning to work on Monday and finding Oliver back at his desk than continuing the fruitless search for the missing will?

–

Saturday flew by, and Anna was in the kitchen on Sunday morning, preparing her guests' breakfasts, scurrying to and fro to lay out the tables in the dining room, when her phone rang.

She snatched it up. Unknown caller. Disappointed, she connected the call, and five minutes later, she took the stairs two at a time. She'd stripped the bed in Aunt Meg's room after Oliver had stayed, but beyond that she'd done nothing else with the room, and now she had more guests arriving that afternoon.

By the time her first guests headed down the stairs for breakfast, she'd made up the bed again with fresh linen, polished the furniture, cleaned the sink and swept the floor.

As she smiled and served breakfast to her guests, chatting about the best walks locally, Anna's mind ran through the last-minute things she needed to do to the new room to ensure it was fully ready: take up a hospitality tray, check all the light bulbs, put out the towels. Popping a fresh batch of biscuits into the oven, she waved her guests off on their day of walking and shot back upstairs.

Stepping back to admire her work sometime later, Anna brushed her hair out of her eyes, eyeing a recently broken nail ruefully as she checked the bedside lamps. Then, she headed for the door, flicking the switch on the main light as she passed. Dead bulb.

'Damn.' She grabbed a new one from the drawer under the linen press on the landing and kicked off her slippers before clambering onto the high bed and, steadying herself for balance, replaced the bulb. She was about to climb down, but then she did a double take. Only a random pattern of shells on the windowsill when you looked at them, but from up here? They formed an arrow.

'Follow the shells,' Aunt Meg had pleaded, even though she couldn't remember why she'd said it. And now Anna could see where the line of shells pointed: to the pink velvet bunny.

Chapter Twenty-Seven

Angry people are not always wise

Jane Austen, *Pride and Prejudice*

Anna snatched up the bunny, turning it over in her hand. Was this 'arrow' what Aunt Meg had meant her to follow? How could this help? Then she noticed the seam at the back of the old toy had been unpicked and badly sewn up again. Hurrying downstairs, Anna grabbed a small pair of scissors and snipped the threads.

Thankful it was the weekend and her usual callers were unlikely to materialise, Anna sank into a chair at the table by the window and slowly pulled apart the sides of the rabbit with a whispered 'sorry'. Some of the stuffing had been removed, and in its place was a piece of chintz-patterned cotton, wrapped around a hard object.

Anna weighed it on her palm for a second, then carefully unwound the fabric to reveal a small, old-fashioned but delicately ornate key.

Getting slowly to her feet, she walked closer to the window to examine it. Anna couldn't recall ever having seen it before. If only Oliver were here… she glanced at the clock. He would be travelling for hours yet, but—

The doorbell rang, and Anna flew down the hall, knowing it was foolish to hope, but as the door swung open to reveal Oliver, she threw herself at him, her only coherent thought as his arms closed around her was that everything would be okay. She could cope with whatever this key meant, whatever the new will revealed when she found it, so long as Oliver was with her.

Appalled as the insight struck her, Anna became aware of being wrapped in a strong embrace. She closed her eyes as emotion filled her. This wasn't a stupid, juvenile crush. She had fallen in love with Oliver. Relishing the feel of his firm chest beneath her head, the steady, calm thumping of his heart, she was filled with the implications of her realisation. It felt so right to be in his arms, feel the strength of his embrace, lean her head against those broad shoulders and inhale the familiar aftershave. How could she face him, look him in the eye, when she had only just discovered how much he meant to her?

She drew in a short breath. Oliver was her boss! What was she *thinking*?!

'I'm so sorry,' Anna mumbled, heat filling her cheeks. He eased his hold on her, which had probably been instinct when she'd launched herself at him. Mortified, she dropped her arms and righted herself, trying to ignore the frisson shooting through her as their fingers brushed against each other.

'So sorry.'

Oliver's expression was hard to read, but then he smiled, and her heart skipped a beat. 'I appreciate the welcome.'

'Come in.' She stepped back, and he walked past her down the hall. Anna willed her heart to behave itself and followed him. 'You're early. I mean, I didn't think you'd be back in Cornwall until this evening?'

Oliver turned to face her, a strange awareness about him. 'Took a train as far as Chester yesterday. Stayed with friends overnight. Felt like stretching my legs once the taxi dropped me off at Harbourwatch.' In better light, she could detect his weariness. Lines etched his face and there was an odd look in his eyes...

'Let me get you some coffee.' Anna busied herself, desperate to think about mundane things and not this massive *thing* and how to deal with it. She glanced over her shoulder. 'Have you eaten at all?'

There was no response, so she turned fully around. Oliver stood by the table, staring at the disembowelled bunny, and she walked over to join him.

'I found it just now. Aunt Meg told me to follow the shells, only I didn't know what she meant, but there it was all the time. I don't know where the key fits.'

'I think I do.' Oliver turned to face her. There was a consciousness about his expression again, and although her heart pounded over his simply being there, Anna's trepidation increased. 'Is Meg's old tea caddy still in the study?'

'The polished wooden box? Yes, but it doesn't open anymore. Oh!'

He pointed at the key. 'If I'm not mistaken, this will do the job.'

'Shall we...'

'I'll go.' Oliver left the room, and Anna turned the ailing toy over to look at its forlorn face.

'What were you hiding, Aunt Meg? Why go to such lengths? Is this because you made another will?' It didn't make any sense. If the second will had come to light earlier, Anna would never have come here, never have known of her bequest... and she'd never have met Oliver.

Not wanting to think about it, Anna hurried over to the now boiled kettle and made herself a mug of tea, pouring coffee for Oliver just as he pushed open the kitchen door. The tea caddy in his hands, he walked over and placed it on the table.

'What makes you think this is it?'

'I have one with a similar key. Quite unusual for them to be so decorative.'

'Oh, right. I'm scared to open it.' Anna eyed the box warily, then raised an anxious face to Oliver. His usual inscrutable expression had returned.

'Only way to know its contents.'

Anna rolled her eyes at him, and the edges of his lips twitched.

'Do you want me to do it?'

Anna handed him the key, praying silently the box wouldn't just be full of more shells.

The lock proved somewhat troublesome, but Oliver soon had it open and lifted the lid. Anna immediately saw the long white document resting on top of the contents, and she tried to clear her taut throat.

'It's there. The will.'

'So it would seem.' Oliver offered it to Anna, and she took it, aware her hand shook.

Everything was about to change. Westerleigh Cottage, the home she'd longed for, the home she'd made for herself, was going to be torn from her grasp. Her life in Polkerran Point – her beloved Cornish cove – would end. There was nothing for her here, with Alex a long-expunged dream, and Oliver – her boss, the man she'd not been aware she was falling for – leaving as soon as the summer was over.

'I can't do it.' Anna's breath hitched in her throat. She wanted nothing more than to bury her head in Oliver's shoulder, have him hold her, kiss away her worries. She held the will out to him. 'Please, can you?'

She chewed on her bottom lip, her insides churning, as Oliver unfolded the will and cast his eyes over the opening paragraphs. Then, he paled.

'What is it?'

Oliver's hand fell to his side, and Anna took the will from his lifeless grasp.

'There's something I need to explain...' He strode over to the window, and Anna looked at the document in her hand. Her heart leapt into her throat.

'It's *you*! You're the one who's going to take everything away. *You* are the beneficiary of the cottage!'

He swung around. 'It's not my choice, Anna!'

Anna's mind careered from one thought to another, but uppermost was the pain in her chest at what felt like the utmost betrayal from the man she loved with all her heart.

Oliver took a step towards her. 'You have to let me explain.'

'No, I don't have to do anything. Besides, what is there to say? You struck up a so-called friendship with Aunt Meg, didn't you?'

'Yes, I did, though there's—'

'Well, it's a bit odd, isn't it? Why would you do that with an elderly lady who lived alone? Was it you, hounding her?' Anna gasped, a hand flying to her mouth. 'You were the one going to the hospice. You didn't even leave her in peace in there!'

'Yes, I went there, but—'

'How *could* you?' Oliver's face darkened, but Anna was too wounded to think straight. 'And you're turning into some… some asset-obsessed plutocrat. Aren't you buying up property in Polkerran?' Anna's mouth tasted as bitter as the words sounded.

'Yes, but—'

'No wonder you didn't need to stay at Harbourwatch, or buy a house here. You were after this one all along. Well, you've got what you wanted.'

To her surprise, Oliver flinched. 'Actually, no, I haven't, but—'

'Veto! That's three buts in a row.' Anna glared at him, the pain in her chest intensifying as his eyes held hers, the inscrutable mask descending over his features. How could she still be so attracted to him when he'd deceived her like this? She'd thought Giles, and then Alex, were the biggest arses she was likely to get involved with. It never occurred to her Oliver would be the worst of the lot.

'Look, I do need to tell you—'

'*You* – you looked through her handbag! On one of your visits to the hospice. That's how you knew the hallmark on that bottle.' Oliver bowed his head, but Anna's heart clenched in her chest as further understanding flooded through her mind in a relentless torrent. 'You needed to find the original will because you had no copy of your own. When you came over that day, when the boys were here…' Her skin grew cold, and her breath hitched in her throat. 'It was an excuse, wasn't it? You were looking for something, not helping me.'

A look of culpability filled Oliver's face, and Anna's distress hit its peak. 'Go. Leave me alone.'

'Anna, listen, I can explain why—'

'Please, just *go*.' She spoke firmly now.

Oliver glared at her a second longer, but Anna felt too wounded to take back her accusatory words and held her own tongue.

'Fine.' He grabbed the will, turned on his heel and strode out of the room, and unable to help herself, Anna ran down the hall, but he'd already slammed the door behind him.

She tugged the door open. It had begun to rain heavily, but Oliver didn't seem to notice as he reached the gate.

Anna drew in a shuddering breath. 'Wait!'

He stopped but didn't turn around, and she held her breath, choking on a sob when he opened the gate without a backward glance and stormed off down the lane.

Closing the door, Anna slumped against it. What had she done? How could she have accused him of such things? *Because I think it's true; I feel betrayed by him.*

'I do,' she said firmly, pushing herself away from the door. What was she to do now? How long would he let her stay?

Anna released a huff of breath. After the way in which she'd spoken to him, Oliver would probably evict her straight away. She looked around the homely kitchen, at her baking tins gleaming on the draining board, the neatly arranged plates on the dresser, Heathcliff curled up on his window seat and that view... the view that cheered her heart every day. How little had she understood that the sight of Harbourwatch had become as much of an attraction as the sea and the sky?

Swallowing back a sob so severe it made her throat ache, Anna strode over to the fridge, grabbed an open bottle of wine and a glass and walked over to sit beside Heathcliff, who raised his head to peer at her, let out a faint mew and then curled up in a ball again.

'Don't judge me! It's alright for you.' She sniffed as she poured wine into her glass. 'So long as I keep you fed and warm, you'll be perfectly content. You don't care about the view, Polkerran or...' Her voice broke, and she quickly took a slug of wine. 'Or *him*!'

The afternoon had progressed by the time Anna's eyes stopped welling up. She checked her new guests in with a bright smile and her usual efficiency, then she retreated to the window seat again. Heathcliff, sensing distress, climbed into her lap, and she leaned against the window, her back turned on the rain-soaked view, watching the room grow darker but unwilling to move to put on the lights.

'Oh, Heathcliff. What am I to do?' Anna felt weary, spent. The thought of having to pack up and leave was unbearable. At least she didn't have any furniture to move, though. The contents of the house would belong to Oliver now. Even the new things she'd bought were technically his, for she'd used a chunk of the inheritance to pay for them.

She knew, however, this wasn't the real source of her distress. It was Oliver. Her having placed her trust in him, believing in him, falling in love with him and who he seemed to be. She felt torn in shreds, destroyed by this revelation her trust had been misplaced. Did the village know he was this scheming and ruthless?

And poor Aunt Meg! To be deceived by someone whom she thought came round to look after her garden, to help maintain her beloved cottage. But then, she'd left him the house...

Round and round went her thoughts, but always they came back to Oliver, and as her disbelief faded, Anna's mind began to clear. She shot up, dislodging a disgruntled Heathcliff in the process.

Her accusations notwithstanding, she had ample proof of his kindness, didn't she? She'd seen how he behaved towards Mrs Clegg; he'd given her and her pets a home, rent-free, and he'd also given paid work to several others...

Oliver had been kind to Anna, too, when she was so distraught over Mrs Lovelace's revelation. Was he that good an actor he could put on a front to try and find the will? And had he even been that bothered about it coming to light? Although he'd tried to support her, help her as best he could, when she thought back to what he'd said it didn't tally. At no point had he seemed like someone desperate to find it. In fact, he'd encouraged her to let it go. And Oliver's shock on reading its contents had appeared to be incredibly genuine...

Anna's stomach swirled as she walked back to replace the wine in the fridge. What if she was wrong? He hadn't denied her accusations, but what if Oliver wasn't as guilty as she thought? Her skin grew cold, and she shivered.

What had she done? Oliver meant more to her than a property! Only he didn't know that. She'd never told him.

Anna's eyes ached with sadness, her throat so tight she could barely breathe, but she had no tears left, and with sudden clarity, she understood what she had to do. She must let him explain. She'd been stupid, a fool. Snatching up her phone, she selected Oliver's number.

Damn. Switched off, as usual.

She sent him a text anyway, asking him to call, in hopes he'd switch the phone back on soon. Would he even reply after all she'd said?

Anna flicked the switch on the lamps methodically, becoming aware of Heathcliff's mewing.

'I'm so sorry,' she said softly as she hurried over to the door to the boot room and filled his bowl with food. She opened the back door, but it still rained heavily, the wind blowing in off the sea.

Walking over to the window, Anna peered over at Harbourwatch.

Then, she flew down the hall, grabbed her Barbour, stuffed her feet into her wellies and shot out the door.

Chapter Twenty-Eight

*Consider the dreadful nature of these suspicions
you have entertained. What have you been judging
from?*

Jane Austen, *Northanger Abbey*

By the time Anna reached Harbourwatch, her jeans stuck
to her legs and her hair was wet through, despite her hood.
She shivered as she let herself in, uncertain whether she
ought to or not, and had barely stepped into the hallway
when the door to the kitchen opened.

Anna held her breath, then let it out in a rush as Mrs
Clegg peered round it.

'Good lord, young'un! What be you about, out in all
this?' Mrs Clegg opened the door wider. 'You're all but
soaked! What is it with you and Master Oliver, running
about in this weather!'

'I need to see him, Mrs Clegg. Is he in the office or…?'
Her voice trailed away as a bleak look crossed the lady's
face. 'What is it?'

'Gone, he 'as. Face like thunder. Threw some stuff in
a bag, changed out of 'is wet clothes but didn't even stop
to dry 'is hair or take a coffee.'

Her heart sinking, Anna leaned back against the wall.
'Gone?' she whispered. 'Where?'

'Wouldn't say. Just took off in his car, 'e did.'

'I— I see.' Anna swallowed on the lump returning to her throat. His phone was off. He'd gone away, who knew where. The message couldn't be clearer. He didn't want anything to do with her.

'Are you okay, dearie?' Mrs Clegg peered at her in a motherly fashion. 'Come into the kitchen for a warm, and I'll make a nice cuppa.'

'No, no, it's okay, Mrs Clegg, thank you. I... er, I'd best get back.' Anna turned for the door, her heart leaden, then stopped. 'I don't suppose he said when he'd be back?'

'Barely got a word from 'im afore he drove off, but 'e was in a mighty hurry to get somewhere that wasn't 'ere.' Mrs Clegg shook her head as Anna turned away. 'Miss the lad, I will, when he's gone for good.'

Anna bade the old lady good night and slipped back out into the storm. Unheeding of the rain lashing her face, her hood blown back by the wind and her hair plastered to her head, she trudged back up the lane.

So that was that. What on earth was she to do now? Leaving Polkerran Point – the cottage, her newly founded business, her life – seemed the only answer. She had no right to stay at Westerleigh, but the thought of leaving so precipitously intensified the physical sense of loss she bore.

Besides, where would she go? Harrogate wasn't an option, even though she knew Lauren would offer affection – and generous glasses of wine. There wasn't room for her now in the lovely house. She would have to start afresh. Perhaps Nicki would look after Heathcliff for her, while she looked for a home elsewhere?

Her mind racing, Anna refused to think about never seeing Oliver again. All she knew was, she had to face up to life somewhere else, and it felt increasingly urgent she find a solution before he reappeared – assuming he would.

Letting herself in through the boot room, she slung her Barbour onto a hook, kicked off her wellies and hurried upstairs to shower and get into dry clothes. She couldn't stop shivering, and a lead weight had settled around her heart. She tied her hair back in a ponytail, wandering listlessly around the house. All her guests had gone out, braving the weather for a night in the local pub, and she felt the silence of the house pressing in upon her. Only the growling of her stomach – no respecter of broken hearts – persuaded her to finally go to the kitchen in search of something for her solitary supper.

It would be a long night.

–

Sadness closed in on Anna like a storm wheeling in from the sea on a winter's day. On the morning after Oliver left Polkerran, she waved off her guests and locked and bolted the door, unable to put on a front for her regular callers, and then channelled her despair into activity, stripping beds, cleaning, making the rooms ready for the guests due in next, but nothing could free her mind from one desperate fact: she would have to leave, and the sooner the better.

She set to, searching the internet for somewhere to rent. She'd need to find a job, so a city or large town would be the answer – and a long way from her beloved Cornwall. The last thing she needed was any reminder of this bittersweet time.

No matter how occupied she tried to be, though, Anna could think of nothing but Oliver, her mind veering between devastating sadness, anger and disbelief.

Taking a break as the flan she'd made for lunch baked, Anna sipped her hot chocolate, but nothing helped to melt the hard lump of sadness that had formed in her breast overnight. How could she not have known she was falling for Oliver?

And why had fate decided that this would be the time she felt all those emotions and feelings she'd read about and longed for? Why was it someone who'd never be interested in her in that way? Hadn't he already said he'd never get married again, that he didn't see himself as father material, that families were overrated? He was everything she never wanted, and yet all she ever needed.

The loss of Westerleigh was nothing to this. She'd find another home, somehow. The thought of leaving Polkerran wasn't tearing her apart; never seeing Oliver again was, no matter what he'd done.

But how could she have got it so wrong? She'd trusted Oliver, relied on him and all along he'd been... what? *What* had he been? He'd appeared to enjoy her company – as much as he showed pleasure in anything. She'd even sensed – just now and again – a connection, an awareness, between them. Or had that been wishful thinking?

The ache in Anna's breast intensified. Oliver had said he needed to explain something, and deep down, she knew there must be a fault in all her muddled reasoning.

The thought propelled Anna from her seat and out onto the terrace. Despite the brightness of the sun, Harbourwatch remained stern and brooding on the cliffs opposite.

'Good riddance,' she muttered under her breath, then a solitary tear trickled down her cheek. She didn't mean it. She couldn't bear the thought of never seeing Oliver again.

'Anna?'

Anna wiped her cheek and summoned a smile, turning to face Daniel, who had come round onto the terrace.

'Hey, Daniel, how's things? Settling into your new home okay?'

'Yes, all good.' He looked unusually serious. 'Anna, what's going on? Saw the big man yesterday, driving out of the village, face like a thundercloud. And your door has been bolted. You look—' he hesitated '—you look awful.'

Despite her sadness, the corners of Anna's lips lifted. 'Thanks.'

He waved a hand. 'You know what I mean.'

Anna joined him by the door to the kitchen. 'I didn't want to see anyone.'

Daniel eyed her kindly. 'Do you want me to go?'

She shook her head. 'Don't mind me. Am I providing fodder for gossip?'

'Mrs L has been chatting with Mrs Clegg. She seems to think her theory's been proved.'

Anna almost snorted. 'She has so many, I'm wary of asking which. Not that Jesus once healed leopards?'

Daniel grinned, but sobered quickly. 'That Oliver and you... well.'

'Great.'

He shook his head at her. 'Most people take Mrs L with a pinch of salt. They know she's only speculating. People care about you, and you've not been yourself for a few weeks, really.'

Anna didn't know what to say to that, so she glanced at her watch. It was already lunchtime. 'Are you busy? Can you stay to lunch? I could use the company.'

'Sure.' Daniel followed her into the kitchen, and she busied herself making a salad to go with the cheese and broccoli flan she'd made earlier. 'Can you cut some bread?'

She waved a hand at the loaf on the breadboard, and Daniel busied himself while chatting about his new cottage, and how nice it was to have his own space after spending so long at his aunt and uncle's house.

'My aunt never stopped complaining about things. My hair. My uncle's habits. Alex's absences...' He threw Anna a quick look. 'That's all over, I take it?'

Alex? Anna could barely recall feeling anything for him. Like many crushes, he'd turned out to have feet of clay. Shame they hadn't set and glued him to the ground. Preferably somewhere tidal.

'Long over. Don't know what I was doing.' Alex belonged to the past, a world in which she'd yet to discover the pain of loving.

They settled at the table, Daniel with a beer and Anna with a glass of her favourite wine, at least, her favourite since Oliver had introduced her to it.

'Cheers.'

'What are we toasting?' Anna took a sip from her glass; it tasted like vinegar.

'My independence? Your... er...'

Anna couldn't help but smile. 'Exactly. Well—' She raised her glass to his. 'Here's to a long and happy life in your cottage.'

'Oh, I'm only there for the interim. I'm going to build a home from scratch.'

Anna cut them both a slice of the flan and slid it onto their plates.

'Won't it cost a fortune?'

'Yup!' Daniel grinned. 'When I worked in the City, I had some big bonuses. And I mean big! They're sitting there waiting to be invested in something.'

'Is that what you used to do? Finance?'

'Yeah. Stockbroker. Got burnt out at work. Had a bad relationship. You know how it is.' Daniel shrugged. 'I upped and left for my sanity's sake. Came here to recuperate. It's been the best possible therapy, but now I'm ready for a new challenge.'

'That's fantastic. Let's do cheers again!' Anna clinked her glass with his, taking a wary sip. Yes, she'd definitely gone off this particular wine.

'I managed to acquire a piece of land with building permission. Oliver has been a great help, too.'

'Why? I mean, he's a historian, not a property magnate.' Anna pulled a face. 'That's what I thought, anyway. I was wrong. He seems to be all about property lately.'

'He's a philanderer.' Daniel winked at Anna, and she blinked.

'Excuse me?'

'That's what Mrs L calls him. She means he's a philanthropist, really.'

Anna burst out laughing, then it became a sob and she covered her face. 'Sorry.' She drew in a shallow breath. 'So sorry.'

Daniel patted her awkwardly on the shoulder. 'It's okay.'

'I know he's kind, taking Mrs Clegg in and finding work for Daisy and Old Patrick.'

'That's part of it.' Daniel rested his fork on his plate. 'I'm ashamed to be a Tremayne at times. They've been buying up property for years, converting them to holiday lets and letting them back to the emmets or selling them at inflated prices.'

'Yes, but what has Oliver done?'

'Lately, he's been getting to the deal first, so he can rent each property at a reasonable and affordable cost to locals – like me and Mrs Clegg.' Daniel winked.

'Mrs Clegg?' Anna frowned. 'How so?'

'Do you remember the cottage she used to live in with her husband? The Tremaynes sold it a couple of years ago, turfed Mrs Clegg out? It just came back on the market, so Oliver snapped it up. When he leaves, he's letting her live there for the rest of her life at the same old peppercorn rent they used to pay the estate.'

Anna blew out a breath. 'Funny how things start to make sense when you know the truth.' Except there was nothing funny about it.

Daniel looked a little uncomfortable, but then he took a slug of his beer. 'It's not the only reason I'm ashamed to be a Tremayne lately.'

Anna took a cautious sip of her wine, waiting for him to continue.

'I think you need to know what Claudia told me last night.'

Anna's brows rose. 'Claudia?'

Daniel quickly explained that his aunt and uncle had asked him to join them at dinner the previous night, to celebrate his land purchase. Claudia and her parents had already been invited round. After dinner, he'd been chatting to Claudia, and she'd told him a few things he felt Anna ought to know.

Anna fetched Daniel another beer and added a bit more wine to her glass. Like it or not, she had a feeling she was going to need it.

'Alex had a top client desperate for this house, a couple of years ago.' Daniel waved an arm at the room. 'Still is, in fact. Hefty commission for Alex if he could seal the deal. Meg Stratfield refused to sell. He visited her in the hospice too but she wouldn't even say who would inherit.'

Anna dropped her face into her hands. Could this get any worse? All the things she'd accused Oliver of regarding Aunt Meg rushed through her mind.

'Are you okay? You're better off without him, Anna.' Daniel spoke quietly, but she raised her head.

'Alex was romancing the house.' Anna spoke quietly. Hadn't his interest and visits eased off soon after she'd found out about the second will?

Daniel looked surprised. 'How did you know?'

'I didn't until now.'

'Claudia didn't approve, or so she says. Alex hoped by slowing down the paperwork for the B&B and keeping you distracted from getting things going, you'd find you couldn't afford to stay and would willingly sell up. Apparently, Alex told her he'll be chasing the deal as soon he knows who rightly owns the cottage.'

Anna smiled hollowly. How little Alex understood her. Well, he would have a challenge on his hands, romancing Oliver.

Then she frowned again. 'How did he slow down the paperwork? Oh!' Oliver was right. She was gullible. 'The delays at the council.'

Daniel looked a bit sheepish. 'Seems Alex started a fling with this girl – an old school friend of Claudia's. I love my cousin, but he doesn't have much in the way of morals. This girl was working for Oliver at the time. Alex wanted her to search through Oliver's papers, see which property he was going after so Tremayne Estates could beat him to it. I don't know what happened, but she left and ended up at the council.'

She hadn't forgotten the young woman glaring at Oliver at the antiques fair. 'I saw Alex with her once. He said he'd asked her to hurry things along at the council, and to be fair, things did happen not long afterwards.' Anna felt numb inside; she couldn't even feel anger towards Alex. So, he'd been cheating on her with this girl all along – or with Anna, if he'd been with the other girl first. No wonder he hadn't wanted to be seen out with her.

Daniel got to his feet.

'Wait.' She stayed him with her hand. 'When did he ever get to see this girl?'

He looked discomfited. 'Claudia seemed to think he spent Sunday afternoons with her when he came down from town.'

Of course he did.

You're such a fool, Anna Redding.

Daniel glanced at his watch. 'Sorry, Anna, I have to get on. Thanks for lunch.' He looked uncharacteristically solemn. 'And I'm really sorry for telling you, but I thought you ought to know.'

'It's fine. I'm glad I know.' Anna summoned a smile from somewhere and followed Daniel back out onto the terrace. 'So, how was it, having the chance to sit down and have dinner with Claudia at last?'

Daniel shrugged as they crossed the terrace towards the rear of the house. 'It wasn't a date exactly, but we had a lot to talk about. She's really interested in my plans for the build. Says she knows a producer on a local *Grand Designs*-type programme and will suggest they contact me.'

They stopped by the gate, and he gave a bashful smile. Was he blushing?

'I thought she had her eye set on Alex.'

'Apparently not. She's hinted she'll go to dinner with me, but says she won't date anyone with hair longer than hers.' He grinned and tugged at his ponytail. 'Thought I'd call on Nic just now to see what she can do for me.'

Anna waved him off. She would miss his cheery company. She hurried back into the house and loaded the dishwasher, then turned her attention to moving the washing into the tumble dryer. Everything she'd heard reinforced her original belief about Oliver: he was a good man. Daniel's visit had opened her eyes further, and it made her feel even guiltier for not hearing Oliver out. Nothing explained, however, why he had been Aunt Meg's choice of beneficiary.

Frustrated, Anna channelled her energies into baking, closing her mind to the confusion spinning through her head, trying to ignore the constant churning of her insides.

By evening, she'd used up every possible ingredient and run out of tins to store her goodies in. At this rate, she'd need to run a doorstep bake sale!

She avoided calling Lauren. Anna didn't want to talk to anyone face to face, but she did send her a message to say what had happened. Her friend was sympathetic but logical, as she'd expected her to be:

> Oh, love. Well, you did say you wanted to feel the heartfelt emotion of being deeply in love…

I know. It hurts!!! My throat hurts. My insides hurt.

Did you ever not trust him?

No – not until this happened.

And now?

I should have let him explain. But he's gone away. And Oliver being Oliver his damn phone is switched off!

So he's not expecting to hear from you…

Or doesn't want to.

Which do you think is most likely, Anna?

When Lauren finally stopped texting, Anna checked her emails. Two of the flats she'd enquired about in Bristol were available to view the next day, so she went round and begged Nicki to look after Heathcliff for the day and resolutely resisted answering any of her questions about where she was going at such short notice and why.

Tuesday dawned, and Anna studiously avoided looking across the cove towards Harbourwatch as she got into the car for the drive north. She was encased in numbness over leaving the cottage, Polkerran, Cornwall. Her all-consuming despair was about Oliver.

It was early evening before she returned. Neither flat appealed, though they were pleasant enough. The views from the windows were of a busy road in the first instance and a jumble of allotments in the second. That wasn't so bad, and at least in Bristol she could still hear seagulls, but nothing would soothe her aching heart, and as soon as she reached home, she hurried round onto the terrace to gulp in the salty air and fasten her hungry gaze on the view.

The day was blustery, the clouds hurried across the sky by an unseen hand, the ever-present gulls circling overhead with their mournful cries. She looked around, then glanced at her watch. She'd better get inside, see how Heathcliff was faring.

Anna returned to the car to retrieve her bag, but as she closed the door, the gate opened.

Oliver was back.

Chapter Twenty-Nine

I am half agony, half hope

Jane Austen, *Persuasion*

Anna's heart lurched so wildly, she clutched her chest, the bag falling to the ground from her shaking fingers.

'It'll be okay, it'll be okay,' she intoned under her breath.

Oliver hadn't moved from the gate. Had he hoped she'd be gone by now? Had he come to take possession? His expression wasn't encouraging, his blue eyes dark with some sort of emotion. Was he still angry with her?

Then, Oliver started forward and Anna's heart gambolled around in her rib cage. He wore an open-necked shirt again and today, if she was not mistaken, he was sporting something closer to a ten o'clock shadow. Damn him for looking so gorgeous.

He fetched up in front of her, but Anna was now fixated on her feet.

'Anna.'

She swallowed hard. No one said her name quite like Oliver did.

'Look at me.'

Slowly, Anna raised her head. How could she conceal her feelings from him? What was louder, her heart throbbing in her ears or the waves pounding the distant rocks?

Oliver drew in a short breath. 'Damn it! I can't think straight when you're looking at me with those big eyes.'

Anna let out an involuntary laugh. 'But you *told* me to look at you.'

'I did.'

Oliver's expression was unreadable, but then he pulled her to him and kissed her soundly. He released her just as quickly, and Anna took a trembling step backwards as he turned away, her fingers touching her mouth. Then he swung back to face her.

'I'm sorry.'

Anna's hand dropped to her side, her lips still tingling from the contact, as Oliver paced away from her, stopping by the railing. She tried to pull her confused thoughts into some order. Sorry? For what? Kissing her? What now? She could stay here, both of them saying nothing. Or she could go to him.

Her feet were moving before she'd even finished thinking about it, and she fetched up behind him.

'Oliver?'

He stilled but said nothing.

Tentatively, Anna reached out a hand and touched his arm, and he turned around. She stepped closer, her eyes searching his face for some clue as to what was going on between them.

Then, he shook his head. 'I'm just sorry. For everything.'

Anna stared at him in disbelief. '*You're* sorry? I'm the one who needs to apologise. I mean, I still don't fully understand, but I should have given you the chance to explain.'

Oliver raised his hands in a helpless gesture, then they fell to his sides. 'I shouldn't have walked out like that. You were right. I've been keeping a secret from you, and I owe you the truth.' He drew in a breath. 'I did come round that weekend the boys were here because of what you'd told me at the office. There was something I needed to find before you did.' He stopped, raking a hand through his hair, and Anna held her breath, her heart clenching as he confirmed some of her suspicions.

He continued. 'But it's not what you think. And once I was here, I couldn't seem to leave. Didn't want to, though I didn't know why.' He stopped again, and Anna let the silence fall between them, not wanting to interrupt. He swallowed visibly. 'It wasn't proof of the second will. That wasn't what brought me over, made me keen to search the papers.'

'Oh?' Anna's curiosity was at its height. 'Then what was it?'

'Meg. She was my grandmother.'

Anna's eyes widened. 'But – but how? I mean she…'

'Yes, I know. She had no relatives. I swear I didn't know, not until about four years ago.'

Oliver looked around, then gestured towards the cliff-top garden. 'Can we go and sit somewhere? There's quite a bit to tell you.'

Confused beyond words, Anna led Oliver round to the large terrace where they both sank into a couple of chairs.

Oliver said nothing for a moment, his attention on Harbourwatch, and Anna waited, her own eyes fastened hungrily on him.

Then, he straightened up and turned to look at her. 'You remember, I'm sure, Meg had an infant sister who died?'

'Yes, of course.'

'Sarah wasn't her sister. She was her daughter.' He raised a hand as Anna went to speak. 'I know, but think about the time. It was 1953. Meg was fifteen and pregnant. Her family did well to allow her to stay with them, but they passed the child off as a sister, and she didn't die. That was the story populated by her parents. The baby was put up for adoption.'

Anna stared speechlessly at Oliver, trying to take in all he said.

'Sarah – or Melanie, as she was renamed by her adoptive parents – was my mother.'

Anna leaned back in her seat. 'And you didn't know.'

Oliver shook his head. 'I found out when my mother died. Came across the adoption records in her papers. Set me off on a trail trying to find her roots.'

'It's like an episode of *Long Lost Family*,' Anna whispered.

'Almost too late. It took time to go through all the necessary procedures to get permission to contact a person of interest in an adoption. There are so many rules—' He waved a hand. 'I'll tell you about it one day.'

The tension in Anna's shoulders eased a little. 'One day' sounded like forever right now, and she held onto it.

'By the time Meg and I met, there was only about a year before her illness began to manifest itself. She begged me not to reveal our connection, and I promised to keep her secret. I think the stigma of the shame of being pregnant at such an age, unmarried, back in the fifties, never left her.' He slumped back in his seat, and Anna's heart went out to him. He looked so weary. 'When you mentioned the stacks of paperwork going back years, I feared that somewhere in there might be correspondence from the intermediary company from when I tried to contact her. I'd made a vow, Anna, to protect Meg and her secret.'

'And you found it?'

'By some miracle, yes. In one of the boxes I took. I wanted to tell you so badly. I almost did, that day we had lunch, but in the end I couldn't. Made up an excuse about needing you to do that research.'

It all started to make sense. Anna eyed him with sympathy. They'd had so little time in the end. 'But Aunt Meg did know you for a good while?'

'Yes, we were properly reconciled. She was sad to know there could be no such meeting with her daughter.' Oliver's face darkened. 'My mother…' He shook his head. 'I was so *angry* with her for not telling me what she knew, for concealing that I had a grandmother who longed desperately for her lost child.'

'It's so sad.' Anna hesitated, then pressed on. 'But you decided to move here?'

'I needed somewhere secluded to write, but I also wanted to be near Meg. Took a lease on Harbourwatch. When the diagnosis came, I set about doing all I could to ease her final years. It wasn't much: continuing to maintain the cottage and the gardens, and then, when she went into the hospice, visiting her, taking flowers, talking to her. She knew me now and again at first, but not for long.'

'I'm so sorry.' Anna bit her lip. 'Did she ever mention me?'

'In the early days, yes. Of course, in her mind, she must have thought she'd already dealt properly with the second will. She never said anything about you inheriting – or me, come to that. I had no idea who would claim the property, or who you were when I first saw you.' He smiled faintly. 'Though I worked it out pretty quickly.'

He looked over towards Harbourwatch, and Anna bit her lip as she studied his profile. This really wasn't the time to wish he'd kiss her again. She cleared her throat.

'And, er, did it cross your mind she might have done this, after I found out about the will's existence – with it being dated after you'd found each other, I mean?'

'Not at first. And when it did, I thought perhaps she'd decided to leave us both something.' He looked over, and Anna held her breath as their gazes locked. 'The search mattered to you. I did what I could, said what I could to help, but none of it was for myself. I almost feared finding it, for what it might mean for you.' He inhaled deeply. 'I didn't want the cottage.'

'I'm so sorry for what I accused you of. I thought—'

'I know what you thought.' Oliver let out a huff of breath. 'Why wouldn't you? I have been buying property in Polkerran, but not because—' He paused, a smile tugging at his mouth. 'What was it you called me?'

Anna shook her head. 'Please don't, Oliver. I feel terrible.'

'But you know why.'

It was a statement, not a question, but Anna answered all the same. 'Yes. Daniel told me what you'd done for him and Mrs Clegg. I also found out Alex was the person trying to force Aunt Meg's hand. But I had tried to see you before I knew any of that.'

'I know. Mrs Clegg told me you came over, when I got back this morning.'

His attention was with Harbourwatch again.

'Oliver?' He looked over at her. 'Where have you been?'

'I've been up to London to visit the Queen.'

She couldn't help but laugh at his use of the nursery rhyme. 'Even I'm not going to believe that.'

He smiled faintly. 'Fair enough. But I did go to London. We'll probably never know for certain, but I think Meg's desire to keep her secret led her to seeking an anonymous solicitor for the new will.' He fixed his blue eyes on Anna. 'I went to see them. I wanted to refuse the bequest.'

Staring at him in disbelief, Anna's heart swelled with love.

'There's a process to go through,' Oliver continued. 'This later will revokes the first, but as Meg's next of kin, the estate is mine to dispose of as I wish.' He leaned towards her. 'You can stay at Westerleigh, Anna. It's going to be legally yours.'

Close to tears, Anna couldn't find any words. How could she have ever thought anything she'd felt for Alex, or even Giles, was anywhere near the depth of feeling she had for this man? Feeling terrible over her previous actions, Anna got unsteadily to her feet. How could she ever hope for him to understand, to forgive her for her stupidity?

Oliver got to his feet too. 'Will you explain something to me now?'

Anna blinked back tears, then drew in a short breath. 'Yes, of course.'

'Why did you react so strongly, not want to hear me out?'

'I owe you an apology for that.' Anna suddenly felt very clear about things.

'I'd prefer understanding why.'

Silence embraced them, with Anna grasping firmly to her resolve, trying desperately to read his expression in the fading light, and failing. She owed him the truth.

'Be warned, you might not like the answer. I— I've fallen in love with you, you see.' Anna hesitated, then the words spilled from her lips with gay abandon. 'I don't care if that shocks or dismays you, or even amuses you. Love isn't something you have any time for, but I had to say it. Be honest with you. I was so... so upset by discovering what appeared to be your duplicity. If I hadn't fallen in love with you, I might have been angry, but I wouldn't have felt so destroyed.'

Oliver swallowed visibly. His shoulders were rigid, and Anna longed to run her hands over them to soothe them.

'So, is that what this is?' He waved an arm, and Anna drew in a shallow breath.

'What *what* is?'

He turned and walked away a few paces, then stopped and shoved his hands into his pockets before turning to face her. The wind barely stirred his hair and his piercing blue gaze held hers for a moment.

'Love. Not being able to sleep. Staring out of my windows every time I pass one, looking to see if there's a light on, any sign of life in your cottage.' He walked over to the wall bordering the terrace, his attention now on Harbourwatch. 'Finding I can't concentrate on my work, the marriage I had fostered with my profession. Finding I don't *want* to concentrate on it. Seeing the life I've built so carefully slowly being dismantled, and not caring, because the hand doing the dismantling is the gentlest, the kindest, and the most precious one I've ever known.'

Oliver turned around, and Anna tried to calm her rapidly beating heart. Was he saying what she hoped he was?

'I thought I'd experienced it once. Didn't rate it much before now, as you know.' His face remained serious, but his voice had softened.

'I thought so too. Or at least, I convinced myself what I felt in the past was as good as it could get.'

'I didn't know, didn't understand why I couldn't stay away.' Oliver smiled faintly. 'I kept trying to think of reasons to call on you, talk to you. And I'm no conversationalist.'

Anna shook her head. 'You simply choose not to be.'

'Fair point. Then, leaving you for the tour, I felt torn away but didn't understand why. Every day I wanted to call you, and when I got your text—'

'I'm still embarrassed by that.'

He shook his head. 'Don't be. All through that long drive images of you kept spinning through my mind. When I saw you in the darkness in the neglected cottage, pale and startled, I had this irrational anger, wanted to protect you but didn't know why. A slideshow ran through my head as the miles passed: you working at your desk and keeping up one of your strange one-sided conversations with Dougal and Thumper. You at the Tremaynes' dinner party. Your face in the firelight when we talked here at Westerleigh.' His face darkened. 'You with Tremayne.' He blew out a breath. 'I knew by the time I'd parked up in the driveway I was in deep, but when we went to the beach, the truth hit me.' He took a step towards her. 'I'm no good at this sort of thing, Anna. I don't even know where things stand between you and

Tremayne, but I've never felt like this before. I can't eat, sleep, think of anything but you.'

Anna could hardly believe it, her throat so tight the threat of tears had returned. 'Alex and I are over.' Her voice broke. 'It's you I love, Oliver. Only you.' She took the remaining paces into Oliver's open arms, and as they closed around her, a tear slowly rolled down her cheek.

Oliver wiped it away with his thumb, his hand moving to cup her cheek as he leaned down and kissed her. The sounds around them – the ever-present gulls, the waves against the rocks – faded as Anna clung to Oliver, her hands sliding up to his shoulders. The feel of his mouth moving against hers, the strength in the arm holding her close, the hand supporting the back of her head all felt so right.

It was as though by coming into his embrace, she had truly come home.

Oliver released Anna slowly, dropping a trail of kisses along her cheek before claiming her lips for one more, lingering kiss, and Anna savoured the pressure of her mouth against his, her heart swelling with happiness as she returned his kisses with equal fervour. How could this be happening?

Ending the kiss, Oliver drew in a breath, then loosened his hold. 'We must have misunderstandings more often if this is how they end.'

Anna smiled, still trying to get her breath back. 'Let's not.' She sobered. 'I was planning to leave. Never come back.'

'I'd have found you.' He pressed a firm kiss on her lips.

Anna smiled at him as he released her and grasped her hand. 'I can't stop smiling. I've gone from the depths of despair to such happiness.' Her tummy rumbled, and she laughed away the embarrassment. 'I'm starving, and all I have right now are more cakes and biscuits than you can imagine.'

With a smile, Oliver took her hand as they walked around to the front door. 'Takeaway?'

He set off for the chip shop while Anna, her heart brimming with happiness, busied herself making coffee. That would help. She opened a bottle of wine, hurrying over to get glasses from the cupboard, then turned her attention to switching on some lamps.

She stood at the window, staring across at Harbour-watch, a soft smile on her face, when Oliver returned, bringing with him the comforting aroma of fish and chips.

They sat at the table to eat, the conversation sporadic, sharing memories of Aunt Meg and sometimes just staring at each other, then breaking into a smile. It felt so right to be here in her kitchen, together.

Leaving the dirty plates for the morning, Anna followed Oliver over to the sofa with the wine bottle. She didn't want him to go, even though he would only be across the water. Would he think her too forward if she asked him to stay?

She suddenly felt overcome with shyness. This was Oliver – he was her boss. They'd been working in close proximity for months now, and here she was, thinking about getting cosy under the sheets with him!

Cosy? Who was she kidding?

Oliver pulled her down onto the sofa beside him, taking the bottle and placing it on the coffee table, and Anna nestled her face against his shoulder, trying to conceal her glowing cheeks.

There was an empty vase on the coffee table. She'd thrown the flowers onto the compost heap earlier in the day, but it reminded her of something she'd been meaning to ask Oliver, and she grasped at it to cover her awkwardness.

'You said you saw me in the graveyard, that first time. There were some lovely flowers on Aunt Meg's grave. Had you just put them there?'

He didn't answer for a moment and she wondered if he'd fallen asleep, and she raised her head to look at him. He was awake.

'No. I had come to tend her grave, but someone else was leaving flowers so I left them to it. Then, I saw you arrive.'

She sat up. 'But the headstone? Did you arrange for it? Plant the spring bulbs?'

He hesitated, then nodded.

Anna took his hand in hers, her fleeting awkwardness dissolving in an instant. Could he possibly get any more adorable? 'And the anonymous donor who covered all the funeral costs, settled all the hospice bills every month? That was you too, wasn't it?'

Oliver stretched his legs out in front of him and pulled her back down to rest her head on his shoulder again.

'She was my grandmother, but no one else was to know. I had to be discreet in case it raised questions.'

Anna pushed herself up again and eyed him lovingly. 'I'm so glad she got to know you before it was too late.' She leaned forward and kissed him. 'I love you.'

He tucked a strand of hair behind her ear, then leaned forward and kissed her back. 'And I love you too.' He glanced at the clock. 'But it's getting late. I ought to go.'

'Please don't go yet. I've missed you so much the last two weeks.' She smiled impishly. 'I'm lost without my grumpy boss.'

Oliver sat up, pulling her round to face him. 'Busy day in the office tomorrow. Conference tour mop-up. Book edits are back.'

'But the boss won't mind if I'm in late, will he?'

Oliver raised a brow, but a smile was tugging at his mouth. 'I think he might be understanding of the mitigating circumstances.'

A sudden image of them making out in the office flew into Anna's mind, and she blinked. How would working together be *now*? She'd never be able to concentrate there again!

'What are you thinking?' Oliver's expression was amused. 'You're going very pink.'

Anna smiled sheepishly. 'About work – the office, I mean. What it will be like now.'

Oliver leaned a little closer, his blue eyes fixed on her. 'It could be a minefield.' His gaze dropped to her mouth, and he lowered his voice. 'All that gossip by the water cooler.'

Her breathing shallow, Anna stared up at him. 'Dougal and Thumper are known for their discretion.' Her words ended in a tremor, as Oliver trailed a finger across her lips and leaned closer still.

'Would you like me to fire you, to make it easier?' He kissed the left of her mouth, then drew back a little.

Anna shook her head. 'It's not difficult.'

He leaned forward again and pressed a kiss on the right side of her mouth. 'What is it, then?'

Her eyes closed as his mouth moved along her chin line and then down her neck. 'It feels—' She let out a small gasp. 'Feels a bit... pervy.'

Oliver's mouth trembled against the base of her throat where it had come to rest. He was laughing!

Anna opened her eyes, then began to giggle. Said out loud, it sounded ridiculous.

Oliver sat back. 'I've been called a few names in my time, but—'

'Not you! *Us*... doing... things we don't normally... do.'

He smiled. 'I'm sure we'll be able to control ourselves. Although I always did find "Dear Sir stroke Madam" a difficult phrase to dictate with a straight face.'

'You'd need a comma after "sir" for it to be an instruction.'

Oliver raised a brow. 'Is that an invitation?'

She smirked. 'Maybe.'

Sweeping her into his arms, Oliver started kissing her again and Anna melted into his embrace, her body crushed up against him, her mouth responding willingly to his, her hands pressed against his back. Heavens, he was a good kisser!

Slowly, Oliver brought the kiss to a close, then leaned his forehead against hers, his breathing uneven. 'I really have to leave. I was barely in the house five minutes. I had to see you.'

'Then don't go.' Anna leaned back so she could see his face. 'Stay with me, Oliver.' Lord, she was being forward again! What had happened to the shyness? But this *mattered*. A lot.

Anna leaned back in his arms for a moment, her eyes searching his face.

'You're absolutely sure, Anna?'

She reached out to touch his face. 'I've never been surer of anything in my entire life.'

Chapter Thirty

We are such stuff as dreams are made on

William Shakespeare, *The Tempest*

Anna woke with a start the following morning, rolling onto her back as memories of the previous night flooded her conscious mind. Oliver was no longer beside her, but the sound of the shower told her why. She tugged his pillow over and buried her face in it, inhaling the scent of him, then flopped back against her own pillow, her eyes drifting closed again.

Images played on a loop in her head: her hands gripping those broad, strong shoulders, the dappled moonlight on Oliver's features, the exquisite pleasure of being made love to by a man she truly adored. She smiled widely.

'Good morning.'

Opening her eyes again, Anna peeped up at Oliver as he leaned in to drop a kiss on her nose before sitting on the bed beside her. He had a towel around his waist and rubbed his head with another, leaving his hair pointing in all directions, and she reached up to smooth it.

'It's a very good morning.' She smirked as he tossed the towel he held onto the floor. 'I appear to be working from home. Is there anything I can do for you?'

Oliver's blue eyes deepened in colour. 'Let me give it some thought.'

She didn't have a moment to reflect on the expression filling his face as he captured her lips with his own, and Anna melted into his embrace, her hands gripping his bare shoulders before slipping to his chest and then to the towel around his waist.

She tugged, and he laughed against her mouth, then raised his head.

'There's a chance we're both thinking about the same… task.'

Reaching up, Anna ran a finger down his cheek. 'If it's top of both of our to-do lists, it would be a shame not to complete it first.'

She kicked off the sheets, then let out a small shriek as Oliver scooped her up in his arms before rolling them both back onto the bed. Awash with anticipation, she gripped his shoulders as he flipped her back onto her pillow. He held her gaze, a smile tugging at his mouth and she reached up and pulled him down as their lips met in a searing kiss. The second towel joined the first on the floor, and Anna happily surrendered herself to Oliver's lovemaking. Her last coherent thought was that it wasn't remotely 'pervy'. It was perfection.

Sometime later, showered, dressed and alone once more, Anna picked up the glass vial they'd found in Aunt Meg's handbag, dabbing some perfume on her wrists before hurrying from the room.

Oliver poured some coffee as she entered the kitchen, and she wandered over to join him at the scrubbed pine table.

'How did you know the perfume vial in Aunt Meg's handbag had a Chester hallmark?' She held her wrist up to his nose so he could inhale the scent as she sat beside him. 'It seemed a shame not to use such a pretty thing.'

'I'm glad you're using it.' He dropped a kiss on her wrist. 'I gave it to Meg, the first Christmas after we found each other.'

Anna's heart was so full she could hardly bear her own happiness. How this had happened, she had no idea, but to be loved by such a man!

She took his hand. 'Did I tell you that I love you?'

Oliver raised a brow. 'I believe you did. You also once told me you loved digging your toes into warm sand, Justin Timberlake and Kir Royale. I'm not sure where I stand in the pecking order.'

Anna leaned over and kissed his cheek, but Oliver moved his head and captured her lips in an intense kiss.

'Heading up the charts, I suspect.' Anna smiled, turning to face the vista from the window. 'It feels strange for you to be sitting here, with that view before us. Normally, I'm looking over there, wondering what you're doing or where you are.'

Oliver grunted. 'I began to think I was going mad, the number of times I stood there staring at the cottage thinking the same.'

Anna tilted her head to one side. 'You mean, you were in love with the cottage? And to think, you had me convinced you weren't interested in the property!' She stood up with a laugh at his expression, but then he was on his feet too, wrapping her in his embrace.

'So, you need more convincing that it's you I love? I can do that.'

The phone interrupted them, and Anna leaned back in Oliver's arms. 'Shall we pretend we're not here?'

'No. Answer it. I'll start breakfast. You may change your mind once you've tried my chilli scrambled eggs.'

Shaking her head, Anna picked up her mobile. Nicki.

'Morning! How did yesterday go?' There was a muted chuckle. 'Or shouldn't I ask?'

'I— Er...' Anna spoke quietly, watching with interest as Oliver opened a cupboard and took out a jar of dried spice before inspecting the limited contents of the fridge.

'Am I right in thinking you're not alone?' Nicki's voice was still amused.

'How did you know?' Anna hissed down the phone, walking into the hall.

'You do know people have to pass our cottage to get to yours? Oliver clasping one of Colin the Cod's paper carriers to his chest is a bit big to miss!'

'Ah. Well, yes.'

Nicki laughed. 'Don't worry. I won't pop round just now. I suspect you have more important things to be... doing.' She snorted.

'On which note, I'll end this call.'

Anna couldn't help but smile. Her heart was too full to care about anything, and she hurried back into the kitchen. Oliver busily mixed the eggs in a bowl, and she walked over to spread her hands across his back, then put her arms around his waist.

'You're trying to distract me so I mess this up.' Oliver stopped whisking and Anna hugged his back even tighter.

'I thought I'd lost you. I mean, I know I didn't have you, but... well, you know what I mean.' She leaned her head against his back, but he took her hands and unfolded them from around his waist, turning to take her in his arms. 'I didn't know I was falling in love with you, Oliver, all I knew was that the feelings I began to have for you were completely different to any I'd had for anyone else in my life.'

Oliver grunted. 'I've been fighting my feelings for you for months. Hadn't got a clue what was going on, but I kept looking for excuses to be where you were.' He raised a hand in a helpless gesture. 'Only accepted the invitation to the Tremaynes because I'd found out you were going – not that I'd have owned up to it at the time.'

Anna rested her head on his chest, listening to the solid thumping of his heart. 'Have you ever read *Pride and Prejudice*?'

A rumble of laughter emanated from Oliver's chest. 'Is this a make-or-break question?'

Raising her head, Anna smiled. 'No. Elizabeth Bennet asks Mr Darcy, near the end, when it was he fell in love with her, and he replied with words to the effect, it had been coming on so gradually, he was in the middle before he knew he'd begun. It's how it was for me.'

Oliver said nothing, but his grip around her tightened, and they remained in a comfortable embrace for a few moments. Then, to her embarrassment, Anna's tummy rumbled.

'Okay. Okay. I get it.' Oliver released her and turned back to the eggs, and with a mortified smile, Anna walked over to lay the table.

It was as they were eating breakfast that the conversation returned to Aunt Meg.

'I wish she'd known. About us, I mean.' Anna popped the last bit of toast into her mouth and chewed thoughtfully.

'Was there nothing helpful in the tea caddy?'

Anna picked up her mug. 'Like what?'

'Didn't you see there were other things in there, under the will?'

'Maybe. I was a bit distracted by the will turning up.'

Oliver got to his feet and walked over to the dresser and flipped open the lid of the box. He pulled out some bits and pieces, including a small leather box, but within a few seconds, he was back, holding out a letter and a couple of photographs.

Curious, Anna took them from him as he sat beside her, glancing at the photos, then smiling.

'When were these taken?'

'Not long after we found each other.' He took one from her and studied it, smiling faintly. 'She wasn't overly familiar with the concept of a selfie.'

Anna raised a brow. 'You, Oliver? Taking selfies? I'm impressed!'

'How old do you think I am?'

Biting back on a smile, Anna pretended to think. 'Well, according to Wikipedia—'

Oliver's lips silenced her briefly, and she smiled warmly at him as he pulled away, but then sobered as she turned her attention to the letter.

It was unopened and addressed to her at the Harrogate address.

'Aunt Meg wrote to me? Why didn't she post it?'

Oliver shook his head. 'No idea. Perhaps she was already getting confused.'

Anna opened it, her throat tightening on seeing the much-loved hand, hearing Aunt Meg's voice as her eyes took in the words.

My dear Anna, for dear you have always been to me,

If you are reading this letter, then you will know everything. Please forgive me for keeping my secret. I didn't know how to tell you. All these years, and all I could think of was the shame I had brought upon my family. I tried to find my daughter, you know? When she would have been about thirty. I went through an agency who acted as intermediary, but she refused to meet me. I don't blame her. Why should she forgive me for giving her up? I never learnt anything about her life until Oliver found me. He promised to keep my secret for me, but I wanted you to know the truth once I was gone.

How can I express the joy he has brought into my life? I am sad I can never be reunited with my daughter, but having a grandson who loves me unconditionally has brought me immense happiness.

I had wanted to leave the cottage to you, dear Anna. I even drew up a will to that effect, but then Oliver found me. I hadn't really thought to change anything. Oliver is a wealthy man; he doesn't need the cottage in the way I felt you might one day, even though he was kin. Ah, you were such a balm to my heart! The child I was never allowed to raise. But time has moved on. I know from our lovely meet-ups in London how happy and settled you are in the north. You have your own life there now.

I'm distressed to say that the Tremayne man – the boy you once admired so much – has become a very persuasive man now, older, confident. He's been pestering, pressurising me to sell up, quite determined to have the cottage.

Oliver has no knowledge of my fears over losing my dear Westerleigh – my haven, my love – but I have had a new will drawn up knowing he will stop Tremayne in his tracks.

I used an anonymous solicitor to maintain the confidentiality of my relationship to Oliver, and now the will is drawn up and witnessed, all is settled.

I am taking steps to ensure only Oliver finds out about the will and have trusted to him understanding my wish for this letter to be sent on to you in due course.

Remember how much I love you, dearest Anna; you are as much a grandchild to me as any of my own blood could be.

With all my love, forever and always,
Aunt Meg xx

Anna had tears in her eyes when she'd finished, handing it to Oliver, who took her hand in his as he read it.

'She never opened the solicitor's letter, so must have forgotten she needed to send the will back to them. It explains why she hid it away – if she was so paranoid about her privacy, her reputation.'

Oliver raised his head when he'd finished reading, folding the letter and placing it on the table. 'At least we know why you and I were the people she told to follow the shells, even though she wasn't sure *why* she was telling us.'

'Such lasting sadness from losing her child. My heart breaks for her.'

A tear spilled over and ran down Anna's cheek, and she hurriedly wiped it away. She was so happy; what was with the tears?

'She wanted you to have the house, Oliver.'

'No. She wanted *you* to. Leaving it to me was an attempt to protect it – put it in safe hands. Besides, you were the grandchild she needed for all those years before I found her.' He held her gaze. 'Marry me, Anna.'

'What?' Anna stared at him in disbelief, her heart pounding fiercely, but then her hopes plummeted. 'If this is one of your "so gullible" moments...'

Oliver got to his feet, pulling her up with him. Then, he put his arms around her. 'That's better.'

Anna leaned her head against his chest.

'I am deadly serious. I had no idea what I wanted.' Oliver's hold on her tightened. 'I felt I knew everything I *didn't* want, but you've shown me that my upbringing doesn't have to colour my future. You had no parents, no loving family, no place to call home, yet you somehow believed it was all worth holding out for. I'd given up, too early, too easily. You've helped me see that the things we assume we'll never have are sometimes worth fighting for.'

Anna leaned back in his arms. 'Are you sure?'

He regarded her in silence, then a smile touched the edges of his mouth. 'I've never been surer of anything in my entire life. Marry me, Anna. Let's make our own happiness and our own home.'

'Can we stay at Westerleigh?'

'If you'll have me.'

Anna smiled. 'I think Aunt Meg would have been happy for us to share her home.' She bit her lip. She longed to say yes, but this was Oliver... 'But marriage? Are you sure? You said never again. And what about children... a family...?' Her voice faltered but Oliver stepped away from her, keeping his hands on her arms.

'When I'm with you, anything seems possible.' He brushed a lock of hair away from Anna's cheek and dropped a soft kiss onto her lips. 'If this is real love, I'll take it gladly and not let it go. My views on families have a low benchmark, but they were never borne of love before. When we are together, things I once derided seem desirable. I'll do my best, and the rest I'll have to work out as I go along.' Oliver took on a pained look. 'Must I ask a *third* time?'

Anna started to laugh. She was so happy, she wasn't sure she would be able to stop. 'No! It's yes! Yes, yes, yes!'

'Good. Because Dougal really does need two parents. Do you think he and Heathcliff will get along?'

Anna had no chance to answer, because Oliver had captured her lips with his own again, but the kiss wasn't destined to last.

'Coooee. It's only us, young'un.'

Anna and Oliver broke apart as a voice floated in from the boot room.

'It's Mrs Lovelace!' Anna hissed. 'I forgot to bolt the door!'

Anna made to step out of his embrace, but he held onto her.

'They will gossip, Oliver!'

'This isn't gossip.' Oliver turned her to face the door, keeping one arm around her shoulders. 'This is fact.'

'Mornin', my lovely. Wasson? Oh!' Mrs Lovelace's eyes widened as she came to an abrupt halt in the doorway, her daughter, Jean, bumping into her back and Phoenix peering over her other shoulder.

'Bleddy hell, Anna!' Phoenix's eyes were round with surprise, and Anna bit back on a smile.

Oliver cleared his throat. 'Er… good morning.'

The ladies walked in, Nicki hurrying in after them, looking from Anna to Oliver, a wide smile on her face. 'Thought I saw people passing.'

'I'm so sorry,' Anna whispered to Oliver, but the arm across her shoulders merely tightened briefly.

'Well, Mum—' Jean nodded over at Anna and Oliver. 'You told us how it was, didn't you?'

'That I did, Jeanie.' Mrs Lovelace turned to Oliver. 'Now, young'un, make sure good care's taken of our Anna. We'm all that fond of her.'

Anna peeped up at Oliver to see how he was taking this, but to her surprise, he was smiling.

'As am I. It's why I've just asked her to marry me.'

Phoenix gasped, Nicki and Jean beamed, and Mrs Lovelace turned smugly to the others.

'There now! All's well with the world. That Tremayne boy always was a wolf in cheat's clothin', but young Mr Seymour here, he's better than that. Didn't I say it just now? He's proper monotonous.'

Acknowledgments

It's hard to know where to start saying thank you regarding this story, which has been so many years in the making – my personal love letter to beautiful Cornwall, a place that stole my heart and soul many years ago. I spent my first honeymoon there (the marriage didn't last, but my passion for Cornwall did), and received my second (and thankfully final) proposal there too, in Nelson's Restaurant in Polperro.

It's a beautiful setting any time of the year, bounded on three sides by the sea. My Cornwall, the inspiration for Polkerran, lies on the south-east coast of the county, between Dodman Point to the west, passing the Gribbin daymark and stretching to Rame Head in the east.

The story's location owes its topography and inspiration to two waterside settlements: Polruan and Fowey, facing each other across the wide waters of the River Fowey. With the river imagined into a bay nestled between two protective arms of land—the cove, as the locals call it—it became the fictitious village of Polkerran Point.

My initial thanks, therefore, go to Cornwall itself – especially the aforementioned town of Fowey and the village of Polruan – with a shout out for the webcams at the Royal Fowey Yacht Club and Readymoney Beach

Shop, through which I'm able to watch the daily activities on the water, keep an eye on the weather and imagine I'm there even though I'm hundreds of miles away.

There are so many people who've helped my dream come true: to write a series of heart-warming contemporary romances set in Cornwall, so here goes!

A massive thank you to all the team at Canelo Romance, for giving me this chance, with a very special thank you to Emily Bedford, who is not only an amazing, thorough and talented editor, but also kind, generous with her time and incredibly supportive.

I'd also like to thank these lovelies:

Geoffrey Hall, for his patience in answering my endless questions about property and Wills, and all in exchange for an Orchard Pig Totally Minted;

Joan Mossop Frost, for the loan of books and advice re setting up a B&B (but mostly for the rosé and laughter);

Christina Boyd, Debbie Fortin and Jane Odiwe, for their help, support and wise words as I wrote an earlier draft of this story;

Jeannie Peters – Cornwall resident and friend – for guiding me on Cornish dialogue;

Jane Cable and Laura Kenton-Weeks – the best writing buddies anyone could ever ask for.

And last, but never least:

Rachel and Tom, of whom I am so proud. Without them, I wouldn't have such fabulous and fun memories of holidays in Cornwall, which have also inspired a love of the county in them;

Julian, for everything he does for me, not least his love, encouragement and support and his ability to make me laugh when the going gets tough. Oh, and also for the silly suggestions he came up with for naming Polkerran.

Despite how ridiculous most were, one even made it into the book! Without him, this dream would never have come true.